PRAISE

Mark Hurst has hit the big time! Big Springs is an adventure you won't want to miss!
Richard Paul Evans
#1 *New York Times* bestselling author of *The Christmas Box* and *The Walk Series*

Every entrepreneur, every dreamer who wants to build a flourishing business, must read this book. Why? Everyone who takes a risk to launch a new business will have the same amazing story to tell. The story about shearing sheep one hundred years ago has a message for today's innovators who need to overcome every obstacle, ignore all the doubters, and break the mold on how business is done.
Alan Hall, serial entrepreneur, Angel investor, venture capitalist

I absolutely love stories that are true or at least based on true events. I find myself living the story and can easily picture the illustrations of the narrative. I am moved by the setting and by the events which transpired. And to know that it actually happened, makes it an even more compelling read for me.
Lee Groberg, documentary filmmaker

The waters of Island Park are thought by many to provide some of the best fly fishing in the U.S. The story of Big Springs is about timing, perseverance, and being in the right spot at the right time. What a setting, what a compelling way to make fishing a sub-plot in the narrative!
Guy Morris, CPA, tax accountant, world-class fly fisherman

Big Springs unfurls across a high, lonely land, sharp in both beauty and peril, where hard-working folk battle the elements and their own conflicted natures. Rich with imagery and insight, Hurst's historical novel gives a fascinating and detailed glimpse into the 1920s in a distant corner of the mountainous American West.
Joyce Holt, author of historic fantasy

The language of the book is as fluid as the rivers in the story, soothing and calming. I expected beautiful prose, but was overwhelmed by the depth of the story that can be read and absorbed on so many different levels. A captivating and profoundly moving read.
Becky Harding, actress, editor, audiobook artist

BIG SPRINGS

Where the River Begins

Mark Hurst

Big Springs

Where the River Begins

Mark Hurst

Copyright 2021 Mark Hurst

All rights reserved.

Producer: K Christoffersen

Cover Design: Mark Hurst and K Christoffersen

Cover Photo: Caryn Esplin of Island Park, Idaho
www.carynesplin.com
https://www.facebook.com/carynesplinphotoworkshops
Back Cover Photo: 25524085 © Richlyons | Dreamstime.com

Interior Design: GM Jarrard and K Christoffersen

Library of Congress Control Number: 2021912277

ISBN: 978-1-60645-280-6 Paperback $16.99
ISBN: 978-1-60645-281-3 Hardcover $22.99
ISBN: 978-1-60645-282-0 $10.99

Version 6/17/2021

CONTENTS

AUTHOR'S NOTES

This is a deeply personal tale set in the late 1920s in a run up to the Great Depression. Some thirty years ago, when I first began thinking about this story, I read *Grapes of Wrath*, John Steinbeck's tragic tale of the Joad Family in the same era. I finished it, put it down, and never picked it up again. I decided it was likely the most compelling book about the Depression ever written. I decided it was one of the best novels ever written. I shelved the idea of writing, convinced I could never add anything of substance to that part of our history or come anywhere near Steinbeck's prose. I resented Steinbeck for a very long time.

Thirty years later, retired to a farm, diagnosed with Parkinson's Disease, I put shaky fingers on the keyboard and began to tell about a time when life, at its core, was about overcoming difficulties, challenges, and beating odds. I now had the time, the motivation, and felt compelled to tell the story. Steinbeck be damned. It is chiefly about my grandfather, Creighton B. Hurst, a man with virtually no education, an orphan at age 13, who somehow found the wherewithal to build a complex sheep shearing plant that changed an industry and employed dozens of people in a remote part of the country.

It's about personal redemption and second chances, set in the rugged sheep shearing camps of the spectacular Yellowstone/Teton wilderness area in Idaho and Montana.

But it is also a story of a different kind. I've tried to give it a modern relevance. I spent the bulk of my career helping venture capital firms, and the early-stage technology companies they finance, find their voice, a resonant message, and a relevant customer experience in today's complex marketplace. I couldn't help letting some of these experiences color the narrative by celebrating innovation, invention, and entrepreneurship. Set nearly one hundred years ago, at the same time it's a very contemporary tale about bold thinkers unafraid to take risks, making even the tiniest corners of the universe better for the people who live there.

It's a strange juxtaposition, the lessons I learned from Silicon Valley and the quiet streams and rugged mountains of Idaho. These two areas couldn't be any further apart. I admit it's a big leap.

The incongruency seemed very logical to me. One setting colored by the other. Both about courage. Both about trust. Both imbued with optimism. Both about starting and stopping, falling and failing, longings and leave-behinds, doubt, perseverance, and determination. In the end, it's about redemption and, to use a more modern tech term, rebooting.

This is a work of historic fiction about the rugged sheep ranches in a harsh and unforgiving environment. It's a story that I created, but it is based on actual events. There are no written records of this industrious undertaking, so I've had to use my imagination to stitch together a quilt.

My family has just two pictures of the shearing outfit. One is a black and white photo of my father age 10, and his older sisters standing with him in the forest. The other is a picture of a large truck hauling bales of wool. In between, there is a whole lot of nothing. No one in my extended family had the sense to ask questions about it all. My grandfather, on whom the story is centered, wrote his autobiography. I have a copy of it. It is twelve pages. And there isn't a single mention of his innovation that dramatically reshaped the burgeoning wool and lamb industry in the roaring twenties. He didn't boast or brag. He would never have wanted to be glorified or celebrated. I hope he will forgive my telling of his story, biased and exaggerated as it may be.

To fill in the massive gaps I called museum curators and visited websites of early sheep shearing in New Zealand, Australia, Idaho, and Montana. I spent time lambing in Idaho, watching sheep being shorn, and consulting with experts around the region about the workings of mechanized shearing. I also talked with numerous people about the cars and trucks of the era, the music of the era, the flavor and color of Yellowstone, and the surrounding areas as tourism and industry grew. I've visited every single place mentioned in the book.

None of this is what I would call research. That would be an insult to researchers everywhere. My efforts were more about wading in the streams, the lakes, the lodges and restaurants of the area, getting a feel for the place and the atmosphere of the roaring twenties. I've fished these rivers, and I've walked these trails.

There may be historical errors and inaccuracies. I tried to be true to the history, but I did manipulate the timeline, some of the characters, and some of the events to enable me to better tell the story. For example, the cowboy song, "Tumbling Tumble Weeds" wasn't written until the early 1930s and not recorded until 1944. The characters in the story knew the song and sang it around the campfire in 1928-29. I missed by just a few years, but the song was a favorite of both my grandfather and my father. It fit the narrative so well that I knowingly fudged the facts.

Sheep shearers and other experts may want to call me and point out errors. Please don't. I tried hard to get it right.

Special thanks to the following individuals, museums, and websites from which I drew inspiration. I wrote the book during the Covid 19 pandemic when most of the small museums were closed. Unfortunately, my visits were mostly web-based.

- National Museum of Australia
- Visit Idaho.com and a story by Gayle McCarthy, "Sheep Tails"
- Idahopress.com: a story by Diana Baird, "The Idaho Sheep King"
- Yellowstone County Museum
- Jarrahdale Shearing Museum, Australia
- Cowboyshowcase.com: a story "Basque Ranching in the Great Basin"
- "This Was Sheep Ranching," a historical look at sheep ranching in the Western US by Virginia Paul
- Heiniger Shearing Equipment, Inc.
- Bryan Lautt, a North Dakota resident and an expert on shearing and the equipment used
- James Perdue, a resident and self-appointed expert on the history of Island Park
- YouTube: video entitled "The Shearers"
- Ron Boyer, still shearing sheep at age 75, from Hagerman, Idaho and I spent an afternoon together talking about shearing equipment, mobile sheds, and the actual procedure for shearing sheep. His insights were invaluable.
- Mark Henslee, a modern-day sheep rancher in Hagerman, Idaho his two sons allowed me to spend part of a day at their ranch during the lambing season where I witnessed the enormous challenges of raising sheep.

- Mike Owsley, the President of the Hagerman, Idaho Historic Museum graciously spent one entire day showing me through their museum and the history of sheep ranching in their remarkable community. I climbed inside an antique sheepherder's camper, watched the lambing process, learned about shearing, and visited the sturgeon fish hatchery. He bought my lunch which was deep-fried sturgeon.
- Dee Bair, a neighbor of mine in Richmond, Utah, is a car enthusiast and restores vintage cars. Dee graciously spent time with me looking at the models of cars and trucks that would have been prevalent in the nineteen twenties.
- Greg Jarrard, a close personal friend, and former business associate has spent time in and around the publishing world for twenty years and helped me find my way through the maze of writing, publishing, and distributing a book. He advises, scolds, pushes, corrects, and doesn't mind my tendency to dream big.
- Becky Harding, close friend, editor, actress, and a successful audiobook narrator gifted me with her insights about storytelling, which were invaluable.
- Jill Hurst, my wife of nearly fifty years, who in addition to feeding me, nurturing me, telling me when to quit, and insisting that I take a shower after a particularly brutal three-day writing binge, agreed to read my very first draft. She grimaced and moaned and groaned her way through it, then told me how bad it was. After that, she tolerated binges, sleep deprivation, crankiness, and my odoriferous office, for the sake of getting it done. She continues to be my strong, steady shoulder.

—Mark Hurst

*"The water sustains me
without even trying.
The water can't drown me.
I'm done with my dying."*

Johnny Flynn

PROLOGUE

A three hundred pound log brushed the top of my hair, no time to duck or jump out of the way. The adrenaline-fueled, fear-driven moment might well have been a lightning bolt or a hummingbird touching down and changing directions. That's how much time there was to make a decision about the rest of my life.

Starting a new career at age forty, logging wasn't my first choice.

Serving in France during World War I meant an exemption from fighting Hitler or Yamamoto as our country was drawn into war again. Logging was deemed a critical industry. Living in the wilderness, cutting pine trees that would become railroad ties, had some allure. Railroad expansion seemed a noble cause. Mountain living was inviting, familiar.

It was a second, or third, or maybe even sixth career choice. Fish-gutter, sheep shearer, working forest fire lines, and bricklaying dotted my resume if I'd ever had a resume. Now, living in a tent again, the pine and cedar forests of Montana were welcoming.

We'd been cutting for a month, a couple of thousand trees stacked horizontally waiting for their ride down the mountain on massive flatbed trucks. Hundreds of tons of raw timber looked like a giant pyramid made of logs instead of cut stone.

Red Borrowman stood just to my right, both of us tasked by the foreman to assist with the dangerous chore of loading logs. Red had been a close friend for fifteen years. Sheep shearing in the Island Park region of the Yellowstone Wilderness area brought us together years ago, and here we are back together, our lives filled with hard labor, mud, sawdust in our eyes and ears, crust around our nostrils, and the constant buzz of saws.

One of a dozen empty flatbed trucks arrived ready for its load. The narrow mountain road suddenly gave way on the south edge and slid awkwardly into the pyramid, a couple of tons of truck pushing against the logs, seconds away from breaking the giant straps holding them in place.

A belt popped like a cannon firing. Logs came flying.

Three or four options flashed through my mind in a millisecond. First, we were about to die. The weight of the logs would crush us instantly. Second, jump away as far as possible and hope. Third, push Red out of the way. None of these seemed much of an option given the way those logs started bouncing like they were made of rubber instead of pine. The sound it made was like my head inside a tympani drum during Beethoven's Fifth.

In less time than a single synapse firing, saving Red somehow made the most sense. Taking one quick step toward the big man, putting my entire weight into his backside, we rolled away from the pile.

That's when the gnarly bark, still clinging to the log, brushed my head and took my hat with it. It lightly touched me as a few hundred others thundered down the steep slope. They took out every living thing in their path. Everything, that is, except me and Red.

Red had two shattered elbows from the fall and my weight on top of him as we both went down. He'd lovingly remind me how those broken elbows sent him to a desk job for the rest of his days.

Some fifty years later, the events of that moment, that brush with death, still haunt me. How was it possible that my otherwise below-average reflexes kicked in, enabling such quick movement? Red Borrowman was still alive. We were both still alive. When you go looking for reasons why these things happen you usually end up down a very dark alley. Dead end. I long ago stopped looking. It just happened.

The only thing that makes sense is that it was my turn to pull someone away from danger the way a good friend pulled me out of trouble, out of a river, many years earlier. The log incident wasn't my only brush with death.

Saving Red's life seemed a chance to repay a couple of debts. Whoever is in charge of brushes with death, or whoever passes out gifts from the second chance department, has been generous. At 6 a.m., all alone watching the sunrise, those gifts are a heavy load. A tender touch.

*The Continental Divide is a little-known,
little-understood geographic marker, an invisible dividing line.
The end of one road and the beginning of a new one.
In the blink of an eye, you change directions.*

CHAPTER ONE

The recliner is pretty much my home. Living in it has become standard procedure—killing time watching two things: sunrises and football. Not much in the way of sports up here in Butte, Montana. Nothing to get excited about and nothing local is televised. My kids got me hooked up with cable TV, so all the Denver Bronco games are available. I never miss one. They should give some serious thought to acquiring a decent quarterback. It might make them watchable again.

The morning of my 90th birthday my grandson is coming over to interview me. I couldn't begin to speculate what it is he wants to talk about. Hopefully not a history of my ninety years on the planet. That would put even a younger man to sleep.

These Butte mornings are always spectacular. They never disappoint. Montana is big and wide, open and quiet. It's a small mountain town at about the same elevation as Denver making us a mile-high city as well. It sits right at the top of the Continental Divide, a geographic term given to the highest point where the North American continent rises up from the west then drops back down to the east. If you look on a map, it's not the middle of the country, but it does divide us. It is where rivers run downhill either East or West, and it's the place where every river is told which ocean they end up in.

It's a little-known, little-understood geographic marker, an invisible dividing line. The end of one road and the beginning of a new one. In the blink of an eye, you change directions.

The early part of my working days was in the mountains around Montana, Wyoming, and Idaho. When I was cutting timber, a group of guys went to check out a spot we heard of in the Teton Wilderness area, so remote hardly anyone went there. Sitting right at the pinnacle of the Continental Divide, it's called "Parting of the Waters," something that sounded vaguely biblical. Moses parting the Red Sea with his stick came to mind. This is different. This is the place up on Two Ocean Pass where you find the headwaters of a small, obscure creek. What you witness *may* be considered akin to a biblical miracle.

It's a very small, inauspicious trickle of a creek, fed mostly by melting snow, and the damn thing is running in *two* directions. Pacific Creek heads west to the Pacific Ocean, and Atlantic Creek goes east to the Atlantic Ocean. *From exactly the same spot.* Now that sounds crazy to anyone who's never seen it with their own eyes. I have. And ever since I've been interested in headwaters, the place where rivers begin, and the direction they take. Living in Butte, Montana, it's possible to view the entire continent, if you know how to look. One day, put a foot over on the east slope. Next day, go over to the west slope, right in the same spot. Choose which way to go that day. It's liberating to think about the freedom of going anywhere, anytime. From up here on my perch, it's all downhill.

My grandson arrived and set up some kind of recording device—a small, silver thing with a microphone sticking out the top, a piece of foam covering the mic. I'd never seen anything like it before.

First thing he said was, "Boy, it's hot in here. Can we turn down the heat just a bit?" He said he wanted to talk to me about sheep shearing. That was surprising. "Of all the things that have happened in my ninety years, you want to talk about sheep shearing?"

"We'll get the whole story another time," he says. "For now, I want to focus on your years working with sheep."

He isn't a journalist, and he's not writing a book. He's actually a veterinarian or soon will be. He just finished up his schoolwork over in Utah at the AC. That's what they used to call it anyway, the Agricultural College. It's Utah State University in Logan, and they have a good vet program. We have a perfectly good DMV school over here at the University of Montana, but this independent thinker wanted to get away from home and convinced everyone it was a better program over in Logan. *Who knows?*

Guess he always wanted to be a vet. His daddy was an animal doc, so he grew up around animals, always crazy about them. I better pause here a minute and tell you his name, which is Wesley Tripp. We call him Junior because his dad is also Wesley Tripp, who we call number two. I'm number one.

Wesley Jr. (I pretty much always call him Junior) is about six-foot-five or so, 250 pounds, big guy, great big old feet and lumbers around when he walks—just like his dad, dragging big, old size 14s on his feet like there were a couple of sandbags hanging on them. I'm not quite that tall, but I was always taller than a lot of the guys I used to know. Kids are getting bigger each generation seems to me.

So Junior got the tape recorder all set up.

"Tell me again, what exactly is it you want to know?"

"I want to dig into your career in the wool industry."

"Wool industry? I didn't work in wool any more than with lamb chops. That's like saying the clerk at the hardware store works in construction. He just sells you the hammer. I worked in sheep. I was just a shearer. And it wasn't what you'd call a career. Very few people made a career out of it."

"Well, Gramps, I think it's an interesting story, and it's the shearing that I'm curious about."

"What the hell for?" I pushed. "It's a lost art, that's for sure. Hard to find a real expert shearer anymore. If that's what you want to talk about it'll be a quick interview."

"It's the animals I want to talk about. Some of us at school have heard a lot about this industry, and there's some evidence that modern shearing can be cruel to the sheep. They get cut extremely short, sometimes cutting their skin. It's very uncomfortable for the sheep. I'm trying to learn more about how it was done in your day and make some comparisons."

"Evidence? Sounds like you're a cop. Did you come to arrest me or interview me?"

"I'm thinking about doing a paper about this, Gramps. No big deal. I met a sheep rancher at school the other day, and it came up. I want to see what's going on. Besides, you've never told me about your days as a shearer. I thought it was time you told me about it."

"Where do you want me to begin?

"Wherever you like. Let me get this recorder going. I'm not an expert at this machine either, but let's see . . ."

I interrupted, "Where is the tape on that thing? Is there a cassette or something?"

"No, it's all digital. There is no tape."

"Well, what is there then?"

"It's digital. It records everything as an .mp3 file so you can move it to a word-processing program where it can be transcribed using voice recognition software."

He might just as well have given me instructions for building an atom-splitting machine. "Get out of my house. Go on, get out of my house right now," I commanded in a voice he knew was kidding. He accepted I was creeped out by all the things technology can do.

"Sorry, Gramps. The only thing you need to do is remember your story and tell it to me. I'll do all the technical stuff. How in the world did you end up as an expert shearer?"

"Expert? No one was much of an expert. Guys came and went. Nobody got trained to do it. Not really, not like going to a University to become a vet. Most of the shearers I knew learned simply by doing it, on-the-job training. We tried to do some teaching, but it was fast and simple, and then we'd throw the trainee straight into the pens to figure it out. A lot of us stumbled into it. There is a course you can take I hear, but I don't know much about it.

"It was right before the Great Depression. Shearing was a good job because wool was in high demand. The army was using wool for uniforms; everyone used wool in those days. Cotton and all the fancy new fake fabrics took over much later and nearly killed the wool business."

Junior asked, "I hear you were a champion shearer? Any truth to that?"

"No such thing," I told him. "I don't have any trophies, no ribbons, no plaques. You see anything like that around here, Junior?"

"No, but Grandma told me you were a champion."

"Your grandma met me long after the shearing days. She died trying to make something out of me that just wasn't there. I was never much of a shearer, more of a foreman over a bunch of guys. It was babysitting as much as anything. I sheared for a while on and off but it was mostly helping a guy run a business. It kept me busy. Besides, I wasn't any good at shearing. It's that simple. It is a real art form that passed me by.

"There were no champions, no competitions. Not like you'd think. We were all working hard to survive, that's all. The shearers got paid by the pelt, so I guess you would say it was competitive. If you cut more sheep in a day than the other guys, you got two things: a five-dollar bonus, and you got to ring the bell as the top gun for the day. Didn't amount to much because 'the gun' always had to buy the first round of beer, and that five bucks disappeared pretty quick. I drank more than a few rounds of beer over the years thanks to the guns. But I was never a champion, and I never had to buy a round for the crew. Fact is, beer nearly ruined me."

"What does that mean?" Junior asked.

"I drank way too much beer. It was beer that got me into shearing."

"What about Prohibition?" he probed.

"There wasn't Prohibition in the early days, right after the war. That came later; but even then, if you wanted a drink, you could get a drink. Prohibition was a joke. It slowed everything down but never stopped anything. I'm evidence that Prohibition never worked. There was never a problem finding a drink."

"That sounds like a good start to the story. Tell me about that, Gramps."

CHAPTER TWO

N ow I had his attention, and so I continued.

"In the early '20s, I was working in Hagerman, a small Idaho town that sits along the Snake River in an area they call 'Magic Valley.' That's another story for another day—how I ended up in Idaho—but there were plenty of jobs there, gutting fish. They had a big plant making caviar."

Junior interrupted, "Caviar? In Idaho?"

"Yessir. They pull sturgeon out of the Snake River that runs down through there. The river comes down from the mountains and runs through an enormous gorge right there in Twin Falls, kind of like a smaller version of the Grand Canyon. Not too many people know about it. It's stunning and terrifying if you hate heights. I do. Evel Knievel jumped over that canyon on a motorcycle back in the 70s, and guys today are always jumping off the bridge with bungee cords and parachutes, and who knows what. The river goes on down just a few miles into this area known as the Hagerman Valley. There are thousands of warm water springs all along there feeding the river, and it's perfect for sturgeon. A company set up shop where they pull out these hideous, snaky looking, half-crocodile, half-prehistoric things. They squeeze the eggs out of them, ship them off to God knows where, and sell them for a crapload of money to Russians or some other exotic place. It's crazy. I did some of the egg harvesting from time to time, but mostly I was gutting fish and grinding up all the bones that we'd sell off to fertilizer guys. Or selling meat to restaurants. Damn messy job, and smelly. To this day, I've still got the 'sturgeon stink' in my nostrils. I can't even think about eating fish all these years later."

"How long did you do that?" Junior asked.

"Probably three years or so, maybe four. Don't remember. Like I said, I drank a lot of beer in those days and don't remember a lot of things. I have to think pretty hard about how I ended up in Idaho. I was from Ohio, and maybe I just liked the fact that these two places had names that sounded the same. I came from Ohio and landed in Idaho. How I got there, I don't know, but I had no better place to go."

"There it is; one of those painful poems you're always coming up with. You should have been a poet," Junior suggested.

"I love poetry," I told him. "Always have. A guy named Ben Porter down at that fish plant had a book of poems. Sometimes at night in the flophouse, he'd read us one or two. Our favorite was "The Cremation of Sam Magee," a poem about a guy who gets cremated up in the Yukon because he was always so cold. That poem sounded just like me, traveling around, doing crap work, looking for a pot of gold. We had a lot in common. In the poem, this old boy McGee pretty much freezes to death. I nearly drank myself to death."

"You used to recite that poem to us, Gramps, and I loved to hear you tell it. Do you still remember it?"

"Every word. But I want to tell you something really quick."

'Don't need to be quick," Junior said. "I've got all day, and it's your stories I came for."

"The poem was written by a guy named Robert Service. He worked up in the Yukon and wrote about the gold hunters and the things he saw and experienced. I always thought he made up this story about cremating his buddy, but it turns out to be true—every word of it."

"How do you know that?" Junior asked like he didn't believe me. My answer, "Because I met the guy, the actual guy."

"You met Robert Service, the poet?" he said, doubt seeping through.

"No, I met the real Sam McGee. He told me it was based on facts."

"There was a real Sam McGee? Gramps, you're making that up."

"Absolutely true story. Why would I make up something like that?"

"Where did you meet this guy?" Junior puzzled.

"Yellowstone. When we were shearing sheep up in Island Park, this area just over the mountain from Yellowstone. From time to time, we'd go over to the national park and have a look around, see some bears and the hot pots and geysers. They were building a bunch of roads there, and they had a pretty big crew of guys. We ran into a bunch of them one night in a bar. After a few beers, more than a few, one guy told me his name was Sam Mc-Gee. The guys all called him Billy because that was his real name—William Samuel McGee. But he liked telling people he was the real Sam McGee.

"I thought you were cremated up there in the Yukon," I said to him. "He was surprised to know that anyone in Yellowstone would have known that story. And then he told me, 'No, I wasn't cremated, but a guy by the name of Cornelius Curtin was. We called him Hurtin' Curtin—kind of a sickly guy. He finally died of pneumonia up there. It's impossible to dig a grave in the permafrost, so the doctor cremated him in a coal stove aboard a ship frozen in the ice. Hand to God, every word of the poem is true. Old Bob Service told me he liked my name because it rhymed with Tennessee.' That's what the guy told me."

Junior still looked doubtful.

"We had an old set of *Encyclopedia Britannica* books. You remember. Grandma got them from a friend. Your dad would use them for schoolwork. She looked up this poet, Robert Service, and sure enough, the poem was based on real people. Have you got time to hear it?"

"I'd love to, but maybe later. We've got a lot of ground to cover. But tell me what you liked about the poem? Why did you memorize it?"

"It was always a personal story about my life. It sounded just like me, wandering around, finding work, and looking for a place to call home. I laid down every night and recited that poem over and over to myself. It helped me sleep knowing that some guys had it a lot worse than me. I may not have been freezing, but it was hard being alone and wandering around for so long, desperate to find something that was always just out of reach. That poem was a voice that spoke for a lot of us on the road who wanted to pack it most days and quietly disappear. It's a poem about chasing something you'll never find. That's exactly what I was doing. I could recite it around a fire, and guys always liked to hear it. It was their story. Every single one of them was a guy named Sam McGee."

Junior prodded, "Gramps, you keep talking about drinking a lot of beer. I've never seen you drink a beer. I didn't know you were a drinker."

"Yessir. Used to be a big drinker. Not an alcoholic, I thought, but drinking was the only thing to do most days. Most of our spare time and all of our wages were spent on booze. I finally stopped guzzling the suds one day. Just up and quit, and never touched it again. That's a good way to start my story."

CHAPTER THREE

Some large construction companies had been building dams on the Snake River and Henry's Lake in those days. These lakes are not too far from Idaho Falls up in the Yellowstone/Teton area. After the war, there were guys coming and going like crazy, taking any job they could. We were all pretty lost, trying to figure out what to do with ourselves. The war ended and thousands of us simply got dropped off—no jobs, no training, nowhere to go. Like taking a bag of trash to the curb. Going home to Ohio wasn't an option for me. Staying out West riding trains here and there seemed like a better idea. One of those trains ended up in Idaho. I had no idea where Idaho was located on a map.

"It was a job working at the fish plant, but it was a bad job and a bad place. Alcohol was readily available if you looked. And so were the girls. Not real girls, but hookers. They were always around. Stinky guys, beer drinkers, and hookers always seem to find each other. I was never much interested in these girls. They looked just about as ugly as one of the sturgeons I gutted all day long, and I want to tell you, that is ugly."

"Hold on a sec, Gramps," Junior said. "Let me quickly pull up a picture of a sturgeon on Google." It took him all of five seconds, and he had a photo open on his computer.

"Oh, man, you're right," he groaned. "It looks prehistoric . . . as much like a crocodile as a fish. They're huge. I thought you were talking about a regular-sized fish."

"They're big, sometimes seven feet long. Their caviar was in high demand. And they kept me employed."

"So, when did you leave Twin Falls?" he asked.

"Probably about '25 or '26. Didn't plan on leaving. Didn't plan anything. Just sort of got by day to day. Here's what happened.

"A bunch of us went over to the Shoshone Falls in Twin, named after an Indian tribe up there. Dickey Parrish had a fairly new Model A Ford, and we filled it to capacity with smelly guys and beer. We called Dickey "Buns" because he had an enormous caboose. We thought the hookers had big butts, but Dickey's was about the same size. He was a good kid and could make people laugh. He was only about 19, but mature-looking, already had a pretty good beard, and he had a nose for booze, no problem finding where to get a drink.

"We stayed all night, not too worried about going to work the next day. It was Saturday night, and we would regularly party as long as we had beer. And we did that night. I have no idea what went on, but when I woke up it was Monday afternoon. A stranger was standing over me to see if I was dead or alive."

"What the hell?' I asked, coming back to life. It felt like fish bones were lining the entire length of my esophagus and the full length of my intestines; the stink of fish adding to my nausea. Who are you?"

"Name's Creighton. You?"

"They call me Tripp. Where are we?"

"Tripp, nice to meet you. This is a storage garage I sleep in. A friend lets me hang out here. Not really room for two, but I dragged you in here because I didn't know what else to do with you."

"What happened?" I asked, and there was a long pause. A deep breath.

"Dickey Parrish was killed last night."

"Buns got killed?" My head went instantly from bonfire to forest fire. "He was just a kid. What happened?"

"There was a knife fight. A bunch of guys from the fish plant got all worked up by some of the construction guys, and Buns ended up with a big knife in his throat. It was still sticking out when they hauled him up the hill."

We both sat there silently for a few minutes. Then I gagged and wretched. It wasn't vomit, that's when bad stuff comes flying out. It was the dry heaves. I hadn't eaten anything in a few days. Sitting there in a small makeshift little shed with a stranger, nothing but rancid air, and the bottom of my stomach coming out my mouth.

"Creighton waited for me to stop retching."

"You were actually downriver just a bit from the fight. You were lucky. Guys were scattering like roaches when the cops finally got there. It was dark and everyone sort of vanished into the rocks. Except you. You were lying face down in the shallows. I thought you were drowned or stabbed. You had a lot of blood running into the water."

"That would explain why this lump on my head feels like a German howitzer exploding in my brain."

"We waited around 'til about three in the morning when it quieted down, and the cops were gone. My brother and I dragged you here. Do you want to see a doctor?"

"No. No. I don't know . . . I don't have money for a doctor. I'll be fine. Was the blood from this lump?" I asked, gingerly rubbing the wound.

"Yes," Creighton replied. "The cut isn't very bad, but you could have a concussion. I don't have coffee or anything to feed you."

"Let's get out of here," I said. "I've got to go see if I still have a job."

Junior interrupted, "Gramps, I've never heard that story. Was anyone ever arrested for the murder?"

"I don't think they ever figured it out. The knife was like the ones we all used at the plant to gut the sturgeon. Anyone could have done it. A lot of guys disappeared overnight. Cops never questioned many of them. The whole thing just kind of went away."

"I still had a job, as it turns out. There were plenty of jobs at the plant after the guys all beat it out of town. The owner of the fish plant was glad to have me back and promoted me to foreman. That was pretty much the end of it.

"A couple of months later, the monotonous world still spinning, Creighton Hurst came back into town. Hadn't seen him for a couple of months and never got the chance to thank him for pulling me out of the river.

"He came into a restaurant where I was having some lunch and took a seat next to me, waiting for me to swallow. A large chunk of extremely dry, deep-fried sturgeon stuck in my throat.

"You have a minute?" he asked.

He saved my life, so I was pretty much going to listen to whatever it was he had to say.

Out in the warm summer evening, quiet as hell on the cliffs above the river, we peered into the gorge, maybe 500-feet deep. No one likes looking into a hole that deep or standing on the edge like that. Especially with two or three beers in your gut. It was easy to imagine a body going over the edge, hitting those jagged rocks. I had to look away. Later that day the phrase, 'hitting rock bottom' came to mind and took on an entirely different meaning. Standing on a cliff that big can change your perspective and give you a minute or two of mental clarity.

Creighton was big, a couple of inches over six feet, but soft-spoken, precise, measured in his speech. He got right to the point.

"I need some help, and I think you're the guy to help me."

He didn't appear to be a bank robber or a bootlegger. He needed help of some sort and assumed I wouldn't turn him down. I didn't. He didn't tell me what he needed, and I didn't ask. I figured jumping off one cliff was just as good as another.

It occurred to me that we were riding in a car that used to belong to Buns Parrish. I assumed Buns stole it, and now there we were heading north in a new Model A Ford, suddenly ghostly and ethereal, an invisible stain of death in all the seat covers, the darkness of a hearse. I didn't ask Creighton how he got the car, and he didn't bother telling me. We didn't say much at all. I didn't know where we were going or what was coming next, but Creighton saved my life, and I was all in. From that day, I never touched alcohol and always did whatever Creighton asked. Dutifully and without questions. And the crazy thing is, he never asked or insisted that I stop drinking. It seemed apparent that he expected this much from me. He was the kind of guy that naturally, effortlessly, made you feel good about yourself, no verbal harangues needed. No lectures. No sermons.

About an hour in, too late to change my mind, Creighton turned to me.

"Tripp, is that what you're called?"

"That's fine, or Trippy. That's what most guys call me."

"Okay, Trippy it is. I have to ask you something. I'm sorry to ask it, but I need you to be absolutely honest with me. Did you have anything to do with the knife fight?"

"No."

"You were drunk. Are you sure? I need to know. I can't abet anyone who is hiding something."

"I'm sure. I don't remember seeing Buns that night. I was downstream from most of the partying. A few of us wandered away."

"There was a fish-gutting knife in his throat. It wasn't yours?"

"No. We weren't allowed to take the knives out of the plant with us. I didn't have a knife."

"You didn't kill him. I've got to ask."

"No," I affirmed, confidently. "I liked Buns Parrish. He was a good kid. I didn't have any reason to kill him or anyone else."

"Do you know who did?"

"No."

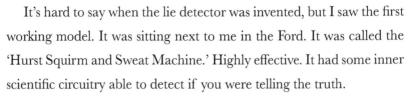

It's hard to say when the lie detector was invented, but I saw the first working model. It was sitting next to me in the Ford. It was called the 'Hurst Squirm and Sweat Machine.' Highly effective. It had some inner scientific circuitry able to detect if you were telling the truth.

I passed the test but remained uneasy. After an appropriate delay to steady myself, I said,

"There is one thing. It has nothing to do with the knife fight, but . . ."
He cut me off.

"Did you hurt someone, kill someone, steal something, or ditch a pregnant girl?"

"No. Nothing like that."

"Is there anything else we need to talk about? If not, the next words out of your mouth need to be 'let's get to work.'"

In about an instant I had some indescribable sense of a boxcar being lifted off my shoulders. This stranger knew me, knew my past and didn't care. And he seemed somehow to be connected to my future. Defining my future. Dragging a willing supplicant into an unknown future. I'd never felt this invigorated, so free, and maybe for the first time in my life, a sense of hope.

Though still very young, my entire life had been spent wallowing in doubt, the dark shadow cast by aloof parents. I left home at seventeen to escape what I thought of as a place filled with downed power lines, exposed wires, ten thousand megawatts dangling above my head, sparking by night, electrical smoke coming out of the head of the stranger hovering over me. A father. An unhinged, mercurial father always just one touch away from the wires, exploding into flames, burning us all to the ground. My parents never gave me a nanosecond of hope. Or a belief in myself. They kept me on death row awaiting execution in the electric chair.

The trenches in France finished the job, snuffing out any sense of optimism. I supposed alcohol would change things, hide things. Alcohol, the madness of a clown, painted face and big shoes, hiding fears and emptiness left behind in Ohio, behind on the fields of Flanders. There may have been some brighter lights around me, but I never saw them because I didn't know what I was looking for.

A complete stranger came along and, boom, in an instant, I got a fresh start."

⁓⁓⁓

The first thing I remember was mosquitoes. I'd curse the high mountain swarms for the rest of my life. But other than that, it was a spectacular place; an area known as Island Park just west of Yellowstone National Park. Shadows fell across the road, the sunlight dimmed as if someone turned out the lights as we drove up the hill from Ashton, Idaho, into a dense forest of lodgepole pines. Mile after mile of dense woods, mostly tree trunks at eye level. The deer ate many of the lower branches, the snow piled up against them all winter killed the rest. The trees at eye level were just trunks, the branches up much higher. The lodgepoles grew tall and straight, a ferocious sibling rivalry, fighting for sunlight. Slender conifers, soldier-like, erect, at attention, row by row by row, no view into the depths of the forest, just thick tree trunks lined up like some kind of a large prison full of jail cells, the bars holding you captive. I suddenly didn't like the jail metaphor.

Over the course of about an hour, we made a slow, gradual climb to 7,000 feet. The temperature dropped about ten degrees from the valley. The scenery, ponds, rivers, and meadows were artfully arranged, ready-made for a Plein air masterpiece. A dozen different shades of green and gray, muted earth tones, a backdrop for ten million wildflowers still in bloom. I didn't know what was ahead for me, but if it included working up here or living up here, I was all in. Twenty-four hours earlier I'd envisioned myself at the bottom of a gorge. The beauty of this place instantly jolted me, pulled me back from the edge, the pungent smell of fish lost in pine boughs and aromas of high mountain air. I was awash with optimism.

It's hard to see at first, the topography, the geological history of the area because of the plush carpet of flora spread out for thousands of acres, hiding a secret below. It is a volcano or at least a remnant of a volcano. A typical image of a volcano is a tall mountain, hole in the top, steam rising out, intimidating everyone living in its shadow. The Island Park volcano erupted millions of years ago and left behind a caldera, a cauldron if you like, an enormous soup bowl now filled with a stew of vegetation. Below it all, lava rock, a broad, deep field of hardened magma—useless, worthless dreck. The caldera now wears a clever disguise—a forest, rolling hills, meandering streams, cleverly hiding the scars below. Nature rolled up a rug and swept the debris underneath where it wouldn't be seen.

Would the volcano erupt again? In Yellowstone Park, just over the hill, it does erupt every sixty minutes at Old Faithful. Not a full-blown eruption, but a reminder, a warning, of tumult and anger boiling below it all.

Ten or twelve miles further up the hill, Creighton pulled off the oiled road onto a barely passable gravel road that a '25 Ford shouldn't have attempted, halting at the base of Sawtell Peak. Sawtell isn't a big mountain like Everest or the Teton range that stuck above the horizon in this area, but it's a hell of a beauty.

About a mile up the trail, Creighton stopped and lifted his nose and took in the scent of the place.

He looked over at me and asked, "Can you smell it?"

"Smell what?"

"Take a real good breath, hold it in."

I followed his orders. The pine tree scent was clearly in the air, but he insisted there was something else.

"It's not the smell of pines. Keep sniffing. It's huckleberries," Creighton said, after an awkward moment. "You can smell them in the air. It's huckleberry season, and in this cool, thin air you can smell them. Let's go."

I didn't smell them, not that day at least. A primitive, secluded forest stretched on for miles along the path, looking to me like no human had ever stepped foot here, pristine and untouched, every step a new vision. Quiet as a goose shedding its downy feathers, the silence was shattered only by brittle branches that cracked beneath our feet, an irreverent disturbance. Pillowy, lime-green moss clung to the north side of the lodgepole pines, as well as numerous other varieties of fir trees, pencil-thin, crowded, all reaching for the sun. The entire hillside was covered in shade from the July sun, deep into the woods, five degrees cooler—a Rocky Mountain summer chill.

"Come over here," Creighton shouted. "Smell that yet? There will be berries here. I can smell them. This is the right place, right temperature. You're about to taste the best thing you'll ever put in your mouth. Come on."

We kept plunging deeper and deeper into the trees, branches snapping, climbing uphill, completely lost, and completely gassed. The air was thin. A knife cut through my chest, a fish-gutting knife in my throat. Creighton walked up those hills like a mountain goat, crazed by the smell of huckleberries. I still didn't smell them.

It took twenty minutes to catch up with this Sherpa of the Caribou National Forest. When I found him, he was sitting there eating berries and filling up his felt hat with the treasure of the mountain. He was never without that fedora, stained with sweat, motor oil, fish guts, and purple berry juice.

"Sit down. I told you there would be berries. I knew I could smell them. You just need to follow your nose. Help yourself."

Fearing some kind of poisonous reaction, I tentatively plucked a single berry, popped it in my mouth, and bit down. Juice squirted out the corners of my mouth, dripped down my chin and onto my shirt, a purple blob as if I'd been stabbed in the chest. Images of the knife fight by the river, my bloody head running into the water, flashed for an instant. Creighton saved my life that night. Now here we were, high in the Idaho mountains, deep in the woods, popping berries like squirrels packing their cheeks full of nuts. I pulled off my shirt, tied it into something of an apron around my waist, and picked berries until the shirt was full. Creighton asked what I planned to do with them. I said I had no idea other than eating them since they were, just as he predicted, the best thing I'd ever had in my mouth.

Seventy years later, I still haven't found anything better than an Island Park huckleberry—unless it's a passel of them baked in a pie with vanilla ice cream melting over the top. I had a grand total of exactly two of those berry pies in my three years working in those mountains. Pie was rare because you could never find those damn berries. Finding gold in the Yukon was easier than finding the rare huckleberry bush.

He then taught me all about Island Park. He said the berries were a pretty good laxative, so go easy. I learned the hard way; that was a fact. Ha! More on that some other time.

He also said that huckleberries were in demand this time of year. Lots of people from the cities came up hoping to find some of the purple delicacies. Most of them went home empty-handed. There are secret places, and if you know about them, you never want to reveal it or there'll be hundreds of people descending on the place.

"Never tell anyone about this place," he cautioned. And I didn't. Then he said, "Don't let anyone see that stash in your shirt there. You could be robbed. Up here, these berries are like the caviar that you used to make for foreigners. Believe me when I tell you these things are like currency up here in these mountains."

"What else do I need to know?" I asked.

"Three things," he replied. "If I can smell the berries in the air, so can the bears. Their sense of smell is about ten times better than humans. They love huckleberries. And blueberries along the river and the wild strawberries and wild raspberries that grow all through this area. You have to be vigilant and cautious about everything you do up here. Hunt for berries, hide from bears.

"Bears? Here?"

"Yep. All through this area. Yellowstone Park is just about thirty miles over that hill, and there are lots and lots of bears. We probably shouldn't be up this high picking berries right now. Is your little apron there full enough?" he joked.

I started running down that mountain, careful not to trip on the underbrush, trying desperately not to spill a single berry, happy to get out before a bear found us with a quart of his preferred dessert. Creighton casually walked down, less concerned despite his warnings to me. This trait came to define him. He never panicked, never seemed worried about much of anything. He was always in control, sure of himself; my polar opposite. He wasn't afraid of anything. His pace was always the same; his temperament always level; his mood upbeat. This was a consistent man, steady, steely, and always shot straight with anyone he met. He was a lodgepole pine, always reaching for the light, strong and straight. I began, that day, walking in his lengthy shadow.

"Second thing about Island Park," he said, "don't go up on the hill picking berries alone. Or out in the forest. Don't go anywhere alone or without telling someone where you're going. The weather here is fickle, and a thunderstorm will come up faster than a pissed-off mama bear when her cubs are threatened. It'll be too wet and too cold. The weather is always going to mess up whatever it is you're doing. And it's dangerous."

Back down the hill, an apron full of berries on board, the Model A bumped and bounced back down the highway, stopping at a bunkhouse where seasonal laborers shacked up. I'd seen places like this before, stops along the way, including my recent past in Twin Falls, a collection of itinerant workers routinely coming and going. The air inside was acrid, sweaty, far worse than a sturgeon farm.

"We're staying here?" I asked him, uncomfortable at the thought of being around that many guys in close quarters. Chaos erupts in close quarters. Knife fights erupt in close quarters.

"No. We're not staying here. I'm picking up someone."

"Still midday, just a handful of crusty occupants lying around popped up their heads and stared as we strolled through the bunkhouse, out to the back of the place, looking for someone. As we walked from room to room, I reminded him he had been outlining three things about this place."

"What is the third thing?"

He paused, turned 180 degrees, and looked me in the eye.

"It'll kill you if you let it. And if it doesn't kill you, it will drive you crazy."

"Oh, is that all? So, if the bears don't kill me, and the storms don't kill me, something else will?"

"Yes," he said in his matter-of-fact voice. "The summers will keep you here, make you fall in love with the place, refresh you, cleanse you, pretty much change you for good. But the winter comes early, about

October 1st, and stays until nearly June. I've seen it get as cold as 50 degrees below zero, and there's usually about thirty feet of snow. It's remote, secluded, not much human contact, and it's been known to send guys right over the edge of Mesa Falls. Call it cabin fever or whatever you want, but just know it's not a place for everyone."

He gave me a moment to ponder this revelation. My mind quickly flashed back to those jail cell bars lining the highway. Something stirred. I was uneasy.

"I'm so glad you brought me up here," I said sarcastically. "Thanks for showing me around. Sounds like the perfect place to put down some roots," I said, mocking him. "Tell me, if it's not too much trouble, what are we doing here? What am I doing here? Tell me there's more than berries and bears and insane asylums up here."

"Sheep," he said. "We're here for the sheep. Let's go."

A younger man followed us as we turned to leave, a teenager I guessed, maybe sixteen. A prominent nose filled up his long, oval face, heavy jawline. On top of his head, a thick tangle of hair, thick black curls fighting with waves, and waves fighting with kinks. A wild sea in a tempest. A quart of motor oil on his hair was losing the battle to hold the curls in place. He wore denim pants I hadn't seen before. Most workers wore chinos, heavy cotton pants, but this guy had heavy pants made from blue denim. His khaki shirt had the top two buttons open leaving a gap that showed a massive hairless chest, broad shoulders, thick, forceful arms bigger than most teens his age. He resembled a pit bull, every inch solid, low to the ground with a low center of gravity. A large, gauze bandage just above his right eye oozed ointment and blood. His hands were also bloody, knuckles raw. These were fresh wounds. I didn't ask about the bloody bandage.

As he got in the car with us, there was yet another new smell.

Creighton caught me sniffing and said, "That's not berries, it's Bryl-creem." He nodded his head as if pointing to the backseat, curly hair all slicked back. The young man spied my shirt full of berries lying on the seat and began stuffing them into his mouth. "Dad!" the boy shouts. "You went up to your secret spot without me again? You won't show your own son your sacred little cache?"

Creighton looked over his shoulder at the boy.

"Doyle, there are secrets a man has to keep, even from his own son."

Our tongues and teeth turned purple from eating an excessive amount of berries. We forced ourselves to stop the binge as we pulled up to the site of a house under construction. Not a house you would see in a city; a log cabin was taking shape. Timber, rough-hewn logs, cut and carefully arranged, were ready to be put into place, completing what looked to me like a 3D jigsaw puzzle. A large tent stood just behind the cabin site, an army tent, heavy canvas in camouflage, an actual war surplus tent that would have been common overseas during the war. The unusually pleasant smell of canvas mixed with pine and freshly cut logs became something of a cologne for me, something I could splash on my face for many years, an integral part of mountain living. A lodgepole pine tree trunk stood sentry in the middle as if the tent had grown up around a living tree. Turns out it was a living tree holding up the tent. Ropes were tethered to surrounding trees, looking for all the world like an enormous spider web.

A makeshift table, also made from logs, was the only piece of usable furniture. Creighton had previously been a timber harvester and knew his way around logs. He fashioned this table and others like it over the next few years with his own hands, never using a screw or a nail to hold them together. High above the tent, large canvas bags dangled from a horizontal log suspended between two trees. These, I was told, were provisions safely out of reach of bears. The tent and two more like it would sleep ten guys each. It would be my temporary quarters for a while. Later on, it would house a team of workers yet to be hired.

My possessions were nothing more than a toothbrush and a change of underwear. Fact is, I never had much more than that; a couple of shirts, one additional set of dungarees. None of it had any value, making it easy to leave it behind in Twin Falls. The boots on my feet should have been retired a couple of years ago, were held together by tape and optimism. They would not survive an Island Park winter.

Add shoes to my growing list of fears and doubt. I followed a complete stranger up to a strange place; not a dime in my pocket; not a woman to fret over me; no family, no friends, no job. Neither the fish plant in Idaho nor family in Ohio was on the list of fall-back options. But anything seemed better than Ohio. Even this tent with no toilet, no shower, no kitchen seemed a better choice. It was an unfamiliar set of emotions, a strange mixture of terror, exhilaration, abandonment, and acceptance. Fear and doubt. A backpack filled with rocks, the trail soft as rubber.

I went from living in, basically, a whore house, to a military tent. How could it be any worse than where I'd been the last five years?

"What twenty guys will live here?" I asked.

"Your crew. Your sheep shearing crew. You're the first tenant of the dorm."

Creighton handed me a blanket and said, "You're on the floor. Sorry. We'll try to round up a cot. It's all we've got for now. Settle in the best you can, and we'll back in an hour to pick you up."

An hour turned into three days. Three days alone with nothing to do. Not a single human being to talk with. Nowhere to get a drink.

Each morning, I watched as people headed for jobs on road gangs, the dams, taking tourists on mule expeditions back into the hills to fish. The guides made pretty decent money without any of the hard labor. I envied those guys. Rich people started coming up this way since E. H. Harriman built a Union Pacific spur. There were always coaches, later on, buses, coming up to Staley Springs or the inn over on Mesa Falls lookout. But they were coming in bigger numbers now thanks to that railroad. Harriman brought the track up this way so he could load up cattle and sheep that were being raised around here. Sheep weren't seen from the highways, from the lodges, from the tourist spots. The bands of sheep were much further on the periphery, invisible, out of sight.

Sheep on the range and fish in the river, hard to spot until you know where to look.

Creighton had vanished. He left no instructions, no tasks to perform, no sense of what was next. I was used to the discipline of following orders but had none. I was an enlisted man again with no clear sense of the big picture.

I wanted to satisfy my curiosity and began walking up the road to Big Springs, a small sign the only indication it existed. Turned out it was more like five miles up and five miles back, dragging secondhand Army boots tested in battle, wounded, struggling to survive. When we first arrived in Island Park, Creighton and I had climbed hills for an hour, chasing huckleberries, and my feet were blistered, oozing, and my arches were throbbing. Standing by the road I raised my arms heavenward hoping someone, anyone in heaven or on earth, would come and rescue me. Maybe bring me a new pair of boots and socks.

No one noticed when I sat in the middle of the narrow road, a Buddha statue, arms folded. I tore off the boots and threw them in the brush, calculating the leather was already halfway to being reclaimed by the earth. Bare feet seemed a better option. The gravel forced me to the cool grass that lined the road, eventually putting me directly in front of Big Springs.

This is one of the really badly named places in the official book of names. It wasn't big at all. It was small. Made me think about another poorly chosen name—the Grand Canyon. Who was in charge of naming national landmarks? The guys at General Motors? Or General Electric. That's all they've got? Grand. General. Big.

It was hard to tell where the spring water was coming from. Just to the left where the road crossed over, the water was coming out of the ground, a slight, imperceptible movement. Not a waterfall or a bubbling fountain, nothing big and showy, just a steady stream of water, one of the largest, continually running clear water springs in the US, a big spring by most standards. Its setting, its size, its silence, had a calming sense about it–pristine, clear. Enormous trout were visible just below the bridge, unafraid, protected by a sign that read "No fishing."

Watercress growing along the banks of the water bounced its bright green foliage in the ripples. The water was colder than Sam McGee's Yukon ass, about one degree above freezing, it seemed. Green moss grew in abundance on the floor of this nascent river.

Other than the berries we picked in the hills, I had eaten virtually nothing in several days. Creighton had abandoned me it seemed. Watercress, I had been told, was edible. The watercress had a spicy flavor, like a mild radish, but did little to fill my stomach, nearly three days empty. I learned the harsh lesson of too many huckleberries and wondered if this leafy herb would have the same effect. I ate cautiously.

I had no idea then that Big Springs would become a place I'd visit often. Any time I felt like walking away from the hard times we would later experience, quitting, giving up, tempted to go on a drinking binge, or when I was just angry enough to wring somebody's neck in frustration, I would head up to Big Springs and stand on that bridge looking down at the huge fish. They hung there, floating as if they were exempt from the pull of gravity, calm and peaceful, making just the smallest movements against the current to stay in one place. I could see my reflection as if I were in the water with the fish, floating, calm and peaceful, effortlessly. I'd known nothing but anger, resentment, and a feeling of being lost my entire life. This place, this water coming right out of the ground every day for the last trillion years, was consistent, steady, and pure. I frequented the bridge many times over the years. It never let me down. It was part confessional, part hospital, where I got healed and found the strength to keep moving.

There were no signs forbidding the soaking of blistered feet. The frigid water stung the open wounds. I contemplated walking in the river to get back to the tent and began calculating the distance, guessing how quickly my feet would freeze. Dickie Parrish's Model A Ford rounded the corner, headlights hypnotized me like a deer, gravel crunched as the car slid to a stop. Creighton hung his head out the window.

"Why are you standing in the river?" he asked, casually as if he was completely unaware I was going to die that night either by hypothermia, or starvation. If not death, then both feet would require amputation. He signaled for me to climb aboard. Missing for three days, I was ready to feed him to the fish. I quietly simmered. The car was silent as we drove back down to the tent encampment.

Creighton said, "Help yourself," as he retrieved a large sack of groceries, threw them onto the table. I did. I pulled some of the watercress out of my pocket and put it on a couple of slices of Wonder Bread with some baloney and mayo. I washed it down with a grape Nehi soda.

"Car troubles," Creighton offered.

With a big wad of bread in my cheek, I replied, "Say again?"

"The Ford busted a gasket, and it took three days to get one from Bozeman. I'm sorry I couldn't let you know. I'm sure you felt abandoned. These cars are going to change the world if they can just keep the dang things running. Thanks for sticking around," he added. With a thud, he tossed a new pair of boots up on the table. "Hope these fit."

"Oh, they'll fit alright," I said. "They'll do fine." And then I blurted, "I was thinking it was time for me to ask what I'm doing up here. If you don't think I'm being impertinent," I groused. "I've got no job; food is scarce. There isn't a soul around. Is it okay for me to ask what the hell have I walked into?"

"Sure," Creighton said in his assured way. "Bring the boots, put them on in the car. There are some dry socks on the backseat. You done with that sandwich?" he asked.

"Yes."

He grabbed the rest of my unfinished sandwich and swallowed it nearly whole. I assumed he hadn't been eating much either.

Back down the canyon a few miles we pulled the car into a clearing that would eventually have a lodge on it. For now, it was a small cabin, dark inside, smoky, as we stepped out of the bright sun, waiting for our eyes to adjust to the abrupt change. The smell of onions and warm bread, and an earthy, almost mahogany tobacco smoke coming from two or three pipes intermingled hung in the air. Mostly uneaten hamburgers sat in front of each of the men at the table, a feast for the weary, unwashed stranger Creighton dragged in with him. We helped ourselves to some of their untouched food without asking and with no complaints from any of them. Years later, I would still be able to conjure up memories of my first burger. It wouldn't be the last burger I ate there at Phillips Lodge. I would thereafter regularly order the rescue burger, a little joke I had with the cook.

CHAPTER FOUR

Creighton warmly greeted each of the men at the table by name. The guys were different than the rowdies I always hung out in the trenches, on the road, the lost, the damned. The men at the table weren't city guys but seemed mature, confident, and upbeat. They were all Creighton's age or so—40, 45, maybe 50. But who knew?

They motioned for us to sit down.

"Fellas," Creighton began, "this is Wesley Tripp. Call him Tripp. He's my foreman. He'll be doing some of the hiring and will be responsible for managing most of the day-to-day work while I finish building the power plant." A table lined with wizened faces stared ponderously at my greasy, uncombed, unwashed hair, ketchup in the corner of my mouth, wet pants.

My face froze, not a twitch, not a blink.

Creighton continued, "Tripp has a lot of experience managing a team down at the fish plant in Hagerman. That's where I met him. He's a hard worker, very loyal, and he's just the guy I need to pull some of this together."

"Welcome," one of the guys said. "Glad to have you on board. What do you think of the wilderness up here? Creighton didn't tell us where you're from."

"I've been down in Hagerman for a few years, but I'm from Ohio, the Dayton area. Went to school there for a while, then off to France. It took me a while to get my head going again after the war and I ended up in Los Angeles. Didn't like the big city, so I just started heading East. Never made it back to Ohio. There were a couple of reasons I didn't want to get back, so I found work along the way, ended up gutting fish and milking sturgeon eggs."

Creighton stopped me before I could admit I had very little experience as a foreman, basically managing three people for three days. He said, "Tripp will be over at the tent for a few weeks taking care of the day-to-day setting up camp. I'm heading down the mountain to Idaho Falls to check on the machinery. I'll keep you posted on my progress but there is a lot to do.

Junior interrupted. "Who were these guys? Did you work with them?"

"Sure," I said. "I spent a lot of time with them. They were all sheep ranchers. There were five of the largest ranchers joined by another six or seven smaller ranchers packed into a small room. There were a lot more sheep ranches in the area, maybe twenty or more smaller or medium-sized, spread out in southeast Idaho, Ashton, DuBois, and some other towns west of Island Park and up into Montana, over by the Madison River."

"Do you remember them, their names?"

"You think I'd forget the names of some of the most important people in my life?"

"Sorry to interrupt your thoughts," said Junior.

"No problem. Let's go."

That day I began to understand what they were doing. They were setting up a business together. That cabin was their boardroom and corporate headquarters. It was the first day of my new career, not just another dead-end job, but something real and challenging. The very best way for me to stay out of bars and away from cliffs was hard work, building something, being a part of something, helping other guys around me.

These guys were about to do some big things in the industry.

The guy doing most of the talking that morning was named Ler Zuninga. He appeared to be the oldest of the group. He had olive skin, not a pasty white guy like just about everyone else up on that mountain. He spoke with an accent, mostly imperceptible, a word or two here and there hinting he was from somewhere else.

Turns out this guy was Basque. I didn't have a clue what that was. After a few weeks, getting to know them, working with them, I learned that Basque people don't have their own country, more like an area in Spain or France mostly. I got to know his son Esteban—we called him Stevie— who became a good friend, a confidant, a fishing partner. Stevie later became a very good sheep shearer. Finding and recruiting shearers would consume me for the next six months.

Stevie's dad, Ler, and a bunch of other Basque families came over to the US in the late 1860s. This was a group that prided themselves on being Basque—not French, not Spanish. When those two countries started drafting the Basques to help fight their dubious wars, they immigrated elsewhere in Europe and the US. They were poor people and landed in Los Angeles pretty much empty-handed.

They found jobs in California and Oregon doing work no one else wanted to do. That included tending sheep. They could handle the loneliness up on the hillsides away from people. They stayed in tiny versions of Conestoga wagons, a canvas covering arched up over the top of a wooden wagon, fitted with a small bed, a wood-burning stove, and a little storage. They didn't speak English, so it was easy to send them out in the wilds where they didn't need to speak to anyone.

You ask anyone, and they'll tell you these guys were hard workers. And smart. Zuninga, the guy I was telling you about, worked in California as a shepherd for a while. He never got paid in cash, preferring to take sheep as payment. He'd get a few sheep, run them with the herds, and after a few years, he had a flock of his own.

There was a lot of controversy about grazing rights in California, so he sold all his animals and came out to Idaho. He had family and friends in Nevada, were all doing well, but he wanted more independence, and finally settled in the Yellowstone area. He probably took one look at the scenery and felt like he was back in the old country, up in the Pyrenees mountains. But the beautiful scenery wasn't the only reason to settle there.

Zuninga would often say he liked the summer range in southeastern Idaho better than anywhere in the world. He would tell me, "It's a great place to raise high-quality lambs, the native grasses more abundant and much more nutrient-rich than Nevada, California, or even the old country." I believed him when he told me his lambs always got bigger and grew faster on the Idaho range.

He ran his herds on land which the government declared open range. The cattle ranchers weren't too thrilled about grazing sheep for free, but that's the way Zuninga and his family got to be big ranchers. When we met, he was one of the biggest ranchers around. Other

Basques came over here from California and Nevada because of the access to this open grazing.

There were other ranchers too, longtime residents who had large bands even before the Basques. Jamie McQueen was, historically, the largest rancher of the area, probably 20,000 head at the peak. His parents immigrated from Scotland to the US shortly after they were married and settled in California sheep country. His father was a third-generation sheep guy, a laborer mostly, and wanted to have his own ranch. The family lived in the Fresno area for most of ten years, saving money and eventually moving to Idaho when they heard about the grazing rights in the Rockies.

Jamie was a shepherd by choice, even though his dad didn't want him up on the hills all alone. Jamie told me his dad tried to send him to college, which he did for a year, but he loved the ranch and was a natural sheep handler from the beginning. What his father lacked in business acumen, Jamie more than made up for. By the time Jamie was twenty-two, he'd dropped out of college and was pretty much running their place. And by pretty much, I mean he took it over and ran it so well his dad willingly let him take the reins. In no time, he acquired the land and the livestock of his neighbor, Smith, a cattle guy who lost his mind and had to be institutionalized. Jamie bought their entire operation from the widow Smith for about ten cents on the dollar with her blessing. He was shrewd and took care of the widow Smith until she passed four years later. He never once paid full price for anything. He had a way of sniffing out smart deals.

Jamie was a kind and patient man, but you didn't want to get on his bad side. I saw him blow his top, kinda like Old Faithful erupting, when one of his wranglers busted a corral fence and let sixty head of quarter horses escape. It took three days to round them up, and McQueen steamed about it for days. He was stern, disciplined, normally calm, and steady on the rudder.

McQueen's herd had problems with shearing. It was slow and tedious; painfully slow as the herds grew in size. Creighton worked with Jamie for a few years, helping with shearing, and they became good friends. Jamie was a very savvy businessman and the first to suggest that the ranchers look for ways to work together to improve the industry in that little corner of the world. All the ranchers in the valley respected his acumen, and he became the lead shepherd, who other ranchers willingly followed.

Wayne Sorenson was the other well-established rancher, third generation. Wayne was across the valley, east from McQueen. He always tried to tell you he was the largest wool grower in the state, and it may have been true. He and McQueen would trade boasts, but it was cordial and in good fun. Sheep would occasionally die, some would be killed by wolves, some would wander away, so no one knew the actual headcount of the herd until shearing and the pelts were counted, graded, washed, and shipped.

Wayne was a shy guy, very quiet, and kept to himself and his work. He had a family of four girls that kept him busy chasing away wolves of the human variety from his girls. Wayne married a Basque beauty, Sophie or Sophia, not too sure, small and dark-skinned. This was kind of like a king of England marrying a princess from Spain to prevent wars, one family marrying another. The Sorensons, McQueens, and Zunigas were collaborators, friends, and family. McQueen's oldest son Xander married one of the four Sorenson girls. None of it was incestuous or wrong and everyone in these three families formed a tight, loving menagerie of grandpas, cousins, uncles, and aunts.

Marz Orazabel was also in that first meeting, the one with the pipe, blowing smoke up to the rafters. I took up pipe smoking in an attempt to look more mature and to imitate the sophistication of this dignified man. My pipe smoking days lasted about a week, sophistication lost in the smoke.

The Orazabel family were all third-generation Basque sheep rancher who first settled the Boise area and then later started a baserri in Island Park. That's what they called farming, I think. He still has family throughout Nevada, Idaho, and Wyoming.

A musician with a musician's temperament, Marz sometimes was a little somber and quiet. Most of the time he was happy-go-lucky, he'd light up a room, and just about knock you over with a handshake or a giant bear hug. He had the olive skin and incredible dark eyes of his fore-bearers, but that's the only way you knew he had Hispanic roots. His English was flawless and his baritone voice booming. Nobody ever heard of straightening teeth in those days, no orthodontists, no braces, so it was unusual to see Marz smile. Great big, white, straight teeth so perfect they looked like they were hand-carved from ivory. Most of the kids had his teeth and his smile, and I envied those beautiful kids. (I took notice of anyone with beautiful teeth. My smile was always more of a closed-mouth grin to keep my mixed-up mess hidden. Lacking a true smile, a stranger might mistake me for an unhappy sort.)

Show up to the family parties at Christmas or Thanksgiving out at the Orazabel place, and you knew you were at a party. Food would fall out of the sky like manna to the Israelites. The most incredible food of any culture, lots of it, and then the music would start with Marz filling the valley with songs of his homeland. Everyone would dine on a massive spread of pintxos, marmitako, lamb stew, Tolosa, and this insanely delicious tomato dish they call basquaise. They made their own sausage so spicy you would fart it out for the next two weeks. We damn near had to ban Basque sausage from our operation. A bunch of guys filling up the air with sausage farts in an enclosed area was bad for productivity. And let me tell you about cheese made from sheep's milk, sweet and soft. The Basques were the only sheep guys that made cheese. No one else took the time to figure it out, just another task. Most sheep ranchers stuck to raising wool and meat, lacking the background in cheese-making. There was no money in cheese, but the Orazabel family had done it for years and it was irresistibly sweet and salty.

I was off alcohol, so I didn't drink any of their home-brewed wines, which I'm told were terrific. No one knew or bothered with prohibition in the mountains. I had to content myself with fresh cider, another thing these families were good at. They did have some kind of dessert with cherries soaked in wine, and I did not turn that down despite my zero-alcohol promise to Creighton. On one occasion, I saw Creighton, the biggest teetotaler of all, eat that cherry dessert. It was good enough to go to hell for.

The other smaller Basque ranchers included Carlos Aguirre, Ander Montoya, and Unai Ibarra. They were all investors and customers in our upstart business and were key to our success.

These were good men, family men, hardworking, and everyone thought of them as the heart and soul of Idaho sheep ranching. It was no small coincidence that Unai Ibarra's name, Unai, is a Basque word for "shepherd." Speaking his name out loud sounded to me like "unique." That moniker fit him well. He was a real character and one-of-a-kind unique. The Basque people on the whole were the kindest bunch I ever met, and they deserved the honor of being called unique. There was a bad apple here and there in these families, but it was rare.

I want to tell you something, Junior, these were some of the finest people I ever met. They were generous, charitable, and so concerned about the welfare of others around them. Many of them had lived in the portable trailers up on the range with nothing but a few supplies and a dog. Just one of these experienced sheepherders would handle 1,000 to 1,200 head of sheep outside, open range, no fences, and they never lost a single sheep. The Basques learned the business and thrived on it.

That reminds me of a story I heard these guys tell. I think it was one of the Montoya boys. Like I said, they virtually never lost a single lamb. One time they did but didn't know it. Nearly two years later that ewe wandered back into the herd, practically blind because the wool had grown all over her face. She looked as big as a hippo. They took 37 pounds of wool off her when she was finally fleeced.

The Basque families loved the sheep and practically knew their critters by name. It was a tragedy when one got lost or killed by a wolf. Old man Montoya would say all the time–actually, he'd sing all the time–a little Basque song that I loved. He translated the words for me: "Stay with the shepherd, stay with the shepherd for safety; the shepherd will keep you safe. Don't wander away my tender lamb. Stay here by my side."

For a long time, we would hear the debates about open grazing rights, but we had no time for politics. A lot of people resented the Basques coming in here with what some of the detractors called 'tramp sheep outfits.' They went wherever they wanted. For the most part, there weren't big rivalries between sheep and cattle guys. They all got along just fine. In fact, a couple of the guys we met that very first day in the cabin had been primarily cattle ranchers and farmers. They saw how well the Basque guys were doing selling both lamb meat and wool, and these hardcore beef ranchers eventually diversified into sheep. More and more of the Basque people immigrated here from Europe to help manage this growing industry. This was a group of very good ranchers. Because they all had the same purpose, the same needs, they figured out how to work together.

McQueen became known as the Queen of Idaho sheep ranchers and ended up with one of the largest sheep outfits in the world. He much preferred being called 'King' but his more feminine title stuck because of his name. He built a big mansion up there like he was king, and I'm pretty sure it's still there. McQueen got acquainted with the tourists coming up to fish, eventually building some private guest quarters. He had become good friends with old man Harriman, the railroad guy.

You've got to remember that wool was a high-demand product all through the '20s. Wages were always good because the production of wool was always good. McQueen had a lot of business connections to Harriman and other industries around the country, and it was through his efforts that the wool merchants eventually started coming out here from the East to buy the wool direct from the ranchers, bypassing middlemen.

Now when I tell you prices were high and demand was high, you've got to remember that this wasn't the case five years earlier and five years later. It was a volatile market and could change faster than the high mountain thunderstorms. It was a high-risk business most of the time, a legal form of gambling.

There were a couple of other Scottish guys at the table that first day. I never did get to know them quite as well. Jamie was their point man. I would guess that if you put all the sheep from the Scottish guys together it was about 10,000 head. The smaller Basque bands about the same.

Combined with the five big ranches there were about 120,000 sheep in the area.

You think about that, Junior. That's a lot of sheep. There were other smaller bands here and there, and sheep ranching became an important economic engine for the entire state. Shearing became an important piece of the equation. Every one of the sheep had to have their wool shaved off every spring. Some 120,000 sheep, fleeced, bagged, loaded on a train to the woolen mills. Do you know how it all came together? Creighton Hurst. He didn't own a single animal, didn't own an acre of land. But he forever changed an entire industry.

CHAPTER FIVE

J unior turned off the tape recorder.

"Gramps, you must be tired. Do you want to take a rest and get back to this tomorrow?"

I looked at him and said, "I think you're the one who needs a break. Why you look plum tuckered out. Been working hard turning that machine on and off. I don't need a break."

We did take a nature break, and Junior needed brain food to keep up. He set off for the bathroom and then the kitchen. As I watched him walk away, I found myself thinking about all those sheep, endless lines of sheep, skittish, mindlessly waiting for someone or something to show them what to do next. I remember every one of them. It would be nearly impossible to know or even guess how many sheep we sheared in the three years we ran that business, but it may have come close to half a million. That might be a little high, but I don't think so.

Junior had me thinking. *Were we ever cruel to the animals?* I know there are a lot of groups promoting animal safety and humane treatment these days. Much of the shearing is automated with inherent risks. It didn't occur to me we were doing anything wrong or mistreating animals.

Our guys were good shearers, and I don't recall even a single case of intentional cruelty or suffering. I didn't know what my grandson was after. I'd ask him about it tomorrow, I decided.

Why would a rancher allow any sheep to be hurt or wounded or mistreated? These animals were like renewable energy, they kept working, growing a new crop each year. When the weather got hot, they'd lose that weight of a heavy winter coat and start all over again. A new beginning every spring. Why would ranchers tolerate any abuse of their assets? *They didn't.*

A bag of Chex mix and Coke in hand, Junior switched on the recorder and asked, "How did Creighton Hurst pull all this together? In the late '20s, money was tight, the stock market collapsed in '29, and yet somehow you guys built a successful business?"

"Yessir."

We were a lot like the Basque guys. We didn't know a thing about the industry at first. We made it up as we went along. People trusted us. Everybody trusted everybody. The growth exploded so fast that we had little choice about working together. There was a compelling need to speed up shearing to keep pace with demand, and Creighton was in the right place when he realized he had a chance to make a difference. He devised innovative ideas and processes, which I'm getting to, but the real magic was the way he got everyone believing it was possible to modernize. His fundamental strength: optimism.

Creighton Hurst didn't go to school past third grade, but he could read and write extremely well. He was naturally savvy. He could look at something and calculate numbers instantly. He had an adding machine in his head and always knew, to the penny, what our costs would be and how to pull out a profit. It was miraculous to me since I'd never balanced a checkbook.

The crazy thing is, Creighton hated sheep. He cussed them every day I knew him. But he knew a good business opportunity, and he knew how to get things done. He oozed confidence and engendered trust in others. He learned how to shear sheep a few years back, working on McQueen's ranch in his more youthful days. He was a respectable shearer, hardworking but restless. He was like the rest of us when we were younger, waltzing Matilda, moving, traveling, exploring, looking for work. He didn't want to raise sheep and a brief stint working on the ranches helped him decide he needed to get out of the pens and try other options. He didn't want to be a farmer. His father failed as a dirt farmer, buried in the soil he failed to conquer.

Creighton lost his mother, his dad, and his stepmother all before he was thirteen. On long stretches of road with him, I began understanding him as he willingly talked about his loneliness, his loss of family, missing pieces of his personal puzzle.

Creighton divided his time between the Island Park sheep camps and the manufacturing facility in Idaho Falls. He had a family down in Burley, Idaho, and vowed to spend more time with kids as soon as the shearing business stabilized. He didn't want any of his kids feeling neglected by their father, abandoned the way he was. However, for an intense period of time, the shearing opportunity in the booming wool industry got top priority, family second. His absence tragically took its toll over time.

Working side jobs, tending to family as much as possible, he still found time to flesh out his plan. The ranchers banded together and agreed to back him. With the money he earned cutting trees, he was able to go to these guys and jointly put together the capital they needed to launch a new venture. It would change everything about the industry."

CHAPTER SIX

For the next few weeks, I became the foreman of exactly nothing. No employees, no sheep, no equipment. Our company operated on handshakes and hope. I was getting paid a little bit here and there but didn't need much money. I finally got out of the tent and began living in a small cabin out on the Sorenson ranch. It wasn't the Ritz, but I had a cot, a warm sleeping bag, and at last a little wood-burning heater.

Island Park, this high mountain haven, is a flimflam man, a con artist. The stunning scenery fools you. Gorgeous sunrises, clear skies, crisp mountain air in the morning. Blink. Thunderstorm. Blink. Deluge. Blink. Ankle deep mud. There are very few days without rain. But all summer long there were afternoon thunderstorms. It's a strange micro-climate, just high enough and far enough north to get every storm that even pretends to have some moisture in it. The area gets about 30 inches of rain; very close to the amount of rainfall in Seattle. Sometimes you'd think it was a rain forest in South America somewhere. It was never bad enough to cause foot rot like the boys over in the trenches in France, but it was always wet and cold. Getting out of the tent, getting off the floor, and into my little shack (it wasn't so much a cabin as it was a storage shed), changed my outlook and my disposition. It was a hint of forward progress. It was a palace.

To use an Army term, the business was operating on two fronts. Idaho Falls was housing the machinery we were developing. Creighton and two mechanics made up that platoon. The second front was getting all the ranches scheduled for shearing. The large ranches were all lined up. We were adding many of the smaller bands, also anxious to modernize. This was in the fall of 1926, heading into winter. Stevie Zuninga and Jimmy Ibarra were helping me out. Jimmy's first name was actually Gamiz, but I couldn't get the hang of saying it the way his mother did, so I started calling him Jimmy. The name stuck. The three of us spent about ten hours a day driving around seeing all these ranches, making drawings and notes on each layout, getting headcounts, trying to forecast how big this would be.

The ranchers were frequently hard to find. There were no phones. No maps. No way to catch a guy other than to go out and hunt him down. We had more than twenty ranches to scout, and we were lucky some weeks to make it to two of them. This was a very busy time. We were preparing to deliver wool in quantities that would make the Aussies and the Scots squirm.

It was a boomtown of sorts. The entire region had a gold rush kinesis about it. Not like the Sierra/Nevada mountain gold towns or the black gold in the Texas oil fields. Those were enormous boomtowns. But it was an exciting time of prosperity here in the mountains of Idaho.

After the war, if there were jobs to be found, guys would show up. Anywhere there was money to be made, guys would show up and lots of guys were drawn to jobs in the Yellowstone area. A few years later there were no jobs. When the Depression hit, the jobs evaporated. It was a booming economy for a time, at least for the sheep ranchers. Then a tragic bust.

There were four things that changed the wool-growing business in this part of the world. First, demand. For a time, the US was getting killed by New Zealand, Australia, and Scottish imports. New Zealand had more damn sheep than humans. Their meat, their wool, was cheap and coming here by the boatload in the early 1920s. The government guys were talking about slapping a tariff on the foreign wool to keep prices competitive. That was like firing a gun at the starting line of a foot race. Or ringing a bell at the starting gate of the Kentucky Derby. Boom, they're off. Ranchers started acquiring more and more sheep. These bands would grow from 1,000 head to sometimes 20, 30 thousand, and more. Breeding was big business. Shearing was big business. But the antiquated, painfully slow shearing process wasn't keeping up with growth.

I was never an expert on wool and the complexity of the industry. I wasn't an expert on anything except keeping a straight face. I had wandered into a massive poker game with high stakes, scrambling to understand the industry. My front row seat was quite a ride.

There was cross-breeding and testing to find the best sheep, the best wool. Softness. Strength. Ease of fleecing. For the most part, up here it was Rambouillet. They were good animals, hearty, strong. Virtually every ewe bore twins each Spring, accelerating numbers. We took very big coats of wool off the backs of the Rambouillet. After a while, there started to be Merinos, a softer wool that most of the manufacturers preferred. Eventually, it was all Merinos.

Second thing was a railroad spur. Harriman brought in an Uptrack for tourism and commerce, making it possible to ship 6, 8,10 times more wool and meat than in the past.

Shipping wool all over the country, eventually exporting it abroad, was easier because we could load up entire boxcars full of wool. If we took it to Bozeman, or Denver, or Ogden by truck you could only get about three tons a week. Those early trucks weren't built to hold much weight, and they were slow. Sometimes it took an entire week to get to Denver. The problem wasn't growing more wool. The problem was getting it to market.

When the train first arrived, we went from three tons a week to 30 tons every three days.

It did get to be one of the leading places in the west for sheep—which was the third thing that caused the change. In time, wool buyers were stationed out here at shearing time. A couple of guys from the east coast would show up and grade the wool. They'd put some red marking on the wool indicating the different levels of quality. Having buyers on-site reduced the time to market which was a big deal.

Junior asked, "And what was the fourth thing?"

"What fourth thing?"

"You said there were four things that changed the industry. You only gave me three."

"I did? Let's see, what was I . . . oh, hell. That's the whole story!"

CHAPTER SEVEN

So there I was, up on the mountain, running around like a jack-rabbit with one leg chewed off by a coyote, trying desperately to keep up with the speed of it all. The ranchers were all working together and treated me like family. We all got along extremely well despite our stark differences and backgrounds.

The Basque guys were second-generation, so their English was good. But the older Scottish guys could be difficult to understand. At times it sounded like they were speaking English but not like I anything I ever heard. Jamie and his kids spoke perfect English, but when I'd listen to the strange brogue of the older guys, I'd just nod my head and walk away. All of this exposure to a new place, new friends, new experiences made me feel at times welcome and at other times still so alone. I could never get past the sense that *I* was the foreigner, the immigrant.

An influx of laborers meant more demand for illegal liquor. Inordinate amounts of time were spent finding, hiding, manufacturing, distributing, and consuming wine, whiskey, and bathtub beer. It was available for anyone who took the time to find it. Prohibition? What Prohibition?

Transportation in this rugged wilderness was challenging. Even if you could get up the mountain on barely passable roads, it was difficult to get around the area, still wild, untamed, rugged. The automobile changed everything. Some of the more well-to-do ranchers had trucks and cars by then, most of them getting better, stronger, more reliable each year. Compared to today's big trucks, these things were like Popsicle sticks. A lot of them were built using wood in the frames. In cities, there were thousands of cars, but up here it was relatively quiet. No traffic to speak of. The boys would all figure out how to pile in one of the cars and get to some of the favorite spots for weekend entertainment. Drunks by the carload.

West Yellowstone was the town where a lot of guys ended up on a Saturday night. It was about twenty miles from Island Park and a bunch of underground saloons sprang up there. This was the western entrance to the national park, and it became a popular tourist town, most of the time overrun with cowboys, construction workers, and weekend bingers stacked two or three high in gutters around town. I feared the gutter.

Bozeman was much farther away, but it was a popular place if you could get there. Gold had been discovered in Virginia City, Montana, and it had its own allure. It was easier to stay close to home.

Clusters of ranch hands, road builders, dam builders, and damn fools patronized the lodges right there in Island Park. Mack's Inn was the best joint, brand new in those years, built right along the river. The alcohol moved around from place to place, a moving target. The blue-collars followed the booze, devoted dogs following their master.

The dance hall at Pond's Lodge, recently completed, was always busy on weekends. This attracted the music crowd, the dancers, a bit more refined than men in boots. I favored boots.

First choice for the blue-collar crowd was drinking, playing cards, and fighting. Some of the fighting was for fun, arm wrestling, that sort of thing. More often than not guys would get into arguments and have a more serious fight. They'd bloody each other until someone pulled them apart or until they dropped from alcohol-induced exhaustion.

Girls were in short supply, but more and more of them started moving in to work in the restaurants and the hotels. No one can tell you where the "other girls" came from, you know, *the other girls*–hookers. They always seemed to be able to home in on the desperate populations. We had a high desperation quotient.

At Mack's Inn on any given Saturday night, at least a dozen guys ended up in the river. Some of them staggered along the boat docks and fell in, some were thrown in there by friends, some lost a bet and had to jump in buck-naked. The river alongside Mack's was painfully cold but shallow along that stretch. No one drowned in this kind, lazy river.

In that cold water, the moss in the summertime was thicker than a pile of sheepskins. Winter would kill the moss, but in the summer, it was dense and slippery. Guys were always getting thrown in the river with nothing on, then come crawling out, drunk and wobbling around on the shaky knees of a newborn lamb, big hunks of moss hanging off their arms and legs like some ancient, bizarre creature that got trapped in the lava flow years ago. The river alongside Mack's Inn was a carnival with sideshows of freaks and human wonders.

Mack's Inn was just down the road from Big Springs. The calming influence of the quiet river was lost on drunk, hungover, under-loved, overworked laborers of the camps, trapped, alone, far from family; very far away from relevance; no inclination for redemption. It was a bunch of buck privates enlisted and fighting another war.

I stayed away from the local lodges. I stayed away from the manipulation of alcohol-induced apparitions. I had plenty of them at my bedside. I could be counted on to help get people home from the binges, ironic that the Tripp name so accurately described the staggering and stumbling of the inebriates.

Pond's Lodge, five miles from Mack's, was growing, evolving. I had very little interest in their dance hall but frequented their store that stocked groceries we needed to feed our small but growing crew. Ponds started out as a commissary for a company out of California that was cutting timber and turning it into railroad ties. The railroads were expanding in the West, and trainloads of trees were leaving this forest every day. Logging was big business. In the early '20s, no one saw signs of forest depletion. No one cared.

Pond's added a restaurant, followed by a dozen cabins, a gas station, and the first post office in the area. It became a popular destination for tourists.

About that same time, Pond's Lodge became the center of my universe.

CHAPTER EIGHT

Week after tedious week of doing things I had never done, coordinating calendars, scheduling all the ranches, running a business, chasing rowdy guys, took a toll on my mental health.

Alcohol used to be a refuge, but it mocked me now as I ignored it. Alcohol used to be my crutch, my support. Sobriety left me unstable. The isolation was harsh, the lack of a woman in my life excruciating. This remote forest, populated primarily by men, had everyone fighting for the one-to-fifty ratio of questionable women, not a single one of which appeared to me to be the marrying kind. These sturgeons were not what I imagined a wife to be. I was ignorant about what role a woman might take in my life and couldn't see that ignorance ending anytime soon. High in the mountains, isolated, some days felt like the top of the world, liberating. Other days, the walls of the caldera seemed claustrophobic, confining, ten million acres of jail cells.

The loneliness haunted me, took me in gauzy dreams to the edge of the massive gorge in Twin Falls, staring into the abyss, teetering. The unsigned contract with Creighton to never touch alcohol became a horse collar. A yoke. A plow. I was a poorly-treated beast of burden.

Weeks and months passed without seeing Creighton. He was immersed in the build-out of our shearing plant. The no-alcohol clause in my contract was shredded, burned, cast to the wind on sweaty, sleepless nights, then glued together in the morning. The hopeful dawn.

Creighton plucked me out of a river, gave me a good job, and I didn't want to let him down. We were fifteen or so years apart in age, but he became the brother I never had, the father I longed for, a friendship I craved. I leaned on him, my new crutch. He allowed me to lean on him. I wasn't the first drunk he pulled out of a river and not the last. This good man showed me what real integrity was. Everyone knew Creighton was honest, fair, and consistent in everything—private or business. In those long weeks when he wasn't around, I continued drawing strength from him. He was gone most of the time leaving me to figure everything out on my own. His shadow over me was as long as a lodgepole pine's at dusk.

Creighton became my religion. Not like saints and sinners, the wounded, the weary, the dying, and the mourners who frequently found illumination in the straight-backed pews. Illumination never found me. I had no idea about churches, less about faith. Nothing about miracles. Eventually, I began considering all options for solace from the madness of the mountains, and it would take me the next fifty years to ferret out even a hint about spirituality, or some force, some source of strength. I didn't know where to look. I didn't know I should be looking. Creighton filled the cracks. He had something about him that was different than anyone else I met. I didn't think I could ever be entirely like him, but I tried; borrowed, stole, purloined from him what I could.

The closest thing to illumination—I suppose that's you could call it that—was standing on the bridge at Big Springs. The placid spot at the base of the foothills on the east side of Island Park, nestled into something of a basin, was quiet and peaceful. Reassuring. Years later it would see thousands of tourists, cars, buses, fumes, tramping, trash. It became a flood, then a tsunami of human masses, tragically overrun. It was nice to have been an early disciple. In the evening, when it got chilly, and the mosquitoes were gone, I would walk to the springs and look down into the crystal clear water coming out of the rocks at the same rate winter or summer, the headwaters of Henry's Fork, slowly making its way down the valley until it joined the much larger Snake River. Two rivers became one, joined by other tributaries along their route coursing through the farmlands of Idaho, eventually joining the Columbia River, then to the Pacific Ocean in Oregon. I'd never seen the ocean and tried to envision where rivers end.

I had to settle for the headwater, where the river began. Big Springs, this natural wonder, was such a place. A beginning. A birth, the water just seconds removed from its cavern, seeing daylight for the first time. Pure water, uncontaminated, consistent, dependable, constant as the North Star, regular as Rambouillet sheep growing a new coat of wool each winter. There was a peace I had not known, the water an elixir that cleansed me, washed away all my grief, and gave me the chance to start over. A personal headwater.

The peace of the water gave me strength to resist the bottle, to resist all the things that damn near killed me in the past. I didn't know what peace looked like, or that it ever existed at all, until I stood on that bridge night after night. I began to see myself in a new way, part of the water. No matter what else happened, I knew I could carry on and become part of something bigger than myself, like this little upstart of a river eventually feeding the ocean, floating along effortlessly, looking at the sights along the way. The trenches of the Marne offensive were, at last, being buried."

"Junior, stop the machine for a minute will you? I need to hit the crapper."

So, we took a minute or thirty to take care of my 90-year-old bowels and find a big Coke. But I stopped the recording for a bit to also gather my thoughts. They'd been coming fast and furious, good memories, mostly. But during that first year, there was a minefield I had to deal with. I needed my strength to keep talking about the events of the first year, loaded with trip lines and booby traps. It was a great experience and a nightmare. A blessing and a curse. A gift and a cruel joke. A lot of memories were coming back, and I couldn't have imagined how raw my feelings would still be after all these years.

Junior shouted, "We haven't got all night, Gramps!"

"Hold your gol-danged horses. I'm coming." Ten minutes later I'd settled back in my recliner, footrest up, headrest back. Every human comes into the world in the fetal position, and from my vantage point, most of the seniors I know exit the world in a similar way, curled up in the La-Z-Boy position. That's how I planned to go. Take me to the big La-Z-Boy recliner in the sky.

"Okay, let's go."

Wesley Jr. turned on the digital recorder with no tape in it. "You sure you're getting all this? I don't want to do this again."

"Yes, Gramps, we are rolling."

CHAPTER NINE

I started recruiting shearers, hiring wranglers, managing my half of the business. Details became a large rock in my shoe, limping, blistering. No time to stop and remove the chunk of jagged lava.

The new language of margins and ROI were as foreign as French a few years ago. I was painfully aware how under-qualified I was. Inexperienced. A dark dread loomed over me most days like I had been stuffed into a burlap sack full of wool. It kept coming and coming, large men stomping it down. More wool, more stomping.

Stevie Zuninga had become a good friend of mine. We shared the same burden, weighed down by too many expectations from too many people. To survive the madness, we would abandon our posts some days and go fishing. AWOL in the river. We loved to fish, but mainly we loved to wade into the river for a few hours to cool down and relax. Our form of therapy was fishing and talking. Our sanity was based on our relationship with trout. A therapist's couch floating effortlessly downstream. We didn't have nearly enough time to do it, but we were able to squeeze in a moment or two here and there, especially early in the morning. We learned a lot about the water, the way it moved, the insect hatches, the timing. The flow. Rhythms of nature. We would practice our backcast and setting a fly on the water, an art form that didn't come easy to a lot of people.

We broke away from the workload and the pressure as often as we could, and I became increasingly confident in the water in stark contrast to the insecurity I felt on land. The lazy, shallow river gained speed and depth as it made a left-hand turn to the West, bubbling, percolating; Coffee Pot Rapids, the water pushing against boots, gently bumping us as we stood nearly in the middle of the increasingly deeper water. In those early mornings, flies were moving around, and rainbow trout were hungry. As the fish started rising to the surface, we had a conversation that became thematic to all the work we would later do.

Stevie got philosophical about where the river goes. I told him it all went downhill toward the valley, trying intentionally to oversimplify.

He said to me, "Trippy, you suppose it's possible to put a boat in this river and ride it all the way to the West coast somewhere, where the river dumps into the ocean? Doesn't matter where. You think we could do that? Put a boat in here and let it drift on down, see where it ends up? We could go to sleep on the bottom of the boat and wake up when it stops moving."

"We wouldn't get very far. (I was, suddenly, so pragmatic.) Just a few miles from where they dammed up the river to make Island Park Reservoir. We'd have to paddle clear across that. I guess you could go around the dam, and then put your boat back in the water and keep going. But after that, you would go for maybe twenty miles and run into Mesa Falls."

"Mesa Falls isn't Niagara Falls, nothing that massive, but it drops one hundred twenty feet leaving a perpetual mist that paints the rock walls a mossy green. A permanent rainbow hovers. It's a beautiful spot for looking, but not a place for boating."

"Stevie, have you ever been down to Mesa Falls?"

"'I've been down there a couple of times. It would definitely be a problem having to go over that cliff in a boat. We don't want to deal with that, but it may be quite a ride."

"After the falls, it's probably good sailing for a while," I suggested, playing along with the ruse. "I've never been all the way down, but I know the river flows past the building where I used to gut sturgeons. Beyond that, I'm not certain.

"You would have to travel through the Snake River Gorge, then figure a way to survive Shoshone Falls. Too many rocks, too many cliffs, too many waterfalls."

"But after that," Stevie persisted, "would we be able to take a boat from there to the ocean?" I looked over at him between casts. Fish weren't biting much, and the conversation got a little peculiar. I wondered what he was talking about, taking a boat clear downriver.

"Henry's Fork isn't exactly the mighty Mississippi, a small river by any measure." I finally said, "Stevie, what are you talking about? What is all this about taking a boat down to the ocean?"

He was continually, mindlessly casting a Woolly Bugger fly over and over again, all the while still talking. His form was terrible, his fly on the water landing with a thud. Finally, he said to me after thinking about it for a moment, "Trippy, my family all came here from the old country. Then they were on the West coast for a time. They are wanderers. They've seen a lot of miles, a lot of land, a lot of different things, and they ended up here, by choice. I've never seen anything. I've never been given a choice about anything. I was born right here by this river, out on our ranch, and have been around sheep my entire life. Twenty-two years of doing the same thing day after day after day and I don't get paid a dime. I work for a family enterprise and I'm nothing more than an indentured servant. They expect me to stay around. My dad says, 'You'll get paid, be patient. You'll inherit all this one day. Don't worry about getting paid right now. What would you do with some money if you had it?' That's what started me thinking, what would I do if I had money, freedom, no chains? What if I got to chart my own course?"

He continued to unload his deepest concerns.

"I'm a wanderer by birth, chained to the shore. I want to travel, escape, see some other places. I want to meet other people. I am tired of looking these sheep in the eye every day. I'm tired of seeing the same people every day. I'm tired of seeing the same scenery every day. I'm tired of getting up early in the morning and going to bed late at night, doing the same things. All for the benefit of other people. It's like putting a boat in this fast-moving water and paddling upstream. Against the current, going nowhere. I don't feel challenged. I'm not learning anything. I feel like I'm accomplishing nothing. I don't have one thing to call my own. There are no real women to date," he trailed off. "Sorry, Trippy. I know I'm prattling on. It seems like time is just wasting away, passing me by. I'm wasting away."

"Passing you by like the fish are passing right by your pathetic fly presentation. In case you hadn't noticed the fish aren't interested in that Woolly Bugger. If you want to try something new and different you could start with a different fly."

He wasn't amused by my levity. He let the fly float in the current.

"What is it you want to do?" I pushed. "What are you telling me?

Where is it you really want to go? If you're serious, let me know. I may want to go with you."

"I don't know, but I want to think that I have a choice. I want to think that I could decide to do something on my own. It's true that I'll inherit that ranch someday, but Trippy, I don't know if I want it. I'd be inheriting land, animals, barns, and burdens. I'd inherit risk. I would spend the next fifty years buried in sheep shit. I may eventually want to run the ranch. It may work out in the end. But I'd like to take some time to decide if that kind of risk, that much work, is what I want. Maybe I do. Maybe in time, it would be a great place to settle down and raise a family. But I don't know right now if that's something I want to do. That's what I'm expected to do. No one has ever asked me what I want to do. I don't know what else I would do. But I want to try to decide that question after I've seen some other parts of the world, met some other kinds of people, had some different experiences."

Change the subject, change the subject, catch a fish, create a distraction, my brain kept circling. Stevie was confused, caught in a back eddy. The confusion I knew far too well. I was an expert in confusion. I was conversant in the language of back eddies, pulled in a swirl most days. Finally, something intended to be counsel trickled out of my mouth. Sincerity lacking wisdom.

"Stevie I've been there. I was desperately lost after the war, wandering aimlessly. Ironic that this mountain filled a gap for me, but it's still a big canyon for you. It has helped me think about the world differently. The mountains may not be my permanent home, but it's a place to start. It's a headwater, where the river begins. It feels comfortable most days. But I understand why you want to see some things. I'm the first to tell you to find your river. I'm not going to tell you, 'Go, get out of here.' And I won't beg you to stay. That's your decision. Whatever you decide to do, I'll support you and wish you Godspeed."

We got some nice rainbow trout that day. (Pale Morning Duns, the preferred menu item of the day.) Nothing big. We threw back smaller ones and kept going after the big ones, exercising the faith of a fisherman. Some days you got only small ones. We were always looking for the biggest fish which we believed was just one more cast away.

Standing in the river, watching it flow by, couldn't help but make even the sanest of people wonder what's down at the end of it. I was tempted to join Stevie, build us a boat, and set sail. Lewis and Clark did that very thing right in this area, checking out the Louisiana Purchase, finding a route to the West coast, paddling upstream until they crossed the Continental Divide.

In a strange twist, talking with Stevie helped me see that I had been fortunate in my wanderlust, ending in a good spot, blessed by hope. The current had taken me away from my demons, my darkness, my desolation. It took Stevie's longing to illuminate the gift I had been handed. If I was a writer, a poet, and I'm not, I could fill up an entire book with the thoughts I had about ends of rivers. Where they led, what possibilities were down around the next bend, any bend, beyond the whitewater rapids. The river never left my thoughts. When things got tough, I knew it was always there in case I needed a quick getaway.

It wouldn't be my first.

CHAPTER TEN

S peaking of gifts, Christina Pond fell out of the sky or crawled out of the river one afternoon. Blink. There she was. Christina was the volcano, reincarnated from the ash. She was molten magma. She disrupted everything in my life for the next few years. Business or pleasure, working or playing, she was part of the experience.

The only daughter of the Pond family, Christina was Lupine, Indian Paint Brush, and Columbine, wildflowers on the hillside, bursts of color, stealing the spotlight from the other natural wonders. You'd never compare Christina to Gretta Garbo or Fay Wray for looks, but you could never forget what a natural beauty she was. My entire adult life had been spent around dirty men. Foul, rancid, muddy men. The trenches in France. Gutting fish. Riding rails. I knew ugly, and I hoped I would recognize beauty. Blink. There she was.

Her beauty was painful if you stared; painful if you looked away. Everything hurt when she was around, and torment when she was gone. It was an impossible face. It was a face with a warning sign attached, big red letters on a yellow sign: 'This girl is not for you. You have been warned.' A hundred guys were lined up behind this circus attraction, so

I made it a habit to always walk the other way anytime she was around. I heeded the warning.

Her family built Pond's Lodge, most of the labor coming from family and friends. The whole family pitched in, girls included. Her hands, her clothes, much of her face was covered in a coat of mud, the maddening mud, the bane. She had the rare combination of red hair and blue eyes. Not the classic emerald-colored eyes or brown. Or hazel. These were deep blue eyes, infrequently given to redheads, a clash of color you would see if the forest was red, set against a green sky. It wasn't natural. Her eyes screamed crass insults to the elements, disrupting the natural order.

You would have to call her petite, I suppose, not small, but definitely slender and girlish. Until you saw her hard at work. All girlishness was gone, lost in a masculine disguise. A slightly crooked smile pulled up on one side, made you wonder if she doubted what you had to say, doubted if she was smiling at you, or mocking you, daring you to try to explain it.

Christina was also painfully young. She would finish up high school in town during the winter months. Summers were spent up in the mountains helping with the construction of their new lodge, located about halfway through the boundaries of Island Park, from Last Chance on the south to Henry's Lake on the north.

She wore dungarees, baggy and loose. A scarf around her head pulled and tugged in a futile attempt to tame her hydra hair. She wore her dad's large work shirts to make sure no one got a glimpse of her curves. Turns out the curves were substantial. She kept them hidden, out of sight of the desperate eyes, including my own. I was in complete look-away mode. Me and my desperate eyes.

Of course, I noticed female curves. Of course, I admired them. Of course, I longed to have a woman in my sorry life. But I had never known any woman long enough to think about curves or any other female anatomical wonders.

Christina Pond. Dubious curves. Questionable warmth. I didn't particularly like red hair. I sure as hell was never drawn to any girl who wore work boots all day. I tried to push away any thoughts I had of Christina. I was too old, too uneducated, and too poor to ever think she might be interested in a backward, awkward, rootless floater like me. I was at the rear of the line of dozens of laborers in that corner of Idaho, all dreaming of being with Christina. Hydra hair began to replace nappy wool in my dreams.

Christina didn't show interest in any of the Neanderthals any more than I showed interest in the prehistoric sturgeons running around the camps. She wore boots like some movie starlets wear high heels. She was comfortable in them, and they defined her. Say something off-color to her, and she'd put a boot right up your Neanderthal ass. She could work ten hours and keep up with any man. The boots sent a signal that she was there to work, not to be admired, and sure as hell not to be messed with.

She never came down to the dance hall, built entirely by hand–hers included–by the Pond family. She didn't like to dance. She didn't like crowds. And she didn't much like the pickins for a dance partner.

With the scarf off her hair, red flames looking for all the world like the torch of Lady Liberty, she walked into the dance hall, closer to running frantically. That red hair lit up the room brighter than the crackling fire in the gigantic fireplace they built a few years back. The fire, the one on her head, burned hot, throwing off sparks at right angles. She either didn't notice the stares or didn't care. She was on a mission. She was looking for her dad because her younger brother Luke had just taken a beating by one of the McQueen boys, Tanner.

Tanner was a hothead. Luke had apparently said something that started a different blaze, and they went at it. Luke was only eighteen and shouldn't have been drinking, but he was. Lots of it, clueless how to handle it. McQueen came close to killing him, but Stevie Zuninga and I were able to stop him and pull them apart.

I helped Stevie drag him in to cabin number 7, the farthest one away from the dance. Clyde Easton and his wife had rented it for a couple of months while he inspected the final stages of construction on the Island Park dam over on Henry's Fork. Clyde opened the door tentatively. His wife, Luanne, saw Luke's battered face. She screamed loud enough to wake every bull moose in the entire Yellowstone area and awakened every other guest in the cabins, tents, and automobile backseats. Easton helped drag Luke into the cabin and onto the bed.

I was anxious to join in the search for the McQueen kid and took off on the run. Christina rounded the corner and exactly that moment— blink. We missed a head-on train wreck by inches. She was frantic, rage burning on the top of her head, her face, gunpowder in her eyes. She came to an abrupt halt and asked if I had Luke. I nodded.

"Is he alive?" she asked.

"He's alive but he's in pretty bad shape," I told her as she walked tenuously into the cabin. She cringed and turned her back to the battered mess lying there.

Most of the guys wanted to round up a lynch mob and swing Tanner McQueen from a tree. McQueen's ranch was to become our largest customer, our business partner, and I selfishly thought about our relationship and whether or not I should walk away from this mess. I had to walk carefully. Onlookers had congregated, and a low murmur rose. Luke was a well-liked kid in the community. The

Pond family was highly respected. The crowd was on the verge of erupting into a mob. Wildlife rangers had called the sheriff, and he was en route. The would-be lynch mob rolled up the rope, quieted, and dispersed.

Christina and I stood there together in the darkness while everyone retreated. There was nowhere in particular for either of us to go. No words, just her labored, angry breathing. Her face now back to a safe pink, her expression blank. Her labored breathing hinted of an eruption-ready geyser.

She turned to me.

"Thank you so much for getting him out of there. Thanks for getting him into the cabin." Then to Clyde and Luanne Easton, "I'm grateful to you for patching him up. Do you think it would be alright to let him sleep here tonight? There is no doctor. I don't have another cabin. I'm sorry to–"

Luanne Easton jumped in, "He's just fine here. We'll make do."

"Thank you so much. I'm very grateful for your help," Christina told her. Pale blue eyes, watery, weary found mine, seared me. "What's your name?" I *knew* my own name. I thought I could *remember* my name until Christina Pond asked for it. My appearance transformed from human to a woolly ram, a look on my face like one of the stupid, expressionless, sheep.

"*Baahh*," I gurgled. Finally, "Wesley Tripp. They call me Tripp."

She said, "I've heard your name, Wesley Tripp. I wonder if you would do me a favor?"

Well, if she had asked me to jump down Old Faithful headfirst to retrieve her scarf, I'd have done it right then and there without thinking. *Baahh.*

"Sure," I managed.

"I want you to take me to Big Springs."

"Okay, when?"

"Right now. Can you take me there right now?"

"I don't own a car."

"I have a car," she said. "Do you drive?"

"I've got a license, yes. Sure, I can drive you over there."

The electric starter of a new model Chevrolet fired up immediately. Night-time temperatures in Island Park that time of year were already near freezing. Christina grabbed a man's coat from the backseat and pulled it on. She put another on my lap. The new heating system, recently installed into automobiles, felt good against the chill.

"Tripp?" she inquired. "What kind of a name is that?"

Baahh. I told her I didn't have a clue about the real meaning or if it even has a meaning.

"My mother said she had some French ancestry, but I'm not sure. My dad insisted it was a German name and came from the guys who sold sausages on the street. Their sausages were made from tripe, the worst part of the cow, so the vendors were known as 'tripes.' I guess they didn't like the association, so they changed it to a person who stumbles a lot it. Much better. Funny, it was true of me when I was young. I was kind of a clumsy kid, teased most days. They called me 'tripmeister.' "

I told her, "The guys call me Trippy."

It was idle chatter. Neither of us had much to chatter about after cleaning up after the fight.

"What do you do up here, Trippy? Most of the guys are either road crew, dam builders, or construction workers. Or fisherman. Which one are you?"

"None of those. I'm basically a sheep shearer. I shear sheep, more or less. I heard myself accidentally struggling with an unintentional tongue twister. She let go a little laugh.

"Seriously, you sure you shear sheep, sir?" She came back with her own version.

"Kind of. I help run a business that shears sheep. We are just launching the business and haven't started shearing just yet. I'm the foreman of a new business in this area. I'm not really much of a shearer myself, didn't ever get too good at it. My boss started the business and I work for him."

She seemed surprised.

"I've never seen sheep up here. I didn't know this was sheep country. Where do they hide?"

"Yeah," I told her. "It's a pretty big business but the ranches are farther up the foothills where all the grazing is and spread out all over the valley here." I waved my hand across the breadth of the landscape like a professional tour guide. She nodded, genuinely curious.

She knew her way in the dark, immediately jumped out of the car before coming to a complete stop, brisk and focused, making her way to Big Springs bridge.

"Why did you pull the two guys apart and drag my brother out of there?"

"The fight had become serious. Your brother was in trouble. I just happened to be there. Lots of guys would've done the same thing."

She looked me over, sternly. "I don't think so," she said. "Most guys were drunker than Luke, and it's possible no one would have bothered. He's only eighteen and shouldn't have been there." She made it sound half question, half command. We both listened to the quiet water, barely audible in the dark. "Shh."

She broke the stillness. "You know, Tanner McQueen will never be charged with anything. Everyone will have amnesia and won't rat him out. The McQueens are a big deal up here, and it's going to simply go away, isn't it?"

I nodded, "Yes. Probably. We don't see much law enforcement around here, once a month or so, not much help. There are fights like this most weekends, very common. The community seems to have its own justice system. I doubt Tanner is going to be much of a problem anymore."

"Do I want to know what that means?" she asked, haltingly.

"I know Tanner's dad, Jamie. I work with him. He's very important to what I'm doing. Tanner is not like his dad. We're bringing together most of the sheep ranchers and modernizing the wool industry. We're changing everything. The construction work will go away; it's already dying down and all these tumbleweed drifters will be blowing away soon enough. But the ranchers will still be here. They've already been here for more than forty years, came over here with just a horse and a dog, and made this place habitable. They're good people. Tanner is a good kid and was raised right. Everyone needs to calm down and not do anything drastic." My bias was showing. Deference to my customer's largest customer was glaring.

"You may not see my dad calm down. He's not going to let this just go away if that's what you're suggesting."

"Christina, I'm not suggesting anything. I have no idea what to tell you. I was glad I was there to help your brother. I've seen far too many of these fights, and a lot of them don't end well. Helping your brother felt like I was repaying a debt. A good man once pulled me out of a river where I was drunk and drowning. He saved my life. He dragged me up on this mountain to help him start this new business, and I got a chance to change my life, to walk into the unknown, and I took it. Best thing I ever did. Tanner has issues but he's going to need a second chance. He knows he made a mistake. Both boys made a mistake. I don't know if you want to forgive them or not. That's a private matter."

"Can I ask you something?"

"Sure."

"Why did you come up to Big Springs tonight?"

She leaned over the railing to try to see her reflection, any reflection here the dark. A crescent moon and a few malingering clouds were no help.

"I've spent three full summers up here now. It feels like I'm like an Austrian pine surrounded by fir trees. I'm the only one. I'm a female surrounded by a bunch of guys all cranked up by booze and testosterone. My whole family lives in a tiny little shack while we try to build up our place and make something out of it other than a dance hall where all those guys come to . . ." she searched for the right words, "to kick the shit out of each other. Someone told me people go crazy from the isolation. There are days when I'm pretty sure I've lost my mind. Winters up here . . . you been up here during winter?"

"This will be my first."

"I want to run back home and never come back some days, most days," she explained. "When I need to reclaim my sanity I come here to Big Springs. It's the only place I can go. It is my cathedral, my sanctuary, my confessional, and . . . sorry, that sounds a little . . ."

Awkward silence as I immediately recognized a common denominator.

"Tripp," she says, "how old are you?"

"Twenty-four."

"Ever been married?"

"Nope."

"Why not?"

I was baffled by her directness. She saw it in my eyes and added, "I'm sorry. I can be a little blunt."

"Because I'm terrified of women like you," I confessed.

"Like me? Tell me, please, what kind of woman I am. I sure as hell don't know. I thought of myself as fairly normal but tonight, I felt something foreign. If the crowd wanted to hang Tanner McQueen, I'd have handed them the rope. I can't believe the anger that rose up so fast. It's not me. At least I didn't think so. Tell me what kind of woman I am."

"Well, not a lot of women wear boots. I've never met one."

"The boots bother you?"

"No, not at all."

"Go on."

"Christina, right now, ten minutes on, is the longest I've ever been with a woman, talked to a woman. And now you're asking me to describe you? You're asking the wrong guy."

"Hmm. Your unbiased opinion may be the best one," she said with that crooked smile.

"I like that you come here to Big Springs," I offered. "So do I. A lot. This is going to sound crazy, but here goes. I've never talked to anyone about this, and no guy in his right mind would ever share feelings with a strange girl." *Baahh.*

"I'm a strange girl, then?" she said sarcastically.

"I mean you're a total stranger to me. Boy, you're making this difficult."

She apologized.

"I'm not good at any of this. It's just . . . "

She looked right through me. Blue eyes are arrows. Hydra hair waves to the stars. I leaned over the railing and talked to the fish, avoiding those blue eyes, a snare, a bear trap. I tried again.

"One day after spending a few weeks completely alone, I came here and stared down into that water. I saw the mountains, the clouds, the trees reflected in there. So was I. I was part of the picture. I was in the picture. It surrounded me. I felt like I belonged here. Maybe for the first time in my life, I belonged somewhere."

She stared at me, expressionless.

"I don't know," I continued, her eyes now strangely encouraging. "It seems so vast here, this unending sea of trees rolling on for hundreds of miles. Yet, it's a very small piece of the universe, this spot. It overwhelms me, at times, trying to comprehend what a tiny speck we are in the big picture. But that day, when I looked down in the water and saw my reflection, I had this sense that I wasn't just a speck in the universe. I was a part of the universe. When I feel alone, I come here, stand on this bridge, and look in the water. And there I am, in the water, moving with the water, a billion other specs headed downhill, on our way to the ocean. I'm in the water. I'm in the mountains. I'm here. I'm a part of it. I matter."

There was a long silence, just the faint sound of the spring coming out of the rocks, creeping along in the middle of the night, as consistent as it does all day. We both listened for a long time.

"Shh."

She finally broke the silence.

"Big Springs," she said almost disgusted. "Big Springs. Have you ever heard of such a stupid name? They couldn't come up with something better than Big Springs?"

I shook my head. *Baahh.*

"I'm cold," she said.

"A better man would have grabbed her and thrown twenty-fours years of chained up passionate heat at her, wrapped her up inside tragically lonely arms. Instead, I said . . .

"Let's go. The car has a great heater."

Later that night I realized how completely inept I was and what a great opportunity I missed. The car has a great heater. *Baahh.*

Shortly after that night at the bridge, I stopped in at Pond's to fill up the truck with gas and grab a few groceries. Christina spotted me before I had a chance to slink away. I hoped she wouldn't remember my incredibly bonkers little speech at the Big Springs bridge. I was certain she thought of me as a drippy pine tree, sap oozing out.

"Where are the headwaters of the Buffalo River?" she blurted out.

This is how she starts a conversation?

"What?"

"Where are the headwaters of the Buffalo River?"

"I'm not sure, why? I've never thought about it."

"The Buffalo River borders our lodge and runs mostly parallel to Henry's Fork," she explained. "They join hands downstream and eventually empty into the Snake River. I've been doing some thinking. There are several rivers and streams winding through here, and you can actually see where they all merge. I've checked them out. I know where they join forces. I know where all the water ends up. I want to know where they all begin."

"I never thought about it," I replied.

"Want to go find it?"

"Yeah, why not?"

"Sure. I've got some groceries, and I've got to drop off a couple of things over at the Ibarra place. How about I meet you back here in an hour?"

Junior interrupted me to ask, "Are you ever going to tell me what the fourth thing was that grew the industry? You got sidetracked by this fiery redhead. I'm enjoying meeting her, but are you ever going to tell me about the business? What was the business you were running? Where was Creighton in all this? You said you didn't see him for weeks on end."

"I am telling you what the fourth thing is. You're just not listening," I scolded my grandson. "I have to tell you all this other stuff because it's what shaped our business. It shaped me. We depended on a lot of different people and contractors and partners and laborers. There were itinerant guys who came and went, and it was hard to maintain continuity. Anytime we thought we were smoothing things out, there'd be sudden chaos, like snow in July. Or broken equipment. Feuds between families were something new. Joint ventures were new. Everything was complicated, and we hadn't fleeced a single sheep. So I'm telling you about the business, the distractions, and what we had to do to keep it going. And, believe me, this girl impacted my life in a big way. She quickly became my main distraction."

"Okay, Gramps, sorry. This is so good to hear you talk about it."

"That's fine, Junior. Some of this sounds off track but it's helping me to recall the chain of events that went on. You might have forgotten I'm an old fart, not as much gray matter as I used to have. It was a very successful business, but it had a lot of ups and downs along the way. All of it matters."

CHAPTER ELEVEN

Driving on barely a dirt road and beating up the car not made for off-roading, we set out to the find the Buffalo River headwaters. Christina asked me about Creighton.

"Tell me more about him. He sounds mysterious."

I told her he was not mysterious or invisible, just gone a lot. He pulled me out of the Snake River and took me in and became my friend. He made me the foreman. I had no relevant experience, but he gave me a chance. I still don't know why.

"Creighton is about fifteen years older than me. He's married and has a bunch of kids, I think, five or six of them. Eventually they all came up here most summers and helped out with cooking and other chores. Kind of like your family part-timing it in two places. They lived in Burley, Idaho, where the kids went to school. It's where they grew up.

"He's away from his family for months sometimes when he's working. We're currently building and pulling together all the mechanical work in Idaho Falls. We found the warehouse we needed, just about halfway between Burley and Island Park and he'll go home as often as he can.

"When we launched our business, he was running his portion from Idaho Falls; I was doing the other half.

"He was smart. He told me once his parents moved around a lot trying to find work. His dad eventually bought a farm but died trying to make a go of it. His mother died a few years earlier, and he told me he was an orphan by age thirteen. Here's a guy with almost no formal schooling, just a couple of years, but he could solve problems without even writing things down. He could build anything. He wasn't made to be a farmer. He was a thinker. He was inventive. They lost the farm, deeply in debt, after his dad died. His stepmother told him there was no reason for him to stay around, so he simply walked away."

"Why did he pull you out of the river?" Christina asked.

"He never told me why he was there. Maybe he saw in me another orphan wanderer and felt a kinship, the lost boys fraternity. He did mention once that another friend, years earlier, ended up in the river and never came out—drowned and washed away. He seems haunted by that. Just a couple of years ago his son, Doyle, ended up face down in a puddle of puke after getting drunk and starting a fight. That happened more than once with this oldest son.

"I don't think he ever went looking for people to fish out of the water. He simply ended up being there when someone needed help. It was uncanny, almost like someone was on a shortwave radio sending him signals. A spy decoding secret intelligence.

"He told me once that's how our business started. He didn't go looking for a way to help grow the wool industry. He knew very little about it. He was in the right spot at the right time, attuned to the right frequency. Other guys could've done the same thing, but he was the one who made it happen. He frequently told me, 'I've got to go. I've got things to do. I need to be somewhere else right now.' He would drop everything and leave. No warning, no notice. Like a butterfly he darted from flower to flower, one task to another. His mind was always working, always figuring things out, and getting them done even when it seemed impossible.

"He was used to scraping and scrounging for food and money. And survival. He never slowed down. Never stopped thinking up new things. He wasn't secretive, not mysterious, he wasn't absentminded. He could see things the way the rest of us couldn't."

"It sounds like you are describing a spiritual quality. A visionary. Would you describe him that way?" she asked.

"Wow, that's a deep subject. I'm afraid I don't know too much about it."

"I don't either," she replied. "It's not something we talk about in my family. I have a girlfriend in Lewiston who told me something once, and she used the word 'spiritual' to describe an experience. It's the first time I ever thought about it. He was in touch with the land, the environment, and had a sixth sense that was hard to explain. She said he wasn't religious but thought of him as spiritual."

I thought about that for a few minutes, then looked at Christina.

"I'd like to think there is a lot of spirituality without religion. I've seen a whole lot of religion without spirituality. I've never sorted it out, and I'm not sure how to go about sorting it out. Hard to describe what I saw in Creighton. Call it spirituality, I guess. Visionary, maybe. Insightful, maybe. Whatever it is, I wish I had some of it. I've tried to copy it and be more like him in the way he handles people and feels their needs. I've never come close. If I figure it out, if I find the secret huckleberry patch, I'll let you know."

"Huckleberry patch? Is that what you just said?"

"No, I didn't say anything about berries." I feigned innocence.

"She is an Indian from the Bannock tribe and had issues with her parents, a lot of pent-up anger and resentment that started when she was sent away to live with white people and get a better education. There were some people in our area who thought it was a good idea to try to make these Indian kids more white. She ran away and got into some pretty bad stuff. She really struggled with her identity, felt abandoned by her parents, and ended up on her own for a while. She told me that one of her tribal elders found her on the streets in Pocatello where she'd been wandering around. He took her home, back to the reservation and spent a lot of time with her, helping get her head back on. He was a guy that kept up the traditions of the tribe, and seemed old-fashioned, in touch with the land, the environment, and had a sixth sense that was hard to explain. She said he wasn't religious but thought of him as spiritual."

I thought about that for a few minutes, then looked at Christina. "I'd like to think there is a lot of spirituality without religion. I've seen a whole lot of religion without spirituality. I've never sorted it out and I'm not sure how to go about sorting it out. It's hard to describe what I saw in Creighton. Call it spirituality, I guess. Visionary, maybe. Insightful, maybe. Whatever it is, I wish I had some of it. I've tried to copy it and be more like him in the way he handles people and feels their needs. I've never come close. If I figure it out, if I find the secret huckleberry patch, I'll let you know."

"Huckleberry patch? Is that what you just said?"

"No, I didn't say anything about berries." I feigned innocence.

CHAPTER TWELVE

D id you find the headwaters of the Buffalo?" Junior asked. "I didn't hear you say whether or not you found it."

"You bet. We found it and had an experience not unlike Lewis and Clark, finding a new river, a new beginning."

Our first visit was late in the fall and the mosquitoes were mostly gone. It's a beautiful, hidden spot. Most of the year you can't get out of the car for all the mosquitoes, but that day was a perfect exception. Unlike Big Springs, with its single source of water rising up out of the ground, the Buffalo River had dozens of separate little springs. The entire ground moved, alive with water, all running downhill toward the Snake. This unusual source of water was hard to find. There was no map, and it took us some effort to find it. Walking around the area was an obstacle course; saturated marsh, peppered with occasional bites of solid ground.

There was no river yet, just the ingredients of a river being gathered together, moving together, thousands of gallons of water and minerals ignoring our presence, moving along, right at our feet. I tried to imagine how much clean, clear water there may be under all the lava beneath us. A bottomless reservoir perhaps, refilling itself each winter, a limitless supply for the flora and fauna strong enough, patient enough to push down through the cracks.

As we stood there letting the silence wash over us, it occurred to me that even during a drought there is plenty of water for the trees, down below all the rock, theirs for the taking. You can't see it, but the headwaters, this place where the river begins, gives you hints that it's down there. You just have to go down and get it.

We did find the headwaters that day and sat in the car for a long time talking. She was so inquisitive about everything including all this amateur geology and how it all worked. She was easy to talk to and helped me see and understand more clearly some of the conflicts banging around in my head.

As we spent time together, I saw two things in Christina. First, a beautiful, young woman with blue eyes that were pale blue in a way that even water and sky couldn't match. Second thing I saw was a rock. She was so certain of herself, so confident and unafraid, so firmly rooted. She was grounded and self-aware, focused on what she wanted from life, a stark contrast to my uncertainty and restlessness. I wanted to be with her, I wanted to be like her. I began to move past some of my own fears, my own doubts. She was showing me how, leading not dragging. She didn't exactly write down a list of how to do it, but I could see it in her. And more importantly, I could feel it in her.

We spent a couple of hours at the headwaters, watching the sun go down. The time passed too quickly. Junior, if it's alright with you, that's all I'm going to say about that little bit of history with Christina. I opened my heart up to that girl, and we had a very sweet and tender romance for a painfully short time.

Can we move ahead? We're still talking about sheep, aren't we?"

Yes, fine let's move on, Gramps. Thanks for sharing this with me. I'm so glad I got to meet Christina after all these years. Your story made her come alive. I can tell your memories of her are very tender."

I quickly changed the subject. We got back to the recording.

Junior, you listening to all this. or are you more interested in that damn phone in your hand?"

It's not just a phone, Gramps. It's like a little computer. While I listen to you, I take notes on this story so I can remember some of the questions I want to ask you."

Okay, okay," I told him, feeling a little chastised for not having a phone or brains enough to operate one.

CHAPTER THIRTEEN

Creighton spent sixteen hours a day designing and building new equipment to shear sheep. Remember, he wasn't an engineer or a scientist, but he came up with a big idea. It's this– think about thousands and thousands of sheep needing to be sheared, basically, all at once. A few breeds would need cutting a little earlier, some a bit later, but enormous herds of sheep all finished growing their wool coats about the same time every Spring. The wool had to come off each year or the sheep would be too hot in the summer heat. It's good for the sheep, and it's good for the ranchers who sell it.

As if that wasn't a big enough challenge, remember that the ranchers in those days had to move all their sheep to a shearing station in many cases miles from where they were grazing. For many years, the large shearing outfits set up camp out in the big meadow. That's the great big flat area you see over on the east side of the highway in Island Park. You follow it along the road on the way over to West Yellowstone. Mountains surround this caldera, this big old soup bowl which the volcano created, pine trees covering everything, rivers running through it. The meadow, by contrast, was flat and bare for miles.

Some of it was swampy but for the most part, it was home to a huge herd of antelope.

People would come just to see this herd. It became the central spot to bring the sheep to for spring shearing. It worked well enough when the herds were small, but with ten times the headcount, ten times the number of cars and tourists, it became impossible to move that many sheep from the hills, then back home again.

Creighton started meeting with the ranchers and presented them with a solution. They loved his concept and formed a consortium to work together to speed up the shearing. With Creighton's creativity and capital from the ranchers, they forever changed the industry.

Orange Nehi soda was Christina's beverage of choice. I preferred Coke but learned to love sipping the syrupy orange while sucking on chocolate Tootsie Roll Pops. This was a frequent event on Sunday afternoons, a large hand-crafted porch swing our preference over church pews.

She was curious, smart, and had a thirst for insights about the world, and our role in it. She deserved to know why our time together was so infrequent, so fleeting. I wanted her to know why I was so busy.

I kept a pair of the handheld shearing scissors in my car. These were the tools they were using at that time, the same tool used for shearing sheep for the last hundred years with little improvement along the way. I took them out of the backseat along with a cardboard box. I was violating my promise to not discuss anything about our plan, but Christina had me fully in her grasp where I felt comfortable. I was done keeping secrets from people.

We sat on the porch, and I looked around as if I were a spy in the war. She laughed.

"What is it? The invasion plans? Or is it the Holy grail?"

I had no idea what a Holy Grail was, never heard of it, so I waved it off.

"No, it's not the holy grail." I let her handle the manual snips. She squeezed the spring-loaded blades over and over as if shearing an invisible sheep. Her hand tired and cramped in less than a minute.

"This is how you shear sheep?" she said.

"Yes. This is how tens of thousands of sheep get sheared every day. It's brutally hard on man and animal. And it takes forever. Now take a look at this," I said, opening the cardboard box.

"What is it?" she asked. "What a weird-looking contraption."

"It's the future of the wool industry," I told her. "And we are very likely the first people in America to have it."

I removed the tool and placed it in her hands, deliberately and reverently, as this was now more important than the Holy Grail.

She turned it over and over, lightly touching every square inch of it. Heavy metal blades and leather-wrapped handle. I couldn't take my eyes off her hand as she inspected every inch. As valuable as this new device was, I wanted to throw it across the porch, into the river, and take her hand.

"Shearers have been using the same old scissors for decades, centuries really. Nobody has ever thought to change to something better. You're looking at a new mechanized tool that will make the hand-cutters completely obsolete. They'll reduce by 300 percent the time it takes to shear one sheep," I pointed out proudly, practicing my sales pitch. "Faster shearing, higher volume shearing, greater margins for everyone."

"Where did you get this? This could be miraculous."

"It is a miracle. I'm not sure of all the details. I didn't get it. Creighton did." I told her the story as I understood it.

"Creighton's grandfather Frederick William Hurst immigrated here from New Zealand. I had to get a map of the world to know where New Zealand was. I'd never heard of it. In land area, it's one of the largest countries in the world, the other side of the planet. They had more sheep than humans, millions of them throughout the country. They had the same problem we're facing–finding a way to have shearing keep up with demand. An engineer by the name of Wolseley developed this, a mechanized shearing tool in Australia. Through some miracle, Creighton ended up with one for us."

"How does it work?"

"I can't show you right now because it needs power. I don't have that right here."

"Is it electric?"

"No, it's not electric. We will be working in enormous camps, outdoors with no electricity. Even so, electric motors aren't powerful enough. We're a few weeks away from having a model ready to go. When we get it set up and running, get the bugs worked out, I'll show it to you. We're close to being able to show everyone. Creighton is building the power plant, and that's why he's never around. He's been working on it for more than a year, all the while taking on carpentry jobs and any work he can get to feed his kids.

"Basically," I explained to her, "there is a series of small rods running down a metal housing. Gears interlock, spin the rods, and move the cutting blades back and forth. It gets its power from a diesel-powered engine. Christina, you're holding the first mechanized clippers in the US."

She looked confused.

"I'm as dumbstruck as you," I said. *Baahh.* Oh, oh. I've been learning a lot about women in the last few weeks, and I was just about to have another big lesson.

"Dumbstruck? You think I'm too dumb to understand what you're saying?"

I stuttered, "It's . . . that's not . . . it's just an expression."

"I know," she added, her crooked smile smacking me in the head. "I'm just messing with you. It sounds confusing, but it is exciting. Congratulations." Her attention went back to the manual cutters, the one-hundred-year-old, preposterously inefficient snips. Two triangular-shaped blades attached to handles, welded at the top forming its own spring. It was a simple, ingenious tool, surprisingly lightweight. A shearer could grab the tool in one hand, hold the sheep in the other and get to work.

"Look at this," I said to Christina, holding the tool and squeezing it open and shut. "Imagine doing this for ten hours, bending over an animal who doesn't want to be sheared, breaking your back in the process."

Christina said, "I assume the shearers developed big forearms?"

"You would be right. These guys were world-class arm wrestlers—they could toss you clear across the room in an instant. Big arms and soft hands. The lanolin in the wool kept their hands soft as the down on those big Canadian geese you see around here. You do not want to get on the bad side of a good shearer. They are very strong, in the arms, their backs, and their legs. It's remarkably hard work."

"Show me your forearms," she ordered. I hesitated and grabbed the buttons on my long sleeves to prevent this highly personal intrusion. "Show me your forearms," she commanded. The rest of the time I knew her, when she commanded me to do something, I saluted her and followed orders. Willingly.

"They're pretty ordinary," I said as I unbuttoned my sleeve and rolled it up. "Just a regular-sized arm. We aren't doing any shearing right now, and I won't be doing much of that anyway."

"You're not a shearer?" she asked, surprised. "I thought that was your business."

"It is my business, but I flunked shearing school."

"School? There's a shearing school?"

"Well, not a real school. But, yes, it does require some training. Even the guys who have sheared for years with these old hand snips will have to learn how to use the new power tools. Part of what I'm doing is rounding up guys who want to learn the new process and get them trained. Remarkably, some of the very best shearers are refusing to change.

"Because of the large number of sheep to fleece every year, we have to attract the very best guys from around the West and get them trained on the new power tools. It's a very simple pitch: we will pay top wages for top shearers who help us speed up the process. The guys will be paid by the number of pelts they cut every day. I'm getting trained to shear so I understand it, but the training is revealing the reality that I'm never going to be good. It's like saying anyone can throw a football–I can't. Anyone can play the piano–I can't. Anyone can lay brick–I tried it once and the wall eventually fell right over. That's why I ended up gutting fish for a living."

"What a sad story, poor little lamb. If you're not a shearer, how will you manage your team?"

"I hope it will work out. I'm counting on being the guy that keeps them employed, keeps the paychecks coming. I've never been much of a foreman or a manager of anything, so I'm hoping for the best."

"Let me feel your hands," she said.

I followed orders, saluted. And for the very first time in my life, I touched a girl, a woman, a creature from another planet. The universe came to a screeching halt. All known theories of physics, time and space, astronomy; all got erased in that moment. Big Springs started running in reverse. The volcano took back its detritus, re-mediated the effluvium. The planets sling-shotted out of their orbits and stars began to collide in a massive cosmic event. The only thing that remained in the entirety of the universe was that hand. That beautiful, young hand.

I placed my hand in hers. She stroked it softly. *Boom!* There goes Jupiter. She turned it over and petted the palm, tracing the creases. Wham! There goes Saturn.

She looked me straight in the eye, pale blue eyes hypnotizing, holding me in her orbit. I didn't blink. I didn't dare blink, afraid I would miss something. I didn't breathe. I was frozen. I stared into the abyss of her face for what must have been a week.

"They are softer than my hands," she said. "They aren't working hands at all. They are softer than a baby's cheek. They're very girlie." She suddenly pulled away. Her hands were much grittier and calloused than mine and she feigned embarrassment.

"You're a laborer, and you wear boots," I reminded her. "You're a bricklayer and a carpenter. What did you expect? Would you like to come and learn how to shear sheep and improve those manly hands?"

Eyes locked again, and I was about to have the first kiss of my life. If the universe came completely unraveled, if every black hole disappeared just by holding my hand, imagine what happened when she leaned in and put her lips on mine. I'll just leave it at that.

"Junior, are you listening?"

"Oh, yes," he said. "I'm listening to every word. Please continue. I've never heard this story. I have always thought Grandma was your first and only love."

"I loved your grandmother very much, in very different ways. We had a great 63 years together. Christina taught me how to fall in love, how to love someone, and get love in return. She prepared me to be a better man and to better understand women. Christina was the second person to save my life and help me believe in myself, the way a really good woman can do. When I thought about all the water that went under my feet over the years, I would always think of her as my headwater, where a river begins."

"Christina, could I ask you to keep this quiet for now? We are being financed by our partners, and they haven't seen this yet. They know about it, that's why they put up the money. But we're going to do a big demonstration for them . . ."

She leaned in and gave me another kiss as though it were the most natural thing.

"Don't worry. That's two secrets I now have. I'm not talking about either one to anyone, anywhere."

We both understood the contract we made with our eyes, just as her brother Luke walked out to the porch. Scrambling, the clippers went back in the box. Back into hiding. But Luke did see them.

"What you got there, Trippy?"

"Gotta run. See you later," I said, jumping up.

"Did I break up something here? What's going on?"

"Nothing's going on," Christina said dismissively. "We barely know each other."

Luke gave us an icy stare.

CHAPTER FOURTEEN

"Gramps, I'm fascinated. But I have a question. This was a very small part of the world, very isolated. It was apparently good sheep country but very far removed from California, or Chicago. Why didn't the big markets have access to this power tool? Why didn't the wool industry here in the states know about it? How did you guys get the very first tool?"

"I can't be one hundred percent certain we were the first, but it's very possible. Wolseley, the company that invented these devices in Australia, was selling the power clippers to New Zealand by then and looking to expand elsewhere. They were pushing into England and Scotland and other parts of the European continent. Wolseley knew they needed to get to the US market, but this was ages ago, Junior. It took forever to make things like that happen. Eventually, everyone had the power tools, but we were ahead of the curve. Even if we weren't the very first, that's my story, and no one has ever been able to prove me wrong."

Creighton's grandfather immigrated here from New Zealand. That's the connection. His kids were all born here in the states and they settled in Logan, Utah. A big bunch of his family ended up in that area, but the old man ended up homesteading in Idaho Falls. The family eventually discovered "white gold"–wool. Grazing was free. Cost of entry was doable with government-backed loans. Family relatives still in New Zealand were encouraged to immigrate and take advantage of the opportunity in the Caribou/Yellowstone/Jackson Hole area. Creighton's father, Samuel Hurst, sent a letter to some family members, encouraging them to emigrate from New Zealand. They were sheep people, after all, and the opportunity seemed attractive.

"Some months later, family members started showing up. No European exodus, no Ellis Island tidal wave. Just a small flock of humble family members ready to work. Ready to raise sheep.

A welcome party of Hurst relatives packed the pavilion at the city park in Idaho Falls, along the Snake River running right through the center of the town. This wasn't as exotic as a Basque party. The new arrivals enjoyed American food, fried chicken, potato salad, fresh-baked rolls slathered with honey butter. Without fanfare, no release of balloons, no skywriting, or cutting of a ribbon, one of the new emigres unceremoniously unpacked the Wolseley power clippers as if just another pair of socks, and set it on the table. Talking, eating, celebrating all stopped. The men at the table recoiled as if the tool was a snake. A half dozen of the men squinted, blocking out the sun with a raised hand, jaws slackened. In New Zealand, the mechanized shearers were as common as a toothbrush, underwear, a belt to hold up a pair of pants. To the Idaho farmers, it was an alien spaceship. No one dared touch it.

Creighton was in attendance at that family reunion. He knew exactly what it was and reached for the clippers. The sea of men parted, making way for Moses. He palmed the leather grip, cradled it in his hand, mentally calculating weight and balance. It is a tiara from the British Crown Jewels. It is a Faberge egg from Russia. It is a gold doubloon from a sunken ship. It is a Ming dynasty vase.

"Is this what I think it is?" Creighton asked.

His cousin said, "It's the mechanized shearers we use to shear sheep. What kind do you guys use? Do you have Wolseley's or some American brand?"

"We've never seen them. We are still using manual snips," Creighton said, his calm voice masking incredulity. His cousin waited for the punch line, wondering if Creighton was the alien. Creighton not only recognized the potential of the power tools, he knew the right questions to ask. How fast can it fleece one animal? How many of these instruments can you get? When can you have them here? How much will it cost to get thirty of them here, immediately?"

That's it. A business was launched over a bowl of Idaho potato salad. That's how it started. That's how prescient Creighton was. Within days, Creighton was scheming and planning, scheduling, organizing, designing, and building the first mobile shearing operation in the country. His inquiries told him everything he needed to know.

Using Wolseley clippers, the large outfits overseas were fleecing staggering numbers of sheep. The average count, using the old manual snips, thirty sheep per day per cutter jumped to 200. Each guy, 200 sheep a day. This was a big, big number, just what the moribund industry needed. It's what the country needed as demand for wool began to skyrocket. The New Zealand guys had the technology for two years, and they were shocked to know that America had never seen them. The

Wolseley company would, no doubt, welcome this open door into the American market.

Creighton sensed the potential instantly. One problem eluded him. What powers it? His New Zealand cousins didn't have answers. They were laborers, not engineers.

Two days later, Creighton had what you would today call a business plan. Back in 1926, he was the equivalent of entrepreneurs we've seen in today's tech industry. It wasn't exactly as big a deal as the computer or the Internet, but in the wool industry, in the shearing world, at a time of robust growth, this was disruptive technology. And Creighton saw it.

He pondered one of two business opportunities. First, acquire a license for the clippers and sell them to every sheep ranch in the US. He didn't know licensing, distribution, selling, or running a business. He rejected this concept and moved on to the second.

He believed if he could power this device remotely, he could take a shearing plant to the ranches, so the ranchers don't have to move the sheep. As glaringly obvious as this now sounds, it was a breakthrough at that moment. Stop the enormous task of moving thousands of sheep. Take the shearing plant to them. In short order, he had a business plan on PowerPoint slides.

Junior jerked his head up, "What did you say?"

"Just kidding. Aren't you impressed I know about PowerPoint?"

His business plan was all in his head, not even on a napkin. This was about three years before the bank industry collapsed, triggering the Great Depression. The timing was perfect. Banks were still making collateralized small business loans, something that dried up just a few years later. He needed collateral, he needed operating capital, and he had neither.

He invited most of the successful ranchers in the area to a meeting one December day in Rexburg. The ones that couldn't make the first meeting got a personal visit and a look at the strategy. Creighton told me he felt like young David standing in front of a group of Goliaths, his only weapon a slingshot and a few stones. The ranchers needed to modernize, they needed to accelerate shearing and time to market, they needed help, and no one laughed when the slingshot came out of his pocket.

His idea is this: instead of taking the sheep to the shearing plant, he'd bring the shearing plant to the sheep. It would all be mechanized, and we'd shear sheep 300 percent faster.

That was the simple strategy. A few hundred questions later, the top five ranchers in the Yellowstone area bought in. Others quickly followed suit. They would use their credit and their ranches as collateral to finance the operation. It was high-risk but with a handshake contract and trust in this unproven entrepreneur, an important new business was launched.

With the help of McQueen and Zuninga, other ranch operators soon joined the group, creating enough critical mass to make the bankers believers. Everyone in the deal left Rexburg looking for large bottles of Bromo Seltzer to settle nervous stomachs. They believed it was the right business strategy, but they must have wondered if they had the right guy leading it. This prominent group felt restless, lined up in pens, nervous about being fleeced.

With a few hiccups, a few twists and turns, Creighton arranged to buy clippers. His connections with New Zealand paid off. His cousin went to work getting as many as he could. Creighton knew he needed twenty or thirty or more clippers long-term, as well as parts for repairing and maintaining them. He'd need at least a dozen immediately, one each for the twelve shearers he calculated would be needed to start.

And he needed the best sheep shearers in the business. His partners in the consortium already knew five or six of the best guys in the area. There were no phones, no fax machines, no email. It was cost-prohibitive to travel all over the country, and there wasn't enough time. Buying clippers, getting them on shore took time. Designing and constructing a power plant was going to take much longer.

"That's just about the time when Creighton pulled me out of the water and put me to work. He had no job description for me, no employee handbook, no clear strategy about what to do next. I had even less of a notion than him. Only one thing to do, get going.

CHAPTER FIFTEEN

My primary job in those early months was to find world-class shearers, and I felt certain we could get the best guys in the immediate area. They all knew each other, they all knew most of the ranchers involved, and always seemed to know when and where there was work. When they found out we had power shearers there were invariably one of two responses. One, *it'll never work.* Two, *when can they be ready?* We wanted the second kind of guy.

Mechanized sheep shearing to some seemed as ludicrous as the notion of automobiles replacing horses twenty years earlier. Mechanized sheep shearing? Why is that a big deal? How hard can it be? There was no middle ground. Bankers, ranchers, shearers either loved them or hated them. While many people saw the potential, others feared getting left behind. To Creighton, it seemed the ultimate myopia. Love/hate; optimism/doubt; excitement/fear; confidence/terror. With any disruptive innovation, there were always early adopters facing off against laggards. Edison faced it. Bell faced it. Ford faced it. Orville and Wilbur faced it. Innovation always attracted pessimists the way Island Park mosquitoes were attracted to a skinny, white Ohio guy hiding out in the mountains of Idaho.

The new shearers were going to have to change their routine if they wanted to modernize and not be left behind. Change was coming and the best of the best embraced the challenges.

Getting my first seven guys on board was a breeze.

A couple of young Basque guys in the area were our first pick because they already knew the process. They grew up with sheep. To some doubters, it may have looked incestuous hiring the sons of our customers. They got preferential treatment because they were highly skilled. Proud. Proficient.

First was Bernardo Velasco. He was shorter than a prototypical shearer. Guys used their legs to hold the sheep steady between their knees, so long legs were preferable, but strength would do. Velasco was powerfully built. Using the traditional hand cutters, he regularly rang the bell wherever he went. He was a highly regarded shearer.

Number two was Tanner McQueen, the guy that beat up Christina's brother. His dad shipped him back to Edinburgh for a time, hoping for a little bit of growing up. He couldn't keep control of his temper. The kid was angry all the time at everybody. Didn't need a reason to be pissed off. He came out of the womb furious at the awkward way he had to come down the birth canal and be disconnected from his mother and stayed mad at everyone. He was trained to use the power clippers by some of the sheep ranchers in the Scottish highlands and came home a little less angry, a lot stronger, and very talented. Jamie was our biggest investor and our biggest customer, so when Tanner came back from Scotland, well-trained, we took him on.

Number three was the Elizondo kid, Tony to us, Anton to his mother. He was a good-looking guy, rugged, with six or eight battle scars on his face. His nose had been broken, so too his jaw. His angular face developed hard edges as doctors kept patching him up. His dark, bushy eyebrows sat on his face at angles, a downward tilt toward the bridge of his nose, making him look perpetually angry or doubtful. His angry eyebrows hid a charming personality and a warm demeanor. When he first started shearing, he was naturally good. His skills diminished for a time after he broke his right hand aiming for a guy's face, missed, and hit a large pillar in a bar in Ashton. His battles made him stronger. He grew up on a Basque farm, and Basque kids knew how to work hard.

Fourth was also a local kid, Jonathan Apidale. Big, strong hands, very little hair, and always sported a big handlebar mustache, carefully groomed. Guys thought his name sounded like Johnny Appleseed. It didn't help that his face was covered with apple seeds otherwise known as freckles. He grew up over in DuBois, and this was an unusually smart kid. Not smart enough to stay out of the sheep biz but smart enough to have gone to the forestry program over in Cheyenne at the University of Wyoming. He wanted to work in wildlife management and got an offer after he graduated. By then he had a baby on the way, and his wife didn't want to leave home. He hoped to get back to the woods, but he learned to shear sheep when he was younger, and he liked what we were doing. He loved the animals and damn if they didn't respond to him better than any of the other new guys. Apidale played some football in high school, and though never much of a standout, he understood the concept of leverage. He played left tackle on defense and knew how to stay low over your legs and drive hard against your opponent. He used this skill and knowledge against the biggest ewes and the orneriest rams. I knew for a long time I wanted him on the team. He would help the other guys learn leverage.

Red Borrowman was number five. 'Red' wasn't a nickname, his mother just liked the name 'Red.' He actually had dark eyes and dark hair, and there wasn't anything about him that was red. His nickname came easy, Ivan the Red, after the Russian guy that banished the Czars and took over that godforsaken country just a few years earlier. Damn good worker, a little older than the others, adding some maturity to our youthful bunch.

A guy named Wright was our number six. He didn't have a lot of experience shearing sheep, but he was on the lam and needed work. He wasn't running from the law, just from his old man. I don't think there was much hate or anger with his dad, he just didn't want to take over the old man's business which was bricklaying. He had been carrying buckets of hod up and down ladders since age six, and he was ready for a change. Shearing wasn't exactly his first choice for a career, but he found us during a fishing trip, hiding out from family. He knew how to work and had the right hands, calloused already. He was a quick learner.

Sabino Arana brought our number up to seven. This was also a Basque kid. I say kid, but he was just a bit younger than me. He was an enormous guy, but the team started calling him 'The Bambino,' an irony clearly lost on this guy. He didn't speak much English. He was one of the more recent immigrants from the old country who came over, sponsored by his relatives, to make more money. He was one of those rare guys who could go up into the hills for nine months, living in one of those small, portable wagons, and stay with the flock without human contact. Eventually, he grew his own flock of sheep and turned out to be just like his uncle Unai. Great guy. Later on, he started being called Sabino Marino after the new kind of sheep we started seeing.

More than half the team was in place. The final five would take a more concerted effort."

CHAPTER SIXTEEN

We were off to a good start, but I needed at least another half dozen shearers to begin. We would likely need three or four backups. It was a slow process. There were plenty of candidates, and I met dozens of them, but they simply weren't right for what we were doing. Many of them resisted the idea of mechanization, laughing at the idea of changing from their beloved old scissors. We had to get the best, so we kept looking, our hunting hindered by the primitive world of snail mail and word of mouth.

I started a training school using the single pair of clippers we had in our possession. We hoped Creighton's cousin from New Zealand, the guy that brought the first Wolseley's to us, would be able to train everyone, but he caught the wanderlust bug and set out to see New York City and Chicago, the real America he had heard about. Creighton and I had both learned to shear using the manual snips but neither of us was very good. We had no experience with the mechanized clippers and struggled to make progress. Creighton was a gifted teacher, and at that point, he was the only one who knew anything about the new mechanized machine.

He was determined to pull this off. He was using other people's money and it had to succeed. He spent long hours learning the touch and nuance of the handheld device. He worked with Tanner McQueen who had experience in the Scottish camps, but he was still a novice and wasn't good enough to teach. We tried to get any helpful tricks from the Wolseley company, but they were on the other side of the world. After three months of wrangling, we finally got a shipment of four more clippers and a temporary power source.

The chief engineer, the inventor himself, made a handwritten list of troubleshooting tips and some techniques for training. Sheep outfits in New Zealand had been using the technology for about two years and we would hear tales about their proficiency. The fastest shearers in the world were New Zealanders but none of them were riding in on a big, fluffy wool cloud to save us. We had to find our own solution.

Creighton took the training list and the crude drawings from Wolseley and enhanced them. He'd inherited a talent for drawing from his grandfather. He didn't draw or paint, at least as far as I know, but he stayed up many long nights, a Coleman lantern for light, painstakingly creating twenty copies of the training techniques and the safety precautions, along with repair and maintenance information. He was like a monk, sequestered away, hand-lettering copies of the Bible.

"The letter from Wolseley also indicated they would have ten more clippers for us shipped by boat by month's end. Our goal was to be shearing sheep during the spring season of 1927. Build an entire sheep shearing plant, hire world-class shearers, design and build the first-ever mobile power station, and be ready to hit the road where one hundred thousand sheep would be anxiously waiting. We were behind schedule before we started.

It was about to get worse.

Our early training was theoretical. We didn't have enough equipment to begin hands-on training. The small group we had assembled was anxious to start practicing on the real thing. They were penned-up bucks kicking at fences. Each of the ranchers in the consortium pulled five of the woolliest sheep from last year's herds so we could make the first attempts at learning the process.

The new mechanized cutters were very much like a barber uses to this very day on the little hair I have left. The Wolseley's utilized a series of two blades that vibrated at high speed, back and forth, cutting everything in its path. What made them different from modern human clippers were triangular blades atop a comb, so-called because it helped push the clippers through the tough, tangled wool, lifting the thick, heavy mat so the blades could get a clean cut. It sounded easy, looked easy, but was much more difficult than we expected.

There were two fundamental problems. We would cut so short it would cut the sheep. And if we kept it too long the pelt would fall apart, like a dandelion in the wind.

Before the training started in earnest, Creighton had some issues to deal with. Nothing to do with the business. It was a personal matter, a family matter that he didn't want anyone to know about. He began the training, but it was obvious his heart–and mind–weren't in it.

The training on live sheep was a debacle. The guys were frustrated and couldn't get past their own muscle memory and the dramatic changes in technique. There was yelling and griping by the entire crew, a mutiny fomented. Creighton could barely keep control. Arana vanished for two days, moaning that the naysayers were right. This would never work. His rationale: 'Manual clippers never break, never clog, never overheat.' To a man, we began slipping on the steep negativity hillside. Creighton and I both had to acknowledge the possibility of failure. It was hard to ignore Arana's simple logic.

The crew grew restless, tense, penned sheep packed tight in a small corral, a wolf stalking around, beady eyes glowing in the dark. They were going to start jumping fences. The team we hired had everything we needed to be successful. To a man, they had the strength. They had the agility. And they all shared one other trait—a natural killer instinct. They wanted to be good. They wanted to be the best. They wanted to be part of transforming their trade. They were able to do the math and count up the kind of money they could make. The crew groused. The wolf lingered.

The equipment finally died. Training would have to wait for a while."

CHAPTER SEVENTEEN

Before leaving town to get back to his family, Creighton met with all the stakeholders–the reassurance tour. Money was, of course, scarce as a black face sheep in a flock of Rambouillet. There was no income just yet. Creighton was getting paid a small amount by then to keep supporting his family, and the consortium was paying me a small amount. Creighton gave up all carpentry side jobs. He was now fully engaged in making it all come together. I had room and board with the Sorensons, so I didn't need much money. I felt certain that I would have better paydays just days ahead.

Our first seven shearers were working with the sheep ranchers as hired hands, helping with feeding and wintering the sheep, maintaining corrals, barns, etc. They were shearers, not farmers. They were craftsmen, not hired hands. They were arrogant. Shoveling shit was an affront.

Cash flow to the enterprise was difficult but it somehow kept flowing, little by little. One of McQueen's banker friends helped us find a solution, a business practice called 'take or pay'. Manufacturing companies all over the world had thousands of looms running full capacity in that era. Wool was the fabric used for everything from women's dresses and men's suits to blankets and Army uniforms. There was a consistent stream of orders for more and more wool. To keep their raw materials flowing and keep the looms running, the mills needed a guaranteed supply chain.

Take or pay is an agricultural term, mostly. Here's an example from today's world. Potato farmers rarely have to shop around for buyers for their potatoes and haggle over price. Their crops are sold before they are planted. Big potato processors, for instance, have contracts in place with growers. Fast food restaurants do the same thing. Farmers have guaranteed sales of their healthy crops at a predetermined price. The buyer pays a penalty if he doesn't take the crop. If the crops are no good, the buyer doesn't have to pay. Win/win. What it gave our business was borrowing power from banks, purchase orders as collateral. Our crop was standing in the field on four legs. Wool kept growing regardless of weather, crop disease, floods, or a pissed off Mother Nature. The harvest was always good.

That's what was happening in wool. The ranchers began increasing the herds when they got guarantees from the mills like Pendleton, Woolrich, and Faribault. Demand kept going up and the ranchers kept buying, kept breeding. According to the plan, the mills would send out their quality control guys to grade the wool and get it on the trains. We would get guaranteed purchasing and advance money because our wool had already been going to these mills via a middleman. They knew our wool was high quality, and they wanted all they could get. Everyone under this new arrangement would make more profit because we would be able to cut out the middlemen.

Everyone just needed to do their job. Ranchers fed the sheep. The shepherds tended. Wranglers wrangled. Shearers fleeced. Wool manufacturers got it to market and turned it into sweaters. Our primary contribution to the supply chain was mechanization. We were there at the right moment in history. Our business wasn't sheep. It wasn't wool. Our business was speed.

It was good business and continued for a couple of years as we rode the wave of demand. We always believed we helped create the wave, those of us who wrestled thousands of ornery animals, breaking backs in the heat, working sunup to sundown. Our little contributions, small as they seemed, made a big difference in the lives of a lot of people. We weren't just a speck in the effort, we knew we were a vital part of it all.

Very few people in the entire region knew about these power tools and the magnitude of changes coming. We hadn't revealed them to anyone. I showed them to Christina and, of course, our five partners knew all about them by now. Bankers as well. Our early trainees knew. But we kept it under wraps for the most part. Our competitive advantage put us well ahead of the competition, for now.

"I knew Christina's brother had seen the tool, but I doubted he would figure out what it was. I knew I had made a mistake by not being more cautious, and it became a worry for me, a lingering concern when I lay down on my cot each night. My worries would all vanish the moment I thought about Christina. Her blue eyes glowed in the night, a wolf in sheep's clothing lurking outside my door."

CHAPTER EIGHTEEN

Meanwhile, Creighton left for a few days. He got word from Burley that Doyle, his now 17-year-old son, was missing. It wasn't the first time he disappeared. This time it was for three days. The kid usually found his way home after a 24-hour binge. With his dad gone so much of the time, Doyle began resenting him. He hated being the man of the house. He resented his sisters. He hated the rigidity, the rules, the expectations imposed by mother, father, family obligations. He grew angrier and angrier with the world. Alcohol became his comfort, his escape from reality. Recreational drinking, partying, innocent at first, alcohol began to control his demon-possessed life and fuel his rage.

Creighton arrived in Burley but didn't go directly home. You can't say he sped down the mountain. Automobiles had maximum of 40 horsepower engines. Today's scooters have more. High-speed was 30 mph. Maybe. He pushed the car as hard as he could, two potential failures looming.

He walked in the front doors of the high school, right past the office of the principal.

Old man Mulka gave chase, barking, "Creighton, you can't come in here like this! I know what you're doing. You can't do this. I'll call the sheriff."

Creighton shouted over his shoulder, "Need his number? I know it. He's my brother-in-law."

"I know he's your brother-in-law, Creighton. Stop for a minute. Wait."

He huffed and puffed and bent over to grab his side, sucking for air. Old man Mulka would run out of energy simply pushing a grocery cart through the aisles. He was probably 350 pounds, maybe a slight exaggeration, but I don't think so. On a 5' 5" frame, he resembled a bowling ball rolling down the hallway. He was unaccustomed to running.

Burley High School was small, built to handle two hundred kids. It was a reasonably new building but had the kind of musty odor that followed kids living on farms; it was in the walls, the sweat-stained memories of anxious teenagers. Creighton's long legs in the short hallways got him from the front door of the building to the classroom he needed in about fifteen seconds.

Hearing the commotion out in the hall, Gene Jones jumped up and immediately ran to the door. He made a desperate prison break just as Creighton stuck out his right leg and sent the kid spinning to the ground. He didn't simply trip. Creighton kicked him so hard he did a near-perfect ten Olympic-caliber backflip, landing first on his feet then right to his butt with a crack. His tailbone was shattered.

He fell back and screamed, "You son of a bitch! You broke my back!"

"It's just your butt," Creighton assured. "If I'd wanted to break your back, you would have been in a body cast three years ago. Your head is next, you little weasel."

Creighton grabbed the kid by his left foot. When the shoe came off, Creighton gave it a toss and continued pulling Jones, his shattered coccyx dragging on the cold, hard linoleum floor.

Jones started screaming, "Somebody call the cops. Call my parents. Get this goon off me. Somebody call the sheriff."

Principal Mulka hollered, "The sheriff's on his way."

Creighton threw the kid in the backseat of the car and said, "No one is going to hear you crying in here so put a sock in it."

Creighton's heavy foot crushed the accelerator and the mighty 40-horsepower engine lurched and coughed and belched a smoky cloud just as the bowling ball rolled up to breathe it in.

Sheriff Ray Mitchell got the call. He told the dispatcher he'd personally go over to the school. He decided there was no hurry, so he stopped at the hardware store to get the new hinges he'd been needing to fix a squeaky door.

Sherm Anderson at the Cassia Lumber and Hardware store told the sheriff he didn't expect the hinge till morning.

"Damn it, Sherm. You told me that a week ago. I may have to lock you up for giving me false information. Now when that hinge gets in you bring it over to me on the double."

"Yessir." Sherm knew Mitchell was in no hurry to get anywhere, stalling, taking his time. Slow and easy was derigueur for Sheriff Mitchell. He sat in the car, savoring every bite of an Almond Joy that Sherm gave him, carefully getting a bite of almond in each bite. With a toothpick he removed the coconut flakes from his teeth, spitting them onto the floor. Certain his teeth were clean, certain he had given Creighton a head start, Mitchell slowly made his way to the high school to investigate another Mulka mess.

Mulka, drenched in sweat, coughing exhaust fumes into a handkerchief, greeted him at the door. "Creighton took that Jones boy and they left thirty minutes ago. What took you so long to get here?" Mulka screamed, spittle flying everywhere.

"Calm down, Mulka. They can't get far. I was busy breaking up a German spy operation out in Declo. Which way did Creighton go?"

Creighton stopped the car and turned to Gene, moaning in the backseat. "Stop crying, you little pissant," he ordered. "Where is he?"

"Who?"

"Don't play games with me, Gene. Where is he?" No reply.

Creighton accelerated the car to the top end, then slammed on the brakes. Gene Jones went flying from his seat-belt-less seat and slammed his face into the front seat. A tooth punched through his bottom lip. As blood ran down his chin, Gene let loose a string of profanities.

Creighton pulled the car onto a side road just to the West of Bill Taylor's farmhouse. He turned in his seat to face Gene.

"Where is he? I'm not going to ask again."

Lip puffed up, bloody, Gene whimpered, "He's over at Dalton's."

"Why is he there?"

"There was a bit of a party a couple of nights ago."

"Beer or something else?" Creighton asked, calmly, handing the kid a handkerchief.

"It was beer, I swear. Nothin' else. No bootleg whiskey, if that's what you're asking."

"Where'd you get the beer?" Creighton asked, now in a concerned, fatherly voice, gentle and calm. "Where'd you guys get the beer, Gene? Please help me. I need to know."

Long pause.

"Doyle stole it. We stole it. Him and I and Junior Larsen got it from the backroom of Dalton's club, out the far end of Overland Drive."

"I know the place. How bad is he?"

"Tom Dalton, the owner of the place found out who stole a couple of his cases, and he tracked us down. The party was at the football field. Doyle was so out of it, Tom was able to lay it on Doyle pretty hard. Doyle had no chance to defend himself. Most of us got clean away, but Doyle was already pretty hammered. He couldn't stand up, much less fight. Or run. Dalton was pissed, and he took it out on Doyle. He's in pretty bad shape."

"Get out," Creighton ordered.

"What?"

"Get out of the car."

"Out here? I want to go with you. Take me with you."

"You can't go with me."

"Then take me back home," he begged. "You broke my back and cut my lip. I can't make it home in this condition."

"Your condition is about to get a lot worse if you don't get out of the car. If you prefer, I will take you home and let your dad know exactly what happened. He will then give me permission to let Sheriff Mitchell take over, assuming your dad doesn't kill you first. You choose."

Gene rolled out of the car to avoid bumping his shattered tailbone. Creighton shoved him the rest of the way, putting his boot right on the cracked coccyx. Gene crawled along the pavement like a dog hit by a car, his whimpering similar in tone. When he finally made it to his feet, he began the six-mile trek back to town. His left shoe was back at the high school.

Creighton watched him for a minute, thinking about his next move. He looked upward, put his nose in the air, took a deep breath, then headed straight to Dalton's club/bar/speakeasy. He was calm and deliberate, grabbed the tire iron from the trunk, took a deep breath.

He paused for the sunlight to clear from his eyes and adjust to the dark, dank room. He had frequented bars, never to drink, but to rescue lost sheep. The same sour smell of vomit, beer, perfume, and PineSol was common in these illegal 'clubs.' In a farming community, there was also the subtle aroma of potatoes and alfalfa trapped permanently in the floorboards. Tom Dalton, the only person in the place, was getting ready for the after-work crowd, the prohibition-be-damned crowd.

"Creighton, I've never seen you in here before. Can I get you a long-neck?"

"What's a long-neck?"

"The bottle has a longer neck. It creates a little more foam."

"Sure," says Creighton. "Bring me a longneck."

Dalton popped a lid off one of the bottles and set it in front of his uninvited guest.

"You know I don't drink."

"No, I didn't know that."

"Longneck," Creighton mused as he rolled the icy brown bottle in his fingers, and used it to wipe his sweaty brow.

"You know," Creighton said, "what it makes me think of, this longneck bottle here? It makes me think it would make a really good Molotov cocktail."

"Cocktail? Creighton, you know I don't have hard liquor in here. Just a little harmless beer," he feebly joked.

"Also reminds me of a German grenade. Did you ever see a German grenade, Dalton? They have a long handle on them, a longneck like this bottle."

"Creighton, just have a beer on me."

"I told you I don't drink."

"Well, this is your first time in here, so it's on me. With my compliments. It'll be our little secret."

Creighton continued, "The German grenade has this longneck on it, and you can flip it as it leaves your hand. More torque, more velocity, more accuracy."

"Creighton, if you're not going to have a drink, why don't you get out of here."

"Okay, okay. I'm heading out, but aren't you the least bit curious why I'm here?"

"Not even the slightest. I'm calling the sheriff."

"Good idea. I know his number. Do you want it? Ray Mitchell is my brother-in-law. I talk to him all the time. In fact, I'm certain he's on his way here right now. He'll probably have a few questions for you about your beer supplier. Grab a couple more longnecks. Mitchell has been known to throw back a couple of beers every now and then. My wife tells me she wishes her brother would leave the stuff alone. His wife as well."

Silence. Long silence. Sheriff Mitchell walked in, paused in the dark.

"Hey Dalton," Creighton said. "I told you to put a couple more long-necks up here."

Dalton grabbed two more bottles and set them on the counter.

Creighton carefully lined up the three amber-colored bottles.

"Hey, Ray. What are you doing here? You know your sister doesn't approve of your having a drink. Neither does your wife."

"I don't drink, Creighton. You know I don't drink."

"I'm having a longneck. You want one? They're supposed to taste better. Dalton here says there's more foam."

The sheriff grabbed a bottle and took a long pull, then looked it over as if trying to find evidence of a major crime.

"I don't see any difference; tastes about the same to me."

A deathly stare from Dalton behind the bar.

"Nope," he declared after a couple more swigs. "I don't drink beer but if I did, I sure wouldn't bother much with a longneck. Still tastes like warm piss to me."

"Well," said Creighton, "if you don't want it, I guess I'll just toss it." Stony silence, Dalton, and three bottles sweating. "You know what it reminds me of, Sheriff? I was just telling Dalton here it reminds me of those German grenades with handles on them. Krauts think they can really torque them out there. You want to try?"

"No, you go ahead. I'll just watch," said the Sheriff, taking another big swig. Creighton stuffed the washrag off Dalton's shoulder, in the longneck to prevent spillage, then took slow aim at one of the shelves stacked with clean glasses hanging on the wall behind the bar. Imitating Dutch Ruether, the ace pitcher for the Yankees, he took a slow wind up then flung the bottle violently at the target. A fastball. Glass shards sprayed all over the bar. Dalton ducked behind the counter, cowering. A second bottle smashed into a refrigerator door. The third bottle hit a chandelier with a Budweiser logo on it. The cheap imitation light fell to the floor in a heap. Sheriff Mitchell made a feeble attempt to slow down his brother-in-law, now behind the counter, tire iron in hand. Dalton stepped aside making no effort to stop him. With a single swing of the tire iron, Creighton shattered three beer tap machines. Handles went flying and foamy beer shot everywhere. Creighton wiped his extra foamy beer-covered face.

"Hey, Dalton, my son is in the garage at the back of your building if I'm not mistaken. Would you please escort him out to the car?" Dalton followed orders. Doyle, stiff from laying on concrete for three days, staggered to his feet.

Like a formal march to the gallows, the four men walked slowly out to the car, Dalton in the uncomfortably close middle. Doyle needed help getting in the car, grabbed his dad's arm for support. Most of Doyle's face was black and blue, his ribs tender. Dalton watched, a smugness tattooing his countenance.

Creighton nudged the bartender, "Go on, bend down there. Doyle has something to say to you. Get close so you can hear him."

Doyle straightened up gingerly, "I apologize to you, sir. It won't happen again."

Dalton leaned in to shake his hand. Doyle cocked his leg and let his size 12 Army boot land squarely on Dalton's face.

Dalton sat in the gravel as the two cars pulled away. When his wife arrived 45 minutes later, his broken nose had finally stopped bleeding. Smugness temporarily vanished.

Three days later Creighton strode into my cabin, Doyle right behind, caught in a jet stream. I had grown used to seeing Doyle bruised and battered and bandaged.

Creighton said to me, "Tripp, meet shearer number eight. He'll be at the training session all week."

"Sounds good to me."

"I don't know what those two guys talked about on the drive back up the mountain. Neither were much for expressing feelings. Doyle had just one year of high school left, and they both agreed it wasn't necessary for him to go back to school. He worked with our outfit for a couple of years and became a decent shearer but felt shearing was penance for past transgressions. It was his father's choice. Their relationship declined.

"Along the way, if our machinery or the cars needed fixing, Doyle would help take care of it. He was like his dad–could fix anything. He was better at maintenance than at shearing, so he became one of our mechanics. He was always in camp. Our head mechanic was usually back at the warehouse in Idaho Falls, helping Creighton build the power plant.

"Deadlines loomed. Falling anvils loomed."

CHAPTER NINETEEN

The warehouse where Creighton and the mechanic hung out became quite a novelty in Idaho Falls. It had been sitting empty for a few years after a guy selling cars went out of business. Selling cars was an easy business to get into–just buy a handful of cars from any of 30 or 40 manufacturers. Put them in a window where they could be seen, and they would sell. The dealer who previously ran a company out of this building sold Auburns, Appersons, and probably Pierce-Arrows, their logos hand-painted on the building's exterior, faded letters a reminder of unrewarded ambition.

Everybody was buying cars. It was another thing to keep them running. They constantly broke down and customers either wanted them fixed or wanted their money back. It was easy selling cars, not such an easy thing to make money. Prices were jumping all over the place like the price of gold in a gold rush. The auto dealer lost his shirt, his house, all his money, and his wife.

He moved out of the warehouse/showroom and there it sat, empty. The city of Idaho Falls took ownership and gave it to us virtually free, hoping that down the road we would succeed and be able to pay sales tax. The price was just right for our fledgling company. We worried about ghosts of a failed enterprise haunting the place.

A large window on the front of the building, designed to show off the fancy new automobiles and became an open invitation to snoop. We had to hang up some big canvas tarps to keep prying eyes away from our contraption. The first thing everyone thought, quite naturally, was that we were bootlegging whiskey. Most hoped we were, others hoped we weren't. The city council guys kept coming around, wishing us well, scouting for impropriety, fueling speculation, and stoking small-town curiosity. We weren't inventing a car that could fly or run for a thousand miles on cow piss. But, with that canvas hanging in the window, imaginations went crazy. We were in the sheep shearing business, working on a new way to speed up shearing—nothing for the townsfolk to get wired up about. There's a feeling people have about being kept in the dark. It drives them mad. A tarp hanging in a window was an invitation to peek and prod. People got nervous, not knowing what was behind the curtain.

One night, one early morning, about three a.m., a dozen or so young high school kids on a dare broke into the place but couldn't see a thing. With the only window covered, there wasn't a sliver of light anywhere. I was sleeping in the backseat of Creighton's car, Buns Parrish's old car parked inside the warehouse. Not sleeping is more accurate, haunted, desperate, trying to remember anything I could about Buns' murder. Nothing would ever come. I was troubled by my doubts. I was comforted by my amnesia.

So, here comes these kids sneaking around. Quiet as they tried to be, I heard them bumping into each other. They had no plan, just bouncing around in the dark hoping to find a secret batch of hooch or a mysterious space capsule.

I watched for a few minutes, then quietly reached up and pressed the horn on the steering wheel. The old *ahh–ooga* sound from the old buggies bounced off the cement floor, raising the decibel levels. I laid into that horn about a dozen times, and for the next three minutes, there was a howling like a couple of wolves, a couple of coyotes, and a couple of bears all trapped in a single cage. It was a symphony of screaming, some of the boys sounding a lot like little girls. One of them finally found the only door in the place, and they all made a run for it.

When the sheriff and the mayor came looking for evidence of who might have staged the break-in, I said it wasn't a break-in cause the door was unlocked."

He told me to lock the damn door next time.

I said, "Yes, sir, good idea." I always went out of my way to avoid the police. I was like a very bad actor, overly courteous to them. The death of Buns Parrish had never been solved, and there would always be a shiver run up my spine when I saw a cop.

One piece of incriminating evidence was left behind at the scene of the crime, the bungled burglary of the warehouse, but they never caught the perpetrators. They tried for a while but could never find the guy who shit his pants and left them in a pile just outside our shop running into the dark wearing nothing but brown streaks on his lily-white ass.

We locked the door after that, especially as the stakes grew increasingly higher.

We never got a rental bill or a tax notice from the city of Idaho Falls. As soon as we started making money and paying off our creditors, Creighton would send the city a check for as much as he could afford. Even if it meant taking less for himself and his family. He figured he owed folks for helping him succeed and he always paid his debts.

The door was locked when Creighton arrived the next morning. When I let him in, he asked about the door.

"What's up?"

"A bear," I told him.

"A bear?"

"Yes, big brown bear tried breaking in."

"Were you scared?"

"No, but there were a few kids hanging around the place, and the bear did scare the shit out of one of them."

"Everything else okay?"

"Yep. Everything is good. Glad to see you made it."

CHAPTER TWENTY

L ate into October, snow was already on the ground. Automobiles in the early days weren't built for snow, and the trucks were worse without any weight on the back wheels. They were always stuck in the snow, or wrecked in the snow, or frozen solid and wouldn't run. One of the biggest problems we faced was cars and trucks. We couldn't keep them running. We had two mechanics making repairs, but getting replacement parts clear up here on the mountain was a big problem. It would remain a problem for the next three years. Automobile manufacturing got better and better, but it was in very small steps. Transportation challenges hampered us continually.

Creighton, Doyle, and a full-time mechanic named Hendershot worked longer hours than anyone on the team. The grime under their fingernails, oil and grease permanently etched into knuckles, a semi-permanent smudge to the side of their nose, branded them as unwashed and overworked. Creighton and his small team designed and built from scratch some of the equipment we would use, imperfect and prone to balky moods. This, along with endless patching, cleaning, holding everything together, nothing ever really got fixed. There were times when the best solution they could come up with was an incantation from the mechanics book of spells, a witch's brew, a temporary bandage, a spider web.

Boise, Idaho, a four-hour drive to the west was next on my list for recruiting shearers. The Basque community in Boise was sizable, and I knew they were harboring several good shearers. I naively thought I could waltz into town and recruit them. When I arrived, they stonewalled me. I made the argument about better pay, mechanization, being a part of changing the industry, all of our best arguments. Nothing worked. They weren't going to let me steal their superstars. I thanked them and invited them to our demo day. I couldn't give away too much information about our equipment, but I did tell them we had machinery that could speed up shearing by 300 percent. More pelts, more money. Those speeds seemed unthinkable to them, and they joined the throng of naysayers who continued their doubtful ways. No way was I getting any of their good cutters.

But they had a change of heart. I stayed in Boise for two days, looking at the sheep ranches, future customers, perhaps. Boise was growing but it was still small enough for them to find me, snooping around town. Enrique Galindoz and his wife approached me as I was leaving my hotel. They were carrying one of those made-in-hell, wine-soaked cherry desserts and described for me their change of heart, their desire to do what would be best for their two sons. They pleaded for me to take two of their boys into this new company where they could experience the exciting change and start making money for their education. They were the shearers I wanted all along, but I wasn't checking their resumes. The dessert was all the reference I needed. I told them to report to me in thirty days for training.

The two Galindoz brothers were a year apart, 22 and 23. They looked like twins, inseparable. They had a great work ethic, they were motivated, they were talented, and I was in the right place, the right moment, finding these two guys. Every once in a while, I got some of that incredible cherry treat from Mrs. Galindoz who learned that opportunity is just like cherries, pick 'em when they're ripe.

My hunch was they learned more about our new power tools, our innovations, from Basque partners in our consortium, and it seemed likely they were sending their boys not to help us, but to learn the new equipment, the new methods. They would be competitors one day, but for now, I snatched their royal jewels.

Over the next few weeks. we continued our search. With the brothers Galindoz and Doyle we were up to ten. We were still in the hunt. I planned on turnover and that was prescient. We would need three or four backups.

Boise, as it turned out, was fertile ground for me. Some kind of a silent signal that only the shearers could hear, announced that I was hiring. Prospective shearers were finding me, seeking me out. One effervescent kid followed me into JCPenney's where I was trying to find blue denim jeans, the new choice of pants, heavier and more durable than cotton chinos. He was very young, maybe twenty-one or -two, and talked incessantly while I tried on pants, cackling like a hen announcing a freshly laid egg.

His granddad had been a sheep rancher, and this kid learned how to shear simply because he was forced to. His family farm ran a small herd of sheep, one, maybe two thousand head. They were so far away from everything that they did their own shearing, butchered their own meat, made their own cheese, completely independent. I was surprised this kid was trying to leave, shocked his family would allow it.

So, Cam Ferguson, joined me for coffee as I prepared to leave town, regaling me with the history of the area, family feuds, his own ambition. He never stopped talking. His motivation: escaping indentured servitude on his dad's place in Meridian. It was the Stevie Zuninga syndrome, something very familiar to me. He wanted freedom. He worked for room and board and not much else, never attended dances or much of anything social, and wanted desperately to get away from home. He wanted to go to college before he got too old, and he wanted to make some money. He left his dad's place, walked away with empty pockets, anxious to travel and expand his worldview. I listened to him prattle and said to him, 'It sounds like you want to build a boat and catch a ride on the river, see where it takes you.' For a moment, he stopped talking and looked at me as if I were an apparition, an iridescent heavenly messenger who knew his innermost feelings.

The transcendental moment faded. Ferguson said, "I'm a better cutter than those two Basque guys you hired. Give me a chance."

The two Galindoz boys had a reputation, they were known and respected shearers, and they came with the backing of the successful Basque families. I knew they were good. But not this guy, Ferguson. I knew nothing about him, and I had no way to know if he was any good. He admitted to having a vagabond spirit, a wandering somnambulist.

"How can I be sure you won't walk away one day?" I asked.

"I will leave," he boasted. His candor shocked me. "I need money and if you guys are paying by the pelt, we will all make a bunch of it. I hear you are going mechanized. I like the sound of what you're doing. If the money is good, I'll be around a while." He reminded me of the reality that no one makes a career in shearing.

I asked him how he knew about our speed, our process and our 'rumored' compensation model. He shrugged. "Word gets around," he said, this time with a smirk.

"Let me see your forearms."

He knew exactly why I was asking.

"Wait, before I roll up my sleeves, I have a better idea," he said. "Come on over here."

A store on Main Street, selling fabric, thread, lace, all the accouterments women need to sew and make dresses for themselves, was already buzzing at ten in the morning. In the '20s, women's hair was getting bobbed, hems were going up, sewing was popular.

Two men in dusty farm clothes drew curious stares. We couldn't have been a bigger distraction if we had been sitting in a chair atop a flagpole. An enormous table filled much of one room. Scissors, fabric, and ribbon were strewn haphazardly, threads and tiny bits of wool flying through the air, visible in the sunlight from the east window. The perfume in the air said this is a female establishment, nothing here for men. Dusty men. Permanent stink of fish guts in my nose, and the continual stench of sheep droppings had weakened my sense of smell, but this store, this touch of femininity, reminded me that there is life beyond camps and trains and boats and dirty animals. A couple of electric-powered sewing machines—gleaming metal showing off the Singer logo—had the ladies all atwitter. Women used to have to pump sewing machines with foot-powered treadles, and here was the latest in automation. Thousands of women at home, as well as factories throughout the world, had all gone to electric machines to speed up the sewing, maybe a half-dozen years previous. The wool industry, lost in the stone age, was shearing sheep with scissors not much different than women used to cut fabric. I could never figure out why some people were resistant to the idea of mechanization of shearing. I was tempted to start hiring women who far more willing to adopt innovation.

This cocky Ferguson kid, a second-generation Scot, was ready to put on a show. Oblivious to the customers, he moved some things out of the way on the big cutting table and pulled up two chairs. He sat down in one, adjusted his underwear and scratched his crotch, twisted the kinks out of his neck, stretched his arms, twirling them around and around about 20 or 30 times, then looked at me. With his nose and a simple nod of his head, he pointed to the other chair, a confident gesture. A dare. A gauntlet was thrown. I knew what he meant, and he knew that I knew what came next.

The ladies had seen this plenty of times and a few of them gathered around to watch. Sleeves up, elbows down, hands locked, we waited for a signal from the woman running the shop, his aunt. The room went quiet with anticipation of a heavyweight fight between Jack Dempsey and Gene Tunney. A dozen or so of the townsfolk trickled in from the street. They knew this kid. They were his adoring fan club. There was no 'ready, set, go' or countdown. The woman stood there in silence for about 10 or 15 seconds, tension building. Wait. Wait. *Boom!* The woman's hand hit the table, a loud thunderclap.

The old trick of rotating your wrist to gain more leverage failed me. His wrist, elbow, bicep, were bolted to the table, permanently. Or welded, completely unmovable. My face was simultaneously two different shades of red. One embarrassment cherry. The other desperation crimson. His arm, forged steel, began to move mine, an inch, then two. His face never changed. He never broke his gaze. He watched me squirm and struggle then calmly, casually, very, very slowly tilted my arm, first

70 degrees, then 50 degrees, then 30 then 10. My shoulder throbbed. An eternity passed. He effortlessly finished me off with a dramatic slam to the table. The women went back to work, and the customers started sorting through ribbons. They had seen this show before.

He continued looking into my eyes, didn't blink.

"I can start today."

When I left Boise, he was bouncing in his seat singing over and over, "I knew you when you didn't have a dime," by Bessie Smith. It was a long drive back home, but this highly energetic young man was a prized possession. Number eleven.

Bessie's song stuck in my head for a long time. I still hear it playing.

To keep this kid busy I would take him all over the area with me, looking for more shearers and keeping the ranchers up to date on our progress. He knew what we were looking for. He knew the industry. He had a high-energy personality that others liked. He knew how to arm wrestle and had a passion for winning. I knew his competitive fire would challenge and push twelve or fifteen other shearers, driving up daily pelt counts. I didn't hire him for his skill, I hired him for his contagious optimism.

We ended up in some pretty distant places. Winter set in, temperatures dropped, travel by car was nearly impossible, but we had to keep pushing car, body, and wits through the deep freeze. No one was shearing this time of year; no planting; not much of any work outside most days. Shepherds tended herds at winter grazing. The ranchers, the hired hands, my crew were all maintaining farms, equipment, animals. And their sanity.

My recruiting trip took me far too often into underground clubs, caverns, caves where seasonal laborers could get daily doses of liquid warmth, antifreeze, to help them survive the persistent winter. Far too many of them never left the caves. I knew them, understood them, but couldn't rescue them. I drew strength from the caves, resolve, gratitude to have been dragged out of one of them. The shearers I was looking for became increasingly difficult to find even though dozens of guys were hungry for a paycheck and some stability. The labor pool kept shrinking.

By February 1927, we had fifteen guys committed. I counted on some attrition. Some guys didn't get along. Others lost patience with the long winter wait. Some didn't like the competitive atmosphere. Some woke from a dream, a heavenly vision, or a hangover, believing they would be happier somewhere else, happier floating downstream in a slow-moving boat. We didn't beg anyone to stay. We were going to stick to the philosophy that you aren't given a spot. You earn it. We knew it would drive up speed. Margins. Profit.

The new shearers gradually started coming up to Island Park, following the retreating snow line up the hill. We housed them in the cabins at Pond's Lodge, three guys in each. They would stay there until it was warm enough to build our movable tent city when we began making our first rounds in the Spring. They became ranch hands for the next few weeks, keeping busy, keeping out of trouble, and practicing shearing techniques with pretend clippers, on pretend sheep that looked a lot like bales of straw.

Crowded living conditions, a cantankerous winter that had no intention of leaving, impatience, isolation, boredom, were a toxic mix of ingredients in the disenchantment stew. Throw in a little jealousy. A pinch of inferiority. Overflowing hormones. It was shocking we didn't have a one hundred percent churn rate.

There were bumps and bruises, but for the most part, and for a time, they all got along. One notable exception was one of the new guys,

Mackleprang, a cave dweller I wrongfully thought I could redeem. Ron Mackleprang. When you say his name a couple of times out loud it sounds exactly like his personality: brittle, twisted, crackle, break your backer, gang banging, plank walker. He was coarse sandpaper, he was pumice, he was prickly pear cactus, he was a pine cone in your shoe, pain in your ass. Everyone on the team had some kind of moniker for him, none of them complimentary, all of them correct. He was the last guy in, and he would be the first to go if he wasn't good enough. He was having trouble with the idea of competing. He insisted he had been guaranteed a daily wage and inferred we had misled him.

I told him to ask these other fourteen guys what the terms were. We told every one of them they had to compete for the job and earn their way up the ladder. It's was a good, healthy competition.

Not too long after the initial season began we needed every one of them anyway. We lost 'prickle pain in the ass' Mackleprang and other malcontents who talked a lot about being the best but could never admit they weren't. Or prove that they were.

We were deeds guys, not dream guys. Whenever a friendly rivalry broke out, one guy would say, dreams or deeds? It was the way to get the mercury rising, the hormone stew brewing. The serious part of the competition became ringing the daily bell and earning the title of "The Gun," the best shearer each day.

We were about to meet the best shearer we had, and we didn't go out and find him. He found us.

He was a black man, but his features were not like what any of us had seen before. This was white man's mountain in white man's world, and we almost never saw a guy of color in the mountains of Idaho. Indians were all around us but kept largely to themselves, blending into the scenery, almost disappearing wherever they went. You couldn't get an Indian engaged in a meaningful conversation beyond weather and wool. The phony, make-believe partition erected by the government, the fake line in the sand, granting them a piece of their own land, kept wounds unbandaged, resentment fresh.

We were a bunch of buckaroos, bunkhouse vagabonds, scattered ashes, proud misfits. If there was a book about world cultures, diversity, etiquette, we didn't have a copy. We were the clueless class, oblivious to even small differences, leery of people not exactly like us. We were all trying to survive. Being kind, tolerant, understanding of people different than us wasn't something we were good at because we'd never been taught how to. The Army didn't do a thing to help eliminate bias. Backcountry guys behaved like backcountry guys: rough, unpolished, mostly undereducated. We were crude. We were strong. We were weak, flawed, frayed. We were fools.

Few, if any, had ever seen a town or a city much farther afield than Montana, maybe the Dakotas. Naïve would be one way to describe our guys. Arrogant would be another good one. But never unkind. Unkind or thoughtless just wouldn't be a word I would want to hear spoken about these guys. They were tough, their backs strong. They would put the weight of the world on those backs for someone in need. I wouldn't tolerate anyone calling them inconsiderate. Brutish, yes. Brash, yes. Thoughtless? Not in my book of etiquette.

But that didn't mean we weren't idiots. That's exactly what we were. All of us. Certified morons of the mountains. There was plenty of learning to do when it came to minorities. Hell, we didn't call them minorities, we didn't know what that meant. We were just a bunch of dopey sheep guys who lived all our lives with people pretty much like us. We loved the Basque guys and welcomed their skill and their incredibly hard work. That's all that a man needed to do–his share. The Basque 'minority' tag never crossed our minds.

So out of the swirl of an August dirt devil, this guy blew into town. It took us three years to find out his story, where he came from because he didn't speak a word of English or any other language. He never uttered so much as a grunt. And there he was standing right in the middle of one of the tents when the sun came up. The guys woke up and found this fella standing over them. Towering over them. Some of our big, strong, Herculean guys became skirt-wearing, lipstick painting ladies in a big hurry, screaming like a 12-year-old girl seeing her first hellgermite.

Junior stopped recording. "A what?"

"What?" I answered back.

Junior repeated, "I said what, meaning what did you just say?"

I looked at him completely baffled. "I have no idea what it is you're trying to ask me."

Louder and slower, "I am asking if you wouldn't mind repeating what makes little girls scream. I did not hear what you said makes little girls scream," he repeated, pronouncing every syllable. It sounded like you said hegermite. What on earth is a hegermite?"

"I said it was a hellgermite. Hellgermite. Junior, how'd you get through animal school without knowing what a hellgermite is? Get out your Googley device and get a picture of a hellgermite."

"Gramps, it's not a device, it's a search engine. And it's Google, not Googley. It's a way to look up information."

He complied and opened a photo. We agreed that the official winner of the universal ugly contest is a hellgermite, not a sturgeon. The official Google spelling is 'Hellgrammite.'

"When I tell a guy he looks like he crawled out from under a rock, this is where that expression comes from. This ridiculous-looking underwater creature lives under rocks. We used to take a fork into the river, slowly lift a rock, and stab one of those buggers to use as fish bait. I have no idea if they were legal to use but they were good bait. We began calling the hookers around town 'hellgrammites and sturgeons.' The fellows, at last, had a choice from the smorgasbord ugly, uglier, hellgrammite.

"Now where were we in the story? Why can't we stick to the story? Junior, stop interrupting me."

"You were talking about this dark-skinned fellow that dropped out of the sky."

"Yes, and that's exactly what we thought. How else did he just show up one day if not by a dirt devil?

It wasn't until many years later that we learned his story. He came up here all the way from southern California, jumping a series of trains, with little thought of where he was going, always looking for a free ride. He ended up in a long string of fights defending the color of his skin with fists instead of words. He found a job working for the railroad, loading lumber on the train that came to Island Park, picking up timber for the railroad ties.

He had been a shearer in New Zealand, which is where he was from, but set out for California gold. Like everybody, he left when the shiny, gold bubble burst. Not knowing where he was headed next, with no idea where to stay or where to go, it was a lucky accident he ended up in sheep country. The wind sort of blew him in. Exactly like a dirt devil.

No one in camp made even a feeble attempt to hide their stares. Nor did I. His skin was very dark, his facial features large, broad, bulging eyes with a threatening feel. But it wasn't just his skin color, or his features, or even his enormous legs and arms that drew so much attention, compelling as they were.

His head, chest, torso, tree trunk legs, and arms were completely covered in blue ink. Tattoos from head to toe. There wasn't a part of him that wasn't tattooed. The designs were intricate and looked like stitching or embroidery, dark blue ink resembling a hand-sewn pattern rather than a painted motif.

His hair hadn't been cut in a very long time and hadn't seen a comb or brush for even longer. It was bushy, thick, very black, and longer by a foot than the way women of the day were wearing their hair. But don't call this guy a girl. When he walked he was confident and strong. His facial expressions never changed, kind of like a dog, same look on his face whether happy, sad, hungry, or angry. He was calm and in control. This guy never changed mood or demeanor: steady, consistent, dependable, and very much at peace with himself. This calm presence was a stark contrast to the mercurial hot heads, alcohol-induced rages, explosive and unpredictable personalities of the white working-class I was familiar with.

It turns out he was an aborigine from Downunder: a Maori. That's what they call the natives of New Zealand, the indigenous tribes, kind of like the Native Americans we call Indians. These Maoris were on the New Zealand continent thousands of years before the white man came. They were treated poorly like we had done to American Indians.

He would not only be a top man in our crew, he would also be one of the best teachers we had. He would never say a word but, step-by-step, he'd show you what to do, making it easy for guys to understand. He had been a shearer for a long time in New Zealand and was a veteran with the mechanized tool. The clippers in his hand seemed miniature, his movements lithe and graceful, fluid, effortless. As it turned out, I did have a bias toward him, and it wasn't racial. It was his size. I wouldn't have believed that a human of gigantic proportions could be so graceful.

He had learned to shear with the new power shearers in one of the largest shearing operations in his country, and he had two years of experience before any of the machines made their way to our shores. He was big and strong and would become a dominant shearer in the western US. Even though the guys didn't quite know what to make of this unusual character, they always secretly admired him. I know I did.

Don't ask me how a guy from New Zealand, nearly seven thousand miles away, with experience in using power clippers, ended up in our camp exactly when we needed him, needed a teacher, a troubleshooter. Almost to the week, we needed him, he showed up. Don't go there. There is no answer. A dirt devil blew him in.

We ended up calling him Kiwi, the name of a highly suspicious fruit from New Zealand. Fruit shouldn't be covered in fur. He never corrected us or ever told us his real name and happily answered to Kiwi. We paid him his wages in cash, like the rest of the crew, but he seemed uncomfortable around money, never had much of it, and didn't have a clue what to do with it. He'd give his cash back to me, and I kept it in a lockbox or in the bank in his name, waiting for him when he finally went back home as quietly and quickly as he had come. Kiwi taught us all how to shear, and he taught me many other things: the power of silence; the value of consistency; the strength of accepting who you are; and the peace that comes from an uncluttered life. I would never again meet anyone this way, totally at peace, without so much as a complete set of clothing on his back or a dollar in his pocket.

I took some of his wages and bought him a new pair of boots, some

Pepsodent cleaning powder, and a toothbrush. The first time he saw it he had no idea what to do with the brush. I made him use it morning and night. Getting him to take a weekly bath was worse than trying to bathe a feral cat. The other guys wouldn't work by him because of the stink. He eventually complied. Most of the time.

Kiwi hated the boots and never wore them. If there was ever a pair of boots made big enough to go around his massive legs, I never saw them. Shirtless, shoeless, a stranger, a lost lamb, Kiwi became our touchstone.

He was strong, confident, but he had a tender side. After dinner one evening, he walked up to Big Springs. Barefoot. The still, pure water mesmerized him in much the same way it did me. When he didn't show up for work that next morning, I went looking for him and found him on the bridge looking into the water. He hadn't moved an inch in eight hours. He wordlessly got in the car and went to work for ten hours without a break, without a word, without a hint at his emotions.

Kiwi was never drunk because he never went to a speakeasy or underground cavern. He was never with a woman because he saw how other men treated women. He had far too much respect for women to treat them like a possession, or worse, a punching bag.

Like the water that flowed out of Big Springs, he was constant and steady. Other guys would come and go, change moods, change attitudes. Kiwi was as dependable as the crystal clear water coming out of the center of the earth. Just as consistent. Just as pure.

CHAPTER TWENTY-ONE

Twelve talented shearers were on board, two other reserves. We already lost one to the winter insanity. Kiwi would act as lead sheep shearer, the others would follow. I knew I needed a few more.

Cam Ferguson had been instrumental in finalizing our hiring goals. Everywhere we went he would somehow find a time and a place to challenge guys to an arm wrestle. He drew competitors like stonefly nymphs draw cutthroat trout. He was the guy to beat. We had the best wrestler in camp. He could fleece any of the biggest rams, and he would be a top-three shearer all season. He would help us shear record numbers of pelts. This was all well and fine. Shearing was his job. Arm wrestling had become his obsession. It was an important part of our pitch to recruits.

And Ferguson was great company on long road trips. He was funny, charming, and kept both of us energized and awake on slow crawls along endless roads.

Helena, Montana was a long drive. Dark skies gave us a subtle head nod as if to say, 'Go ahead if you dare.' Fresh biscuits from Mrs. Sorenson's table, wrapped up in a napkin would have to suffice for a long day. Two black coffees, more in a thermos, fueled the drive. Ferguson smelled the coffee and drained a full cup before getting seated. He opened the thermos and gulped more, oblivious to the temperature straight out of the container. The drive was about four hours and our goal was to make it up and back in a day. Our coffee clearly wasn't going to last.

Transforming our theoretical startup business into a working enterprise seemed overwhelming most days. It would have been easier to change a Model T Ford into an airplane or change an airplane into a heron, or a sheep into a stallion. Details were stacking up, timelines were shrinking, panic was multiplying. Herds would be coming down from the range in a matter of weeks, panic would quadruple.

Pick a crowd, a big crowd, say Yankee Stadium, bleachers full to get a look at Babe Ruth and Murderers Row. Churchill Downs in Springtime at the Kentucky Derby watching Black Gold wear the roses. Let's say it's twenty thousand people, all men, all of them need to be shaved. All of them looking at you saying, 'Could we get this done right now.' That was our morning ritual, sheep in pens, ten to twenty thousand at a time, ready to be fleeced. All at once. All in one place. It's like poking a stick in a termite mound and watching the frantic insects chaotically react to the exposure. Spring lambing, castrating, docking tails, branding was in store for the young ones. Shearing was next for the older animals. An unproven new venture was on the verge of colossal failure, or monumental success. My only thought: get this car moving. I'm going to need more shearers.

Our entire crew was working at menial jobs, shit shoveling servitude, earning room and board and a modest wage, anxious to begin the work they were hired for. Creighton was virtually done with his machinery, his power plant, and we were ready to begin testing, teaching our guys. Earlier attempts at training were a Titanic failure. We would soon enough have a full complement of tools, backups, spare parts, manpower. *Why did I still have nightmares about drowning, a knife stuck in my throat?*

We believed we would have all the clippers we needed and were told we would have them on time, coming on a ship from New Zealand. Wild stallions in the stable, meantime, were kicking down fences. Time was running out. *What could possibly go wrong? Keep driving.*

"Did you drink all the coffee, you greedy slob," I said to my energetic over-caffeinated partner. "Man, I need some coffee. Whose idea was this?"

"I know how to keep you awake," he said as he launched into an A Capella version of "Keep on the Sunny Side."

"That song will keep me awake just long enough to find the nearest cliff to drive this car off," I screamed. He wailed away. Halfway through, I joined them singing the song originally written in 1899 by Ada Blenkhorn, but popularized by The Carter Family and Johnny Cash.

There's a dark and a troubled side of life
There's a bright and a sunny side too
Tho' we meet with the darkness and strife
The sunny side we also may view
Keep on the sunny side, always on the sunny side
Keep on the sunny side of life
It will help us ev'ry day, it will brighten all the way
If we'll keep on the sunny side of life
The storm and it's fury broke today

Crushing hopes that we cherish so dear
The clouds and storms will, in time, pass away
The sun again will shine bright and clear.
Keep on the sunny side, always on the sunny side
Keep on the sunny side of life
It will help us ev'ry day, it will brighten all the way
If we'll keep on the sunny side of life
Let us greet with the song of hope each day
Tho' the moment be cloudy or fair
And let us trust in our Saviour away
Who keepeth everyone in His care
Keep on the sunny side, always on the sunny side
Keep on the sunny side of life
It will help us ev'ry day, it will brighten all the way
If we'll keep on the sunny side of life
Keep on the sunny side, always on the sunny side
Keep on the sunny side of life
It will help us ev'ry day, it will brighten all the way
If we'll keep on the sunny side of life
If we'll keep on the sunny side of life

We sang our way into Helena, Montana. We'd been up since five a.m. The first item when we arrived, bathroom. Second item, coffee; fill the thermos, and keep it away from Ferguson.

The third item, track down a guy named Gavin Kirkpatrick, the shearer we had heard about. He met us in a bowling alley where he was working, the prototypical, small-town facility with five lanes, manual pinsetters, beer-stained floors, cigarette smoke, and stale bacon grease trapped in a windowless, concrete box, the final refuge of failed athletes and failed marriages. Midday, not a single ball on hardwood disturbed the funereal atmosphere.

It was a very long, tedious trip, and Ferguson and I were both tired, hungry, and in a rush. The tragedy of this dump made us long for green mountains.

When we found our guy, we got right down to business. I took out the box that held the power shearers, opened it up to show to him. Instead of the power clippers, the box held a piece of dark brown pumice. Lava. Hardened volcanic magma.

The tool was gone.

CHAPTER TWENTY-TWO

Junior turned off the recorder, stretched, rubbed his face, then walked out of the room. "Gramps, I've got to have a break. This story just got very interesting, and I don't want to miss a word of it."

He came back in with two Coke bottles and two baloney sandwiches. We ate silently for a few minutes. I drank that entire 8 oz. bottle of Coke nearly in three swallows. Dumped it down my throat, let out an enormous belch ready to start talking again.

I spent most of my life, all ninety years, drinking about a liter of Coke every day. It replaced beer as my beverage of choice. I always had one with me in those shearing days. I'd get a dozen bottles from Christina and pack them in a wet blanket to keep them cool. They would sit in the river if we were close by. Stealing Cokes from the stream became a popular version of hide and seek during our travels. A bottle of cold Coke became currency and salvation. From that day on I never stopped drinking Coke. I made it to age ninety because of Coke and chocolate, I'm certain of it. Doctors won't tell you to use this diet, but I rarely saw a doctor in ninety years, and I'm certain it was the Coke and chocolate.

144 | MARK HURST

"Junior, did you ever hear about my little Coke incident?"

Junior got very intrigued. All sorts of stories were coming out about shearing and, even though this was a fork in the road, he let me roll.

"When did this incident happen?" he asked.

"Just a couple of years ago, not back in the sheep days."

"It's not a historical memory about the sheep camps? Now that is getting sidetracked. Please go on. I hope it's not one of your endless stories. We need to stay on track."

"I'll be brief. One day I started feeling sick. I was getting near ninety, and I was very tired. I had some chest pains. I was sure a cold Coke would make me feel better. I pounded a big old cup, but over the next hour, the pains got worse and worse. Your Grandma Ruby told me I had to get in to see the doctor. I refused. Ruby insisted. Ruby won. I called our son John in San Francisco. He was a doctor so I thought he could tell me what was wrong. He asked why I was calling him during his office hours.

"'I'm sick,' I said.

"'Sick, what's the matter? Dad, are you okay?'

"'I'll be fine, your mom told me to give you a call.'

"'She did? You both know I'm a psychiatrist, not an internist. This is not my expertise. Why do you need a doctor, what's wrong?'

"'I'm having a heart attack. I'm sure I'm having a heart attack.'

"John paused, then asked me about my symptoms.

"I explained to him why I thought I was having a heart attack. He and I ruled out heartburn even though heartburn sometimes feels like you're having a heart attack.

"'Dad, how much Coke do you drink in a day?' Dr. John, the shrink, asks.

"'What's that got to do with anything?'

"'How much Coke do you drink in a day?'

"'Probably a liter.'

"'A full liter of Coke every day?'

"'Yeah, so what? It's healthy for you.'

"'Dad, it's not healthy. I think it's the carbonation. Your body is sick of dealing with carbonation. It's telling you to stop. The carbonation is getting trapped in your organs, and you can't process it anymore. It's built-up pressure, not a heart attack. You have to stop drinking Coke and eating chocolate.'

"I said, 'You're not a real doctor' and hung up.'"

Junior and I both fell into hysterics, close to tossing up the baloney sandwiches. He looked at me, completely baffled, watching as I poured another glass of the brown sugar water.

"So you never thought about quitting?"

"No. I gave up beer. I'm not giving up Coke. Let me have this little vice. I need some chocolate."

"Did you ever think about drinking Diet Coke or maybe a glass of juice or something?"

"No, I didn't ever try Diet Coke. Who wants that crap? Just the 'real thing' for me. Besides Diet Coke has the same amount of carbonation, so what have calories got to do with anything?"

"Can we get back to our story, please? What took you down that side road all of a sudden?"

"I'm sorry, Junior. It's just that when that fake heart attack happened, I truly thought I was dying. We laugh about it now, but it was terrifying. I have to finally confess just how much it scared me. I'm old enough that any little thing could finally take me out, and I realized at that moment just how fleeting everything can be. Sitting here with you, recollecting these stories has touched me deeply. I'm truly grateful to you, Junior. These were such challenging times, such difficult times, but so rich and lasting and fulfilling. We watched the world modernize, and change, and mature. Despite a depression, a tragic war, and a whole lot of trouble shearing sheep, we came out better and stronger than when we started. The world had transformed and so had I. It's been good to reminisce.

"Junior, coming here, talking to me, I think you may have had motives other than the care and protection of sheep. I think caring for sheep is important, and I hope I can be of help to you as you begin your career with animals. I'm extremely proud of you. More than that, you've allowed me to talk about my life. You have me talking about the one, deepest emotion I carry around with me every day.

"You want to know what it is? It's you. This story is about you and the other grandkids. You and your dad and mom. It's a tale about the family I almost didn't have. I was dead and buried when a great man pulled me out of a river. I was a drunk. A contemptuous, shiftless drunk. I can't tell you how far down in a giant pit I was. I may have witnessed the murder of a good friend and was too drunk to remember it. I abandoned my family in Ohio, abandoned everything because I thought I knew better than anyone. I was so arrogant, convinced I could do things myself. I found out I can't. I didn't know how badly I needed the love and support of others to lift me and hold me and be by my side to protect me, guide me, teach me.

"You're my life. You are the end of this story. You are my history and I'm glad you're helping me talk about it, sharing the journey that ended up right here, me and you eating crappy baloney sandwiches and belching Coke. My little fake brush with death reminded me how quickly some things change. The Coke incident made me feel like I beat death for a third time, and it took me back to that mountain, to those rivers and springs and the tall pines where I became a man. I was given a second chance by a complete stranger who had an unearthly ability to reclaim people and give them second chances. And he did it so effortlessly. I'm alive because of him. I've spent all my life trying to live up to that, and I've always done the best I could to be like that. To be like him.

"This is probably more than you wanted to hear. I'm sorry about that. It's just that I don't want to forget a thing. There's so much that happened in the shearing years, so many people that shaped me, strengthened me, and taught me. A remarkable man took me in his arms and held me very tight and sheared a heavy coat of wool off my back, then loved me and cared for me and let me start fresh and clean.

We sat in silence for a few minutes then Junior, all six-foot-five of him, grabbed me and held on to me for what seemed an hour or two. It felt like he hugged me for an eternity. And that's exactly what it was.

Junior finally regained his composure, and as he punched a start button on the recorder, he asked, "What happened to the clippers?"

"Oh, yes. I forgot where we were. The missing tool."

I was angry beyond angry, somewhere very high on the fury scale. Beyond fury. Beyond eruption. In the instant I opened that box, I broke a molar. No kidding, I cracked a tooth. We rarely saw a dentist in those days and my teeth were already in bad shape. I clenched my teeth together so hard I felt and heard a tooth go *pop*! I grabbed my jaw and stood up, casting curses on the bowling alley, Helena, Montana, sheep, mud, sleepless nights. Ferguson grabbed my arm and ordered me to sit down and shut up, a captain barking orders to a buck private. I obeyed, slinking away onto one of the hardwood lanes, feeling like a bowling pin, a twenty-pound ball rolling my way. The day began at five a.m., no food, no coffee, and we still had a four-hour drive back to Island Park ahead of us, cracked tooth, stolen tool, breached security. What a terrific career choice I made.

Ferguson was calm, grinning.

"Let's start over," he said to this guy Kirkpatrick, standing uncomfortably close to his face. "Look, I don't have a ton of time. My partner over there is a little on the edge. Let me ask you something. You're a shearer, right?"

"Yes."

"How long you been doing it?"

"Couple of years, maybe three. I gave it up, though, and did some work on the roads up in Yellowstone but my mom got sick, so I came back here. I work in the bowling alley mostly at night. My dad runs the bank here, so I help care for Mom the best I can. But yes, I'm a shearer. I was a shearer."

"We need only the best cutters. I hear you used to be pretty good. Are you any good? Yes, or no, I have no time for bullshit."

He paused. "I'm stuck here with Mom. Doesn't matter if I'm good or not. I can't leave here right now."

"Listen," Ferguson said with authority, "we came all the way up here to see you. That's how serious we are. The plan was to show you something, revolutionary. It got stolen, and we didn't know until we opened that box just now and found a rock. That's a little problem we've got to take care of. I'm certain you'll want to go back to shearing when you see what was supposed to be in that box."

Kirkpatrick stared straight ahead, not a blink. His heavy mustache gave a slight twitch that gave away his otherwise perfect poker face.

Ferguson continued with a sales pitch like he was P. T. Barnum himself, or one of the tonic sales guys that would come through town from time to time selling phony cures. Ferguson was smooth; Ferguson was persuasive; Ferguson was desperate. Kirkpatrick was unphased as Ferguson moved in to seal the deal.

"What we wanted to show you was a new mechanized tool. It's a power tool that replaces these. He held up the old hand scissors. Kirkpatrick had seen plenty of them before. The new tool will allow us to shear 200 sheep per day. I'm guessing if you were any good you could do 30—with these old things. That about right?"

He nodded.

"So, you got paid ten cents per pelt, $3 a day. You'll never be a rich man making $3 a day. Or managing a bowling alley. With the new power tools, you'll be able to do 200 pelts a day. Twenty cents per pelt. I don't know if you went to school and if you know much math but . . ."

"My dad's a banker. I know how to count. I told you I can't leave my mother right now but thanks for the offer."

"It wasn't an offer. Nobody's offering you anything. You'll have to earn a spot. Maybe you haven't got the balls to compete. That's fine. I heard you were good. We're leaving. Enjoy the bowling alley. Say hello to your mother."

With that, we were done. The cracked tooth was now in about four pieces, shattered, my lower jaw throbbing, swelling up like an unmilked ewe. Ferguson took the wheel so I could curl up in the backseat and whine the whole way home. He didn't start the car.

"What are you waiting for?" I screamed.

"I'm waiting for that Kirkpatrick fellow. Right now he's throwing on a coat and headed for the door of that mortuary, excuse me I mean the bowling alley. That door is going to fly open any second and he'll come running after us."

Ten seconds. Thirty seconds. Two minutes.

"Do you have the thermos full of coffee?" Ferguson asked. "I hope this guy has the sense to bring coffee."

Another two minutes, then three. "He's not coming. Let's go," I said." "He's coming. He's coming. Hang on."

"While you're waiting, oh mighty seer, I need to tell you there's no way we can afford to pay that much per pelt. You had no authority to offer him that much. We'll never make any money at that level. We have to make a profit somehow. Have you ever had the concept of profit explained?" I asked, broken tooth screaming. "We have to make payments on the loans for the equipment, repairs, costs you know nothing about. We're not paying that much; the ranchers aren't going to pay that much."

"They are now," Ferguson said, looking past me at the building, counting backward, seven six, five, four, three, two, one, and right on cue as if rehearsed, Gavin Kirkpatrick came flying out of the bowling alley, one arm hanging onto a jacket, the other reaching for the car door, onto the running board, into the backseat just as Ferguson floored the gas pedal.

Kirkpatrick screamed from the backseat, "Let's go get those clippers."

In unison, three guys started singing, "I'm sittin' on top of the world, rollin' along, singin' a song," trying to imitate Al Jolson.

CHAPTER TWENTY-THREE

We didn't need Sherlock Holmes to figure out who took the clippers. A visage of Luke Pond appeared on the hood of the car, an apparition, a target to aim for, running him down over and over. Luke had seen the clippers, and it would be easy enough to figure out what they were. A part of me believed he was too young and too stupid to do us any damage, but I had an uneasy feeling that he could blunt our launch and tip our hand to competitors. Our unique, competitive advantage was about to disappear. I was going to be embarrassed in front of our partners because I had been reckless in caring for our most important asset.

"Ferguson, put some lead in your shoe and get this damn car going. Have we got enough gas?"

"I sure hope so," he said.

We pulled into Pond's Lodge at dusk, setting sun and mountain silence irrelevant, invisible, lost in the smoke of my burning rage. It was a long haul, and we pulled in, running on empty. Empty gas tank and an empty cardboard box.

"Where is Luke?" I yelled, to no one in particular, pacing like a nervous panther, frantically looking for Christina. A dynamite fuse hung out my back pocket waiting for a spark, ready to annihilate the entire store, the entire valley.

Christina was unloading groceries onto the shelves, dropped a can, and ran to me reaching for the fuse. She had never seen my angry side, yet knew instantly I was panicked. And she knew why.

Calmly, she reached for my hand. Bomb diffused.

"I need to find him."

She said, "Come with me."

"Christina, where is he?" I struggled to speak, pushing words carefully through a swollen jaw. Between rows of canned goods in the storage room, she pulled off her apron, tucked a loose strand of hair behind her ear, reached up, and kissed me. Forgetting my sore jaw, I grabbed her desperately tight as if I was clinging to the only tree left on the cliffs above Shoshone Falls, feet dangling, jagged rocks five hundred feet below extending their bony fingers, desperately holding her in my embrace for what seemed like twenty minutes, twenty years. Neither of us had any intention of ever letting go. Without a word, I knew she had been worried. I felt the worry. She felt my rage. We had a new language that no one else knew. We spoke it silently to each other each time we were together. Warnings, longings, disappointments, hopes, fears, delights, anger, sadness, all transmitted like an invisible wireless radio signal between us, activated with just a look or a slight movement of the head, a single touch, a lengthy embrace.

"Help me reach this top shelf," she commanded. Her slender waist was firm, small, and it was the first time I had my hands around it. She seemed featherlight, her work boots the only thing keeping her tethered to the ground.

From the shelf, she retrieved a large Prince Albert tobacco tin, opened the lid, and pulled out a cloth wrapped around the missing clippers. I rubbed my chin, then my whole face. Then I took off my hat and rubbed my hair like a dog. She picked up all these cues from the new language. Anger, frustration, revenge. Her eyes responded, stay calm.

"Luke isn't coming back. He's gone." Her next words were unspoken: You don't have to go looking for him. You won't have to hurt him. He won't cause you any more grief. "And your secret is safe," she added out loud.

She knew how important the clippers were to our success. She knew we were on the verge of launching the business and how vital it was to keep them under wraps. She knew I erred in showing her the tool. She knew Creighton and the ranchers would question my judgment.

Christina reminded me of the disappearance of Tanner McQueen, who vanished in the dust of the assault some weeks ago. She reminded me that the vanishing of ghosts was getting to be commonplace in these mountains. She then filled me in on the details.

"My dad had to drive to Salt Lake City to pick up more groceries at the wholesaler. He took Luke with him and Luke didn't object. He seemed pleased when they got to Salt Lake and Dad handed him a Greyhound bus ticket to San Francisco. They didn't embrace, didn't shake hands, didn't speak about it at all. Dad simply got in the truck, picked up his load, and drove home. Luke was gone.

"Luke did break into your place to steal the clippers. He had no idea what to do with them, so he hatched up a scheme primarily to disrupt you. He took them out to Ander Montoya, clueless that he was your business partner. Montoya listened attentively to the feeble sales pitch, cleverly guiding Luke toward the bear trap he'd set, oblivious it was there at his feet. Luke asked him for money to buy some more of the tools. He had no plans to shear sheep, only to sell clippers at a profit to the other ranchers in the area. They could be partners and make good money. Montoya asked where he would get them all? Who was his supplier? Luke said he had an unlimited supply, bluffing, but couldn't reveal the source."

Montoya asked to see the clippers. He looked them over then asked, "These don't run on electricity. I'm curious, what powers them?"

Snap. The bear trap closed around his ankle. Even Montoya still didn't understand the full picture. No one did.

"Interesting," Montoya mumbled, then, "Here's an idea." With the dry throat of an amateur con man, Luke tried to swallow, stay calm, stay in character. *Montoya's impressed,* he thought. Montoya wrapped the tool in a cloth and put it in the tobacco tin. "Let's go," he said to Luke. "I know exactly what to do."

Montoya's truck was painted a rare, dark blue with the Montoya name on the side and a crude drawing of a sheep. They drove straight to Pond's Lodge.

Luke said, "What the hell? What are we doing here?"

"Where's your dad?"

"My dad? No. I've got to go. Give me the tobacco can."

"Let's go find your dad. Where is he?" Montoya asked, calmly.

"I don't know. How should I know? We can't show this to my dad."

"I have no intention of showing it to your dad. Come with me."

Montoya grabbed his arm as Luke tried to pull away. Montoya had a hold on that arm like a pit bull with a ham bone in his jaws. Montoya had the arms of a shearer. Pond walked up just as his son fell to the ground, arm trapped in a vise.

"Mind telling me what you're doing with my son, Montoya?"

"Ask your son."

"Luke, what the hell is going on?" Luke was silent.

Pond was patient as he said, "Let go of his arm."

Montoya complied, but Luke was still on his knees.

Luke's dad ordered him to stand up.

Montoya finally, after an uncomfortable silence, said, "This boy took something of mine. I found out he took it, and I thought you would like to know."

"What is it?" Pond asked.

"I can't show you. I have it here in the tobacco can."

"Why can't you show it to me?"

"I just can't."

Pond turned to him. "What is it? Why were you trying to steal it?"

Silence.

"It's a new way to shear sheep. A new mechanized tool," said Montoya. "It will help our industry. A lot of families will benefit from it. So will you. But it's so new no one else knows about it. Your boy there doesn't really know what it is or how it works, but he tried to convince me to buy it and finance a business to sell them."

Looking up to the sky, Pond stared at the clouds as if they would somehow spell out an answer for him.

Luke tried to reason with his dad and said, "Dad, I didn't—"

"Quiet," his father ordered. "Montoya, if you won't show it to me, how do I know you're telling me the truth?"

"I can't show it to you, but I'm telling you the truth. In a couple of weeks, I'll be happy to show it to you, the entire operation."

"Thank you, Senor Montoya. Thank you very much for bringing my son here. Please wait here for a moment."

He returned from the store with four oranges in his hand. Citrus this time of year, this far away from warm climate orchards, were bricks of gold stolen from Fort Knox. "I wish I had more to give you," he offered.

"I can't take all four. Please—"

"I want you to have all of them. It's too small a price to pay for your kindness to me. Thank you. Via con Dios." The two men shook hands and went their separate ways.

———

"The next morning my dad drove Luke to Salt Lake City. He's gone–poof–gone," Christina said.

"Thank you," I told her. How is your father?" I recoiled when Christina leaned in and gave me a peck on the cheek, the entire left half of my face swollen, throbbing. The kiss nearly made it feel better. My mood was certainly better. The four-hour drive back from Helena was brutal, my angst worse than the pain in my mouth. One small kiss and the universe resumed its natural order. *This girl, this . . . what was this girl trying to do to me?* I rubbed my face, then scratched my scalp like a dog, again.

She tousled my hair and said, "Good boy."

CHAPTER TWENTY-FOUR

The snow was beginning to melt, the frozen ground beneath showing signs of life. Ice on the lake started moving, creaking, cracking, the symphony of the mountain thaw. Bears and wildflowers stretched and yawned, coming out of hibernation. With no hint of the fragrance of pines in the air, my sense of smell reverted to sheep shit and fish guts, sour socks, and unwashed men.

Although it wasn't spring yet, even on that day in April when the high temperature for the day reached a balmy 40 degrees, there was hope in the air, a highly contagious malady. Don't be thinking about summer yet or the weather gods will smack you down. For a moment, the day looked good, felt good.

It would be a good day for shearing sheep. The real shearing wouldn't begin for a couple more weeks, but we loaded up about three dozen sheep, a few from each of the partner/ranchers. A small caravan of sheep, shearers, tools, trailers, and trucks paraded down the mountain to the warehouse/manufacturing facility in Idaho Falls.

Thirteen shearers were on board, antsy and anxious to begin. (We lost two backup guys to what I began to call the winter dreads.) If it storms today there will be snow instead of rain. April in the mountains. The caravan pressed on hoping for the best.

I had agreed to stop in Ashton to meet with an additional shearer, a guy named Hans Herrmann, a transplant from Germany, second generation. For the most part, Oregon had been his home with a variety of stops here and there. He grew up on the west coast, raised by a father who came to the US before the outbreak of WWI. US citizenship didn't diminish the stereotypical strict sense of German order and discipline. His tall frame, his demeanor, board-straight back, eyes looking past you, suggested seriousness and exactness, a wooden soldier at his post.

Hans was a tree guy, timber cutter by trade. He started out on the West coast felling trees and moving them to the sawmills. He got in a bit of trouble with the daughter of the Coos Bay, Oregon mayor, Glen Graham. When the local police chief came looking for Hans, he had vanished. He decided it was a good time to join up with the railroad tie company in Island Park. He was adept at handling big saws, big timber. He could wield a two-sided ax with the fluidity of a heron, the torque of a pile-driver.

When a larger-than-most pine tree fell at his feet, inches from crushing him, he felt insulted by the insolent tree lying in a tangled heap where saws couldn't touch it. Hans, gloveless, spit on both hands, rubbed them together, and attacked the beast with alacrity. The log fought back. The ax landed on a veteran knot in the grain, as old as the tree, hardened by age and pine gum. The ax deflected, like a stone skipping on water, slicing through the leg of his dungarees, taking about two inches off his calf with the simplicity of slicing a thick slab of homemade meatloaf. The blade missed his bone and didn't sever any of the large arteries. A quick, clean, slice of meatloaf went flying like so much pulp. Blood flooded the calf, swamped his boot.

He calmly took off his shirt, pulled the sleeves tight around the wound, finished his shift, and limped home. He washed and bandaged the wound but woke up in the night in intense pain. With no phone and no car, he hobbled on foot down to the ranger station about two miles to the south. The US Forest Service maintained a Yellowstone regional office there stocked with emergency equipment and first aid supplies. The Rangers fired up a truck and drove him to Ashton where there was a small makeshift hospital at the house of the only doctor in town. It was one of the few hospitals in the whole area.

In pajamas, slippers, bifocals on top of his head, the doctor took one look at the leg, cleaned and dressed it, gave him a tetanus shot, some penicillin to stave off further infection, and orders to stay off the leg for six weeks. The Ranger took him back up the mountain for the night.

Thunder rumbled the following morning, a fleet of trucks carrying the timber crew he'd been working with, crawled up Two Top Mountain Road where they would be cutting timber for railroad ties. Hans wasn't on the truck. His injury kept him grounded. His job that summer was gone. And all his wages after he paid the doctor.

He didn't know a soul in any of the other cities and towns. He had no other skills. No family. No friends. No income. Near starvation, he met a ranch hand from the Warm River area. Hans overheard him talking with a couple of guys about the shearing season coming up. Hans asked if there was any work.

There was plenty of work. Hans wasn't a shearer but his 6' 7" frame, powerful shoulders, and intimidating, steely-eyed stare was a Norman Rockwell *Saturday Evening Post* cover of the perfect sheep shearer.

"'Sure," one of the guys said. "We've got work." For the next two years, Hans worked for the Neuberger Brothers Farms in Ashton. Enormous fields of potatoes and alfalfa, wheat and barley, orchards filled with apple trees, about 800 head of cattle, a matching number of horses, and a good-sized herd of sheep gave this thousand-acre farm the look of a patchwork quilt, a variety of textures and colors lining Warm River.

The Neuberger sheep herd was getting larger each year, now numbering in the thousands, as demand for wool and lamb meat soared. The herd was too big to move so they had started doing the shearing themselves. A couple of his guys were reportedly very good.

Hans would do year-round chores, mostly for room and board, outworking any of the other permanent and seasonal crew. When the shearing season started, he was assigned to be a wrangler, no small task. Moving herds of sheep from the fields to corrals and getting them into the shearing pens was one of the toughest jobs in the camp. It was eight to ten-hour days wrestling stupid sheep who always had a look of ignorance about them. Either ignorance or innocence, maybe a cross of both.

Hans could lift up any good-sized ewe, effortlessly toss her around, keep her moving. He became overseer, master, field marshal, general, and dictator of the kingdom of the pens. Nobody ever got in his way or disagreed with him.

Kent Neuberger's office was a natural history museum, filled with memorabilia, awards, and ribbons curating the history of horse breeding and training. Unannounced, without knocking, Hans entered the large room which housed three or four buffalo heads, elk, deer, and other varieties of rare, wild game you could only get from Africa. The stuffed heads with their glass eyes glared down at the big German making him feel uncomfortable, the way the morose hobby of mounting animals as trophies makes nearly everyone feel. Kent put down his pipe and looked up at the big man.

"Kent, I've got something I want to show you. You got a minute?"

"Sure, how's the leg?"

"The leg is fine, no worries."

Hans pulled from his shirt pocket loosely folded drawings and notes, a plan to build a new system of fencing and pens. His design eliminated hard 90-degree corners by adding some curved lines. This was meant to keep the sheep moving. Sheep didn't have the sense sometimes to turn a corner. The fencing plan would be three parallel rows, each with rounded corners at the ends, moving the animals into the shearing pen at three times the speed according to his estimates.

More importantly, Hans had designed a clever way of attaching all the fencing together, sturdy but flexible. In other words, it would pull apart so you could move pieces of it around to any number of configurations.

"It could be portable, movable," he said to his boss.

"Portable? Why the hell does it need to be portable?" Neuberger quizzed. "We're not going anywhere. We shear our own sheep right here. Just go put up the fencing sames we've always done."

Neuberger chose the status quo, no need for innovation, no need for improved efficiency. As his headcount increased, productivity slowed. Moving large herds from grazing to pens and back again added three weeks to the process. He was slowly being overwhelmed, yet the status quo remained status quo. *Who needed modernization?*

Hans retrieved his drawings and was dismissed before showing his boss the best part: an ingenious snap-on connector that he made from salvaged copper tubing and leather strips.

Hans had worked closely with Kent's regular shearers, two of them good friends. The news about mechanized shearing was widely known. Anyone remotely connected to shearing knew about Creighton's new venture and understood that disruption was on its way. No one knew details, the scale, the process. But everyone knew something was happening. Everyone except Kent Neuberger, the ignorant, indifferent look of a sheep on his face after being deserted by three key employees.

So, on my way down to the warehouse, I stopped to meet with Hans who was with two of his buddies. They offered to buy me lunch, and if someone wanted to buy me lunch, I was happy to hear what they had to say. Hans opened his drawings and gave me his pitch,

"I need a piece of lemon meringue pie if I'm going to understand this better."

As long as they were paying for lunch, I figured I'd have the pie. Besides which, I really did need a moment to let it all sink in. Portable fencing? No one had ever thought of that and the connectors were remarkable. The materials for the connectors cost virtually nothing from the scrapyards, and we could break down and reinstall fencing anytime, anywhere. We were already going to be out the cost of the lumber, so this was an ingenious concept. I let my enthusiasm simmer. Three large men sat opposite me, eyes shifting back and forth in a silent Morse code conversation.

"Hans, are these two guys any good? I need good shearers, not dreamers."

"They're as good as any I've seen. They're the reason I never got the chance to learn how."

I took my time eating the pie, scraping the meringue off the plate with my index finger.

"You sure you boys don't want some pie. It's incredible."

"No thanks," Hans answered for them all.

I wiped my mouth, blew my nose into my napkin, retrieved my custom-made, hand-carved toothpick from my shirt pocket, picked at my teeth, sucking bits of pie crust and the remnants of chicken-fried steak out of my mouth. I deliberately stalled. The three guys remained silent.

"Hans, you'll get paid the same amount as the gun each day. You make the shearers look good, speed up the process across the board, and you'll get paid what they do. You two guys, Frick and Frack, any trouble leaving Neuberger?"

"No."

"We'll be paying 20 cents per pelt, bell ringer gets a five-dollar bonus. And then I asked, "Do any of you arm wrestle?"

I grabbed my hat and headed for the door. "You coming?"

I was supposed to stop in Ashton for twenty minutes and interview a potential shearer, then hustle down to Idaho Falls. Two hours late, I arrived at our warehouse with three strangers in tow. Our entire crew, miffed at the delay, glared at me.

"What you got there, Trippy?" Creighton asked.

"I call them Frick and Frack and the Kraut. They'll be joining the team."

Speaking of teams, Creighton, now being called "General Hurst," gathered everyone around an old Plymouth parked there in the warehouse, jacked-up, axle resting on bricks, one tire removed. There on the axle was a contraption that looked like a torture device. A big leather circular band was attached to a system of pulleys and gears resembling a tangle of fish line, or Doyle's curly hair. A jointed, metal version of an octopus tentacle dangled from a hook. Two large rubber mats covered the floor.

A half-circle of very large men formed around the machine. Creighton launched into a training session he had been preparing for the last three weeks. His blue eyes, paler than a cloudless July afternoon, gave an intensity to his face that day. Sometimes, in the light of day, his eyes were such a pale blue you could see no color at all. It was discomfiting, hypnotic to both men and women. His baritone voice gave him a commanding presence in front of these men—a General sending troops into battle. We listened, I have to say, reverently, more like a church meeting than a workday. He was passionate as a Bible-thumping revivalist. Salvation, healing, redemption were ours for the taking. Along with large paydays. *Hallelujah. Amen.*

His hat, the sweat-stained, omnipresent fedora, was filled with numbers, then passed around the circle, each trainee pulling out a number.

"When that number gets called, you'll come up here and shear a sheep," Creighton announced. A murmur went through the boys. There wasn't a sheep in sight. When the hat came to Hans Herman, he passed it on without taking a number.

"Take a number," Creighton ordered.

"I'm sorry, sir. I'm not a shearer."

"Not a shearer? Then what are you doing here?"

I whispered in his ear. "I'll explain it to you later. He may be the most important man in the room."

Creighton looked at me with those blue eyes, the left eyebrow making a gradual upward motion that I knew to mean 'better be a good explanation.'

Number seven was pulled from the hat. Stevie Zuninga, lucky number seven goes first.

Stevie walked, tentatively to the front and planted his feet on the rubber mat. Creighton handed him a pair of old snips, the de facto choice of the old school, still the only choice for ranchers across the country. Following the script, I exited a side door just out of view of the team and reentered walking a sheep on a rope as if it were a dog show. The sheep's hooves slipped on the concrete floor making her look like a very bad skater on the ice for the first time. The sheep gained traction as it stepped onto the rubber mat. The rope off, Stevie grabbed the animal, ready to throw it onto its back and begin.

"Wait, wait, wait," Creighton barked. Everyone laughed, a little tense, uncertain. Through the same back door, Kiwi walked in with a shaggy sheep in tow. Kiwi was in native Maori apparel, which is nothing more than a cloth sarong and burlap booties on his feet. His dark skin glistened with lanolin, blue ink alive and waving. He stood confidently, slightly hunched, arms curved suggesting a warlike threat or a Sumo wrestling match. He led his big buck calmly to the mat and stood parallel to Stevie, turned his head, and stuck out his tongue.

Kiwi was so proficient, so incredibly adept with the clippers that he became our number one shearer and Creighton's best friend at working out bugs in the system. Creighton knew exactly what we needed when he snatched Kiwi away from the tents and took him to Idaho Falls with him to prepare for this very day. They were both well-prepared and were putting on a great show.

A swift move of the arm from right shoulder to left hip, Kiwi reached into the pouch strapped on his belt as if he were packing a Colt 45 in a holster. He looked like a gunfighter in a Zane Grey book. It was, in fact, a gun holster that he'd modified. The mechanized power clippers were drawn, quickly attached to one of the skeletal arms, and the gunfight at noon was on. The entire group was spellbound and silent.

Creighton fired up the Dodge. The rear wheel began turning, pulleys and gears all in sync.

"Ready? Trippy, you got a second hand on your watch? Start the time when I give the signal with my hand."

Stevie looked over at the strange-looking dark-skinned man, then over at me as if to say, 'What the hell am I supposed to do?' Creighton lowered his hand.

Stevie grabbed the ewe, tipped her over on her back, and started cutting with the traditional, soon-to-be-obsolete scissors. Sabino Bambino hollered out, "You lay them on their back so you can kiss them on the lips." This put everyone at ease.

The wool went flying. Stevie was a very good shearer and worked hard to prove he was more than Daddy's boy. He was exactly our kind of guy, driven to succeed. He held the ewe firmly between his knees. The animal didn't flinch, didn't blink. Kiwi was doing the same thing, slowly, confidently, but with the new power clippers. As quick as it started, Kiwi turned off his clippers, unhooked the device from the tether, returned it to his holster, bent down, and held up an entire pelt, totally intact, with barely a scrap anywhere on the floor. All this with the grace of a ballerina. A very large, dark-skinned, tattooed ballerina.

All eyes went to Stevie who had barely one-third of the pelt off. He had finished one leg, working his way across the animal's chest to the other leg. Kiwi left the scene of the crime and grabbed a sandwich from the food table, swallowed it nearly whole, licking his fingers while Stevie was still cutting away. It made the moment more dramatic, more tense.

Fifteen long painful minutes later, Stevie held up the floppy remains and pieces of a pelt, raggedy but still intact. A cheer went up, mostly in mocking fashion, more like cheering on a dancer in a burlesque show. Stevie politely bowed. The tension eased.

Stevie was a world-class shearer, destined to become one of our best. His time of 27 minutes was impressive. The guys knew right then that he would ring the bell plenty of times down the road. Stevie was the guy to beat.

Apidale shouted out a question but Creighton cut him off. No questions. Save it. Next. Let's go. He drew out the number nine. Galindoz rolled his head and did a very slow blink, his body language hinting 'Why me?'

He steadied himself on the mat, traditional snip in hand, intuitively scraped together a few of the loose pieces of wool with his foot, and slid them off to the side. The black mat was already getting a little slippery.

Another ewe was readied for Galindoz. Kiwi was ready with another ram, heavier, more rambunctious than the lighter females, plugged in his tool, raised it over his head, mockingly, big white eyes bugging out against that dark skin. His tongue stuck out, mockingly. He thumped his chest. Creighton gave the signal, and the two adversaries began.

Galindoz finished in 32 minutes. He had a very fine pelt, mostly in one piece. Kiwi stood, expressionless for 25 of those minutes, observing the strokes of his rival, his movements, his personal style. Everyone had little movements and cuts all their own. There was no single 'best way' to shear a sheep. There were some general guidelines, but each guy would put their own touch on the process. Some techniques were fine, others would change with the introduction of mechanization.

Three or four more guys came up, all very good cutters, and got embarrassed by the Aborigine who was now standing in a far corner of the warehouse.

Creighton returned to center stage. No one sat down. These guys were used to spending all day on their feet. The next four hours passed quickly, the revival tent filled with excitement. It was a revelation.

Not every guy got to compete against the machine that day. Kiwi bested them all by an average of twenty minutes. But they would all get a chance to shear. For now, Creighton demonstrated how the machine worked.

Kiwi brought in another big ewe and walked her over. Creighton was going to teach the class. Since Kiwi never spoke a word, Creighton had to learn the techniques in silence. A nod, a twitch, a hand gesture meant good, right, wrong. A grunt meant 'I'll show you once more, cement head.' Long nights were spent by the two men here in this building, learning, improving, and developing the best way to do this. A complex effort done in stony silence.

Creighton effortlessly pinned down the ewe and fired up a second set of clippers. The lamb's two rear legs were tied together. This isn't what typically happened, but the demonstration was going to take nearly an hour and the animal would get tired and restless. I helped hold her still while Creighton went through a step-by-step training regimen.

At the end of the demonstration, Creighton asked for questions. Every single hand went up simultaneously. The room crackled with energy, electrical bolts inside a thunderstorm. Every single one of the guys was practically wetting their pants like a little kid who plays out in the yard and ends up peeing himself rather than taking the time to stop and take a bathroom break. They were six-year-olds dancing as if a scorpion crawled down their boots. Shits and dams and hells were flying like wool.

Creighton answered all the questions but one. Gavin Kirkpatrick, who was one of the last guys in camp and had not seen or heard of

Kiwi yet barked out, "Hey who's the darkie? What boat did you just drag him off?"

Creighton and Kirkpatrick didn't know each other yet, never met until that instant. The revival tent went silent. Exposed power cables arced. Creighton's pastoral eyes illuminated. His voice wasn't loud, but it was clear, calm, deliberate.

"What's your name?"

"Kirkpatrick," he squeaked.

"You come from Helena?"

"Yessir. Just got here."

"Welcome. What do you think of the demonstration?"

"Very impressive. It's exciting. Can't wait to get to work."

"Good. It is exciting. I hope you are successful here," Creighton said, warmly. "Let me just tell you something. Kiwi here is not a darkie. Don't use that term again. He's not African. He's not a slave. The fact is he is your master. He is your superior and mine. You'll treat him with the same respect you give me and Tripp. He's the best shearer, and he is the expert. He taught me how to work this new equipment, and he's going to teach all of us how to do this the right way. He doesn't use words so watch and learn. Okay?"

Creighton faced the entire group and continued, "Kiwi comes from a place called New Zealand, and that's where we got these mechanized clippers. You guys may be the first in the entire US to have them. Kiwi has used them for two years and is as expert as you'll ever see. And he's better than any of you. Get used to it. If any of you can't learn from him and do this the right way, I've authorized him to remove one of your arms and feed it to the dogs.

"We're done with questions. Let's get to work. Nobody is guaranteed a job here. You have to earn it, so get in here and start earning."

Five hours later, enthusiasm still high, the work was just beginning. The table from which Kiwi had been mockingly eating was now spread with egg salad sandwiches on home-baked bread. A young girl was keeping the table stocked. She and her mother brought in baskets filled with carrots and celery, dill pickles, slices of roasted lamb, and lemonade.

The food wasn't as inviting as the power tools. Two dozen hungry men detoured past the food, a direct line to the clippers and the machine powering them. Each one of the new mechanical marvels was scrutinized with the thoroughness of a doctor looking for a hernia. Over, under, held up to the light, touching the sharp teeth and every screw. These large men were looking at every detail, the way your roommate helps you look for ticks on your body at the end of the day.

Also under the glare of all this machismo was the young girl at the food table. These guys averaged 27 years of age. This girl was maybe fifteen, but going on thirty, stunning, even at this early age, and she seemed naively oblivious to the stares. Creighton was not. It was his daughter, Carma, one of six kids. He looked around the room making mental note of the too-long looks.

"Don't even think about it or these new power tools will give you a different kind of shave. Everyone hear me okay?" A moan and a laugh from all. "Get some sandwiches," he commanded. "We've got a long night ahead of us."

For eight more hours, until three in the morning, each of the guys took turns learning the new contraption. To some, it was intuitive, comfortable. Others had to retrain their brain, muscle memory attuned to the rhythm of the old, manual scissors going clip, clip, clip, slowly moving in a pattern around the animal. The new cutters would, with a single arc of the arm, cut as much wool as 30 snips of the now antiquated scissors.

One by one they improved and accelerated their times. The forty sheep that the ranchers had sent down with us were cleanly shorn, our test drive mostly successful. By the end of the training, we were collectively beating normal shearing speed by a factor of 300 percent. The bankers would love it.

Everyone grabbed a wool skin, took off their boots, and found somewhere to sleep for a few hours. We all got maybe four hours before Creighton rang a big old bell and put us back to work. With no breakfast.

Sluggish, hungry, all excitement gone, the trucks were loaded, the convoy headed back up to Island Park. Creighton said to me, "Let someone else drive your truck. Do any of these guys have a driving license?"

"A couple of them, yes."

"Ride back up with me and Montoya."

No one realized Montoya was even in the room. He was there representing the other partners who were busy getting ready for spring lambing season. He had been completely quiet the whole time but paid rapt attention the entire 17-hour day.

"I want to hear what Montoya has to say," Creighton said, walking to the trucks. "And I want you to tell me about the two new guys and the German freak you dragged in here today. Do they understand the whole privacy issue?"

"They're good," I said confidently. Hopefully.

"You got all six of the clippers? I never want those in any other car or truck than mine, right?"

"They're already on board. I'll have to sit on them for the next three hours but, yes, they're on board."

"Good, it will keep you awake. Montoya and I have a lot to talk about.

CHAPTER TWENTY-FIVE

On cue, the spring storm we feared was lurking. It didn't feel like April. It felt like we should go back to sleep in the warehouse and try again tomorrow. We made an ill-advised run for the hills.

Rigby, Idaho, just ten miles north, is as far as we got before the flurries started. In southeast Idaho when flurries start, it's a simple warning flag that you're about to get clobbered. Ten miles further, near Rexburg, the big German timberman in the sky swung an enormous double-bladed ax, a single blow, opening up a hundred-mile gash in the storm clouds. It didn't go from flurries to a light dusting then to a cozy winter snowstorm with large flakes and kids building snowmen and catching flakes on their tongues. Storms up here don't behave like that. These storms don't like children. When a cloud gets full of moisture up here, it's more akin to a bad case of winter diarrhea. When a storm hits it doesn't just snow. It erupts. It explodes. Temperatures dropped twenty degrees in an instant.

In ten minutes, three or four inches of snow accumulated on the ground, completely covering the highway. Thirty minutes more, damn near a foot. The wind was blowing out of the North, probably all the way down from Alaska.

"Now, Junior," I said as I took off my trifocals and rubbed my eyes, "what kind of car do you drive?"

"Beg your pardon?"

"What kind of car do you drive?

"It's that GMC Suburban there in front of Broadbent's place. Why?"

"That's a pretty nice outfit for a college boy."

"Yeah, it's good. It's nearly seven years old and has 130,000 miles on it. Dad gave it to me when he got his new Ford F50."

"How much power does it have?"

"I'm not real sure of the specs. I think it's General Motors' big five-liter, but I don't know the horsepower, one hundred fifty, maybe four hundred or something in that range."

"Four-wheel drive?"

"No, it's what they call all-wheel drive. It's pretty much always in four-wheel mode."

"Heater, air conditioner?"

"Yes, and it has heaters in the seat."

"We had heaters in the seats in our day."

"Really?" He knew something corny was coming.

"Yeah, we called them rocks. If we were lucky, we'd heat up a couple of rocks on the top of the woodstove, wrap them up in blankets, and the ladies would hold them on their laps. Didn't last too long but it helped out a little bit.

Junior just shook his head. "Didn't you and Grandma take a potato to bed with you? Heat it up and put your feet on it, I think I heard you say."

"You bet. Nothing like a hot potato in bed. And in the middle of the night, if you got hungry, you could reach down there and have a few bites." Junior had heard that joke before apparently.

"So, there we were in the Model A with a very sorry excuse for a heater. It had an engine about the size of today's sewing machine motor, no four-wheel drive, one very dubious wiper blade that froze up twenty minutes into the storm, and tires that—well, today you might confuse them with tires on a baby buggy. It was a fragile piece of crap.

"We didn't sit there and wonder if we could outrun the storm. That decision was already made. We were stuck, unable to move forward, impossible to turn back.

"We had come to a complete halt, not even off the side of the road. We were right in the middle of the highway. Now you might be thinking a snowplow may come along and run right into us, right? We didn't worry about that too much for one simple reason." I paused.

Junior piped up, "What simple reason?"

"There were no snowplows. Hell, even the very best vehicles in those days had a max of about 40-horsepower. Everything had a hard time getting up those mountain roads. Nothing was powerful enough to push heavy, wet snow. They couldn't get any traction even if they had the power."

"So what did you do?" Junior asked

"I never became a praying man, as you know. This may have been a good time to start. But remember, this wasn't even a winter storm; this was a spring storm. That was the good news."

Prayer was ruled out. It was not widely practiced in sheep camps. Men spent too much time invoking God to curse annoying animals, curse the weather, curse the mornings. They knew how to invoke God for damnation, not for miracles. There was a small chapel right there by Mack's Inn, usually with a few cars parked outside on Sundays, so I assumed they had services. I met a Catholic priest once but couldn't be sure where or when he preached. A couple of Mormons would come around trying to get us in the water, but otherwise, there wasn't a whole lot of religion. Hearts were not changed that day.

Perhaps God punished us that day for not being better people. Sure seemed like it was a punishment. Maybe more like a curse. Probably stupidity, acting smarter than a storm, ignoring red flags. But there sat Creighton Hurst, calm as a well-fed heifer chewing her cud after supper. He had no fear. He'd seen this a time or two. For the longest time, he just sat there quietly with his hands on the wheel like he was still driving, his brain spinning like a kid's wooden top.

"I hope those other guys stay in their cars." His first words in an hour. His only words.

They didn't. The strenuous training down in the valley completely immersed us in wool and wonder. The only thing we'd eaten in the last 48-hours was an egg salad sandwich and a carrot or two. We had good coats on and good gloves that the Bannock Indians made from elk hide. I hoped everyone in the other cars had good gloves. They didn't. We were extremely hungry and tired. Here we were stuck about seventy miles from home. In a blizzard. A hard, freezing blizzard. In April.

Creighton said, forcefully, "We'll just wait this out. Hunker down, stay in the car, and try to stay warm. Don't go to sleep."

Unfortunately, the other trucks couldn't hear his warning. Stevie Z, peered through the frosted windows and decided we had stopped just outside of Rexburg. He knew the area and insisted he knew of a farm nearby. That was the first mistake. Out on that stretch of road, there is nothing nearby. Farms and empty BLM land spread out for hundreds of miles. You might bump into a farmhouse if you walked around for the next five days, but in this storm, there was little chance of finding anything. If snow blindness didn't kill you, frostbite would. The temperature dropped to 25-degrees, wind chill knocking a dozen degrees off that.

Ferguson and Apidale tried to talk him out of whatever he was thinking. "What exactly are you hoping to do?"

"We can't just sit here. This storm could last all day," he said. "The rancher I know will have a tractor and horses. He'll be able to pull us to his place so we can wait out the storm. I know what I'm doing."

"You don't know what you're doing. You're out of your mind, Stevie. Don't go." Ferguson was pleading.

Stevie pulled his coat up around his face, feigned bravery, rejected insanity. "Somebody has to do something. We can't just sit here."

He headed south, the opposite direction we were traveling. Ninety minutes later the storm quit as fast as it started. The sun came out. It wasn't a day at the beach, but the spring sun began to slowly melt the snow.

These spring snows were as short-tempered as a wasp at a picnic. You're going to get stung. It felt and looked like a storm you'd see up in Alaska or the Yukon where old Sam McGee froze to death. The snow had piled up quickly on the roads, but the roads were reasonably warm thanks to a few days of decent temperatures.

We cleared the snow off the windows of the vehicles, ready to roll. The roads were passable, although the snow was still very heavy, very wet. It quickly turned to slush. We were well ahead of the caravan but decided not to turn around to find the other guys. It may have been a mistake, but we were low on gas. We always carried a couple of cans of extra gas, and we were going to need it. The sun would be gone in an hour and the roads would refreeze.

In the slush, facing headwinds, the Ashton Hill was laborious, adding more than an hour to the trip. Last Chance on the southern end of Island Park finally crept into view. Nothing much more than a wide spot in the road where the river is slow and wide. Last Chance became our first chance.

A small, one-pump gas station opened about a month ago. As cars started to increase in number in those years, so did gas stations and diners everywhere. This little station was going to make a lot of money if they could keep gas tankers coming up here. For now, it was a sanctuary. The homely little shack was an alabaster mansion with peacocks strolling gold sidewalks.

Caviar and champagne were not available. We dined instead on beef jerky, bread and jelly, Tootsie Roll Pops and coffee. No one seemed hesitant or embarrassed to be huddled together under sheepskins, sipping coffee, sharing body heat. A very long hour passed. Finally, the rest of the caravan came slogging along.

Creighton stood with hands on his hips stretching his six-foot-two frame up as high as he could, watching them come into view at the crest of the slope. He bowed his head for about thirty seconds and stood right in the middle of the road, his feet soaked by the slushy wet snow.

The trucks pulled into Last Chance and began filling up gas tanks. "Is everybody okay?" Creighton shouted, running to their aid. Very large arms and legs began poking out of the doors, like a chick breaking its shell, slowly emerging. Joints popped and creaked as they untangled.

Creighton asked again, "Other than too many big bodies in too few trucks, is everybody okay?"

The entire team went silent, leaderless. No one spoke. "Hey," Creighton implored, "is everyone here?"

"Yeah, we're all here," Ferguson answered, speechless for the first time in his life. But Stevie is in bad shape."

"Stevie? What happened? This is Ler Zuninga's kid. Please don't tell me Ler's kid is hurt."

Creighton's demeanor went from anger, to fear, to heartbreak, to concern, back to anger, the complete gamut of human emotions on a carousel—up, down, up, down, around, and around.

"Frostbite," Ferguson said. We're not sure, but it's probably frostbite.

"Frostbite?" Creighton threw his felt fedora hat onto the slushy pavement. "What in heaven's name happened?"

"Stevie thought he knew the area and tried walking to a farmhouse for help."

Creighton doubled over with his hands on his knees as if someone sucker-punched him in the stomach. He let out a huge moan, rubbed his stubble, moaned again, then took a breath.

Stevie was the very first of our shearers to give the new clippers a try. At the big training the previous day, he drew the number seven out of the hat. Lucky number seven. After all, he had been through in his personal life it looked like he was on the move up the river like the spawning salmon, getting back home. He had come so far only to have this setback. The crew, from then on started calling him 'Seven,' a name they gave him out of respect, and it was their way of saying things were going to get better.

"'Where is he?' Creighton asked.

"'Over there in the Chevy.'"

"Stevie was curled in the fetal position, coats piled on top, still shivering.

Creighton placed a hand on his shoulder, firmly gave a squeeze of reassurance, and said, 'Let's get you warm. Don't worry about a thing. We're going to get you back to work. I need you. We all need you. You hear me, Stevie, we need you."

It was as bad as we thought. We got hot coffee in him and made him comfortable enough to get home.

Ferguson, the most talkative person in the group told us how Stevie believed he could get some help, get them off the road, get them warm. Everyone tried to talk him out of it. There was no bravado. His heart was in the right place.

The only reason he didn't die out there was that he knew he was in trouble about fifteen minutes into his walk. He turned around to come back but lost his way. He ended up out there in the cold for about an hour and a half, walking in circles as the winter gods watched, laughed, applauded. The temperature had dropped to just twenty-five degrees by then, an angry storm on the mountains wreaking some kind of ancient revenge.

We got everyone moving from Last Chance back to base camp. The day was shot. The crew built a large fire and stayed by it until about two o'clock the next morning. Montoya and Creighton stayed with Stevie at the doctor's office in Ashton. The doctor said he'd lose a couple of toes and two fingers on his right hand. That news landed on us like an avalanche that broke loose and buried life, limb, and hopes. Stevie sobbed. The winter gods grinned.

This was our best shearer. He had a chance to be one of the best in the world. His times would easily beat already the best in Australia and New Zealand. He could match Kiwi pelt for pelt, and we hadn't begun the actual fleecing.

He returned from the hospital a few days later with just three fingers on his right hand. We had spent the better part of a year getting this outfit ready to run, our attention so focused on building the right equipment, we didn't ever think about our most important equipment breaking down. We could always replace a belt or a pulley, but we couldn't replace a ring finger and a pinky on a right-handed sheep shearer.

"Did he ever shear again?" Junior asked.

"Oh, he sheared again. It took him about a year but eventually, he developed his own method and became a good shearer. He was never again the very best, the way an athlete is never quite the same after blowing a knee. But Stevie outworked every single man that came and went through our plant over those next two years. No one ever worked harder. Even though he was a shearer he pulled extra hours moving pens, packing trucks, whatever needed doing. He never slowed down, never stopped moving. It seemed to me it was his personal form of penance, working off his debt, believing he had let us down one too many times. He didn't complain when we relegated him to a backup role in the shed. He became our best trainer when new guys came along and made everyone in the company a better part of the crew."

"Creighton underwent a penance of his own. It took him several months to stop blaming himself for the incident. He told me repeatedly his regrets about putting business ahead of people. He believed he put the entire squad at risk during that freak storm. He took a private oath to never again make efficiency, success, and, profit the basis for any decision. On the band inside his fedora, he stuck a piece of paper where he had written a list of his priorities. 'Number one: people. Number two: everything else.' "

Junior glanced over my shoulder to take a look at an old piece of wood, a gnarly hunk of pine bark hanging on my wall. Your grandma hated that thing and begged me to throw it out. But I kept it all these years."

"It's the number seven isn't it?" he said. "That's been hanging there forever, and I never knew that it was something other than an old scrap of wood. I thought you had no trophies or awards from the shearing days. What do you call it?"

"What do you think I call it?"

Junior and I finished up for the day, had some chili and flatbread. I learned to make chili from an old Mexican who used to work on the crew from time to time, and I learned flatbread from the Basques. Still cooking it myself.

CHAPTER TWENTY-SIX

We didn't need Sherlock Holmes to figure out who took the clippers. A visage of Luke Pond appeared on the hood of the car, an apparition.

"Good morning, Gramps. You ready for another day of storytelling," Junior said, energized as he charged in.

"You're not sick of my stories?"

"I've never had so much fun. You are incredible, and I can't wait to get back to these events. It is fascinating. Let's get started."

Back in camp, we all got restless. We had a grueling training session, a short boot camp of sorts. We were Olympic caliber athletes, feet in blocks, awaiting the starting gun in the one hundred-meter dash. Get out of the way. We wanted to run. There would be plenty of issues down the road, but at this moment, spirits were high. We felt a confidence that had mostly eluded us, marching into unknown territory where failure wasn't an option.

The inventory of clippers and spare parts were now locked up in a safe we had installed in Sorenson's house. We treated them like they were the very last copy of the US Constitution or top-secret military invasion plans. We weren't letting them out of our sight now. And we were waiting for six new clippers coming from the manufacturer in Australia. We desperately needed additional clippers. Ander Montoya agreed to go with Kiwi to meet some of Kiwi's relatives who were immigrating to the US. These immigrants, people we had never met, would be carrying the equipment. Carrying our future. What could possibly go wrong?

Ander Montoya stayed involved at what you would call the management level doing a lot of things neither Creighton nor I could do. Like going to pick up the new clippers. The partners made Montoya their go-to guy. He was a valuable part of everything we did.

Kiwi and Montoya were scheduled to meet the boat in San Francisco, a four to five-day trip for us if we were lucky. We had six clippers in hand, ten more coming. Without additional equipment, we would never meet daily quotas. Wool buyers would fall short, the entire supply chain would blow up, and some one hundred thousand sheep would be wearing enormous wool coats until Christmas. One hundred thousand sheep, as it turned out, was a painfully poor estimate.

The contractor that had sheared up here for thirty years wasn't coming. He got bumped by this brash, new, innovative company using untested, unproven machinery no one had ever seen. There was no fallback. No contingency. No quarterback coming off the bench. We were the only option. The jilted contractor made it clear he would exact revenge. Rumors swirled from Yellowstone to New Mexico that C. B. Hurst & Co. Mobile Sheep Shearing was about to trigger the worst catastrophe since the volcanic eruption a million years ago. Creighton, McQueen, and Montoya spent much of every day calming the nerves of all the stakeholders.

We didn't want to take a chance on having a trucking company, or anyone else, deliver the precious cargo. Montoya and Kiwi agreed to make the arduous trip to the West coast. Montoya continued to be the liaison for the consortium. He had everyone's confidence.

Kiwi didn't speak a word the entire time. There were no radios in cars, nothing to do but watch the road, large sections of which still had no paved surfaces. It took them four very long days to get there, sleeping in the car and surviving on some Basque flatbread, sheep cheese, and two bottles of pears Creighton's wife had put up last summer.

The long drive back home with three additional people—a man, his wife, and son—would test the mettle of car and driver. Kiwi's relatives, his very large relatives were coming. There also had to be room for the ten ingots of gold they would be delivering—ten rare earth minerals, the crown jewels—ten brand new power cutters from the Wolseley company. It would be crowded far beyond the capacity of the '28 Studebaker, but we weren't sending another vehicle. We didn't have the manpower to spare.

Hungry, tired, impatient, they crawled into San Francisco, over-whelmed by the size of the city. They got a glimpse of the Golden Gate Bridge, but there wasn't much to see. It had been under construction for ten years and wouldn't be completed for ten more. They could see the towers rising out of the water, not much else. The rest of the city pulsed and teemed, more cars in one block than the entirety of the state of Idaho. A gold rush, silk from the east, and international shipping had made this city one of the most important in the world.

Kiwi and Montoya couldn't find the docks. That sounds impossible, but they couldn't find the docks where the ships came in. Montoya had no sense of direction. He came from a village in the Pyrenees and a mountain outpost in Idaho. Kiwi was helpless because he didn't speak and, we assumed, couldn't read. They were deer in headlights, hypnot-ically frozen in place. The crowds and noise seemed deafening, their ears attuned to mountain solitude. Montoya and the Kiwi could not have felt more out of place if they had been shepherds leading a flock of sheep through New York's Times Square.

You would think that all roads lead to the ocean on the West coast, a decent deduction. You would simply bump into it if you kept heading west. The ocean had to be there someplace. Nonetheless, they got lost. But that was just the first challenge.

The second challenge, far worse, the '28 Studebaker couldn't make it up some of the steep hills they built that crazy city on. The gas tank in this poorly designed machine was under the driver's seat. There was no fuel pump. When the car attempted to climb the hills, the gas would settle to the back of the tank, unable to feed the engine.

The third challenge, they ran out of gas. It wasn't like there was a gas station on every corner back in those days. You had to plan out your gas situation, and they didn't.

Te fourth challenge, the boat came in on time. Because our boys were hopelessly lost for nearly four hours, all the passengers had gone, the boat and the docks were bare. No New Zealand Kiwis in sight.

Another hour ticked by. Find gas. Find a can to carry gas. Find a place to park the car. Montoya began frantically searching, stopping anyone he could find, begging for help. Kiwi trailed silently behind. The main offices of the shipping line were about a mile down the Embarcadero. Surely they would have these foreign people in a waiting room. They didn't. No one had a clue where they might have gone after they cleared immigration. Two more hours went by and still no sign of them.

Out of the blue, Kiwi sat down. He folded his massive legs into a pretzel and plopped down on the side of the road. He didn't move, didn't sleep. His eyes were closed as if sleeping. Montoya paced, frantically. Ten, fifteen minutes passed. Kiwi jumped up, pointing to the east, turned to Montoya, and spoke the first words out of his mouth in nearly a year. No one had any idea what those words might have been. I wasn't there, but Montoya assumed it meant, 'I know the way.'

And he did. Some of us guessed Kiwi prayed and got some flash of light; some of us guessed he got lucky. Since the entire trip had been anything but lucky, we ruled that out. A couple of guys guessed they smelled their way to each other since the Kiwis didn't care very much for baths. Perhaps it was his ancient link to Maori days of tracking and hunting, drawing on his instincts. It's hard to say.

When Montoya told me the story and all the details, he said, 'All of a sudden Kiwi went from panic to calm, got up off the ground and started walking, upright and confident. He didn't look at a street sign. He kept his head down as if following a trail of a deer, or as if someone had painted a yellow line on the road to mark the way. In no time Kiwi and Montoya strolled casually into Lafayette Park as if that had been their destination all along. Sitting there in the middle of that park, in the shade, on the ground with legs crossed, were the missing Kiwis. They greeted each other with smiles, some Kiwi words and strange noises, hugs, and grunts, and bumping foreheads. And a bit of crying. And that was that. Kiwi, our Kiwi, told them it's time to go and pointed the way.

They had no luggage, just leather bags hung around their shoulders. And one large bag that held ten boxes. Ten new Wolseley power sheep clippers worth more than the amount of gold Sacramento prospectors might find in ten years. Montoya wanted to hug all three Maori's but was tentative, awkward. Kiwi nodded approval. The big father picked up the much smaller Montoya, arms pinned to his side, twirled him around, and set him back on his feet, breathless, dizzy, laughing.

Getting all this cargo into an undersized car, very large people, too much weight for an under-performing car, was the worst part of the outing. Four days coming, eight days back. Overheating on the Utah Salt Flats. Changing tires in Pocatello, Idaho. Bathroom breaks and strenuous reloading of human cargo, four times each day.

Creighton and I barely ate or slept for eight very long days. This put us more than a week behind schedule.

CHAPTER TWENTY-SEVEN

K iwi and his relatives were safely back in camp. So were the clippers. We now had a complete inventory of tools and spare parts, blades, and combs. Doyle inspected them, tested them on the machine hooked to the Plymouth wheel, and pronounced them ready to go.

When we got back from training in Idaho Falls, the first order of business the next day was to figure out what the big German was talking about. We had been building fencing for a couple of months, but we wanted to see how Hans' new plans worked.

It was very clever, its brilliance in its simplicity. Hans took scrap copper tubing and fashioned it into a simple, interlocking latch, dangling from a leather strap. He would set up a section of wood fence, put two pieces together, wrap the strap around the wood, and lock it in place with the two connectors. Five seconds each.

What this meant was we could save one entire day on set up; another day saved on tear down. We had to bring our own pens because the pens at the ranches would be full of sheep home from the range. Also on-site, large crews were castrating bucks, inoculating them, docking their tails, filling pens by the thousands. We had to create our own operating theater, part of the contract.

The original plan was to have sections of fence built, stack them on the flatbed truck or in trailers, and transport them around. That plan required digging fence post holes and/or nailing two wooden feet onto the bottom of the posts for stability. Taking it all down, pulling nails, loading, actually took more time than setting them up. Hans' invention, seemingly insignificant, was vital to our success.

I thought of my boat ride home from France, an enormous passenger vessel powered by two propellers below water. Two small propellers moving tons of weight, effortlessly. I told Hans his contribution was our small, nearly invisible propeller, efficiently moving animals, something unseen, under-appreciated. This fencing with curved pens and snap-on fasteners was every bit as important to our success as the clippers. Speed was changing the way the shearing industry works. We invented speed.

Having our stand-alone shearing station also meant having our own sheds. The weather was so unpredictable that we had to shear inside. Prior to this, shearing was done primarily outside. The third part of our success was designing and building mobile, indoor facilities. Creighton and his guys built two mobile sheds that enclosed the clippers, the workers, the wool. On one end of the sheds, sheep came up a ramp, a shearer waiting for it in their personal workstation, grabbed it, rolled it on its back, and removed the pelt. Newly fleeced, the animal was shown the exit door, a chute to the side of the shearer. If you thought of it as an assembly line in one of Henry Ford's car factories, it was the right idea. Smooth, simple, efficient. Other workers would collect the wool, keep the floor clean, stomp the wool in burlap bags, and other chores to keep shearers working.

The entire operation was untried, untested. Ranchers fretted. Competitors and laggards scoffed, waiting to pick up pieces of the impending disaster. As these ranchers increased their herds by the thousands, it became impossible to move that many sheep across rugged terrain, up and down hills and gullies, crossing any number of streams, down highways now crowded with cars. It meant miles and miles of traveling. When we came up with these plans to reverse the process, take the plant to the ranches, it was new to everyone. It hadn't been done. It had no precedent from which to learn. We were making it up as we went along. Writing the book.

Creighton saw the end from the beginning and every step along the way. He remained confident if a bit tense. After the spring blizzard nearly killed one of our guys, he spent more time with the shearers, understanding them, leading them, inspiring them. Everyone leaned on his strength.

Hans pulled off the assignment to get the fencing done two full weeks ahead of schedule. Hans would be like this. Didn't matter what he was asked to do, it was always done right and on time.

The pressure and stress were unrelenting. Any number of us had lived with stress in the war and survived. This was war. Sheep ranches were our battleground. The difference, no bullets flying overhead. Our biggest enemy? Ourselves. A lot of people were counting on us to succeed; twice as many who wanted us to fail. These Rambouillet sheep would have a huge crop of wool on them after a long winter, and it had to come off before the heat of summer. The wool market wasn't waiting for us. When the buyers came out here to grade it and pick it up, we had to have it there. Trains left with the wool onboard or without it. Deadlines were deadlines. A firing squad stood at the ready.

Portable pens ready to go. Check.

Two self-enclosed shearing sheds, six stations each. Check.

The power plant was built, tested, and ready to go. Check.

Clippers were tested and ready to go. Check.

Twelve of the best shearers in the West, ready to go. Check.

Backups standing by.

Our team honed their skills by bringing a few sheep in from the fields each week. Using power from the back-tire contraption we had temporarily rigged up, each guy would practice, then talk about ideas for improvement. The armatures and equipment didn't have all the leeway and flexibility they needed, and speeds got worse for a time. But the kinks got worked out thanks to Kiwi's teaching and a very good captain, Stevie Zuninga, who the guys respectfully referred to as Captain Seven.

We felt like we were ready, and it felt good, knotted stomachs, sleepless nights notwithstanding. Fifteen to 18-hour days left me drained. I needed to see Christina. I needed her strength. The only time we had together during those hectic days was an hour here, a few minutes there, hikes in the forest, or standing on the bridge at Big Springs talking. Every minute we shared brought us closer and closer together. We knew there were some big decisions ahead, looming like a dark, afternoon thunder bumper. The kind of storm that makes you run for cover.

These issues would have to wait. The biggest challenge was she wasn't yet nineteen, and I was twenty-five. This was no big deal to her or to me, but it was going to be big with her dad. This isolated, high country environment may not be the ideal place to raise a family. All these issues had to be put in a Prince Albert tobacco can and stored on a backroom shelf for now. Christina promised to attend our demo day, the unveiling, the big show: opening night on Broadway.

Mid-April, the fields were reasonably dry. A very wet winter, a very wet spring brought wildflowers out of hibernation–ten thousand varieties, ten thousand colors, soft, watercolor edges against the pines, against purple peaks. Lavender chicory, coneflowers, columbine, fleabane, and bright orange poppies woven into a tapestry of color spread over the brown rock below.

A small crowd of thirty or forty onlookers gathered over at the Sorenson's ranch to see the unveiling and a trial run. Our entire team, now numbering nearly thirty, was ready to roll. A row of high-end cars, some of the first to come in colors other than black or gray, lined the perimeter, neatly arrayed, reflecting the warm April sunlight. Three or four of the cars were having mud removed by their drivers, like a ewe that was having her heavy coat fleeced. The mud refused much the same way a sheep does. This was a long way from civilization. The fancy cars, private chauffeurs, the spectacle of it all was in sharp contrast to the rugged rawness of the wilderness. Still not quite comfortable with it all, I think I heard the lava groan. Sawtell shrugged.

We were not at all surprised to see E. H. Harriman himself there. He had become an investor, clearly understanding the potential of all the freight that could come out of these mountains. The crew was oblivious to the pomp. To them it wasn't a show, it was removing hobbles from prized racehorses.

And there were the bankers. I'd never met them, but Creighton knew them. The Sorensons, the McQueens, and the Basque families had done business with them for many years. To pull this off they had borrowed money locally: Blackfoot, Idaho Falls, and Boise, but also from a bank in Chicago of all places. There had to be bankers. There had to be operating capital. Creighton's early idea seemed simple enough, but it became apparent early on that it was too big to be bootstrapped. The first revenue would go straight to servicing the debt. Bankers wouldn't wait any more than sheep can wait to be shorn. My uninformed mind, ignorant to such matters, began to think of interest on loans as a different type of fleecing.

I'd never borrowed a dime, still haven't. Built this house and three others with my own hands. So, I didn't understand it at all, not a bit surprising. This group formed a consortium made up of Creighton, Jamie McQueen, Wayne Sorenson, Ler Zuninga, Unai Ibarra, Marz Orazabel, and some of the other Basque families. They had good credit. The Idaho banks would do the lending to the group, guaranteed by the Federal agricultural loan assistance group out of Washington, DC. That was a lot of pilgrims in a small boat, but everyone was on board.

Why were so many onlookers gathered to watch us? We assumed there would be a small group, but it became quite an event. During the time we were building everything, demand for wool had gone crazy. I don't know the numbers, never did. All I knew was that the herds got huge. Not just here, but in Nebraska, Wyoming, California, New Mexico, and especially Nevada. The Mountain West had become sheep country. Speeding up shearing had become a hot topic, and here we were trying our best to make that happen. Mechanization in Idaho became the epicenter.

When the Depression hit, banks would shut down by the hundreds. We were a bit oblivious to how bad it got. Hidden away in a forest, on top of a mountain, in a corner of one of the least populated states in the country, we were largely ignorant. We kept working. We were deemed 'essential' by the government. It's what kept us going for three years. We got the financial help we needed, right when we needed it.

Together, about twenty ranchers from this area, large and small, all pledged collateral against the loans. They all got shares in the consortium. They liked the idea of investing and getting some return on their money. Far more important, getting wool to market in a timely way. That's where they would make money. Wool and meat gave the ranchers a dual income. Most of them were farmers and cattlemen as well. They employed dozens of farmhands to keep this robust economic island viable and vibrant.

A rare, cloudless morning dawned, brisk, calm, fragrant, a perfect day for christening our new baby. Cloudless for now, always wary of the thunder bumpers that are famous for spoiling picnics. And unrehearsed spectacles.

The entire group of guys in suits and ties turned around when they heard a small parade of trucks rumbling down the gravel road, circus elephants, trunk to tail.

"First was a big Harvester International truck, a covered back, pulling a trailer. With a staff in hand, tattooed body gleaming with a new coat of lanolin, Kiwi, the Aboriginal warrior, stood astride the cargo, presiding over the invading forces.

The second was a Ford flatbed carrying our massive power plant, covered by a couple of big tarps. The third one was a newer model Chevy truck, smaller, pulling a small trailer. Three other trucks all pulling trailers completed the caravan.

No marching band, no baton twirlers, no fireworks, no ribbon-cutting, but nonetheless it was a sight to behold, this grand entrance like some parade down Wall Street. Couldn't have been any better if there was ticker tape and confetti raining down.

As the trucks pulled to a stop, the crew went to work immediately. In one hour the fencing was in place, normally a 12-hour task.

Two large trailers were unhitched and put in place to the left of the holding pens and the chutes. The onlookers seemed puzzled, the blank stare of a sheep, as a door on either side of the big trailer opened up, tilted down, and became ramps covered with old rubber tire strips for traction.

In less than thirty minutes, an entire shearing plant popped up, on-site, the first of its kind mobile plant was operational. No one had moved a single animal, but on cue, there they came, about 200 of them being led by two English sheepdogs and one shepherd with a staff in hand. The sheep, following a lead, politely, efficiently filled up one of the holding pens.

There was no speechifying, no spectacle, just an incredibly efficient bunch of guys ready to shear. If the bankers, the Feds, and the railroad guys were impressed, they didn't show it. I don't know the right word, but it didn't look to me anything like excitement. More like faces chiseled out of granite with permanent frowns on them.

These prominent men, with their expensive, hand-polished shoes, now colored an Island Park grayish-white, made the stone faces on Mount Rushmore look like they were having a party. Abe Lincoln telling a joke. This was serious business for them. We all knew how serious it was by the stern looks, deep lines in furrowed brows that looked like cursive writing: "doubt."

Creighton and a couple of guys jumped up on the flatbed and removed the tarps. Kiwi attached clippers to armatures inside the two sheds. Kiwi was wearing only his sarong and holster. The big wigs pushed closer, faces brightened, a hint of a smile on each face. They didn't know how close I was watching them.

The tarp on the back of the flatbed truck went flying, and the large Cummins diesel engine came to life. After fourteen months of preparation, the big power plant was ready for its debut. Belts and pulleys, armatures, and gears conjured up images of a Rube Goldberg contraption.

The diesel roared, black sooty smoke belched out of the modified exhaust pipe, dissipating in the mountain air. Kiwi and five others stood in one shed, six other nervous shearers in the second. We had twelve guys on board, practiced and ready to go, three others still in training as backups.

This included Creighton's son Doyle who, for the most part, had stayed sober. He was already eighteen and beginning to get control over his demons and his temper. He was an excellent mechanic and had become a good cutter, as well. Doyle stayed with the Cummins throughout the demo.

The onlookers wanted a closer view of the sheds. As if raising the curtain on a Jenny Lind concert at the P. T. Barnum circus, I rolled back the canvas awning revealing the entire horizontal workings of the shed, shearers at the ready, center ring, Kiwi the ringmaster. The entire operation was on full view, exposed to all.

We knew there were spies in the crowd. Two of them came from the shearer who lost the contract. The others were shearers we had met. They made no attempt to disguise themselves. They were waiting in line to come to work for us. The price per pelt that we would pay would easily triple a season's wages.

Everyone knew it. Once we got going, our plant would become the kind of company that other out-of-work shearers would flock to.

⌇⌇⌇⌇⌇⌇⌇⌇

"Whoa, Junior," I said. "Sorry about that really bad pun. It was so bad!"

Junior rolled his eyes. Back to the story and the best day of my life. To that point anyway.

~~~~~~~~~~

The Cummins engine hummed, power clippers buzzed. Twelve guys simultaneously drew their weapons from holsters, a posse in a shootout. Sheep marched through the pens, effortlessly around curved sections, up the ramp into the newly-minted sheds. The dignitaries and the stockholder/ranchers now jockeyed for a closer look.

In seven minutes, Kiwi's first pelt was off, held aloft by one of the Hurst boys. The sheep was summarily dismissed down a chute to the holding pen on the other side. We heard small, appreciative applause but these onlookers weren't exactly the applauding type. For the most part, they stayed quiet.

E. H. Harriman and his driver turned and headed for his car, two of the four bankers followed. One pelt done, and they bolted like they had a hat full of huckleberries with a bear on their tail. They had seen enough. The rest of the visitors stayed glued in place. Creighton and I made eye contact, each of us sending a signal that said, 'What does that mean?'

As three of the fancy cars headed back to the highway, everyone looked at each other wondering what to think of the abrupt departure of four of the most important guys. Did they like it or hate it?

Within seconds Creighton was waving his hand shouting, "Let's go! Let's go! This isn't a party."

An average of seven minutes per sheep times 200 sheep: the entire demo was done, every animal completely shorn and out the door in two hours. Two hundred pelts in a burlap bag, stomped and bundled, ready for market. The amount of time to shear one sheep would dramatically decrease with experience over time. For today, seven minutes was miraculous. The spies retreated into the shadows and vanished, vampires caught in the morning sun.

The demo, two years in the making, was over. Except for eating. The smaller trailer was opened, and Creighton's wife Mary and two daughters started dishing up chili and fresh hot Basque flatbread and chilled cider and wine courtesy of the Basque families. No one had time for Prohibition.

The big diesel engine coughed and sputtered to a halt. Every pulley, belt, clipper, and armature was thoroughly checked, tightened, and oiled, ready for tomorrow. Day one, done. Two hundred sheep down, a hundred thousand to go.

CHAPTER TWENTY-EIGHT

The winter of 1927 came early, just like the UP train, right on schedule. No one ever thinks of winter as a blessing. After a grueling first year, winter was a reprieve, a commutation. Shearing went remarkably well. We had the magic formula. We had the right team, the right equipment, the right process. We forever changed the wool industry in this country. None of us cared about innovation, modernization, and forward progress. We were too worn out to imagine ourselves as anything special. We felt anything but special. We were exhausted from our first summer.

People all over the country wrote us letters, but no one had time to answer them. No one had the skills. A reporter from the *Wall Street Journal* tracked us down. New York for hell's sake. How did that happen? It was quite a story when we thought about it years later.

We cut down standard shearing time by more than two-thirds; we took the shearing station to the ranches and saved each owner a couple of weeks' time moving the herds. Because the ranchers didn't have to move the animals, it saved on labor costs. With operating costs down and wool in demand, everyone made more profit. And this was just before the Depression. For a lot of us, the twenties roared.

Shearers regularly came looking for work. Word got out about our success, and we had a steady stream of replacements in the queue. Guys from all over the area walked in and out of our revolving door. That first year we didn't have to hire any new cutters. Our twelve guys did great. Better than great. They attacked their work every day with more and more intensity. They spent hours honing their blades. They improved their movements. They worked together to find the most consistent cuts, and developed methods still practiced today. Every day, every hour they found ways to reduce their times. They challenged each other. Pushed. Dared. The internecine conflict flourished.

It wasn't just work. It was a craft. It was an art form. We didn't go scouting around for shearers ever again. They came to us. We were paying extremely high wages, and everyone wanted to join the band. We couldn't take on every guy and their Aunt Ethel, so I put Cam Ferguson in charge of swatting flies. We always suspected some of our guys would eventually move on, our little flocks of North Americans, vagabonds, 'Waltzing Matilda' types. Prone to moving. Prone to drifting. Prone to building a boat. I kept my eye on some of the other caterwaulers, just in case.

Winter was cold and miserable. It was also a welcome change of pace. Winter days could actually mean longer work hours because there was so much we had to do to refurbish and repair. In summer, when the sun went down, the work stopped. In the winter we would be inside the Idaho Falls warehouse preparing for the following Spring, working longer hours. Some of the shearers went home if they had a home or a family. Some stayed on as laborers out on the ranches. Every one of us became cramped claustrophobes longing for open spaces. Longing for the pine-scented mornings and campfire smoke-infused dusks.

We were locked into doing the twenty farms in the consortium the following Spring, and that was good. We knew we had work all lined up. Our dance card was full. No one was getting rich, least of all Creighton. He sunk every dime he had into the project. Even though the operation was profitable, Creighton was paying off the machinery, the trucks, fencing, spare parts. We would unexpectedly burn through most of the belts on the power plant every two or three weeks.

We ran fast and hard. Bills were always paid on time. The bank loan was always paid on time. The last one to get paid was Creighton.

He drew down what you'd call a salary, more like a living allowance, just enough to get the family by. I got to know some of his kids, and they never complained much. They'd come up most summers to help out a bit, the girls in the cook trailer, Creighton's wife, and the two younger boys. We always had good food; simple stuff but plenty of it.

Simmering below the surface, hot magma bubbling, his oldest son, Doyle, began to feel the emptiness of an absent father, the freedoms it gave him, and he began to expand a resentment he was not aware of, roiling in the deep.

Over the next three years, Creighton's family shrunk. As soon as the older girls were about seventeen or eighteen, they bolted. I'm not sure where they ended up, but I never saw them again. Except for the youngest girl, Carma. She was that fifteen-year-old girl that sent shock waves through the camp the very first time she showed up a couple of years back. She was no longer a little girl; now a mature seventeen-year-old, raven-haired stunner.

Junior interrupted., "Gramps what about your girl? Christina? Was she around? Did you two continue to——"

"To what?"

"To date, I guess. You know, to court."

"I don't think anyone would call it a courtship. She was still so young. I didn't ever have a confrontation with her dad, but he had made it clear I was too old. She had too much ahead of her. 'Hey, I'm the 25-year-old virgin here,' I wanted to say. 'You ain't got no worries with me.' I kept my distance from her dad and heeded the advice of a friend: 'Keep your zipper up and your mouth shut.'

I'd see Christina periodically, far too infrequently. In the summer, we were working 12-hour days, the entire crew falling into bed in a comatose state, near death. On the weekends, Christina and I would spend time together. There were no movie theaters, ice cream shops, or anything of culture. There was the dance hall that the Pond family built. I tried it out a time or two, but I was as awkward as a young lamb on a lanolin-covered wood floor. Remember my nickname, 'Trippy.' A couple of girls made me dance from time to time, but I wasn't much for chasing other girls, mostly flighty tourists at the dances. The visiting females added variety to the scenery, a refreshing change from the sturgeons and hellgrammites, but I wasn't out to catch anything.

Christina went back to Lewiston for her senior year of high school, now eighteen. She was a good student and wanted to go to college after that. She loved kids and dreamed of becoming a teacher. Already accepted to the Albion Middle School, she pushed hard so she could graduate high school early. For most of the winter months, I wouldn't see her.

She would quite naturally go to dances or to the movies in town with some of the boys her age. I figured that was the right thing. I didn't have a picture of her hanging on my wall. I wasn't one to carry her photo around in my wallet if I'd ever had a wallet, which I didn't. But I remembered that face of hers, that crooked smile. I remembered every touch, every embrace, her smell, her calloused hands, her unladylike boots, her slender frame draped in work shirts.

And every other detail. Didn't need a photo. Every time I shut my eyes, there she was in full color, red curls swirling in the pools and eddies of the Buffalo River. A siren, half-bird, half-woman, luring me to destruction with the sweetness of her song.

We made Ponds one of the regular places to get foodstuffs. Mary would bring a load of provisions up from Burley, and Ashton had a good store, but for the everyday stuff like milk, eggs, flour, and salt, we would buy at Ponds. I was glad to have a reason to frequent the store. There wasn't a single moment of reacquaintance needed, no refresher course on our secret, silent language.

Deliveries kept her busy stacking shelves, but she would say to me, "I've got a lot of new inventory, would you like to help me?" This was code for "meet me in the storage room." We did a lot of catching up with each other behind cans of corn and Spam.

She was always keen to know about our business, and I loved telling her about our progress. She was glad to be graduating high school, but she wouldn't talk about what was next. I didn't ask. Beware poison ivy ahead.

There wasn't a single thing either of us could do about our age gap so we acted as if were a hot pot along a Yellowstone trail. Don't step off the path. It wasn't indifference, just the way of a bachelor like me. A rover, a loner, a gypsy, just barely more than a hobo in a freight yard, like so many other postwar floaters, just a breath away from a breeze, a moment or two away from waltzing Matilda, not a single one of us contemplating marriage. But those dreams about water and red hair and blue eyes and blue skies kept me in flux about my agenda. For the very first time, I had an agenda. Nightmares of war, nightmares of drowning in alcohol, knife fight terrors, were still commonplace, but they began to recede as Christina increasingly brightened my nights.

Occasionally a live herd would come to the dance hall, but it was primarily records we'd dance to. I liked the cowboy songs. 'Home on the Range' was both a hymn and an anthem to me. I loved to watch guitar players move their fingers around the strings and the frets. It was hypnotic. The harmony of voices blending, the rhythm of the strumming guitars was easy for me to feel and internalize. Modern songs of the '20s were either too tragic or too cheery. Western tunes were authentic. They told a believable story. They told my story.

I gave the guitar a try once. A new shearer with a guitar on his back joined up with us in our second year. He showed me the fundamentals, and I could pick up a tune here and there but not much. The guy with the guitar wasn't much better than me. He knew a grand total of three songs and sang them over and over around the campfire at night.

"Tumbling Tumbleweeds," a popular cowboy lament, was a favorite of mine, but when he started playing it for the fourth time, Apidale didn't want to hear it. It was a Saturday night, late, and Apidale had a bunch of beer in him. He wanted to sleep. When that tumbleweed song started over again, Apidale jumped out of his sleeping bag and headed for that guitar, intent on throwing it in the fire. Apidale nearly ended up in the fire himself before reaching the noisy songster. A couple of guys had to pull him out. He tried again but the guitar guy went running, screaming like a girl. "You leave Patty alone," he screamed. "Get out of here, you lousy drunk. Leave my Patty alone."

The guys all had plenty to drink and were star-gazing, letting the globe spin for while, feeling the full weight of gravity and booze. They cheered Apidale on. "Get him, Appleseed, get him. Look at him run. Go man go. He's in love with his guitar. Patty Patty Patty." The guitar survived, as did the guitarist who was in camp with us for two of the three years and learned maybe one new song in all that time. The guys changed his name to "Patty," and that's what we all called him from then on. He never complained about the name change. I always wondered if the curves of the guitar, narrow in the middle, conjured up images of a girl he left behind; a girl named Patty, hard to tell. I never asked. "Tumbleweeds" became our unofficial company song. Apidale tripped on a raised tree root and spent the rest of the summer nursing a broken toe. "See them tumbling down."

That's about how things went. Long summers in the camps, pulling everything up every couple of weeks, moving it all around like a circus troop, big tents and all. There was very little time for a private life.

Everyone worked hard and played hard, surviving, not prospering. We'd listen to the radio when we were in town, hear all the news. The big bank crash was up ahead, like whitewater rapids that you don't see coming or the huge ravine where Mesa Falls made its plunge. But in '27 and '28 the economy was still good. The wool industry got bigger and bigger each year. The herds grew exponentially each year. The sheep grew a new coat every year, and it had to come off. We couldn't stop cutting. The government-subsidized us a bit, so even if the pelts were piling up, that wasn't our problem.

Saturday nights were lively if you liked lively. Increasingly, our crew would be down at Pond's dance hall. Some of them, anyway.

Sunset Lodge up the road on the north end was always a favorite spot for the guys. The large pool hall was a magnet, a very popular place, money changing hands back and forth all night, hustlers and hellgrammites in abundance. Pool halls in front, illegal booze out back.

All of the alcohol there at Sunset was bootlegged, of course. Wool and timber going out, booze secretly coming in, courtesy of Union Pacific. Alcohol still flowed, even in these remote spots.

Turns out Doyle was a pretty good shooter at pool. Throughout his high school days, he didn't like history class, he hated algebra class, and preferred the pool hall in downtown Burley, Idaho over high school classrooms. He became a very good pool player and an equally talented hustler. He spent a lot of his free time at Sunset Lodge. By then Doyle was also a good shearer and a very good mechanic. He never rang the bell as I remember, but he kept up with the guys and made good money. Somehow, he always ended up with more cash than just about anybody, taking bets and hustling guys at pool. His game improved, his bravado increased with a few drinks in him, keeping him loose, fluid. His skills always left him with a roll of bills stuffed into his Levi denims.

Doyle had no sense about managing his money. His idea of a bank depository was cash in your pocket. Most of the guys in our group were sending money to a wife or a mother. They needed a few bucks now and again for a drink or a game of pool, but they didn't pay anything for room and board, so living was cheap.

A couple of the Basque guys put away every nickel they ever made. They were just like their fathers. They started buying lambs each spring, ran them with family bands, and in a couple of years they would have their own small band. Doyle, and for that matter, many of our guys never grasped the concept of saving for the future. For the most part, they didn't understand the meaning of "future."

It wasn't long before other large shearing companies around the west and around the country started buying the power clippers. The entire industry changed. Some US companies reverse-engineered the Wolseley. Wolseley had no US patents. Power clippers showed up everywhere. It's hard to know if anyone duplicated our mobile plant right at first. It was pretty easy in the end to figure it all out. But for three years, our innovation and experience kept us ahead of the curve. We always got the best shearers. They were well paid, the very top of the scale of wage earners, and everyone knew we ran a cash business.

Doyle always had that big wad of cash, never put it in the bank or sent it home. Each time he made a wager at pool, he'd pull out that wad and flash it around, daring others to take him on. He was popular, he was despised. He was respected, he was envied. He was a target. One Saturday night, the pool sharking at Sunset Lodge took a serious turn.

A big bunch of guys came passing through, a dozen or so, as I recall, on their way to the Army depot down in Ogden, Utah. They weren't Army guys, civilians, as far as I know, hired as contractors to work down in the munitions warehouses. They had all been working back in Chicago, well-trained in the logistics of moving military stuff around. The Ogden Depot was ramping up munitions depleted after the war.. Leading up to the Depression, there were plenty of military and civilian jobs there. I heard it said that there was a fair amount of illegal hooch on the Army trainloads coming through Ogden. The cops couldn't bust an Army train, and Ogden became a wild town in the '20s.

With these Ogden guys and some hotshot tourists looking for a game and a drink, Sunset Lodge was swarming, a hatch of flies just emerging on the river, skittish, aimlessly buzzing. Sweat, booze, smoke, vomit, rancid perfume, boots still with traces of dead trout, all of it overcooked and simmering in the July air. The crowds grew more noisy and more rowdy as the night went on. Doyle was center stage, taking on all comers. He lost a game or two, but not more than that. It was part of the hustle. Everyone wanted a shot at him.

By the end of the night, everyone was sloshed and started stumbling out of the place. Doyle had a few drinks but not much. He still had his wits about him. He had taken a bunch of money from the Ogden guys, ended for the night, and had a round of drinks together; buddies, pals, Doyle's new, best friends, all agreeing to a rematch in the near future.

A reverse hustle was underway. Two of the Ogden guys were standing by Doyle's car as he walked out. He knew immediately he had walked into a trap. He turned around to walk the other way and three other guys were coming at him from that direction. He made a quick mental calculation. He had been shearing sheep and had added extra muscle to his already thick frame. He had become a good boxer over the years, and he figured he could get out of any scrape with two guys. In most fights, he could escape three guys. But this was a gang of nearly ten, now in a circle around him, a pride of lions at a feast.

"Doyle, this is easy," one of the guys said. "Toss over that wad of cash in your pocket, and we'll all go home." Doyle was calm and expressionless. One knee began to bounce. A drop of Brylcreem and sweat dripped down his forehead.

"It's a nice little wad of cash you got. You should never carry around that much cash especially since a bunch of it is ours. We're going to need a little of it back."

Doyle said, "Why don't you greasy Chicago guys go on back to the hellgrammite holes you crawled out of and take your Army munitions bullshit with you?'

Doyle was stronger than they thought possible, like an enraged bear upright on two feet protecting her cubs, teeth bared, huge chest puffed out, massive claws at the end of huge, hairy arms. Then silence. Rubber tires on gravel. Moonlight and crickets. Mountain stillness. A crack in the lava rock.

Sunday morning, calm arrived in camp with the sun. Squirrels click their tongues, a killdeer screech, the only sounds. The river ran stealthily in the background. *Shh.* Quiet, clear skies over the entire Yellowstone region awakened the ancient caldera, sleeping peacefully. An elk trumpeted "Revile."

The low rumble of a car engine broke the quiet. The owner of Sunset Lodge made a slow, lumbering crawl out of the car, paused, and took a deep breath.

Creighton watched the man pull up, peered over his bowl of oatmeal, and stopped eating. He knew exactly why this man was here. The two men shook hands.

"Thanks for bringing him here," Creighton says. "I've had to drag him home more times than I can count. I'll come and pick up the car later today if that's okay."

"Yes, the car will be fine there."

"Much obliged."

"Creighton, look, I'm sorry about this. I think he was out all night laying in the gravel. I had no idea he was out there. I didn't see him until about an hour ago. I came right over."

"Do you know who it was?" He stared blankly up at the hills.

"They're gone, Creighton."

"Who was it?" Creighton insisted.

"Creighton, listen to me. They're gone. Gone. They weren't Army, but they were civilians working down at the munitions plant in Ogden. You'll drive yourself mad trying to find them. They're gone."

Creighton worked a hand-carved toothpick and chewed on the remaining bits of oatmeal, spitting small bites to the ground. He pushed his thinning hair back off his forehead and faced the morning sun, now casting an orange light, more like an evening sunset, morning and evening trading places, as if the light could somehow go back in time and prevent this.

Creighton's tanned face stopped at a line where his fedora normally sat. The orange glow of the morning made the two tones of his face more prominent, the upper third a pale white. The wrinkles of the aging skin on his forehead, exposed now without his hat, cast deeper shadows than the morning before. They were no longer wrinkles. They were gorges a river had cut into stone.

He listened to the silence of the caldera. It groaned and cracked, the ancient lava underneath his feet, restless after a couple of million years of hibernation, came to life a bit, if only for a moment, stirred by the energy now in this good man's soul.

If you were a newcomer to the area, you wouldn't be able to hear those sounds. You'd hear the rivers and creeks humming along over the rocks on their way down the mountain. You'd hear the occasional crack of an aging tree finally laying down its brittle branches. And you'd hear the cry of the osprey diving down plucking trout out of Henry's Fork, the bugle of a bull elk, the rush of wind under the wings of a sandhill crane awkwardly getting off the ground.

These were the natural sounds of nature, the obvious sounds, always there. Anyone could hear them. They were all around and easy to pick up by the casual ear. They were on the surface.

But, in order to hear the voice of the ancient rocks, the ancient volcanic tuff below, you had to train your ear. It was a different wavelength, a different frequency. It didn't speak often but when it did, those with wise ears, the trained ears, attuned ears, heard it whisper and murmur and moan as it attempted to give counsel and consolation. It never said the same thing twice. This demanded attentiveness. Creighton, and a few of the other authentic Idaho natives, never wrote any of it down. You had to take it in, absorb it, and let it become a part of your lifeblood. It was far too sacred to ever share.

I asked him about it. Once. He kept his vow of silence. But on that day, that morning as the earth was speaking, as he stood there looking at the sunrise, he told me the rocks wept with him. Both he and the earth had a deep dark fissure in their core that would never heal.

Ancient voices struggled to find words of solace, but there would be none that morning.

Creighton and Apidale pulled Doyle's lifeless body, already stiff from a long, cold, Yellowstone night, out of the car and put him on the wooden table that Doyle himself built from the timber that surrounded us.

"Trippy, go get a tarp and cover him up. Mary will be awake soon. So will the kids. I don't want them to see any of this." His voice was calm. His face, stone. His hands trembled.

CHAPTER TWENTY-NINE

I want to say camp got back to normal, but it never came close to being normal again. We all worked hard to help soothe the sorrow Creighton and his family were struggling with. Creighton could find no comfort. He pushed us beyond limits we thought impossible. The entire camp needed and wanted to be pushed in an attempt to move on from the tragedy.

We had just arrived at the Ibarra ranch for a full week of fleecing. There were only about three thousand sheep here, but Andrew Aguirre's ranch was adjacent, just over the hill, and it was easy to bring their herd of two or three thousand over and combine efforts. This allowed us to set up just once and shear two complete bands without moving.

We were on schedule to get the spring shearing done. We would need every hour. As the summer went on, some of the sheep were longer and shaggier and should have been done at least a month earlier. Our shearers were stronger now and had more stamina, so cutting even the heaviest coats seemed normal. No one complained as pelt counts soared.

We went late into July, in a three-week period, finishing up all the smaller bands and preparing for McQueen, the largest ranch with a little more than 20,000 head. This is where we would end our summer shearing. August had its own monsoon type of weather, more moisture in the air, more afternoon thunderstorms. Moist air and rain would shut us down. We pressed on. Speeds increased almost daily. We were averaging five minutes per pelt. Elsewhere, shearing the old way dragged on at warp turtle speed, anathema to the naysayers and the viziers who predicted our failure—and our bitter competitors praying for our demise.

Late into the month, wake-up calls got earlier. We needed every hour of daylight. Mornings were brisk. By brisk, I mean cold. By cold, I mean damn cold, like a porcelain commode on the north side of an iceberg. Frost on the ground, on the tent, on the fences. Our shearing began with frost on the sheep, an impossible task. Speeds picked up with the final arrival of the sun.

As the camp came to life, coffee aroma wafted through the tents. The smell of Mary's bacon and pancakes dragged weary bones out of bed, out of the three big Army surplus camouflage tents, bones creaking, yawning, and working their necks and backs, getting the kinks out. Most of the guys made their way to the table with a sheepskin wrapped around them for warmth; big, tall, upright sheep gave the sense they had been cutting for so long that they became one with the animals, reverse anthropomorphism.

For a long time, even the heavy schedule wasn't allowed to disrupt Sundays. Many of the consortium members worried that Creighton's hard and fast rule about no work on Sunday would put them behind schedule. They had learned to trust him, and no one ever argued about it.

None of the cutters ever complained about a day off. They were making more money than at any time in their lives, and they loved having a recovery day.

Sunday mornings with more quiet time frequently meant more idle time, more getting one another's nerves at times. The crew was better when they were working. If they were idle, petty arguments would break out, sometimes moving to serious ones. Tempers would flare, and more serious fights would break out. Not so much fisticuffs and head bashing, more wrestling on the ground, rolling in dirt. Big, strong men refusing to give an inch. Someone would eventually break it up. It was usually harmless. Creighton called it a bad case of MSB. Symptoms included restlessness, anxiousness, and short tempers. For years we called it by that name, MSB, and I assumed it was a medical term. Years later I learned that Creighton made up the term MSB to describe a condition known as "massive semen buildup." Others would call it piss and vinegar. Lots of names for it. It was simple pent-up energy that needed to be harnessed.

It took about fifteen minutes for Junior to regain his composure when I told him about MSB among the men. He'd never heard it called that. It was good to see him laugh after listening to my much too-long ramblings. When I wondered out loud if Junior had a bad case of MSB himself, he would neither confirm nor deny it.

Sunday was a patch-up day. Fixing machinery and fixing our human assets, bruised, bent, banged up. Everyone had wounds on their hands, cuts from the blades now sharper than ever as honing improved. There wasn't much in a first aid kit. Mercurochrome for cuts and scrapes, nothing like Advil or Tylenol to relieve chronic aches and pains. We had some aspirin from time to time but, for the most part, the only medicine was a bottle of "stop crying like a baby" or a vial of "go tell it to the sheep." Creighton invented that medicine and had a patent pending on it. He would often say, "You can get better in September. Meantime, buck up, lamby boy."

Bottles of bogus liniment would invariably show up in camp. The contents were always mysterious, their healing power dubious. You could rub some of the concoctions on sore shoulders, thighs, lower backs, the places that were always sore, and pretend it made you feel better. It didn't. It smelled like turpentine because it *was mostly turpentine*. The sheep hated the smell. We were working in close quarters and nobody wanted that smell all day. Liniments were banned. Healing meant getting stronger and stronger. Everyone on the crew learned to heal fast or to work through pain.

It seemed ludicrous to some that liniment was banned. Compared to the smells of the camp, it was eau de cologne. We would be in one camp for an average of two weeks, longer for the big herds. Six, eight, ten thousand stinky critters coming and going in the pens, sheep biscuits piling up, constant mud from all the rain, dogs everywhere, diesel smoke in the air, and a gang of dark, hairy Basques, some kilt wearers, one big German, a dark brown Kiwi, and a bunch of misfits lucky if they bathed once a week. Here they were in the shed every morning at seven, working their butts off all day, August heat warming that shearing shed up above a hundred degrees. Women wouldn't come near the plant. Neither would the dogs. Hell, I didn't like to go around there much, and I was the foreman.

Making repairs was an everyday occurrence. Creighton and his mechanic, a guy named Hendershot, now a full-time employee after the passing of Doyle, dealt with any number of ailments on the equipment. The clippers we used were efficient, but there were always issues. Repairs included tearing a few of those clippers apart, putting in a new gear, and some oil. The power plant, with all its moving parts, was being patched up night and day. The shearers were always looking for ways to gain an edge over the others and would spend hours sharpening. This meant that most of them adopted one pair of cutters as their own and treated them like a baby. Over the years shearing companies would provide the machines, but the guys would have their own 'jewels,' the name they gave to the blades and the combs because they were so valuable. It was their livelihood and their reputation. They wanted to control the quality of the jewels. Sharp meant speed, speed meant money. Equally, speed meant prestige and bragging rights.

The power plant did a lot of coughing, and chugging, and complaining, but did its job remarkably well. Creighton designed and built the entire thing, and with the help of good mechanics, it became quite a wonder to see. Word got out, and we regularly had visitors. Tours were part of my responsibility, a ridiculous part of my portfolio given my awkwardness and clumsy speech. The governor of Idaho even stopped by to have a look. He wanted to see for himself how this new endeavor found its way to the center of a major industry, the tentacles of which had created a lot of jobs and increased the tonnage of wool going out of Idaho. The mechanized clippers were a marvel, but the mobile power plant was the star of the show.

H. C. Baldridge, the governor in those days, loved to fish. He had come up to stay with McQueen, a good friend. McQueen had given a lot of money to help old Henry get elected. The governor was a big supporter of the wool industry and helped get payments from the Feds to keep it going. McQueen made sure the governor went home with a big catch of trout, courtesy of the two young Hurst boys, now world-class fly fishermen.

Another newspaper guy came all the way over from California. Creighton, in his normal quiet way, talked to the guy and answered his questions. He was generously shown the entire camp and the equipment. The reporter interviewed Wayne Sorenson to get a rancher's perspective about this new mechanized method. The journalist left with a promise to send a copy of the story he was writing. And he did.

We picked up mail from Pond's Lodge which had become an official post office. There in the pile of bills was the *Fresno Bee* newspaper. I worried about this kind of public exposure giving away our secret inventions and our process. So were the investors. Creighton, in typical fashion, wanted to show it off. He was very proud of it all, anxious to share it with anyone who may want to build their own outfit and help put people to work. Creighton's connection to the New Zealand company that made the clippers was so random, so fortunate, he would tell me 'those clippers fell right out of the sky.' Creighton felt an obligation to share everything he had learned.

He would regularly remind me that he didn't choose to shear sheep. He had other skills. He told me once, "I didn't know I would be the one to modernize an industry. It simply came my way. Somehow I knew what needed to be done. I think all of this, the portable station, the automation, the skilled shearers, came along, and I was fortunate to be the guy willing to give it a try. Sharing all this, showing everyone the system, is why I did it. It was meant to be shared, meant to lift others."

Junior stopped recording when I stood up. I fetched the yellow, brittle newspaper story, put it in front of him, and told him to read it out loud. There was Creighton Hurst, a black and white photo, standing by the power plant, pulleys, and belts, and the crazy octopus legs coming

out of it. The picture had a caption: "Revolutionizing the wool industry, a new invention speeds the shearing process up 300 percent."

Junior read the article:

*"Out in the wilderness of Idaho, in the spectacular region known as the
Yellowstone/Teton Wilderness, far, far away from absolutely everything, an
enterprising businessman has invented a remarkable machine that powers mechanized
clippers, speeding up the process of getting wool to market. The inventor, Creighton
Hurst of Burley, Idaho, isn't exactly Carnegie or Rockefeller, Edison or Tesla, but his
clever contraption is nonetheless a remarkable achievement. This quiet man willingly
gave away all his secrets and wants to share the success with all comers.*

*"We went out to one of the ranches where there were thousands of head of
sheep lined up to be fleeced. It looked to this reporter like an impossible task to get
these temperamental animals sheared, but what I witnessed was nothing less than
a small miracle. The operation ran smoothly and with a precision that was in
sharp contrast to the chaos I wrongly expected. I ruined a perfectly good pair of
'city' shoes tromping around in the mess of such an undertaking. I was oblivious to
the smell, the mess, the noise, and the diesel smoke as I walked around, mesmerized
by the speed and the strength of the men and their astonishing efficiency in a most
challenging environment. I happily ruined my shoes."*

I looked at Junior and said, "I'm pretty sure Creighton never saw
or read the article. It was never important to him what others thought
of him or his accomplishments. When the newspaper came in the mail
Creighton handed it to me, unopened, and said, 'I hope this helps other
shearing outfits figure out how to change their business.'

"Everything about the industry did change. We never believed we
started the avalanche of change, but we were content knowing we may
have pushed the first snowball rolling downhill, and we knew we were
on the cutting edge of the change. That pun was intentional, Junior."

Junior rolled his eyes.

CHAPTER THIRTY

" So went the daily grind, shearing day after day after day, endless rows of identical-looking sheep bleating and bunching. One particular morning as the guys were putting on their booties–"

"Booties? The guys wore booties? Junior asked.

"Well, that's what they called them."

The shearers were always looking for an edge, always coming up with something or other to make the job easier, faster, more productive. The burlap booties reduced sliding on a lanolin-coated floor. They also replaced shoes with laces, frequently getting caught in the blades. Lanolin was a blessing if your girlfriend liked soft hands. It was also a curse.

Hamish Fagan, a shearer from Scotland, worked his way from standby to the shed. It took him two full years to earn a spot but he hadn't bothered making slip-resistant booties. Head down, fur flying, the ornery ewe between his knees decided she had enough of the nonsense and made a sudden leap for freedom.

The animal seemed to sense Fagan's rookie handling. No experience, no booties. When the ewe jumped, Fagan's left foot went sliding. His entire leg folded in half, and we heard the crack of bone even above all the machinery noise. His own body weight and a hundred-thirty-pound ewe slammed on top of the leg. Three guys started immediately vomiting when they saw the bent leg, a couple of bones sticking out.

An enormous amount of blood began to pool. Fagan immediately passed out from shock. Hans, the big German, who years ago had a leg injury of his own, took off his shirt and tied the sleeves around the thigh, pulled it tight to slow the bleeding.

The worthless suspension of the rickety old Plymouth was never more evident, each bump a sledgehammer, each pothole a moon crater. The doctor in Ashton was an hour away. Not a hospital, barely a clinic to treat sore throats, they could not begin to care for an injury this serious. The doctor's wife passed out, the doctor himself a pale, pasty white.

Sprained ankles were fairly common, a twisted knee, sore hip, mild and curable maladies didn't slow down our crew much. We didn't need inspectors or government agencies enforcing safety rules. We knew the dangers. The guys made their own rules. Accidents were minimal so this horrendous leg break spooked us all. Safety was something we always tried to emphasize."

"Junior, you wanted to find out if the sheep were poorly treated. They weren't. Neither was our shearing crew. Keeping humans safe became a top priority. These shearers were like today's athletes, better than anyone else in the world, and we had to protect our assets."

"Did the kid ever get back to work? Do you know how it turned out?"

"Oh yeah, sorry, I forgot to tell you that part of the story. He lost that entire leg. They removed it damn near up to his hip. Every blood vessel, tendon, and ligament got mangled. A gray, Hamish Fagan cloud hovered over the sheds every day. Red Borrowman made a little wooden sign and hung it over the door into the shed. It said, 'Hamish Rules, a reminder to be careful all the time. That's where the booties came from. The newspaper reporter missed a good story about innovation of another kind, insignificant as it may have seemed."

<hr>

The guys in camp each had their personal challenges. The second summer was a long, strenuous shearing season and tempers could flare quickly like a lightning bolt hitting a stand of tinder-dry forest, setting it ablaze. It was impossible to stop lightning and it would be just as hard to extinguish the blaze it starts. There would be massive forest fires in these woods from time to time, and we had our share of fires right in camp.

Tanner McQueen developed into a very fine shearer. He was with us through the first two years. His dad, Jamie McQueen, had by far the largest herd going into year two. The majority of ewes that are bred give birth to twins. It's rare when they don't. The herds multiplied quickly year over year, so our workload increased exponentially. Jamie helped keep the bankers at bay when prices started dipping and demand eventually plummeted. He was the voice and the conscience of the consortium. I grew to admire his firm leadership and integrity.

It was no small matter when we started having trouble with Jamie's son, Tanner. I didn't want to run to Jamie and tell him Tanner was in some kind of trouble. I didn't know what his own struggles were, but it was my job to make sure he was keeping pace with the other shearers in camp. We were adding new equipment and new shearers to keep up with the workload, and if he wasn't making his daily count, we had new guys who could. We would have to make a change despite the fact his father was our partner.

Tanner had always been a conscientious worker, no problem in the cutting shed or in the camp. When we packed up to move from one camp to another, he was willing to take on even the smallest of tasks, helping our laborers do their job. He always seemed to want to prove that he wasn't just daddy's boy. He had earned everyone's respect.

But whatever burden was weighing on his mind began showing up in his work. He was making a lot of mistakes, slowing his count. I tried to encourage him without screaming and shouting. The gentle approach didn't work. I tried taking the verbal strap to his back. That didn't work. I tried the "arm around his shoulder, let me help you, psychological counseling, everything will be okay" approach. That didn't work. I asked the team captain, Stevie Zuninga, to see if he could help, peer-to-peer coaching. That didn't work. Tanner was, daily, on some other distant star, far removed from reality.

The other shearers in the shed began hassling him, and it escalated like a small fire, unspotted by the watchman in the fire tower. Tanner wasn't making numbers, and his teammates let him know their concern. Their idea of encouragement was heckling, trash-talking, humiliation, using the trick boys and men have used for years: calling him a sissy. This was the flashpoint of the ensuing forest fire. He became known as the skirt wearer. "All the Scots wear skirts. Time for you to wear your skirt to work."

"Scots don't wear skirts; they are called kilts," Tanner responded defiantly, defending his entire clan.

"Kilt, skirt, they're both the same," Ferguson called out. Ferguson started riding him hard, innocent fun in the beginning. In-house discipline eventually turned nasty. Ferguson's cocky air versus Tanner's gentility was a wooden boat hitting a sharp boulder in white water.

Tanner brooded and seethed for days; his focus gone; his confidence shot.

In the quiet of an early morning, the entire camp asleep, Tanner took the clippers that Ferguson kept in his holster which hung on his cot. He had gathered sand from one of the washes in the river and quietly put a couple of hands-full into the blades of the clippers. He cleaned the leather handle and put the tool back in the holster.

Ferguson routinely hooked up to the armatures at his station and grabbed his first ewe as morning cutting got underway at daybreak. The clippers let out a screech. The entire shed heard it. Ferguson started again. Screech. Third time, screech, then the smell of smoke coming from the clippers, the motor stopped, the acrid smoke of an electrical burn filled the room.

"Son of a bitch," Ferguson screamed. "Who the hell put sand in my machine? There's sand in my machine and somebody put it there!" Justice in the mountains never waits for evidence, no "'innocent until proven guilty" rules. Ferguson had Tanner McQueen by the throat in seconds. McQueen tried to use the clipper blades as a retaliatory strike, swinging violently at Ferguson's head. Apidale stopped his arm and pried the weapon from his hands. Ferguson's face was as red as the victim in his clutches. McQueen was on the ground, Ferguson on top of him with a knee in his chest. "McQueen, I'll kill you, you little skirt-wearing shit!"

Eleven guys were ready to let Ferguson finish him off. Mountain justice. Tanner passed out, face turning white, then blue. Ferguson tightened the vice, violently shaking the ragdoll in his clutches. Elizondo jumped onto Ferguson's back, pulling on him. "Ferguson, he ain't worth it. Let him go, he ain't worth it." A couple of guys agreed and pulled Ferguson off. McQueen, gasping for air, staggered out of the room, his invective just a growl from damaged vocal cords.

The emotionally drained crew struggled for an hour or two to get their equilibrium back and take a tentative first step back to shearing. I didn't wait for Creighton's leadership. I gathered everybody together and said, "This is my fault. I should have kept McQueen out for a day or two to let things calm down."

The guys rumbled and groaned. "It's not your fault. Tanner McQueen was a blight on this place," Fitzpatrick proclaimed.

"It's a setback, certainly not our first," I reminded. "We'll get our rhythm back. But this is my fault. I accept full responsibility."

Tanner was preoccupied, bothered by something, and I couldn't understand him. He needed help. I should have spent time with him, try to bandage whatever scars he had. I couldn't see the wounds or the scars because I didn't know where to look.

The restless crew, breathed a collective sigh, each one sucking in air to quiet the adrenaline, finally settled, but the focus on shearing was completely shot.

I was able to finally catch my own breath. "Guys, there is no place in these sheds for violence. There is no place in these sheds for personal issues. Whatever problems you have, leave them at the door. You bring them to me, not to the shed." Then reality hit. "Let's get to work. We're an hour behind schedule. We're going to make our numbers today even if it means shearing by lanterns."

Over by the pens, the wranglers were frozen in place after the fight. The entire crew was restless. The sheep were restless. I scanned the faces.

"Landuay, come with me." Tex Landuay slowly came to the front. "Let's go. You heard me, get over here. Pick up those clippers and get to work. You're up. If you're not ready, tell me right now. Do not go in there if you aren't ready. No shame in admitting it." I waited for his answer.

"I'm ready. Thanks, boss. I *am* ready. I won't let you down."

I took a quick look at Kiwi. He shrugged his shoulders, tacit approval.

I moped around for days, putting on a good face. Here was a chance to pull a drowning guy out of the water. I didn't know how, didn't know how to read the signs, see the blood running in the water, be there when a guy needed me most. This was one of my gloomiest periods because I failed a good man, and I failed myself. I longed for the voices from the rocks, but they didn't make a sound. Not a sound that I could hear.

My insecurities and fears of being an unproven leader of men didn't melt away that day, didn't magically wash away in the current of the rapids. Nor did I gain any strength. But I felt two things: honest humility and clarity. These were the only two things that matter in any of the job leadership training schools. In the midst of chaos, I found my legs a bit, though it was still like a sheep trying to escape, hooves skating across slippery floors, like a kid wearing ice skates for the first time.

Jamie would later thank me for my patience with Tanner. He told me Tanner had some issues with his temper while in the Scottish Highlands. "He never quite conquered that Scottish temper. It got him in trouble with his crew and with a family he knew overseas. I personally thought he was ready to come back. I got it wrong."

That was it. I didn't ask for any details, just accepted the painful, visible sorrow on the face of a very loving father.

I never saw Tanner McQueen again.

CHAPTER THIRTY-ONE

After the Tanner McQueen incident, I decided to take the afternoon off. It was a difficult time for us all. It weighed heavily on my mind. We could keep the floors clean, we could prevent slipping by wearing booties, we learned how to keep blades razor-sharp, we could keep the power plant running, and we were highly efficient in everything we did. But it was challenging to keep the human machines running. They became run down and occasionally needed fixing. It took me a long time to be able to spot inner turmoil or emotional breakdowns and determine if a guy was leaving his issues at the door.

It takes a lifetime of trying.

Creighton insisted I take some time off. He was good at checking my blood pressure, taking my temperature, diagnosing the need for a break. The two younger Hurst boys, Wendell and Wayne, led the expedition that day.

The boys took me to one of their favorite spots, right above Coffee Pot Rapids. The shallow, lazy river at that point stops being lazy and picks up speed. The water is deeper as it comes thundering around a sweeping bend, hits the boulders, and produces the biggest whitewater of the entire stretch of Henry's Fork. Just before the rapids, deep pools swirl along the bank.

The Hurst boys could drop a fly onto a pin head if you asked them to. I asked around and was told there was a hatch of Pale Morning Duns, so I tried slapping a few of them around for a long time with no results. A rogue breeze sensed my awkwardness and decided to play a trick on me. A sudden gust grabbed the fly and the nearly invisible, monofilament leader, and flung it right back in my face just as I started my backswing. The tiny fly hit me in the cheek and sunk deep into the skin, teaching me how it feels to be a fish. It appeared to me that the only thing I would catch that day was myself.

The boys came over with a pair of cutters and adroitly snipped off the loop of the fly where the line is attached. With a pocketknife, Wayne scraped off the colorful threads that ornamented the fly. Instead of trying to drag or cut the sharp barb out of my skin, he adeptly pulled it out backward. *Clever, quick, like his dad,* I thought.

A Parachute Adams fly, with upright white wings, a proven performer this time of year, and one you can see clearly on the water was today's recommendation. I immediately started catching fish, returning small ones back to the water for some more growth and a second chance. I kept six for dinner.

The boys knew exactly what to use for an attractant. They taught me how to read the river. Watch the water. Get down low and focus. There will be tiny, imperceptible little insects floating along, just hatching from larvae laid on the bottom of the river. You see what's there, and you find a pattern that matches it. No sense putting something in front of a fish that they'll never eat. You just need to be able to spot the right insect. They are right there on the surface, and all you have to do is look.

I was dazzled by the simplicity of their approach. Like all fishermen, I wanted just a few more casts of this amazing fly, just one more attempt to get the biggest fish of the day. I moved farther into the middle of the stream. The noise of moving water grew louder at this spot. Wayne shouted to me, "Careful there, Trippy. Don't get out too far. The current is pretty strong out there." What I thought I heard was, "Go out a little farther." Instead of encouragement, he was warning me.

He no sooner said it than I slipped on the moss, got my rubber boot tangled, and the current gave me a push. I went face down into the freezing water. The rubber boots immediately filled with water and pulled me down. The current accelerated, dragging me downstream towards the rapids.

The boys, who fished the cold water without waders, immediately ran to the shore instead of deeper into the water. They nimbly climbed over rocks and fallen logs positioning themselves downstream from the rapids. Instead of going into the water after me, they got ahead of me and waited for me to come speeding by, completely submerged and held down by the weight of the water in the boots. They knew exactly where the current would drag me, where back eddy's swirled, closer to shore.

At exactly the same time, the two boys grabbed the soles of my boots and dragged me into the shallows where I came up coughing water, a hundred pounds heavier from the water in my waders. I couldn't move from the weight, the shock, and the icy cold effects of this merciless river. The river seemed so calm in so many places, but in an instant, it turned villainous and tried to kill me.

We got the boots off and sat for a time, all three of us trembling and shaking as the adrenaline levels started dropping. Wayne broke the silence. "Should we head back or try just a few more casts?"

I thought he was joking. These two kids were serious fishermen. I just had a near-death experience, and they were ready to resume fishing. At dusk, hungry fish started rising up to the surface and the boys caught dozens of fish, none bigger than the pathetic figure on the river bank, freezing cold, tucked into the fetal position, shivering.

Twice now, I had been pulled from a river by someone named Hurst. We got back to camp and handed the fish to Mary who willingly added them to the evening menu.

Creighton spotted me, still wet and freezing. He looked at the boys. They both give a casual, nonverbal shoulder shrug.

We moved camp the next morning, and I was glad to be busy tearing down and packing up. That was one of my responsibilities, moving the traveling circus. I dreamed all night of being underwater, tangled up in monofilament fishing line, big-eyed fish watching me squirm, green moss strangling me. I stumbled through the day.

With a checklist in hand, we performed every task and made the move over to Marz Orazabel's place. He had 6,000 head ready to shear. We set up the entire operation with a fluid efficiency that would make synchronized swimmers envious. All this in one day. We had our process as sharp as our blades. The team was beat. Dusk settled, so too, large male bodies in tents; *thud, thud, thud,* lodgepole pines felled.

Then dawn, no longer an artist's painting, rather, a harsh reality, a stern taskmaster, a painful rebirth. Big, lumbering bodies, much slower following the drudgery of a move, followed the aroma of the coffee pot, their noses the only thing that worked early in the morning. The grasses were wet with dew, pine needles poked at aching feet not yet ready for boots.

Camp was never like the Army or an athletic locker room where we got marching orders and speeches, assignments, and pep talks. Everyone knew their jobs. No one needed motivation. Big paychecks were our motivation. But Creighton rounded up all the strays and firmly shouted, "Listen up. We're short a guy again. I'm going to take Eddy into the shed and let him cut today. He's been a wrangler with us all summer, training on the side. I think he's pretty close to being ready. Kiwi thinks he's ready, but, Kiwi, please keep an eye on him," Creighton admonished. "Harry, Sam, he'll be down at your end so please see if he has any kinks to work out. That's it. Let's get to work."

Any time you had to babysit a new guy it definitely meant you weren't ringing the bell that day. Helping a guy out, spending time helping him learn was fine, but your personal count would usually be short that day. Maybe even three or four days or the whole week.

The crew was generally happy to have a new guy; if not happy, then tolerant. A trainee would be assigned to the cob hole, the worst spot in the sheds. The top shearers loved a new guy in the cob hole. If a rambunctious sheep came along, or if a ram had big wrinkles or clumped fiber, the "gun" could exercise his option to send it down to the cob hole. This was known as passing the buck, a term still used today.

The guys' feet were frozen in place, moaning and muttering. "Eddy?" one of them said, loud enough for Eddy Carlisle to hear. "Eddy-never-ready?" Creighton wanted to put Eddy in the shed.

The collective voices mumbled, "Nothing against Eddy; he's a good kid. Why another replacement? That's two in two days. Who's missing? What the hell?"

Everyone looked around, Creighton already halfway to the truck to power up the Cummins. No answer.

Who's missing? Everyone was doing a headcount.

"It's Bradley," I told them. "Bradley's not here. Let's get to work. The sheep aren't going to shear themselves."

"Where's Bradley?" someone else asked. "Trippy, what's going on? Where's the kid?"

"Honestly, I found out about this just now. The only thing I know is that he took the six o'clock Greyhound to Salt Lake last night."

The guys finished putting on their booties and slowly made their way to the shed.

Eddy shouted, "Anybody got an extra set of booties I could use?" Tattered old booties went flying.

Bradley was a very good shearer, always top five in pelts. He was lively, energetic, and entertaining. Everyone was sad to lose a friend, lose a good team member. No one ever saw him again, and it wasn't until years later that Creighton finally told me what happened.

Bradley was an amazing young man. He wasn't a real big guy, maybe 5' 9. Not a ton of muscle, but he was wiry and quick. And good-looking. Even if you were a herder, a rancher, a shearer, or a guy that cuts timber or wrestles bulls in the rodeo, maybe drills for oil, or pours liquid steel, a man's man, a tough guy—doesn't matter—you would agree with me that this kid was striking to look at. Movie star—better than movie star looks. And he was oblivious to it. Girls swarmed like bees to honey.

His dark complexion, a few shades lighter than Kiwi, was a stark contrast to the freckle-face whiteness of Apidale and other pinkish complexions of the European imports woven into our quilt. Stubble on Bradley's face, damn near a full beard every three of four days, grew faster than the moss at the bottom of the Buffalo River. He never wore a hat, leaving his long hair unshackled, waves allowed to do whatever they wanted, something different every morning. His name was Ezekiel Bradley; Zeke to most, Bradley to some. He loved the girls, and everyone started calling him "Easy." Then "Z," and eventually "Easy Bad Boy" instead of Ezekiel Bradley.

For much of his, life he dreamed of flying. He joined the Air Force at seventeen, left the Kentucky coalmine town where he was born, and never went back. He feared the bottomless black holes in the earth and loathed the expectation that he would be a coal miner like all his brothers.

He washed out of the Air Force and rode trains around in California, ending up at a sheep station in Elko, Nevada. You'd be right if you guessed he followed a girl to Elko. Nothing else would attract a man to Elko. He charmed his way into a job and learned how to shear. Never put down roots anywhere and at age 23 didn't seem the type to ever put down roots.

He was the back-slappiest guy I ever met. He loved to talk, but never about himself. He'd sit there and ask you questions about yourself, dark eyes looking straight at you. I admired his genuine interest and his willingness to listen, a skill I tried to emulate. He could get in any card game or pool game because everyone liked having him around. Everybody was drawn to his energy, his cheery spin on life.

This included Carma, Creighton's youngest child, third daughter. She had been coming up here to the camps for two summers. She was now seventeen, and her dad was looking for a way to put bars on the windows and locks on the door of the trailer where that family slept, keeping her in and predators out. If humanly possible, he would have tied her in a bag, raised her high off the ground, and attached the bag to a pole to keep her away from hungry bears.

Everyone in a two hundred-mile radius knew about Carma. Men were on a constant lookout for just a glimpse of her, like a Yellowstone gray wolf in the hunt for dinner. She was that pretty. And her curves—whoa—I can't say more than that. Creighton didn't want to hear about her curves. Especially from a bachelor like me. He knew she was a beauty and didn't need me or anyone else to point out her features.

Carma worked in the kitchen trailer with her mom, and she became a good cook. Doyle was gone, and Creighton never got over that loss. Everything about him changed. It showed in his eyes. More furrows harrowed his brow. His family, now more than ever, was his top priority. Not the sheep, not the business, not the profits or the losses, paying the debt, or servicing the always irritable machinery. Family dominated his every waking moment now. Especially Carma.

The two boys that fished me out of the water also spent time in camp during the summer months. They pretended to work, cleaning the floors, sweeping up wool pieces. They tried stomping wool into burlap bags, but they were skinny kids and didn't have enough weight on them to pack it down. For the most part, they went fishing. That's how they knew where to take me a couple of weeks earlier. Hell, there were grown men who'd come around asking them for advice. Like huckleberries, you kept secret spots and secret bait to yourself. They would recommend a Woolly Bugger or a Renegade knowing full well it was an Elk Hair Caddis the fish preferred on a given day, something entirely different the next.

They had Mary hand-tying flies for them in the evenings, testing them out by day. Fried rainbow trout, potatoes, and onions were on the menu several times each week. There was no licensing and no limits on how many fish you could take each day. To these boys, a "limit" meant you had to stop when you couldn't carry any more in your creel.

The men worked hard, the family worked hard, days were long.

There was very little socializing during the week because there was very little to choose from, no cars to get you anywhere, and a clear mandate of no hangovers in the shed. Even a hint of a hangover would bump a guy from the shed for one week. Without pay.

There would be dances at the different camps we traveled to. Carma and a few of the guys would go dancing once Carma turned seventeen. The Basque families especially loved the dances. The music at the events was rooted in the unusual tunes from the old country. There were fiddles, guitars, and a couple accordions. The music ended up being a very strange blend of Basque ballads, cowboy crooning, touches of bluegrass, and that annoying "I'm Sittin' on Top of the World." I hated that song.

Everyone, including old Grandpa Aguirre, wanted to dance with Carma. I've never been told what an actual "Belle of the Ball" meant, but she was a very popular dance partner. Christina would come around most Saturdays, and I tried to let her know when we moved camps so she could come. We didn't care too much for dancing, but we loved the music. We loved the atmosphere. We loved these families. We loved our quiet moments together at river's edge.

Carma and Easy were doing a lot of dancing. The other guys were jealous, but it wasn't Easy doing the hogging. Carma had a shearer's grip on the guy. She was intoxicated with his dark curly hair and magnetic personality.

The intoxication got her in trouble, an emotional hangover not allowed in the Hurst trailer.

The entire operation came to a wet, muddy halt one July afternoon. Rain was common most days. We could work for a while inside the sheds, out of the rain, but wet sheep have to dry out. Rain killed our productivity, but it was our reality. We built weather delays into our timetable.

Cobbling together new booties, sharpening blades, cutting each others' hair, and calculating their lost income to a rainout, the crew groused and grumbled. I was mindlessly whittling away at a wooden stick that refused to reveal an inner life form, nothing but random chips flew off my knife, spraying the tent. When the rain slowed down, hinting at a full retreat, I did a headcount in case we could still do a half-day's work. I couldn't find Easy Bradley. It wasn't supposed to be a day off, but he may have gone fishing with the two teenage Hurst boys. A little rain never stopped those boys from fishing.

The tents were warm and dry, rain on the canvas creating a soothing white noise. I always slept better in the rain or to the sound of the river. The water moving over rocks was the best lullaby ever sung—its melody full of optimism, effortlessly moving downhill, fully aware of its final destination.

As the rain decided to stay for another hour, still no sign of Easy, no sign of Carma. Mary's eyes turned a dark shade of gray, the palette of the storm, her mouth pulled tight. She and I met at the lean-to where Creighton spent most of his days patching equipment, having pointless conversations with inanimate objects, winning some arguments, losing others. The slow day was a perfect time for needed repairs. Creighton saw the gray in Mary's eyes and immediately asked, "Where is Carma?"

Intuiting a fold in the universe, I told him Carma was out hiking, probably with Ezekiel. I called him by his real name around Creighton who didn't like to think about what his nickname suggested. Especially at that moment.

"Hiking? It's been raining most of the day. Did anyone go with them?" I shook my head and shrugged my shoulders. "Help get these pumps back together and back on the truck," he barked, already halfway in the car.

"What is this silver metal thing you just handed me?" I yelled as he drove away. With his head out the window, he shouted back over his shoulder, "Have you got wool for brains? It's called a wrench. Figure it out."

Hendershot, the full-time mechanic, stopped him at the road. "Creighton, I don't know where those two may be, but I'd start by checking the fire tower."

"Fire tower?"

"Just a guess. It's only a mile hike over that ridge and maybe they went there to get out of the rain," he offered.

"The fire tower. What makes you say that?"

"Lots of guys go there with girlfriends. The Forest Service closed it a few years ago and built another one on some other mountain. The old one is open. You just have to jump to grab the first rung on the ladder and up you go."

"Do I want to know how you became an expert on an abandoned fire tower," he asked.

"The fire tower?" he stammered. "I've been up there a time or two to have a look around."

"Can we drive into it? Will it be accessible in this rain?"

"Not likely. Not today. There was a road for a while, but it's been closed for two years since they shut it down. The road is pretty much overgrown. In this rain, I wouldn't get anywhere near it with a car or a truck."

"Can you show me where it is from this side?"

"No, I don't know my way in these hills."

"Come with me and show me where the road is. Trippy, I've changed my mind. Get the other truck and follow me." I held up the wrench, waved it back and forth.

"Get the other truck, now."

By then the crew was passed out in the three big tents catching up on some badly needed rest, oblivious to an impending shootout. I desperately tried to force the battered war surplus Willys to keep up with Creighton and Hendershot in the much faster '27 Dodge truck. I didn't want to miss the road into the fire lookout tower. I didn't want to miss the firestorm. From camp, the fire tower was about two miles as the crow flies. By automobile, it was five miles to get to the road and another mile on muddy roads. We walked in the last half mile, a misty rain still falling.

Halfway down the road, two human figures, silhouetted by the mist, were climbing down the ladder, ghostly apparitions haunting the pines. They were scrambling. My guess is that up in that fire tower they saw or heard us coming and were hustling to make an escape.

Creighton picked up the pace and calmly walked up to the fugitives, wet, freezing. Creighton wrapped his jacket around Carma's shoulders, a tender, soft touch to help her stop the combination of shivering and nervous shaking. Easy was uneasy, dancing around in a Roaring Twenties flapper kind of dance, jacket-less, trying to keep warm. Creighton asked, "How's the view up there?"

"It's good," said Easy.

"See any fires?"

"Nope, no fires today. It's raining."

"Oh, thank you. I hadn't noticed," Creighton mocked. "See anything else?"

"Not really. You can see Henry's Lake from up there. Mostly just a lot of treetops."

"Daddy, we were just talking," Carma said.

"What about?"

Easy chimed in, "We were talking about books." Creighton raised his notorious left eyebrow.

"Yes, books. Carma loves to read, and we were talking about books. I love to read too as it turns out."

"You're a reader? I haven't seen you reading in camp."

"Yessir. There aren't very many books in camp."

"What book were you talking about?"

"Well, Carma said she just finished reading *Little Women* (that was true) and we were talking about that."

"Did you know that those girls were all married by the time they were fifteen or sixteen?" Carma offered. "They got married very young back then."

Creighton replied, "Yes, they married young. Also died a lot younger in those days," he said with a bite.

"Trippy," he turned to me, "please make sure Carma gets back to camp, will you?"

"Creighton," I said as I grabbed his shoulder, paused, knowing the next thing out of my mouth was either going to confirm that I, indeed, had wool for brains, would permanently damage my relationship with my boss/partner, or possibly to save a man's life. I've always, always followed orders. But on that day, I broke protocol.

"I thought we had a 'second-chance rule,'" I reminded him. "This is a great kid, Creighton, and a good shearer." I pleaded my case. "We need every cutter we can get right now. This loss would hurt."

Creighton looked past me into the forest for a moment then turned his head so the electric-blue eyes met mine. I was immediately blinded. "Will you make sure she gets back to camp? Hendershot, you three go on back now. I need those pumps done and back on the power plant. I'll see you in just a bit," he said, almost cheerily.

Scolded by the principal, reprimanded by the judge, three soggy culprits shuffled muddy feet back to the car. Carma turned to see what her father was going to do next. She opened her mouth to speak, guilty air dissipated in the mist.

A leg of lamb on a spit over hot coals dripped fat into the heat, the aroma familiar and welcoming as the three of us pulled into the water-logged camp. Wet socks, wet blankets hanging on makeshift lines, dared the clouds to return. The eyes of some thirty guys for the first time that summer looked away from Carma, desperately looking at their feet, their books, their blades, the mountains, anywhere other than staring at the stunning young woman, dripping wet, her dress limp as wilted as socks on the line, her demeanor soggy, bedraggled. They didn't dare look, fearing they might turn to stone. The crew tried to hide their pity and spare her any further embarrassment.

The very small kitchen, normally welcoming and aromatic, at that moment, seemed confining, the same dimensions as a prison cell. If there were tears, they became part of the rain, both retreating.

"Start chopping those potatoes and get them in a pot, quick. And peel some onions," Mary instructed, emotionless as if this was any ordinary day in the kitchen. "And wash your hands before you start," Mary said as if Carma was still a child.

Business as usual in the kitchen; business as usual in the repair department where Hendershot and I were working. When Creighton returned, he asked me if I'd put the pump back together.

"The pumps are ready to go."

"That wasn't my question," he replied. "My question was, did *you* put the pump back together like I asked?"

"Here's your wrench back," I said as I slammed the wrench in his palm and skulked off.

"This isn't a wrench; it's a pair of pliers."

"Whatever. The pumps are ready to go."

Deep into the forest, I had a conversation with myself, an arm wrestle, pushing and pulling at the same time, the trees encircling me to watch the event.

"When I want someone fired, they stay. When I desperately need someone to stay, they are sacked," I remembered saying to the squirrels who mockingly giggled back at me with their annoying chant. Stay/Leave. Second chance/Hit the road. Welcome back/Here's your bus ticket. The rules seemed flexible, arbitrary, glaring contradictions from the one man I had come to believe was as consistent as gravity.

CHAPTER THIRTY-TWO

Eddy Fessenden, the young, new replacement, put in his first full day. Whereas each of the guys was averaging about two hundred pelts a day, Eddy had one-hundred-twenty. Not too bad. By week's end, he was up to 130, and the rest of that summer he was cutting 145. Still short of the tallies of the other guys, he stayed with the camp for a long time trying hard, but never ringing the bell.

Creighton's favorite thing was hearing that bell ring. To him it was a grand cathedral, five or ten bells in the belfry, pealing out for all the world to hear, the sweet sound of profit ringing through the caldera. The bell was the sound of competition driving up volume. The sound of success. He loved the bell. He loved watching a younger guy come into camp and earn his way.

Creighton believed in earning things. The government was subsidizing the wool industry, and it gave our partners confidence. He would become an FDR Democrat in the '30s. He supported getting people back to work when the Depression hit. But he was also an entrepreneur and preferred to create a business free of government regulation–build it up, create jobs, *real* jobs, with employees who wanted to work hard.

He knew these were tough times that required tough measures, but he feared that too many government handouts would create a workforce dependent on government. It troubled him, but he never spoke about any of it disparagingly.

Creighton never held a regular job, never punched a clock, never collected a steady, consistent paycheck. He got along by finding ways to work for himself and create jobs for others. He always thought of his workers as family. The ranchers, the truckers, the merchants, and others in the community were extended family to him. Everyone knew his unspoken creed: "Nobody gives you anything. You get exactly what you give. Stop waiting for someone to take care of you and get going."

He had taken Ezekiel Bradley into that family and felt betrayed. There were no rules posted in the tent about how to conduct your personal life, but everyone knew we were family. That meant hands off his kids. Zero tolerance for being stupid. Make a mistake in the shed, keep trying; mistakes happen. But break the family trust, and you were gone.

If a guy was one of the top shearers in the entire country—and we had any number of the best guys pass through here—it didn't matter. Laziness, drunkenness, rudeness, and dishonesty were always testing his limits.

Womanizing was a conundrum to Creighton. He was never one to impose his morals on the guys. He couldn't stop guys chasing girls any more than you can stop the Snake River from making its way to the Columbia, or the Columbia making its way to the ocean or the ocean from a rising tide. You can dam up a river here and there, take some of its water, but you have to put some of it over the spillway to keep it flowing. The river always wins.

He wasn't a prison warden and didn't crack the whip when it came to womanizing. He'd often say, "Always treat a woman with respect, act like a gentleman. If a girl is pregnant, do the right thing and marry her. If you marry her, take care of her." And then he'd say, "If you're single," looking right at me, "well then, heaven help you."

I'd learn years later that after getting the two love birds down from the fire lookout tower, Creighton drove straight to Mack's Inn. This is where the Greyhound bus stopped every other day picking up passengers for Salt Lake City and on to Nevada, then on to the coast. A curiously parallel route taken by the rivers. Violating the family trust was a crime, zero tolerance, and came with a mandatory sentence of banishment.

Creighton stood there as the 6 p.m. bus pulled away, making sure Ezekiel Bradley, otherwise known as Easy, was on it. He watched the taillights disappear around the bend and down the hill.

Carma spent another week in camp and worked twice as hard at chores to try to win her father's approval. I knew for a fact that he loved that girl to painful extremes. He wasn't always the most demonstrative guy in the world, but he loved Carma, deeply. She spent the next few years living in California with her oldest sister, Effie. They both got a lot of work as fashion models and learned to design and sew. Creighton had a few photographs from those days of the two girls modeling, and it was something to behold. I don't think I ever saw women more beautiful than the Hurst girls. If I'd been their dad, or someone else was their dad, there would be fire lookout towers wherever these girls went, putting out a fire before it scorched and blackened the entire forest.

CHAPTER THIRTY-THREE

"The rest of that year was a real humdinger," I said to Junior.

He broke my flow and asked, "What exactly is a humdinger?"

I looked at him exactly the way an old guy looks at a youngster who asks stupid questions.

"What do you mean, what is it?"

"What is a humdinger?"

"I have no idea. Why does it have to have a meaning? It's just a word. It means what it means, whatever you need it to mean. It doesn't need to mean anything. It's an expression, it's colorful. You got a problem with my mastery of the English language?"

"No, Gramps, your English is mellifluously radiant."

"Arrogant schoolboy. Let me rephrase it. The rest of that year was a real doozie."

"What's a doozie?" Junior mocked. I told him to look it up on his Googley thingy.

Not only did that wet spring finally give way to summer, it was a record-breaking hot summer, the start of a drought that lasted about four years.

The forest was baking in the sun. The timber was dull gray, pine needles prickly, stiff. With no rain, the mud was gone, leaving instead a fine, gray, powdery dust that constantly filled shoes, eyes, nostrils, and most meals. Even light breezes would stir up a dust cloud depositing grit on the lambs' wool, in our shed, in our clippers. Although we would gladly trade dust for rain and mud, it felt as if the entire forest might just blow away on the next breeze. The trees, dejected, shoulders slumping, may have welcomed a strong wind to carry them to the west coast for a change of scenery.

New to pine forests, I wondered how the trees survived harsh conditions. Thirty feet of snow, elk, deer, moose, antelope feeding on their branches all winter. Drought in the summer. They had a secret. There was always plenty of precious water underground. That was the miracle of the caldera. Trees seemed to grow right out of the lava rock, the Targhee tuff below their feet. In fact, they did grow right out of the rocks. During a drought, they worked extra hard to send roots down deeper and deeper to get to water. Humans can't see the water, but it's down there. And the roots knew they had to get to it, even if it meant pushing down through the ages-old lava beds.

The trees struggled for a few years during the drought, but, eventually, the forest bounced back, just as it has for eons. The trees were stronger for it, roots deeper, anchored, and secure.

I learned to love the strength and amazing resilience of these trees. I had taken up wood carving to help pass the time in the evenings. The lodgepole pines gave me the perfect wood for my little hobby. Tops of trees fallen in the forest are round and straight, the result of a fierce battle against brothers and cousins, standing shoulder to shoulder, fighting for sunlight. Pine trees have knots where the branches had grown, hard spots to work around, and test your patience. But pine is reasonably responsive to a sharp knife. I learned how to carve animals, then human figures, rough and inexact. Shaping and watching a little person come alive from the wood filled my sleepless nights, carving by dim lantern light. The lantern cast awkward, unreliable shadows. The knots in the wood created unreliable grain and texture. Some of the pieces would surprise me, turning out different than what I thought they would be. The wood seemed to have its own opinion. That made the figurines better in my mind, a little imperfect, maybe a little rough around the edges, each one unique, each one emerging from the wood their own way, not mine.

The knife I used wasn't a carving knife, just an old thing I picked up along the way. I spent as much time nursing blisters on my fingers and palms as I did carving, so I started wearing gloves. It reduced blisters but prevented me from feeling the grain and texture. Creighton occasionally watched, curious to see if an animal or human figure would emerge from a stick.

"Try this," he said, holding a high-quality pocketknife with three blades folded into the handle.

Sharp tools were mandatory in the world of shearing, and all the guys became very proficient at sharpening. A couple of them acquired what was called sand and glue wheels. They would put an edge on any blade thinner and sharper than the Gillette razor company could only dream about. Callouses, never-ending blisters, frustration were painful evidence that I was slow to learn the value of "sharp."

Creighton opened one of the blades of the pocketknife, placed it on his forearm, and cut a swath of hair. The blade was covered with his blonde arm hair.

"The knife is yours, Trippy. I want you to have it. Make something for me."

Three or four quick cuts with the new knife were an epiphany, a revelation, the difference between old manual snips and the power of mechanization. I still had to put the blade in the right spot on the wood, but the blade moved seemingly on its own, shaving, chipping, cutting, shaping as if it knew what the wood wanted to be. The rough cuts were made easier. Shaping was simpler. The fine details improved with each little cut.

"You let me struggle at this damn hobby for a year without showing me a sharp knife?" I said.

"I've been gonna give that to you for a while," he answered.

"Been gonna" became a catchphrase, secret code between us, that meant, "Sorry, I'll do better next time." It was shorthand for two men communicating patience and understanding, apologizing, and moving on.

"Sit down here, Trippy. Been gonna show you how to sharpen a knife." The blades did get dull after completing one or two pieces and needed constant sharpening.

Sitting around the fire, I attended a lecture with the master teacher, the professor of sharpening, the Ph.D. of the blade. An oily, gray towel opened to reveal a whetstone: flat, rectangular, some kind of pumice rock, new to me.

"There's two secrets to a sharp knife: patience and polishing. With this whetstone, you are taking off small little metallic burrs, honing the blade. You can't see the little irregularities with your eye, but they are there. Polish them off and your blade returns to its crisp edge."

He put the stone to his mouth, spit on it, then patiently for the next twenty minutes carefully pushed those blades up and back, up and back, up and back, a rhythmic *shh, shh, shh*, like the sound of a wire brush on a snare drum. He wiped some gray muck off the blade: spit and microscopic metal. Finally, he pronounced it sharp and reminded me, "Patience and polishing." Hair effortlessly came off my arm in clumps.

"Never carve toward yourself," he said, treating me like a nine-year-old.

"Junior," I said, as he turned off the recording device with the mysterious digital whatever. "I've got something for you."

A green cupboard where Grandma kept napkins and all sorts of kitchen things had been hiding, for many years, one of my hand-carved human figures, the last one I had in my possession.

Knee-to-knee with my grandson, I told him, "Junior, this is the last piece I have in my collection. I gave away everything I made as Christmas gifts to people I worked with. Didn't have much else to give.

"This one I tried to make look like Creighton Hurst, but I could never get it right. There's no real way to capture him. I want you to have it. None of the other grandkids will have one of my pieces. I wish I had more. And here is the pocketknife that made it. Take this and always remember that it constantly needs sharpening if you're going to use it to shape men. Patience and polish."

CHAPTER THIRTY-FOUR

Junior and I ended the brutal inquisition. We were both a little tired and decided to would get back to it the next day. He had some schoolwork to attend to and ended up being gone a whole week. I was glad for the time. I had to prepare myself for the next round. I was going to tell him about the worst thing that ever happened to me. This would be the first time I had ever talked to anyone about it.

During our break from recording, I remembered worrying about the business as we moved along. Our first year, demand for wool was at an all-time high. It was cyclical, but we hit it just right, kind of like being on Henry's Fork of the Snake River when there was a big May Fly hatch, or Stonefly Nymphs were emerging. Bring a very large creel.

England had a large wool industry, Scotland as well. Combined with all the wool coming from Australia and New Zealand, we had a lot of competition and pressure on pricing, but still plenty of demand. The US output was high. Always plenty of work and demand from the ranchers for more and more shearing left us in a constant vortex, the swirling, turbulent flow of capitalism. Every rancher across the country was increasing the size of their herds and competition was fierce.

The danger to the growers was getting the herds too big, knowing that this level of demand wouldn't last forever. A big old bubble was going to burst at some point. The ranchers didn't want thousands of head of sheep grazing on harder-to-find acreage, paying more to cut all the wool, being strapped with high wages, and not being able to make money when the market shifted and prices plummeted. We all knew there was going to be a correction. Our business strategy was simple: When the fish are biting, keep throwing out May Flies, or Pale Morning Duns, or the especially effective Elk Hair Caddis. Keep the cutting blades sharp, the crew alert and healthy, and keep shearing.

I was able to spend more time with Christina in '28. She had done her first year of college at Utah State University instead of the much smaller Albion Normal School. She was now more determined than ever to be a teacher. She also longed to be a mother. Her hints were hard to miss. I was willing to help her out in that regard but we both managed to keep our relationship proper. My love for her deepened because of that. She was focused on her plans and goals, firmly in control of her emotions. My emotions, on the other hand, were up and down, highs and lows, deep gorges and mountain peaks, rainstorms and droughts.

The herds all through the Yellowstone area nearly doubled, each ewe throwing twins every spring. The numbers were staggering. The line of additional backup shearers dispersed, ranches throughout the west were all now competing with us for talent. I spent most days in the sheds, my feeble shearing skills sorely tested. I could get fifty pelts a day, an insult to the experts, but every one counted. Creighton came in for half days. We asked Mary, in the kitchen, and Hendershot, the mechanic, to give it a try. They kindly refused.

Our busiest season left very little time for me to court Christina and even less time to fish and to do some woodcarving. We tried to see each other as often as we could. In her spare time, Christina was reading novels, devouring books: *Beau Geste* by P. C. Wren, *Babbitt* by Sinclair Lewis. She would tell me about George Babbitt and his struggle with conformity, a concept that resonated with me even at my simple, nonintellectual level. I wasn't much of a book reader, but I admired her passion and envied her intellect. It took me most of a summer, but I did read *Showboat* by Edna Ferber, lighter reading, so I could pretend to be literary. I struggled to answer the pop quiz Christina gave me.

One way to spend more time with her was to take her to church. Her dad approved of that. He didn't much care for organized religion himself, but he didn't like people working or playing on Sunday. The store, the bar, and the cafe at Pond's Lodge closed on Sunday, a big day for the other lodges.

Christina had a lot of questions about religion, but I was too mentally deficient to even understand the questions. "Ask George Babbitt," I suggested.

Christina was like her dad, a curious, casual observer from the pews. Our Sunday getaways included lunch on a blanket and a nap under the pines. We did, from time to time, take a swim. She made sure not to get her hair wet and give away her secret to her dad.

Neither of us was particularly shy, so swimming in underwear seemed natural, comfortable. There were times of course when I'd loved to have taken her in my arms and never let go. But we were content simply to be together. Any heat we had cooking pretty much cooled off and shrunk right up in that icy cold water if you know what I mean.

On far too many occasions, and out of necessity, Sunday became a makeup day for the shearing crew. We were behind schedule. It was getting increasingly warm, dry, and brittle due to the ongoing drought. The sheep were hot and restless, badly in need of fleecing. One makeup day became three; then there was no Sunday, no Tuesday. Every day was twelve hours of nightmarishness, one day bleeding into the next.

The sweetness of Christina's role in my dreams gave way to the recurring horror story of sheep taking over the world, keeping humans in holding pens, dogs controlling our movements. Rows and rows and rows of endless sheep glaring at me with those stupid smirks.

Some days it seemed like we would shear a ewe, and she would go to the end of the line sporting a new coat. We had another six hired hands doing nothing but moving pens, moving sheep, tromping wool into bags, and loading it on trucks. We had three new shearers we were trying to train on the job. Kiwi tried to give them a crash course—a literal crash. Rushing them wasn't the answer.

The rookies were slow at times, awkward, weak backs and legs, far too often cutting the sheep's shallow belly vein. That meant time out, grabbing a needle and some catgut, every one of us preeminently qualified medics on the battlefield. It frequently meant blood on the pelt, ruining most of it. Getting new guys up to speed was tedious and painfully slow, but no one complained. No time to complain, no time to gripe and moan, no time to think.

With patience and perseverance, any number of our recruits became proficient shearers. A young guy named Aroet Cassaday signed on. We had no idea about that first name, so we started calling him Butch, after Butch Cassidy, the train robber we read about in the papers. The spelling of the last name wasn't the same, but it stuck. He became a very good shearer, shocking the entire camp when he first rang the bell. He also had a head for business and later started his own outfit in Colorado, complete with power plant and mechanized clippers. Creighton didn't consider this a breach or a rip-off; he considered it a compliment. Creighton walked Butch through every pulley and wheel, every nut and bolt, and the two of them traded ideas on how to make everything better in version two. Creighton knew the country needed the technology, and he was content to have launched a revolution. Rather than burying Cassaday, he praised him and celebrated his success.

We regularly got some talented shearers, and it turns out, some had brains as well. But not everyone was suited to the grind. Desperate as we were, almost no one got fired.

Luke Pond, back from exile, several inches taller, twenty pounds heavier, walked into our camp over at DuBois, Admiral Hess's place. Luke knew we needed new guys, hiring virtually anyone in boots.

Hess had grown his place into an impressive operation. He snatched up the land and animals when his neighbor, who was also his brother-in-law, died of pneumonia. This left Hess's sister all alone. She deeded everything over to her brother, the Admiral, and lived with his family until she died about ten years later. He combined the two spreads into one massive operation. They diversified into farming grains, raising cattle, and adding to the very large herd of sheep.

We called him the Admiral not because he was ever a sailor, but because he bought a very strange, very large boat. It was far too big for Island Park Reservoir, now filled to near capacity because of the new dam finished two years earlier. It was big, and it was ugly, more like a garbage scow—flat, shapeless, and painted bright orange. It had come from Lake Michigan and had enough dents and scrapes to make it appear ready to sink without provocation. The Admiral loved it and spent time running it around the lake. I had a ride with him one afternoon. The big, old brontosaurus lumbered around the water, its aging back and hips complaining the entire day.

I was making a pitch for him to become part of the consortium, but he preferred his independence. I was surprised to find out there was some bad blood between him and our partner McQueen. I had no interest in the details. Hess had emerged as one of the top three largest sheep ranchers in the area, gladly retaining our services with no objections from our partners.

We had been camped at the Admiral's place for a week, half of his 12,000 sheep fleeced. Another week to go. Luke, driving his daddy's navy-blue Chrysler, emblazoned with the Pond's Lodge name on the side, made a dramatic entrance, stopping at the pens with a one hundred-eighty-degree spin of the car, dust of the drought falling on the sheep. Not a wise way to reenter our world, dust and rocks and arrogance spraying.

He politely watched us work for an hour before we took a break for lunch. Stuffing cold potato salad and cold roast beef into my mouth as if it was my very last meal on earth, our quick lunches were the unfortunate reality of our workload. Lots of folks in city jobs took an hour-long break. We took ten minutes if we were lucky. If you remember your math, a ten-minute break is equal to nearly two full pelts. That slim margin often was the difference between second place and the gunner.

"What do you need, Luke?" I asked between bites. "What are you doing here? I thought your dad banished you from this area."

"He's okay now. I came up for the 4th of July celebration and thought I'd fish a bit. I hear the Royal Wulf and Gold Hare's Ear are working well down Box Canyon, so it should be good. (He had no idea what either fly was.) Want to come?" he asked, pretending we were buddies. Pretending he knew how to fish.

"Thanks, Luke, but you can see . . ." I simply waved my hand over the tableau, food flying, guys throwing back Coca Cola like thirsty camels at the oasis filling their humps for a trek across the Sahara, the holding pens overstuffed with 1,200 sheep to do just today. "Sorry, no fishing today."

"That's why I wanted to talk to you," he said. "You're busy. You need help. Seems you've been hiring additional shearers. I think I could learn to shear. I've been around here for a long time, and I know what to do."

"Oh, you've watched us, and you're ready to go? Well, okay. Just give me a minute, and I'll get you all set up. We've reserved a slot for you in the trailer. I'm so pleased you waltzed into camp just in the nick of time."

Luke picked up on the sarcasm. "Look, I know you and I have had our differences. Let me give it a try. You know I did get some training over at McQueen's."

"That was with the old hand snips, and you quit after two days. That's not experience, that's called entitlement. You think people need to hand you everything your little heart desires. Doesn't work over here, pal. These guys earned the right to be here."

"I know I can do it," he said, now a bit desperate.

He watched me throw down the entire contents of a 12 oz. Coke in four large swallows, cram a big crust of bread in my mouth, and walk away, hollering over my shoulder, words muffled and muted by the giant mouthful of food, "Go away, Luke. Come back when you're sober."

Gray dust covered his daddy's brand-new car as it lurched for the road, flying gravel his parting shot. Drunk at 1 in the afternoon. I rated his odds of wrecking the new Chrysler at about 2:1.

Three of the hardest weeks of the year were behind us. We were back on schedule. The entire team, now numbering nearly forty, was ready for a break. I agreed to go to a 4th of July dance at Pond's Lodge dance hall with Christina. I'd dance, I'd sing, I'd stand on a fence in a pink tutu and do backward somersaults into a vat of sheep dip if Christina asked me to. I agreed to go.

This meant three things needed to happen. First, scraping three weeks' worth of dust and grime off my very weary frame. Quick dips in the river once a week were the only baths we had. Soap was optional.

Second thing, what to wear. My entire wardrobe consisted of dungarees and sleeveless flannel shirts, sweat-stained, threadbare, and lifeless.

Third, I would probably have to dance. I would rather have an angry bear chasing me down the mountain for stealing huckleberries than dance. Neither Christina nor I liked dancing, but I was certain we could find plenty of things to do, including making some fireworks of our own to celebrate the holiday.

We finished up at the Hess place ready to celebrate the holiday. I was typically the last guy out of camp, shutting down for the day. A young girl approached me just as I was finishing up. She was cradling a new lamb, barely a week old, already weighing nearly as much as the six-year-old blondie holding it. "Hi, Stella." I leaned down to her level. "What have you got?"

"This is for you," she said, holding out the animal.

"Me?" I asked.

"That's what daddy says. Her name is Snow White, after a book I read. You take her and give her to Christina. She'll love Snow White." She delivered her line tentatively, sad to part with even one lamb.

"Why on earth would your dad want to part with this charming little princess?"

"Because daddy says you are the best. He knows how hard you work and never have time to yourself. Daddy says you should get your own flock of sheep."

I thanked Stella who ran off quickly before I could see her tears.

"Admiral, this is a kind gift." I found him in the enormous red barn, fussing over a new propeller for the engine of his boat.

"July 4th cruise on the lake tonight," he said, polishing the blades. "You should come."

"This is very thoughtful of you. I don't think Stella was very happy about parting with Snow White."

"Stella will be fine," he answered. "We have plenty more. I thought now would be a good time to start your own family." I thought about Christina and blushed. "I mean a sheep family. You can't shear sheep for the rest of your life. No one makes it a lifetime career. I'm just saying you can start preparing right now for the next phase of your life."

I've never been sure if it's a step up or a step down to move from shearing to ranching. I wasn't ready for it just then. Of course, I didn't know what "ready" meant.

"Take your time. This little lamb is yours to keep." With a quick snap, he fastened a tag on the lamb's ear and swabbed a large red letter "T" on its back. "She'll run with our band, grow up, and you can decide later what you want to do. You'll always have your first ewe, and she'll likely throw twins next spring. I'm going to save thirty acres right over there on that eastern slope. I'll lease it to you for a dollar a year. There's a lot of feed going to waste up there, and I'd be glad to have you as a neighbor. I'd be honored to have you as a neighbor.

I've never known a finer man," he said, extending a very large, very oily hand.

The Admiral somehow sensed the feelings I had, standing at a crossroad. This was the second time in three years someone helped me believe in myself, believe that there was a future for me.

The Admiral knew how tired I was. This kind of work beat us all up beyond exhaustion. He knew I had other things on my mind. I suddenly remembered Christina.

I would be late but still had to shower and change. I stripped down right there in the pasture running an ice-cold stream from the hose at the watering troughs, all over my translucent white body. Creighton's wife yelled, "You pervert, there are children here. Go get some clothes on. Christina will wait for you."

I had no idea how she knew I would be seeing Christina that night. We tried to keep our "relationship," or whatever it was, a secret but it was widely known by then.

The only child in sight was 18-year-old Carma, and she was whistling at me, throwing semi-hard sheep biscuits my way. I turned the hose on her, and Mary came at me with a broom. Mary feared Carma would be scarred for life at such a sight, a pale white sheepherder running for cover from flying sheep turds.

I reassured Mary shortly thereafter, "I'm sure Carma will not be scarred. Seeing me naked in a cold shower was nothing. She's tough." This is the young beauty that joined the wranglers one day, knife in one hand, teeth pulling on the ram's sack, helping to separate the young bucks from their testicles. I watched her grab a bowl of the balls and fry them in a pan with onions and butter for her lunch.

"Carma is as tough as they come. Maybe we should get her trained to be a shearer." Mary's expertly-honed butcher knife glistened in the sunlight as she held it over my head, a French guillotine blade waiting for a signal from the executioner.

A new shirt from the Montgomery Ward catalog was neatly folded on my cot. "Mary," I yelled, sticking my head out of the tent.

"You're welcome," she said. "Get out of here, you pervert. Don't keep Christina waiting."

Christina greeted me warmly, wiping shaving cream from my ear and onto my dungarees. It was a surprisingly intimate thing to do. She then turned and introduced me to a friend from high school. A male friend. A handsome male friend wearing glasses and a UNM sweater. "University of New Mexico," he said before I had time to ask. A schoolboy.

"I'm a friend of Christina's," he offered. "The name is Edison. Like the inventor. Ed. Nice to meet you. Thought I'd come up for the 4th and see what's going on at the dance."

"Great," I muttered to myself, the sweater and glasses screamed intellectual. I cleaned my boots, nervously, on the back of my Levi's, tugged at the stiff collar of the new shirt. I'd never been in love, never dated a girl before, twenty-five years old with zero experience dealing with jealousy. Christina saw the confusion of a virgin swirling in my eyes, grabbed me by the arm, and escorted me out the door.

"He's a friend, Trippy," she reassured me after reading my not-so-subtle body language, the complete spectrum of emotions–fear, rage, confusion–all over my face.

"A neighbor actually. His farm abuts Dad's down in Lewiston, and they're farming it for us while we are up here. I grew up with Ed, rode the bus to school with him every day. The family is up for the week, fishing. I don't suppose you could break away from Creighton for a day and show him the secret fishing hole and your secret stash of huckleberries.

The berries are in season, I think."

"How would you know?"

"I can smell them in the air." She pointed her nose in the air, took in a deep breath. "Isn't that what the experts say?"

"I may have heard something like that. It's possible." I tried to pull her close, but she pretended to squirm.

"Christina, I, we, this . . ." *Baahh.* "Christina, we may be falling in love. I suspect we are falling in love. I'd do pretty much anything for you. I will absolutely take Mark fishing, but I'll never show you where those huckleberries are. A man has his limits. Even in love."

"Love, is it?" she said imitating an Irish brogue. "Are you sure it's love, darlin'? Seems to me you're more in love with the sheep. That's where you spend all your time."

"Oh, that old wives' tale," I said, responding to the ages-old rumors.

"Well, if you won't take me to huckleberry heaven, the relationship is lost." She pivoted and said, "Have a nice life."

"Before you walk away, I want to give you something."

"A present?"

Snow White had climbed all over the seats of the car, opening gashes in the upholstery, depositing fresh biscuits everywhere. Ignoring the mess, I took a red bandanna from my pocket and tied it around the lamb's neck to demonstrate the little lamb's patriotism.

Christina lit up, blue eyes against the red bandana, fireworks exploding all over her face. She began kissing the little lamb, and it was obvious I wouldn't be able to get her attention back if I threw her in Big Springs. In an instant, she was in love with someone else. The lamb, not her friend Ed.

"Christina, Admiral Hess gave her to me. She's now yours. That tag on her ear will help us find her. She'll run with the other 12,000 sheep in the Hess band, but she's yours to keep. A year from now, I'm going to start my own flock. Hess is going to let me use thirty acres of prime grazing, and we can raise a whole flock of Snow Whites."

That was the end of that conversation, the exclamation point, a lengthy kiss, a squirming lamb between us. Unspoken were these questions: *Did I just propose? What fool proposes without a ring? What about her desire to be a teacher? Does she want to be a rancher's wife?* Neither one of us wanted to talk about any of that for the moment, commitments just a little too complicated on this day of independence. I would, much later in life, learn the meaning of irony.

The dance hall was patriotically decorated, red and blue bunting draped along the wall of logs, the fragrance of the mountains inside and out. Cigarette smoke mixed with the woody smoke of pine logs burning in an enormous fireplace, gave the room a mysterious look, hazy, doubtful. The yellowish logs around the room that made up the walls of the building were dead and dried, horizontally stacked, like the pile of raw timber that nearly decapitated me years later. The slumbering, or deathly repose of the logs, ninety degrees different than the upright, vertical way trees in the forest naturally grew, seemed to say to me, "You're in the wrong place."

Locals, vagabonds, tourists, and fishermen crowded the room. Christina and I pretended to dance. We pretended to socialize. We pretended we were happy to be there with 300 other people. She never let go of Snow White, our three-way dance partner for the night.

Flasks started magically appearing from dungaree rear pockets, from purses, from belts. Alcohol livened up the party, threatened me, beckoned

me. Time for us to find some privacy, escape the noisy, claustrophobic celebration. Christina pushed the lamb into my arms, dashed for the restroom
with this charge: "I'll be right back, do not lose that lamb." It appeared to
me that the lamb was her date for the night. I was the chaperone.

While she was gone, Luke came strolling in, drunker than earlier that
same day. His eyes were blue like his sister's, but while Christina's eyes
were filled with life and joy and hope, his were hollow, empty, sinister.

"Let me hold your little pet, Trippy," he slurred.

"It's Christina's lamb."

"Christina's? How nice. What a thoughtful guy you are. Hey, Trippy,
have you given any more thought to teaching me how to shear sheep?"

"Lucas," I said, calling him by his full name, "this isn't the time—"

"I know, I know, I know." His head bobbed, words ran together.
"I'm sorry. We'll talk later. You and my sister are a fine couple. Enjoy
yourselves. We'll talk later."

"Yes, Luke. Thank you. Please come see me when you're sober and
we'll talk about it." I was fluent in the language of drunks, any number
of dialects, any idiom or nuance. I authored textbooks on the language
of inebriates.

"You got a deal, mate. That's what they call each other down in New
Zealand, isn't it? G'day, mate."

"I think that's Australian."

"Tripp, let me hold the lamb for a minute 'til Christina gets back. I
want to show you how much I care about sheep."

Even Snow White seemed uneasy around Luke. I reluctantly handed him the nervous lamb.

"Nice touch with the red bandana, you old romantic." He cradled
the lamb like a baby. "Nice job. Hey, Trippy, hard to believe this soft

little wool coat will be a massive pelt of wool someday. I want to show you a little secret. It's a new way to remove the wool. I learned this from a friend. Now don't peek."

With his back turned, he pulled a cigarette lighter out of his pocket, fumbled around, dumping lighter fluid on the red scarf. Click, the bandana and the wool caught fire instantaneously. Lucas held the torch aloft shouting to the crowd, "Happy 4th of July."

I jumped at him. Like a discus thrower at a track meet, he spun around and sent the little lamb flying through the air, slamming her into the eastern wall of the dance hall. The burning lamb stumbled, staggered, ran, crazed and terrified. I ran for the animal just as Christina returned to chaos, the entire east wall ablaze, Snow White charred black.

The log structures in the '20s followed no fire code. They were built with dry, aged timber, and sealed with Varathane, highly flammable either liquid or dry. This coating was barely two years old, still not completely absorbed by the logs. The combustible sealer on dry lumber exploded when the fiery ball hit it with a massive whoosh sounding like 10,000 sandhill cranes taking off all at once. Panic filled the room as fast as the fire. Three hundred revelers pushed to the door. The only door to the hall. One door, the only way out. I grabbed Christina and yelled, "Take my hand, and don't let go." She looked me in the eye, then pulled away. "Snow White!" she screamed.

I tried to grab her, but something hit me in the face. I dropped to the floor.

An oxygen mask covered my nose and mouth. My throat was parched.

I was lying on the grass, no idea where I was. My head throbbed, and I collapsed in a heap when I tried to stand. A woman grabbed my arm to catch me as I passed out again.

A large American Indian wool blanket covered me when I finally regained consciousness. My legs and arms trembled as I stood up and surveyed the scene. The smoke and oxygen finally cleared out of my brain. I regained my footing. Tenuously, flirting with passing out, I started walking, dragging my feet, shuffling, each foot with a 200-pound sack of potatoes attached. The diminished crowd huddled together staring at the chimney, the only thing left standing. The rest of the lodge was gone.

In the three hours, I was unconscious, it burned completely to the ground. There was no attempt to save it because there were no firefighters, no bucket brigades, no hydrants, no pumps in the river. It burned so fast there was nothing to do but get the people out.

Get the people out. Christina. I've got to find Christina.

"Where is Christina? Have you seen Christina?" I was grabbing people and screaming Christina's name. A lot of the people at the dance that night were tourists and others I hadn't seen before. None of them knew Christina. Nobody knew anything. No one was in charge and everyone was dazed. My eye socket began to throb. I didn't run into something in the smoky room. The last thing I had seen in the smoke and the confusion was Luke's fist coming at me.

CHAPTER THIRTY-FIVE

For weeks, the brick fireplace at Ponds Lodge stood erect in smoldering, black debris. It looked like some kind of ancient Roman ruin. The County Fire Department finally knocked it down for safety reasons.

Christina had taught me about irony. That's what came to mind as the worthless, hapless, invisible fire department was now worried about safety.

The Pond family built that structure brick by brick with their own hands. Christina carried bricks and mud when she was just thirteen. The family soul, the family spirit was gone. They felt like they'd been beaten by some unknown, invisible enemy they could never have seen coming, unable to defend against its rage. Their own son.

In the end, seven people died in the fire. The victims included two women who, two weeks later, still hadn't been identified. Two men I had met at the Sunset Lodge, regular victims of Doyle's pool room hustle. Additionally, Christina's friend Edison was killed. So was Christina's brother Luke. So was Christina. And the lamb, Snow White.

Creighton picked me up at about 3 a.m., the early hours after the fire. He kept the Indian blanket around me. He didn't ask any questions. I wasn't in the mood for questions, and I didn't have any answers. He was well-acquainted with my ups and downs, my strengths and my weaknesses, my darks and my lights. He knew the depth of my feelings for Christina. His words of counsel seemed, to him, as worn out as the combat boots I wore the day I arrived, so he didn't bother.

This would be the second time Creighton rescued me from near death. I desperately needed someone by my side at that moment. In the weeks to come, more than ever, I needed to borrow his strength. I needed his arms. I needed his heart because mine was in tatters, in ashes. He was the most giving when I needed him most. The loss of a son had recently shattered him, but it prepared him to buttress me. I needed a father.

I was in a dark place for a very long time, as if I was trapped, standing in the smoky aftermath of the smoldering fire, breathing in smoke, unable to see my hand, my feet, people around me. Unable to see any way out of the blackness. I would remain lost in that smoke for much of the rest of my life. Not just a week or a month or even a year. I felt most of the time like the smoke was never going to dissipate. The smell of fish was gone, replaced by the acrid smell of charred human remains. I began to wish I had never been pulled from the river. I wished I had wandered closer to the edge of the Snake River Gorge. I wished the fire . . . I couldn't finish that thought.

Creighton tried to get me to take time off to recover. He didn't have the right words, and I had no idea what recovery would look like or feel like, or what form it would take. *What was I supposed to do?* Work was therapy; work was numbing; work was the only thing I had. Work rescued me once, and I had to hope it would again. There was a Greyhound every night at six o'clock. The ocean seemed most days a tempting escape. I thought about Stevie Zuninga's boat.

Lingering questions burdened me for days and years. They still do. Christina was gone and wasn't coming back. As painfully obvious as that was, as often as I repeated this logic, these facts, this attempt at closure, the guy in the mirror, the reflected image there threw them back at me, coldly telling me it couldn't be true. It was convoluted logic that can only come from a reflected image. It was backward. And I listened to it. I believed it. I rejected it. I believed it. I rejected it. I had questions but couldn't get answers. Hate, resentment, revenge, and a seething anger were always seconds away from erupting. The ancient volcano simmered beneath my feet, and I screamed at it, begged for it to erupt, and dared it to pour hot magma all over me and entomb me in it. My screams bounced off the lava and dissipated into the mountain air without a sound.

I turned to Big Springs, my trusted counselor, my confidant. This had been my quiet place, my place of reflection, and it became the place where Christina and I shared our most intimate thoughts and feelings. It became our cathedral and our confessional. When we went there together, we better understood each other and the promise of never-ending water, of calm, of solace. Even our smallest problems would disappear because the water knew them and felt them and took them from us, carrying them far enough away that we forgot them.

At Big Springs, we could concentrate on the love that grew between us because we weren't encumbered by self-pity, self-doubt, by the hatred of others, by the jealousy of others, by the mistakes we made, and the offenses we gave. We left it all in the water where it vanished in the wash. We never felt perfect, but we always felt perfected. We never felt we were better than anyone else, but we felt better about ourselves. We felt changed. We felt renewed. We believed we had grown and improved in small ways. We always had moments of elation and enlightenment, moments of clarity, and a taste of pure joy that neither of us found any other place.

After the fire, after Christina died, Big Springs could bring me neither a balm nor a cleansing, nor a fresh start. No redemption. Very little hope. I felt alone, I felt betrayed, I felt abandoned. The river was no longer a river but a large rope strangling me.

I began to resent the spring because it let me down when I needed it most. It was worthless to me now, the silliness of the springs. I decided it could no longer be called Big Springs. It was a horrible name to begin with. We had laughed about it. Now, so completely devoid of love and compassion, it didn't have an ounce of credibility left. It was so diminished in stature that I began calling it "Tiny Springs," "Worthless Springs," "Piece of Shit Springs."

I'm sure Christina would've felt the same way, desperate and deserted.

Here in the Caribou National Forest, this extraordinary place where the pines roll on forever from the Idaho border, through Montana, across the Continental Divide, the rivers follow their ancient, exacting course, dutifully following orders. They are George Babbitt ruled by conformity. I had no course, nowhere to go.

The edges of the forest extend all the way to Canada, but for the arbitrary borders of men, in one continuous topographical wonder. Volcanoes buried it for a few million years, but it eventually became more spectacular because of the massive eruption. Over the centuries, forest fires, like the volcano, regularly scorched vast acres of this macrocosm, leaving behind ash and charcoal. Each fire destroyed old life and created a more fertile environment for a century of renewal and rebirth. "This is the natural order," I had been told. Destruction, restoration. Desolation, renewal. This was science. This was fact. This was bullshit. Science, facts, evidence were no comfort to me. I could feel only desolation, the heat of the still-smoldering ashes.

If you could look down from a tall enough fire tower and see this incredible place all at once, there wouldn't be this or that national park, or artificial boundaries drawn by men. The lakes would have no names. Sawtell Peak would be just a peak. The rivers would roll around anonymously, winding and intertwining with other rivers, feeding each other, strengthening each other. They wouldn't need names. They would never need praise or adoration for the things they did. It was their duty to water the land. It was their privilege. There would be no need for maps because there would be no roads to navigate. There would be only this natural wonder, this simmering caldera, and scientists wouldn't have to bother wondering what goes on underneath it all. Caught in this vision, this view from the fire tower, everything suddenly seemed bigger. The forest, the water, the mountains, the cosmos, the enormity of it all, crushed me, leaving Big Springs minuscule; my reflection in it a diminished, irrelevant spec again. The big lie.

The first time I came to Island Park with Creighton, he taught me to smell the berries in bloom. I pretended to, but my nose was never sensitive enough to pick up the fragrance. Creighton smelled it, felt the pulse of the land, and it talked to him. He felt something very few people feel. I would spend the next sixty years looking for it.

I wanted to tell Junior something I'd never told anyone because I was never able to figure it out: how to get over a loss, moving on and trying to put in place pieces of the puzzle that make up the rules of living and dying. My thoughts have been just my thoughts. I may make a mess of it.

The Continental Divide decides which way a river runs. The rivers have no say in the matter. In those shattered days and months, people would tell me I treated rivers as though they were living, breathing entities. That's exactly what they were to me—living waters, their course irrefutable, acknowledging obstacles in their way, then moving on. I envied them. I had no set course and lacked the strength to get over obstacles. The rivers mocked me.

Some people try to tell you the earth and the stars and the universe came together with a great big crash. Somehow all the elements for life randomly fell into place. The miracles of life, the complexity of it all, and the perfect way it harmonizes make that crash theory preposterous. It makes everything seem meaningless like we're all a great, big accident. There has to be something beyond randomness.

Some people like to tell you that the elements have always been around, that they evolved into the world we now live in with some incomprehensible way to organize themselves. There's no life on Mars or Venus we're told. No water, too hot, too cold. Only planet Earth has a formula that is perfect for life. Bad things happen–floods, hurricanes, earthquakes. Volcanoes blow their tops. Death. That's not perfect conditions for life as far as I'm concerned.

Then there's the group that tells you God made it all. He gathered clay and some bones, some oxygen, and water, stirred it all up, and made this planet in seven days. This is a fable someone dreamed up to help intellectually challenged people like me understand it all; an allegory to make God a little simpler. I don't want a simpler God. Sorry. I don't want to think of God as a guy up in some golden palace, on a diamond throne, pulling levers to make it rain so much the ground can't handle it. Or turning off the rain until half the earth shrivels up. Or flipping a switch to turn on a volcano. How can I comprehend a god, much less fear him or love him, if he snaps his fingers and a fire breaks out in Pond's Lodge? How can I forgive a god if he allows seven people to die while I'm passed out, helpless, worthless, unable to rescue the one person who has helped me go on living?

God forced me to carry around that weight all my life, loving a woman and hating her brother, delighting in imagining that miserable son of a bitch burning. A god of love doesn't create people and then burn them up like that. No god would ever do that. God didn't start that fire. A devil did. But it seems to me that God didn't try to put it out. It seems to me on that particular day, he sat on his throne and watched it burn, let it burn so that someone like me would be desperate enough to give up and seek his help. I sought his help plenty of times. He never came around and explained to me why he didn't put out the fire or why he turned his back at a time he was needed most.

I stood on that bridge, alone, freezing cold, all night long and didn't move an inch, just like Kiwi would do from time to time. It's hard to say what Kiwi found in the river, but I knew what I found that night. Water. Elements. Just another very ordinary river. This was no longer a headwater. It was dead water. Thirty or forty feet into the edge of the forest, I found a boulder that weighed about 75 or 80 pounds. I raised it over my head and dropped it on top of the big, pampered fish, sinking some of them to the bottom, sending a dozen others flying to the banks of the river, flopping around on the ground, desperately trying to breathe and get back in the water. I stood over one of the fish and waited for the last flop, then kicked it into the middle of the road.

Almost nothing was left of Christina's body. They found her teeth and some bones. Teeth and bones and ashes. Elements.

Christina's parents and I sent her ashes down the river. I dumped them in Big Springs and watched them wash away down past the bridges, the roads, the lodges, the cabins, the wild country, the dams that men made to hold the water back, the waterfalls that dropped water 200 feet and kept moving until the river reached the ocean. I had to believe, I forced myself to believe, that Christina wasn't just a spec of ash in the river; now she was the river. She wasn't just a speck in the universe; she was the universe. She wasn't just a part of me; she was in me, every cell, every drop of blood, every strand of DNA was part of her, flowing through me, forever part of me.

I heard her voice, unmistakably clear to me one day, saying go back to Big Springs and quit trying to be a philosopher struggling to figure everything out. You're not smart enough to figure it out. I resisted, but her voice that day stayed with me.

I took her advice much later, back to the bridge, after many years of mourning, and stared at the water coming out of the center of the earth somewhere. It kept coming and coming and would keep coming for a million more years. I knew that the only thing any of us could do was take it in and let it bathe us, cleanse us, and carry us downstream. I raised my nose in the air, took a deep breath, and for a fleeting second, a synapse firing, I smelled the huckleberries in bloom. I smelled those damn berries. And then it was gone. The water was no longer just wa-ter. My reflection was back in it. I was still part of the water, not just a drop in it.

CHAPTER THIRTY-SIX

I missed my friend Stevie Zuninga in the days that followed. Christina was gone, and with her, I lost my headwater. Then Stevie walked out—

"Wait, go back," Junior pleaded. "You told me about your buddy Stevie a long way back in your story. The two of you talked about drifting away. You mean, he did it? He escaped? He left? I assumed it was just a fantasy you both had. I assumed it was just idle talk."

"It was never idle talk for either of us. We were both young and impatient. I stuck it out and got back to work, always the best way to clean out the bags of wool in your head. Yes, Stevie left."

There were many days in the aftermath of the fire that I wished I had gone with him. He didn't tell me he was leaving.

Stevie was my confidant. When he left, I had no one to talk to. Creighton was my rock, but sniveling and self-pity have their limits. Creighton and I shared the common bond of loss. The relentless weight of hollowness.

I thought about Stevie and the time he and I stood at the river and talked about exploring other things, seeing new places, walking away. I was proud of him, concerned about him. His Basque family was so good at what they did, they had created a large, successful operation that would thrive for generations. It was a big blow to Ler Zuninga, and for that matter, to all the Basque families, when Stevie, the heir apparent, one day, took that boat. In the end he, didn't go too far away.

The Basque families were from the old country, regions in Spain and France. They later settled in California where fruit was plentiful and were experts at making cider. Everyone loved it. They also learned to make wine in small batches for their own use. Personal use was a gaping hole in the prohibition laws. Anyone could purchase unlimited amounts of grape juice and produce their own wine.

Up in the harsh environment in the Yellowstone area, there wasn't a lot of fruit growing. The growing season was too short. Down in the valley, just a couple of hours away, fruit grew abundantly. There's a strange micro-climate down there, more temperate than neighboring communities. Warm water runs right out of the rocks.

There were a lot of fruit growers in Hagerman; watermelons, stonecrops, and apples. The Basque guys in Island Park made frequent runs to Hagerman to buy fruit for their cider and their small batches of wine.

Turns out Stevie decided he wanted to get down there and open a little cider business. He knew how to make cider as well as he knew sheep shearing. He likely decided he could buy all the apples he needed to make cider and sell it. He hoped he could save enough to float down-river to California, or wherever the hell some of the rivers led him. At a time when we desperately needed him shearing with us, he was gone.

The fruit growers were glad to have him around because he was buying a lot of their produce. It wasn't long before he concluded that cider-making was just a couple of steps away from being able to make wine; just a couple of steps away from making beer. He grew up learning both.

He became a bootlegger. Wine and beer, none of the moonshine that got all the attention of the goon squads in the East and the deep South. In the Hagerman Valley, this tiny little anonymous community and surrounding towns, law enforcement was sparse, especially Federal law enforcement. His beer was passable. His wine decent. Decent wine and beer were good enough for thirsty drinkers. This was never going to be California wine or the quality of alcohol produced in Basque country over in Spain and France. Stevie was using everything but grapes. Quality wasn't the issue. Nobody cared as long as it was alcohol. Nothing else mattered. He had plenty of customers, his unaged product in high demand. Wool, lamb chops, alcohol, all in high demand. All three bubbles were about to burst.

Stevie did this for the better part of a year. We missed having him in camp. I missed him. He was far and away our best shearer, and he vanished overnight like the 24-hour bloom of the wild Penstemon growing in abundance on the hills. He never quite got over the shock of losing two fingers and wondered if he could ever live up to the lofty expectations of others. He worried about living up to his dad's expectations. His Dad's road map.

The day he got frostbite, he lost a lot more than fingers. He lost his way. He lost his self-esteem. I knew about losing one's way. I'd been in that hole and didn't want to have that happen to me again. Stevie had to go through it. He knew those two fingers were never growing back and he must have wondered the same thing about his self-esteem.

Stevie never really found what he was looking for downstream. He did come back to the camp a short time later. Just when he thought that there was no law enforcement in these remote communities, someone figured otherwise.

A couple of preachers in the area finally ratted him out. Preachers uniformly jumped on the Prohibition bandwagon. When their congregations started shrinking, they knew alcohol was somewhere nearby with competing doctrine and dogma. A preferred form of absolution.

Religious, pious zealots led the fight to get Prohibition in the Constitution. They thought that people were going to hell with drunkenness, and there were times when I found myself agreeing with them. As much as I despised their piety, their message had resonance with many of us who had, indeed, gone to hell. I'd lived in hell. I knew all about its size and shape, its colors, its length and breadth, its fire and brimstone not unlike the cauldron burning right beneath our feet, manifesting itself with regularity in this Yellowstone region. Siding with the preachers' logic was easy. Sermonizing, self-righteous indignation, loss of free will, not so much. That was a fight for another day by another group of people. In that moment, Stevie was in serious trouble.

The Feds came in and shut him down. Baseball bats and tire irons, crowbars, sledgehammers, and double-bladed axes destroyed everything. His little venture was being dumped in the same river that brought him here. He didn't make much money, not what you would call profit. Certainly not enough to sail away. Emotionally, financially, and in every other way, he was in bad shape.

Stevie was arrested, but not locked up. His dad, Ler, came down, bailed him out, and brought him back home for a while. He felt about as low as an old, worn-out Border Collie sheepdog who just lost his status to the younger dogs. He had little motivation to do much of anything.

The preliminary hearing in Boise was brief. Prosecutors cut a quick deal, another absurd trophy for the overmatched Feds. Stevie got probation and a hefty fine which his dad was happy to pay. He told Stevie he'd have to pay back every dime, so I was thrilled to see him come back to work. Stevie told me he needed to be worked hard. I obliged him by having him clean pens and bury the dead ewes and stillborn lambs: garbage detail. I made him earn a spot back in the shearing shed. And he did, much to the chagrin of a couple of the less-talented guys.

He beat the Federal felony charges but dragged around an invisible ball and chain for many years. His right hand and left foot, where fingers and toes had been removed, were always cold. This was his jail punishment, a life sentence with no parole, reminding him daily of his failures. He hid his mangled hand in a pocket wherever he went.

On a couple of occasions shortly after that, we got back in the flystream, but Stevie didn't have much enthusiasm for it. He continually looked downstream.

If his father and some of the other Basque families ever seemed embarrassed by this golden boy running off and making illegal alcohol, it never showed. Their resentment, their anger, their concern, their private discipline stayed private.

The Basque families all came together to welcome Stevie home. Sheep ranchers from all over the valley, some people I'd never seen or heard of, showed up at a big party to welcome Stevie back. The massive Zuninga spread came alive with the smell of txistorra in the air, leg-of-lamb on a spit over the fire, dripping rendered fat to the coals.

Fresh bread baking outside in cast iron pots put an aroma into the air so strong that it seemed to fill the entire valley, vanquishing even the smell of pine gum for a time. No one would have been surprised to see wildlife encircling the ranch hoping to grab a bite of whatever was cooking, a dozen different odors swirling around the caldera.

Out came the accordions, the guitars, the fiddles; out came young girls in native dress; out came cider and wine. Stevie had been arrested and was close to getting tossed in jail for making illegal booze and here we were at this party, everybody drinking celebratory Basque wine. Prohibition outlawed the sale and transportation of alcohol, not its consumption.

The Basques were as good at making wine as they were at raising sheep, crops, and making money in the wool industry. Island Park, this wilderness area, secluded and shrouded, was miles away from Prohibition, appropriately an Island unto itself. The County Sheriff hoisted a glass of wine to the reunited family.

CHAPTER THIRTY-SEVEN

"What's next?" That was our unofficial motto. We were not much different than a circus troupe, pulling up stakes going from ranch to ranch setting up camp, getting the wool off enormous herds of sheep in the very short summers of southeast Idaho. Knees creaked. Backs buckled. Muscles throbbed in the morning, throbbed when a ten-hour day finally concluded, and then throbbed all night.

Even after we'd finished the quota of sheep for the day, there was always clean-up, repairs to the equipment, sharpening blades, loading trucks, unloading trucks. Always, *what's next?* Never, *hey, what should we do today for fun?*

Every day was a ten or eleven-hour shift, six days a week, and sometimes seven if we fell behind schedule. On Sundays, Creighton gave everyone their choice. He preferred to allow everyone a day off and let them go to a church service if they wanted. Virtually no one did.

Some of the guys would fish on Sunday or just take it easy. Some of them would write letters and stay connected the best they could to a mother or a girlfriend. A lot of weekends the guys would try catch-

282 | Mark Hurst

ing up with their accounting if you want to call it that. Some chose to send some money home each week to help out the family. It was hard times for a lot of families as the country slipped into a depression. Some of the guys would put part or all of their wages in the bank, saving up to start their own cattle or sheep ranch, maybe a farm, open a little store, maybe go to school, build a house and settle down. Everybody had a dream. None of those dreams were about shearing sheep for life.

There were dreams, to be certain, but seldom goals or plans on how to achieve them. We were paying top wages, especially as wages elsewhere around the country dropped and unemployment soared. No one was a millionaire, but still, wages seemed to disappear like the water in the river, flowing away, effortlessly downhill.

Some of the guys had no idea how to save or didn't care to save their money. It disappeared within days of getting paid. Sometimes it was gone even before they got paid. A bookie or a pool room hustler was always hanging around collecting debts. I tried to teach them how to avoid debt and to avoid the temptation to keep making bets they couldn't win. They didn't want to hear it from me. Keep a section of portable fencing between Tripp the foreman and Tripp the human. Whether alcohol, gambling, hellgrammite hunting, or personal finances, the giving and taking of advice was to be avoided the way one avoids stepping off the trail in Yellowstone, ending up with a foot caught in a three-hundred degree hot pot.

When it came to advice, it seemed to me there were three types of people. We saw this in our men. The first type was a person who'll come around asking for advice because they have a need for answers. They're typically good listeners willing to learn from others. They don't mind admitting that they need help. These people were like a ball of clay. You can help shape them, mold them and make changes.

Then there was the type of person who'd take advice even if they weren't looking for it. You'd say to them, "You want a piece of advice?" And they'd say, "Sure. Anything, if you think it'll help." These I called sponges, soaking up help from others as fast as they could.

And then there were people that didn't want your advice, didn't want your opinion, didn't want a thing from anyone. These I called cement-heads. Nothing got through to them. No matter what you did, or what you told them, they didn't hear a word.

Three types of people: Clay. Sponges. Cement-heads.

That third group, the cement-heads, was familiar. It would have been my mother's favorite description. She wondered if my ears worked, or if I had been stricken with a childhood deafness she didn't know about. I was unable to hear frequencies that included advice: taking advice, heeding advice. My mother surely would have preferred a ball of clay to a block of cement, assuming she could decide my future. In those angry years, it seemed neither of us had a clue about the future.

School wasn't my thing, living at home wasn't my thing, and Mom's advice—worthless. With no crystal balls or road maps available to me, getting out of town became the best option, even with no end goal on the murky horizon. So in camp, for the most part, keeping my mouth shut in the whole advice arena was the preferred approach. The crew were peers of mine. Many of the guys were the same age as me, some older. They knew my background, my history, my aimless past, and rejected the advice of the hypocrite. This meant it was difficult to be a mother or brother figure—or any kind of role model to them—trusted enough to dispense advice or counsel. Creighton was clearly a father figure, a stern taskmaster with a look that made you sit down, shut up, or beg for mercy. Years of imitating "the look" never worked. Nothing on his face moved with "the look." His lips didn't purse, no eyebrow popped up or down, no downward tilt of the head, no scowl, no furrowed brow, just a deep penetrating stare that would go in through your eyes, come out the back of your head, do a 180-degree loop and come right back again and smack you in the head with the equivalent of a two-by-four followed by a five-hundred-watt electrical burst down your spine. It was a look that would singe your eyebrows and leave you clean-shaven for a couple of days.

The crew saw me as their foreman, never their friend. They respected me but probably didn't fear me. Most of the time it was okay to be their peer, free from advice or any counsel about saving their money, blowing it all, the dangers of gambling, the perils of alcohol. Let them get beat in pool. Let them booze away the weekend. It was time to stop caring. Here's the only rule: at 7 a.m. be sober, and be at your station cutting wool. And make your numbers. That's it. Get the wool cut. If you don't want the job, there are a few thousand guys out of work who would love to take your place.

There was no such thing as a paycheck. It was a cash-only economy. I left the issues of taxes for another day, for other people. It wasn't my responsibility, and I didn't want to know about it.

We helped the Bank of Blackfoot, Idaho set up direct deposits like they do today. We'd be at the bank first thing every Saturday morning. This was the bank where all of our operating capital was kept, the government loans, the investor dollars, and the final payments we would collect when we had finished work at one of the ranches and moved on to the next.

George Lampropoulos, the Greek who ran the bank, would open the doors at eight a.m. sharp with two armed guards and a pile of money. Creighton would make a deposit, the Greek would enter it into the ledger, then look at the first guy in line, and say, "Name?"

"Marquardt," the first guy in line answered.

The Greek would say, "Cash or deposit?"

"Deposit," Marquardt said.

Cash would go from one pile into another and get recorded in the ledger. There would be a running total in the ledger. Each guy could see his total, make a note of it, either in their head or written down on some scrap of paper they found.

"Next."

"Red Borrowman."

"Cash or deposit?"

"Three hundred in deposit, twenty bucks in cash."

"Apidale?"

"Half cash. Half savings."

And so it went, down the line, one after another. No one left until it was all done. Everyone would stay in the bank until every transaction was handled. There were no secrets about how much money each of them made. It was all right there in the ledger. Wages were pretty even depending on who had the most skins each day.

There were always guys making less money because they cut fewer pelts. It was never an issue. If there was jealousy or resentment, it was subtle or under the surface. They all knew the rules when they signed on. They knew that if they could improve day by day, they could make a few extra bucks. Our pay-for-performance model drove competition and excellence.

There was a reason we all went to the bank together and stayed at the bank together. There was a significant amount of cash coming in and out of that bank on Saturday mornings. Ever since Doyle was killed with a wad of cash in his pocket, we were skittish, twitchy, antelope in wolf country. Everyone was cautious. Everyone was vigilant. We erected a fire tower where we looked out for each other, took care of each other. If one of the guys was drunk, drag him home. If he was broke, loan him a few bucks. The hustler, stand by his side to make sure both he and his opponents were shooting straight.

For the most part, the bank business on Saturdays was a matter-of-fact event. The armed guards never fired a shot, but their presence was intimidating. On one occasion, we got a surprise that reminded us how dangerous a cash operation could be.

A different variety of hellgrammite, uglier, dirtier, creepier, crawled out from under a rock and was hanging around the lodges trying to bum a drink, or a meal. None of us knew him. No one had ever seen him. We were all putting in backbreaking, 10-hour days, every day, and as a group, we had come to resent a freeloader. He was a mosquito. An annoyance. A bloodsucker. A painful reminder of our past lives.

He heard about the cash payments being made at the bank on Saturday mornings. Everyone knew about it. It wasn't a big secret when thirty guys came into town all at once, went to a bank that was open on Saturday for a single customer, under armed guard. It was obvious what was happening. We never tried to hide it.

This grifter hooked up with a girl vacationing in the area with her family. She was very young, very vulnerable, in a big hurry to grow up. She was intrigued by this dangerous stranger and his tales of escaping small-town isolation and small-town eyes. He talked her into driving him to the Western Union Station, adjacent to the bank at Mack's Inn on Saturday morning so he could pick up a money order and get it deposited in the bank.

Early Saturday morning, her family still asleep, she crept out of the tent and drove to the appointed rendezvous point. She had told the grifter she was sixteen and had been driving for two years. In Idaho, they licensed fourteen-year-old drivers so they could help drive trucks and tractors at potato harvest.

"Works for me," he said. "You sure of yourself?"

"Yes. It's a 10-minute ride. No big deal. Come on. Get in."

Leaning forward so she could see over the steering wheel, this undersized accomplice peeled out of the gravel driveway by the ranger station and headed over to the little branch office of the Bank of Blackfoot, part of the compound there at Mack's Inn by the river.

"How much money you got coming in?" she asked.

"Never mind that, keep driving."

"Well, if you are a good boy, and buy me some beer with some of that money, I might meet you at the fire tower later."

"What's a fire tower?"

"How much money you got coming in?"

"I told you to shut up about that."

"Okay, okay. You buy me some beer and later on, I'll teach you how to spot a fire."

"Okay," he said with a doubtful nod. "How old are you?"

"I'm sixteen. I told you that already."

"I thought you said you were fourteen."

"No, I said a 14-year-old could legally drive a car. I didn't say I was fourteen."

"You look fourteen."

"I'm sixteen. You going to buy me some beer or not?"

"Sure thing, my little Idaho Spud. Let's go get some beer."

We heard all the details from the sheriff after he interviewed them, a blow-by-blow account of the planned heist.

This genius walked up to the bank as it was opening, looking for the Western Union station.

"It's around the corner," said the Greek.

"Oh, I thought it was here in the bank."

"No, I just told you, it's around the south end there. Besides, the bank isn't open on Saturday."

"Then why're you unlocking the door?"

"Around the corner," the Greek said with authority.

"But I got a wire transfer coming in, and I'd like to open an account and deposit it here today. Could I do that one thing?"

Just then, Creighton walked up with his bank bag and deposits. The Greek reached for the door handle to escort Creighton in for the Saturday banking when this pea-brained John Dillinger imposter grabbed the bank bag from Creighton and headed for the getaway car. The bank bag contained about fifteen dollars in petty cash and some deposit slips. It happened so fast that Creighton didn't react. He took off his fedora, scratched his head, watching the bandit escaping on foot. Steve Wirth, a big old Army vet standing guard duty, cautiously put the thief in the crosshairs of his .270 caliber deer rifle.

"You really going to shoot him?" Creighton asked. "I made the payroll deposit a week ago, and there's no money in that bag."

"You want me to shoot him? I'm ready," Wirth said.

"How far you figure he can run and still drop him."

"300 yards maybe more. You tell me when."

"Okay, I'll tell you when."

The young girl, unaware of the robbery in progress, sat in the family Studebaker, engine idling, popping her Black Jack chewing gum. She heard her partner screaming, "Bring the car, bring the damn car!" Gears grinding, she found reverse and started backing toward the sprinting crook, the slow pace of the novice driver, unsteady, weaving big "S" curves.

Creighton grabbed the arm of the big marksman. "Wait a minute. There's a girl in that car."

"How about I shoot a tire?" He had his itchy finger on a trigger he hadn't pulled in twenty years. "I can hit that tire."

The inept, would-be Butch Cassidy jumped in the moving car shouting orders, "Let's go, let's go, let's go!"

"You robbed the bank? You didn't say we were robbing the bank!" the hysterical girl shrieked. She started punching him with her closed fist, yelling, "You son of a bitch, you robbed the bank! Shit, shit, shit! You didn't say we were robbing a bank."

She hit the gas, popped the clutch all at once, and the car lurched, jerked, and bounced awkwardly away from the building, out of the parking lot, down the slope, picking up speed. Backward. She forgot the car was in reverse.

She would've gone all the way to the bottom of the river, but she ran into a row of red canoes piled up on the bank of the river. It slowed her watery plunge, but too little and too late. Canoes went flying, birds took flight off the water. A high-pitched scream from inside the car made even the trees cringe. Pumping the brakes furiously, the car hit the slippery mossy-green boat ramp and slid backward into the river.

The Greek, Creighton, Wirth the rifleman, and the thirty of us who came to get paid stood silently watching the spectacle. The car kept sinking deeper into the river. The girl was hysterical. They both finally crawled out of the windows and into the water, screaming for help. None of us moved. It was apparent neither could swim. It was also apparent none of us had any intention of getting wet and rescuing a couple of lowlifes intent on stealing our payroll.

"Think we should grab 'em?" one of our guys offers. No reaction. "They may drown."

"What a tragic loss that would be."

Borrowman made a move for the river but pulled up short when Creighton grabbed his arm.

"They're fine. You ever been swimming here off these docks? You ever fished here? The water is maybe three feet deep, four max. They're not going to drown. And," he muttered, "that makes me furious."

"What, that some incompetent petty thief tried to rob us?"

"No." He turned and looked at me. "They're messing up a perfectly good fishing hole."

A small newspaper article featured a picture of the car being towed out of the river. A reporter would occasionally come around if there was some news to report, but there is never much news in this Yellowstone wilderness. The reporter missed most of the action, but she did write about that drifter trying to rob the Island Park branch of the Bank of Blackfoot, aided by a 13-year-old girl who "stole" the family car.

That was the end of attempted heists of the camp payroll. Steve Wirth was still there every Saturday morning ready for sentry duty, but he rarely put any shells in his gun. Most of the shearers began making larger deposits, keeping less cash in their pockets.

CHAPTER THIRTY-EIGHT

Junior and I laughed for a while about the bungled bank job. We turned off the recording machine and caught our breath. It made me forget what we were talking about. He had to remind me what came next.

I was completely lost in the story of the robbery, polished and exaggerated after so many tellings, about ninety percent true.

Junior looked up from his notes and said, "You started to talk about Saturday night entertainment. You got sidetracked. Again. I'm trying to talk about sheep, and you told me all about bank robberies."

"Well, that's part of the story. Nobody had ever run a crew this big, and no one had set up a way to make weekly payroll. Everyone was plowing new ground."

"Saturday night entertainment," Junior poked again. "Yeah, yeah, yeah."

It was a lot of the same thing, day after day. We were a bunch of restless bucks, castrated, fleeced, penned up, living out of sheep camps for four months with very few options for escape or relief. At the first of summer, the guys ran around like crazy on weekends. Later on, they would run out of energy, too exhausted to chase booze, betting, and Betty's. News about the Depression reached us occasionally. We all started paying attention and started holding onto our money. We all preferred to hang around camp on the weekends. Mary started making a big pot of chili influenced, in part, by the native Americans, combined with recipes from some of our Mexican hired hands. Peach cobbler in a Dutch oven was worth staying around for.

There were always a few poker games going on in the tents. A couple of guys learned to juggle sheep biscuits. The Gamiz brothers mastered the art of ax throwing. Fitzpatrick invented Olympic events: Twenty-pound shot putting with boulders; discuss throwing with the lid to Mary's Dutch oven; javelins made from the tall, straight tops of lodgepole pines. A few guys liked reading, leisurely avoiding the Olympic games, studious and saving money for the fall semester at university. They passed around a handful of books they arrived with, each book read three or four times.

The size of a man's arms, his overall size, and strength were all part of a litmus test we used when hiring the crew. Arm wrestling skills mandatory. This became the favorite Sunday pastime. Creighton sanctioned the events. He didn't typically compete, but one lazy Sunday morning, right out of the blue, he said to a couple of the guys, "You know I learned to shear a long time ago?"

They looked surprised. He held up a pair of the old hand snips, squeezing them in and out. "This is how real men shear sheep. You girls have been spoiled by the power clippers." *Snip, snip, snip*, he taunted them. "Most of the sheep ranchers in the industry still use these sorry old things. We may be the only outfit in the country using power tools.

My guess would be that you spoiled brats aren't quite as strong as the older shearers. I wonder how you would fare against these other outfits.

Ibarra courageously confronted Creighton, playfully poking his sternum, chest-bumping, and backing him into a wall of teammates. Ibarra, four inches shorter, said, "Show me your forearms, old man."

Cards, money, chips of the ongoing poker game scattered as Creighton cleared the table, placed his elbow down with a thud. "Who's first?"

Chairs went flying. All three tents emptied, the entire crew in one tent pushing and shoving for a front-row view. A Coleman gas lantern smashed to the ground starting a fire in the dry, July brush. Mary, who was tending the pot of chili, deftly put out the small blaze with her dishtowel. She rolled her eyes and scowled at the ridiculous antics of this older man taking on the boys.

The game was on.

Arm wrestling started out as a harmless diversion among our little group, something to pass the time. It eventually became more important than ringing the bell, the victorious right of the top shearer. Word got out that we were having contests at the Sorenson ranch on Sundays. From there it exploded. Big crowds would gather to see the jousting, the gladiatorial games in the Roman Coliseum. The weekly event quickly became the most entertaining form of legal gambling. When the dance hall burned down, locals and tourists needed a new form of entertainment. The crowds increased, Basque wine flowed, fleecing flourished.

Creighton was older than most of us, nearly double some of the team, but he could regularly throw down an arm or two and enjoyed the diversion as much as anyone. The shearers loved it. They were innocently unaware of how strong they had become. Creighton knew. He watched them grow from rookie to pro, to world-class expertise. He knew and understood his crew, better than they knew themselves. Not just their physical strengths, but their emotional strengths and weaknesses, their moods, their loneliness, their inner turmoil. He had lived every pain.

Our guys were in very good physical shape. They spent long hours, in grueling heat, wrestling sheep that didn't want to be wrestled, skittish animals frightened by the chaos, the chugging of the diesel engine, and the noise of the power clippers.

The arms of the shearers were visibly large. They would remove the sleeves of their shirts to allow for greater arm movement, exposing firm, sculpted muscles. Their legs were twice as strong as most men, standing all day with 200-pound bucks between their legs, pinned to the ground.

Creighton wasn't a gambling man, and he wasn't a hustler. He never went to the bars or the pool halls except to occasionally pull a guy out and take him home. But he was a competitor, a fierce competitor, who hated to lose. It was a fun thing at first, a diversion for the boys. By the end of summer, we had construction guys, road guys, arrogant fishermen from out of state, most of the sheep ranchers, their families, and their entire crew including the Basque herders down from the hills, attending the Circus Maximus.

We didn't put up fliers to promote the weekly events. We didn't do anything to promote it. Word got out and people started showing up, no invitation, no ticket required. The crowds expanded each week, and it didn't much matter which camp we were in, they'd find us. It was a badge of honor if you could beat a sheep shearer, known for their strength, agility, and endurance. They could go all night.

Creighton may have known, or he may not have known the unintended consequences. Hard to tell, but an interesting thing happened.

Instead of pool, cards, booze, and women, the camp started to build camaraderie and a bond.

They were working together, learning about trust and what a family bond should look like. No one condemned pool or cards. Hell, I saw Creighton one time clear a pool table in eight shots. Creighton left to the preachers and the moral crusaders the condemnation of the vices that buried his oldest son. He was a quiet moralist, never imposing his will on others. His preference was diversion, allowing the guys to figure out for themselves how to avoid white water, to step back from steep cliffs. Running a little enterprise, turning a profit, giving and following orders, building teamwork and cooperation, designing and executing a strategy, were skills they didn't know they were learning. Like powerful arms, they didn't know how strong they were becoming.

The wrestling brought combatants and onlookers from as far away as Indiana, Chicago, Minneapolis, lawyers, doctors, professionals who came all summer for the world-class fly fishing on the Madison River and Henry's Fork of the Snake River. They were good sports, happy to be the first to part with their money. Red Borrowman could toss most of them damn near back to the Hoosiers.

The shearers designed a clever plan to get some of the cash from the tourists and the campers and the regulars who came back every year. Other shearers around the area, equally strong, became fierce rivals, but in the end, they became our partners, co-conspirators helping all of us make more money from visitors. We never cheated, robbed, or rigged the bets. It was the "Harmless Hurst Hustle." The plan relied on one thing: vanity. Outsiders thought they were tough and wanted to take home the pelt of a shearer much like taking home a trophy fish. A stuffed elk head on the wall. The strategy was simple: give them a stage to showcase their vanity.

We would take on all comers. We let a few of them win a time or two. When I say "we," I mean "them," my team.

I had become mostly a pencil pusher and a problem solver. I didn't have muscle in my body, not like my guys. Truth be told, I was terrified of these guys who could rip an arm out of your socket, roast it over the fire, and have it for lunch before you realized it was gone. I continued to be a cut man, a cornerman, and a keeper of the bets.

That's how we ran the show. We would let some of the outsiders think they were good. When the betting pot got a little bigger, and the bets always got a little bigger, my boys would pretend they were too tired and switch to their left hand.

Attention professional con men: left arms were stronger. Left arms, typically, held the sheep. Right arms did the cutting. These young bucks were thin, lithe, low in body fat from sweating off calories all day every day. Slender frames disguised their strength.

Here's the secret to arm wrestling: the legs. You transfer torque up through your legs into your torso, then down your arm, and into your wrist in exactly the way we brought power from our diesel engine: down through the armatures and into the clippers. Transference of energy. The art of shearing included the science of physics. So did wrestling. The key: torque and timing. And quickness.

No one could beat our guys when they began to use their left arms. The crowd would want their money back, tricked, fleeced. My guys, barely breaking a sweat, threw every single challenger over to the Bannock Indian Reservation.

Speaking of Indians, one Saturday night someone came up with the idea of leg wrestling. We heard it called Indian wrestling. We didn't ever see Indians doing it, and we didn't want to anger the tribes by insulting them. They were also wool people, growing it, carding it, and looming it themselves. We helped them shear when they needed extra help. They were neighbors, they were friends, and we didn't want to disrespect them by calling it Indian wrestling if they never did it. We referred to it as leg wrestling. As it turns out, it is very popular in India, something of a national pastime.

Similar to arm wrestling, two combatants lay down on the ground facing away from each other, arms locked. On the count of three, they'd lock legs, one trying to throw the other ass sunny-side up.

Creighton loved leg wrestling, successfully tossing most of us with ease, those brave enough to take him on. But there was another champion in camp. He just didn't know it yet.

He was a big guy from Hyrum, Utah. He joined the shearing crew at the beginning of our third year. He was a farm boy capable of throwing 100-pound bales of hay six feet up onto a haystack. His legs were massive tree trunks that made him look like a tractor, big wheels on the back coming out of a giant butt. So we called him "Tractor."

He loved the name.

Creighton took on all comers, the guys wanting to show up the old man and take some of his money. After he threw all ten challengers, the betting stopped. Tractor was thinking he'd wait a bit and get Creighton tired out. The boys egged Tractor on, their last hope against the tyranny of management.

"Left or right?" Creighton asked. Tractor suggested one each, best two out of three.

The money started flying again, good money going on the much younger man with the visible assets. There was only one fan club on the sideline, Team Tractor, cheering on their Herculean warrior. "Off with his head!" they cried.

"To the lion's den with him!"

The first match, right leg, lasted about 40 seconds, neither man able to finish off the other at first. Tractor outlasted the boss, twenty years his senior, and gave him a final toss. Every single guy started pulling pockets out looking for more cash. Creighton grimaced and wiped grass and dust off his face.

It took about three seconds for the old man to toss Tractor, on the left side. Less than three seconds, maybe a millisecond. Tractor came up spitting grass and mud, bloodied scrapes on his elbow and chin. It was so fast Tractor barely remembered it. He came up looking like he didn't know north from south, up from down, Idaho from Indiana.

The crowd noise died down by about half. The rumblings were somewhere between disappointment and doubt. Surely the old man couldn't win the final round.

One apiece. Tractor had actually won that first round on the right side with ease. He let Creighton think he had a chance, holding him long enough to wear him out. Money now was split, the odds changing by the second. The boys began to quiet down. *Would Tractor have the sheep testicles to toss the old boy? Would he break the old man's neck and shut down the business?*

Creighton cracked his neck, stretched his hamstring, and waved his arms. "Here's what I'll do," he announced. "Everyone, hold up the money you've got. Come on, hold it up." They all held up a fist full. "Put it all here in this hat. Trippy, pass the hat if you would, please. Fill it up, boys. If Tractor beats me, I'll personally double the money in the hat, and you will all get a share. If I win, the money goes to bed with me. He looked over at Mary who turned and walked to their tent refusing to watch the older man snap his neck.

Every last penny went into the boss's ratty fedora. Double money on a sure bet.

Tony Elizondo grabbed Tractor by the shoulders, massaging them, keeping him limber. Borrowman wiped the sweat off Tractor's face and tended to his scrapes like a corner guy in a Jack Dempsey fight. Their boy was ready. Round three—a fight to the death.

The two combatants fidgeted on the ground, squirming with nervous energy. The twilight sun, orange as Kokanee Salmon swimming upstream, was retiring behind Sawtell Peak. The river joined in the event sounding very much like the applause of a crowd enjoying the gold medal round of an Olympic event. The applause died down, reverted to its normal end-of-day hush just as the fight ended.

Creighton was tired. He felt the twenty-year difference in his hamstring, tightening, cramping, not a soul to give him aid. He hobbled to the lonely corner of the victor.

He was older but wiser and somehow found an extra gear, an extra kick, determined to beat the much younger man. His fierce competitive streak had taken over common sense. He flipped the big man over and held him there an extra few seconds until Tractor couldn't breathe, then let him go, jumped up, and extended a hand.

Groans went up as if it were the end of a Yankees/Dodgers World Series baseball game that went twelve innings, and ended with a walk-off home run. The guys started off to their tents, all of their money on Tractor, now thoroughly beat. "Guys, hold up," Creighton cried out. "Tripp, how much is in that hat?" He was going to gloat.

"I don't know."

"Well, count it. Divide it by thirty. You can do that much math can't you, Trippy? Give everyone in camp an equal share. I think we've discovered a very, very interesting new activity next week at the wrestling matches. Tractor, get that left leg in shape. We're going to make a lot of money next week."

Yankee Stadium gave up a thunderous ovation for the boys of summer.

CHAPTER THIRTY-NINE

"Those wrestling matches were a great experience. Every day the crew came to work in a better mood. Our shearing picked up the pace.

"At the end of a long summer, exhaustion fraying nerves, no time for relaxation or a day off, we needed a diversion. It was a fun pastime and helped the guys earn a little extra money. In the long run, it was a bonding experience, all of us pulling together.

"I remember a night at the wrestling event you'll want to hear. I won't embellish it too much, and it comes with a warning. It might make you proud of your grandfather, or embarrassed, or shocked. Maybe disgusted. You want to go on or just call it quits?"

Junior answered immediately, "You kidding me? Of course, I want to hear it. And I promise to withhold all judgment."

"Okay, here's what happened at the wrestling matches one night, late in our third year."

As the gawkers and gladiators started filing in, our boy Tony Elizondo overheard a couple of guys talking, boasting to just about everybody, that they could win some money tonight. Tony heard them say, "We'll get some money either by winning some bets or getting rich the way we did that night over at the Sunset Lodge when we rolled that arrogant prick, Doyle. You remember the guy that won a bunch of money hustling pool? What a dope, flashing a wad of cash around like that. I wouldn't mind running into that guy again. I won't be surprised to find some other simpleton tonight we can roll."

Tony followed these guys around, casually, seeing what they were up to. They chatted up a couple of younger girls from Nebraska out here seeing Yellowstone with their family. These two guys told the girls they worked for the Army in Ogden, Utah, boasting that they were in charge of bullets and guns and grenades, puffing their chests and bragging. The girls weren't impressed.

As the wrestling matches got underway, Tony quietly told me he found the guys that killed Doyle.

"What?" I said way too loud. "How do you know that?"

"I overheard them boast about robbing him. They talked about rolling him. I doubt they know he died."

"Are you sure it's the right guys?"

"They were hitting on those girls right there," he said, pointing with his nose. "The big guy boasted about working for the Army in Ogden, but the girls weren't exactly swept away. The big guy is going to challenge a couple of our guys and said he'd win some money either on a challenge match, or the way they rolled a guy one summer. They knew Doyle's name."

My eyes glazed over. I stared into the darkness waiting for some vaporous apparition to appear and tell me it was okay to do what I was thinking about.

Tony interrupted my pondering. "Should we have a little talk with them?"

"See if there's any way you can get more details. We have to be sure it's the right guys. Don't let on what you're doing."

"What am I doing?

"I don't know yet. I'm thinking, I'm thinking."

Tony got in a preliminary match with the smaller of the two Ogden guys and lost, intentionally. Afterward, Tony said to the guy, "Hey, I remember seeing you out at Sunset Lodge a few years back. I think you got absolutely fleeced by a pool hustler. You guys got worked pretty good."

The Army guy asked, "Did you know the guy?"

"No, I didn't know him. He used to be around here a lot of times hustling guys like you. But I haven't seen him in a long time. How much did you lose that night? I remember you guys losing a ton."

"Oh, we got our money back. If you ever see the guy, tell him I said hello." Tony reported this to me.

"Good work," I told him. "Don't say a word to Creighton. He doesn't believe in revenge. Go get Tractor, Red Borrowman, and the older Galindoz kid, and meet me around the west side of the shearing shed."

"Every one of our guys is lined up for grudge matches," Tony cautioned. "They won't want to be pulled out of the lineup."

"Tell your two Ogden boys there's some side action behind the plant if they want to make some real money. And go get our other guys. They won't mind delaying their matches. I'm certain of it. There's still plenty of time, and this is more important. Now go on," I ordered.

Tony walked away in stealth mode. I half-whispered, half-shouted, "Bring two clippers."

The reply from our guys when I told them what we were doing was, "Where and when?"

The better part of an hour passed as we set the trap. The bouts continued in the center ring. Tony soon came over, leading his prey and the two Nebraska girls, one on each arm, anticipating the show Tony had promised. The team and I had set up a table, and I invited them to sit down.

"I hear you might be up for a little side action, higher stakes, bigger pot." As I said it, I flashed an enormous wad of cash that our guys rounded up. The eyes of our victims lit up. This was like setting a stonefly nymph in front of a cutthroat trout that hasn't eaten in a week. They knew this lure, and they would bite.

Sleeves up, elbows down, feet planted, "Sure," they said, confidently. "Bring it on."

About fifteen minutes later, they had won a lot of cash from us. We turned up the juice and won some of it back. Money changed hands a dozen times as we switched to left hands. We cleverly let them walk away with a small pot, eventually getting all our money back. And most of theirs. We weren't concerned about winning or losing. Our goal was setting the hook.

The girls, on cue from Tony, giggled and said, "You boys might be interested in another little side action." I nodded my approval to the girls who took them inside the shearing plant.

I fired up some Coleman lanterns and started the power station. "I wanted to show you what we do in here. Here's the bet. I'll shear a sheep, and then you can see if you can beat my time."

The big guy said, "I ain't taking that bet. You guys do this for a living. Ain't happening."

"Look at my arms," I offered as I rolled up my sleeves. Red Borrowman rolled up his sleeve revealing a cured ham where biceps normally appear.

"Those are shearing arms. Mine are chicken wings?" I pointed to our crew. "These are the cutters. That's why they beat you so handily. We wear long sleeves all night so nobody sees the size of their arms. It's part of our scam, our hustle, and you boys just got worked. I'll give you a chance to double your money."

The large wad of bills sat on the table in front of them. I'll bring a couple of sheep in here, and you and I will go at it. I don't shear. Never have. I swear I don't know more than you. I'm the foreman, and all I do is clean up after these guys."

They were intrigued but still didn't take the bait until the two Nebraska Corn Huskers egged them on, daring them. I offered them a flask. Alcohol, testosterone, bravado, greed kicked in.

"Why not," they said. They were certain they had a backup plan to get their money back.

We plugged in the clippers, and I gave them both a quick lesson. Finally, one of them said, "Well, let's get this going. Let's get a couple of sheep in here and give this a go. Win or lose, this'll be fun."

"They're already here," Tractor said. "The sheep are standing right in front of me."

The two goons were slow to catch on. They tried to run but alcohol made them stumble. We were, of course, much bigger and stronger than even the orneriest of 200-pound bucks. Two of our guys easily held each of them down while Ibarra and Red removed every stitch of their clothing. Everything but their socks.

Their beards were the first to go. Then all the hair on their heads. The massive pelt of chest hair of the big guy went flying. Arms, legs, armpits. We rolled down their socks and shaved their legs. "I'm better at this than I thought," I proclaimed, arms overhead.

The girls were somewhere between hysterical, terrified, and anxious to see what came next. The big guy threatened, "You have no idea who you're dealing with. Have fun with your little joke. You have no clue what I can do to you guys. Did I mention I manage a munitions depot?"

Red Borrowman dropped his sizable knee into his chest, whispered in his ear, "I'd hold very, very still if I were you. The next cuts are tricky. Our reputation depends on the sharpness of our blades, you know what I'm saying? Hey, Ibarra, you ever nick a sheep?"

Ibarra shouted back, "Not too often, but occasionally we make a mistake and cut the wrong thing. Mostly accidents don't happen."

"What's the main cause of accidental cutting?" Red asked.

"It's usually when a big ram thinks he's tougher than me and won't hold still."

"Yep," Red says. "That's about right. It's usually a big ram. I suggest you fellas hold nice and still so we don't slip and cut off the wrong thing."

Red and Ibarra proceeded to slowly, cautiously, remove every hair in the entire man region. The victims hurled warnings of retribution.

Before letting them up, I said to them, "You guys walked into the wrong hustle tonight. Just like our buddy Doyle Hurst walked into your trap two years ago."

The two goons stopped moving, trembling, completely fleeced, cold temperatures and terror a frigid combination.

"Doyle died that night, and the entire Idaho criminal justice system has been looking for you losers for a long time. Don't show your face around here again or we'll give you a much closer shave."

Borrowman offered, "We usually turn rams into eunuchs. You sure you don't want me to finish the job?"

Uncertain, tenuous, tempted, I shrugged my shoulders.

Tony had retrieved the tool used to tag sheep ears. He had etched the letter "D" into the tags he had prepared, and with an efficient "*Pop,*" the ears of our two stooges were pierced. With a pair of pliers, the tags were firmly, semi-permanently attached, and the two newly fleeced goons were adorned like any self-respecting pirate. Blood dripped down their flabby, white bodies, and this was the breaking point for the girls, lost to the forest.

Before we released them, Red grabbed a swab and a bucket of paint used to mark and grade the wool. Sadly, the large orange letter "D" painted on their chests would wash off in two or three months. Stark naked, shivering, they joined the newly fleeced sheep in the pens. Lights off, engine killed, we made it back to the wrestling matches just in time for Tractor to win his final heat.

The Ogden boys must have hunkered down with the sheep for the night to keep warm. No one was ever sure how they got back to Ogden, or if they ever did. I would sure like to have a picture of two naked guys hitchhiking back down the mountain. We did leave their socks on. We weren't entirely without manners.

Junior interrupted me and asked, "Did Creighton ever find out about it?"

"I don't think he ever knew. He asked me the next morning after the wrestling matches if I heard anything over by the pens. I told him Tony thought he had seen a wolf lurking around. He took the dogs over but didn't see anything.

"'Wolves? I didn't know wolves are this far west.'

"'Maybe it was a coyote. Or a cougar. Or a skunk. Who knows?'

"By the way," I said to Junior, "One of those Nebraska girls was very impressed by the way Red Borrowman handled everything. She spent a few evenings in the fire tower with Red that summer. She came back out here the following year to work with Mary in the cook trailer. The preacher from that little church over by Mack's performed a marriage ceremony on the bridge at Big Springs. The preacher told Red and his new bride the springs were a good place to start a marriage, fresh and clean."

CHAPTER FORTY

We discovered that, just like any other business in the world, your biggest asset is your workforce. The mechanized machinery changed the industry, we paid good wages, but guys still came and went, three or four abandoning ship each season, looking for their next spot, their next nightmare. Replacing good shearers was always a challenge. We had seen guys blow in on a breeze, fall out of the sky, or turn up out of nowhere. Other times we had to grovel and beg.

A guy named Spackman came into camp our third year. He didn't blow in, no dirt devil. A forest ranger brought him in, half-naked, half-frozen. The majority of the shearers were rough-edged, but it was apparent Spackman had spent time on a whetstone, polishing, sharpening. He was very bright. He already had a degree in engineering and a good job. He left his job, lost his girlfriend, and nearly lost his highly-educated mind.

He met the girl at the University of Utah when he was studying, and she was in the nursing program. When she got pregnant, her dad unceremoniously shipped her off to Jackson Hole, Wyoming. This is a spectacular place, in the Teton Mountains, maybe one of the most beautiful places on earth. It has the perfect climate for grazing sheep on the open range. We didn't shear that far away, too long a haul for all our equipment. Maybe next year we would find a way to expand our reach. There were a couple of big sheep outfits over there, one owned by a guy named Rampton, wealthy, and well-known in that area. He was friends with the pregnant girl's father and agreed to take the girl in until she gave birth, and the child was placed for adoption.

She had been living in the Rampton home for a few months when Spackman left Utah and tracked her down. The owner wasn't around much, so Spackle (that's what the guys ended up calling him), was able to find a job on the ranch, toiling away in anonymity. He tended and wrangled sheep for a while, cleaned pens, mended fences, made himself useful, remaining invisible. He watched the house from a distance, hoping for just a glance of his girlfriend, who remained oblivious to his presence on the ranch.

It was rare that a laborer could pick up the techniques, the nuances of shearing, just by watching. He did. He even started making suggestions, entry points, geometric equations, balance. The guy could write a textbook on shearing, and he hadn't set foot in a cutting shed. The mechanized equipment was new in Wyoming, a couple of years behind Idaho and the world. There was no one to train them, and the shearers struggled. The foreman welcomed the input.

"You've never done this?" he asked.

"No."

"You want to give it a try? Let me grab a couple of ewes."

The big shot engineer calculated everything but the weight of the animal. His geometry was astonishing, movement and technique flawless.

He was a natural, gifted shearer, but his anatomy resembled frat boys, CPAs, bookworms, bankers, and other indoor chair-warmers. Said another way, he was a weakling.

He wouldn't give up. He lived like a skittish coyote, one eye on his kill, the other on a hawk circling above, working, learning, improving, and staying hidden from Rampton. The small group of shearers loved the guy. Their technique improved, and Spackle set the pace for speed and precision.

Spackle and the foreman, a guy by the name of Carter Moudry, became good friends. They talked of a shearing school, teaching, selling equipment, building a business.

"Carter, can I ask you a question? A favor actually," Spackle said, standing by the pens, brainstorming.

"I don't know," he answered. "What kind of favor? You don't want me to kill anyone do you?"

Spackle paused, much too long a pause.

"You didn't answer."

"Sorry," Spackle snapped out of a mental detour. "I may end up a dead man, though."

Moudry was baffled at this response.

"Listen, Carter, I'm sorry about this. This may cost us our friendship. I hope not. I think we could build a successful business together. I'm having a hard time asking this favor. It may be too big."

"Give it a try."

"I haven't been truthful with you. I came here, found this place, and got a job under false pretenses."

"You're not criminal on the run? Not a prison escapee?"

"No, no. Have you seen the tall brunette living at the house?"

"Yes. The pregnant one? Oh, no." Moudry immediately connected the dots.

"She doesn't know I'm here. She never comes out to the pens. I've been avoiding Rampton. He agreed to keep her here, away from me. She is due in a few weeks, and I want to be there for the birth. I need to talk to her. She has no idea I'm here."

Moudry cut him off, shook his head, spit a big wad of chewing tobacco. "That's a big favor. That's a *damn* big favor. Why didn't you say something? If I help you, we're both dead men. If not dead, then unemployed."

"I need to talk to her father in Salt Lake City," Spackman explained. "I'm sure Rampton could make a long-distance call. I want to marry her. He's got a phone in the house, right? He could do a long-distance call. I need to talk to her father."

Without a yes or a no, or even an acknowledgment, Moudry walked away.

The cabin that housed the shearers and the hired hands on the Rampton ranch was vibrating, shingles rattling, ten guys playing an orchestral piece of snoring, harmonious snorting. Spackman was wide awake. Laundry hanging from rafters cast an ominous shadow when Moudry entered the room carrying a lantern.

"Spackle, you awake?"

"Yes. I haven't slept all night. Can't you hear this racket? Of course, I'm awake. Listen, I'm sorry . . ."

"Tomorrow morning, ten o'clock, go up to the house. Rampton will have your father-in-law on the phone. He agreed to talk. Don't be late."

"Moudry, I owe you one."

"You're damn right you owe me."

At 9:45, pacing like a ram in the queue for castration, Spackle was pale, palms wet, oily hair tucked into his hat. His dungarees were stiff, dirty, last cleaned three weeks ago. *It's just a phone call, nobody will notice dirty pants.* A well-dressed man, clearly not a ranch hand, poked in the tent. "Hey, Spackman," he said, overly enthusiastic, "come with me. We've had some trouble making the long-distance connection. It's not quite the technological marvel we hoped for just yet. No worry, I'm going to drive you to a neighboring ranch. The call is set up and ready for you."

Ten minutes, fifteen, twenty, the big Lincoln Continental sedan was going sixty miles per hour, unheard of speed. Spackle knew there was no phone call waiting, knew there was no stopping the car.

Spackle was found at the top of Sawtell Peak, the big patriarch presiding over this valley. He damn near froze to death. He was walking down the mountain when a ranger spotted him. That's how he became a shearer with us. The ranger dropped him off in camp like you might take an ill-mannered dog and dump him in some remote location. Like a war veteran, lost, forgotten.

The pregnant girl was gone. Moudry, the foreman was gone with her.

Spackle's catatonic stare ended, his three-day hunger strike ended. His first words, "Is this a shearing camp? I can shear. I'm a very good shearer."

Aguirre was recovering from appendicitis and laid up for a few weeks. We needed an additional guy. We always needed backups. I looked at Spackle's skinny, frail physique, half-starved, and questioned his ability to shear.

314 | MARK HURST

His quiet, soft-spoken manner became even softer, darker. He brooded night and day. But his technique became the new standard. His count never dropped.

The guys let him wallow, longing for that girl and her baby. He was frequently distracted. This was a job where you couldn't afford to be distracted.

Spackle inevitably made a mistake. He hadn't been sleeping, two or three hours each night, underwater with grief. He completely lost his concentration, buzzards circled above his head sensing that grief was on the verge of killing him. Two hours into the morning shearing, his physical and mental state imploded. Lost, somewhere in a fog, he had pinned a big ewe to the ground with his knee and kept her there for twenty minutes instead of the six minutes it normally took. None of us noticed he was haphazardly moving his clippers, cutting more air than wool.

His eyes were open, but he was in a nightmare, sleep-walking through a nightmare, glassy eyes affixed on an invisible vanishing point, his head in some parallel universe. He had leaned into the animal so hard and for so long that the ewe stopped breathing. He didn't notice the lifelessness, just kept cutting. He removed the tattered pelt then pushed the lifeless animal down the exit chute. Robotic. Motionless. Deadman walking.

Apidale immediately straddled the dead animal, tried to get her upright, desperately shaking her head, harder and harder, faster and faster. No response. Shearing stopped and every single guy went down to the dead animal.

There were occasional deaths. It happened, but this our very first negligent death. We had been warned it could happen. With the old type of blade cutters, it happened a little bit more often because the guys had to hold an animal down in an unnatural position for so long. We virtually eliminated negligent deaths once the sheds were mechanized. This was our first death in two years.

I paused and looked at my grandson, Wesley Tripp III, Wesley Junior, the veterinarian-to-be. I pointed out that this was the only time I ever saw cruelty to animals. And it was a true accident. We were well-trained. There would be occasional cuts, other injuries, but it wasn't the norm.

"Hell's bells, my barber accidentally nicked my ear once, but I didn't jump up and have him arrested for senior citizen abuse.

"We cared for the animals. We were required to keep a needle and catgut thread by our station at all times, and we all knew how to use them to patch an occasional cut. There was never any abuse. This loss was a tragedy for all of us."

"Thanks, Gramps," he quietly replied. "That's very helpful. Thanks for that story, it's important to my research."

So, at that moment, I was as livid as I ever got. A foaming mouth on a rabid badger comes to mind.

"How small is that brain of yours?" I screamed, my forehead ram-butting his. I was enraged, ready to take his power clippers to the jugular in his neck.

Spackman erupted. "Go to hell, Tripp! Every one of you go to hell! This place is a living hell. This place stinks, and I'm sick of every one of you and these animals. I hate these damn animals, walking around all day in sheep shit."

Pent-up anger, resentment, loneliness, and testosterone combined, the slumbering volcano erupted. Hot magma flowed out. Gray ash covered the forest. He flailed at the air, and his clippers sailed into the trees. Arms swinging, sheep shit flying, the tantrum of a three-year-old. Completely hysterical, he jumped on my back, hanging on and punching me on the right side of my face, the face of the enemy. He wanted to punish all of us. He blamed us for sending his girlfriend away. He blamed us for everything even though we did nothing but take him in and give him a chance. His rage blinded him to the facts.

Even Creighton, the vizier, couldn't tell which of us was more crazed, hysterical, demoniacally possessed. Creighton and a team of guys pulled us apart, both of us leaving deep tracks in the dirt, boot heels gouging as we were dragged to separate corners. Creighton had never seen my temper like this. No one had seen me like this. I had never seen myself like this.

Fully restrained, Spackman wept, sobbed, screamed, his face covered in snot and dust. Tractor held my arms behind my back, and I screamed back, "You are out of here, you shit for brains. You are gone. Get out of here, now. Don't pack a bag. Somebody get a truck and take this garbage to the landfill. Drop him in the lake. Do something, get him out of here. Let go of my arms, you morons."

A referee got between us, ended the fight.

"Walk away, Trippy," Creighton demanded. "Walk away. Let me handle this."

"What do you mean you'll handle it?" I retaliated, shoving him. My fists were was cocked, ready to hit him.

"I'll handle it. You're too angry, and you need to cool off before deciding what to do."

"There's no handling, there's no deciding. That guy is gone. It's handled."

The whole camp had gone dead still, including the sheep killer. Everyone wanted to know what would happen between the two partners. No one had ever seen us go at it. We didn't need to fight because we were normally so supportive of one another. Just not in that moment.

"Tripp," he said, now with more force, "let's take a walk." I resisted but finally conceded rather than make a bigger scene in front of the team. We disappeared into the trees.

"Creighton, I'm the foreman, your partner in the business, the boss, the guy with the whip. I am supposed to be the voice of authority and in ten seconds all of that has been undermined. You just took my legs right out from under me. You made me the bad guy. How can I ever get the respect of the crew if you don't let me handle it?"

"I know, Trippy, I could have handled it better. We both could have handled it better. I'm sorry. But it would be an even bigger mistake to throw him out. We both have to calm down."

"Are you out of your mind?" I implored. "He killed an animal and was trying to kill me. He has to go."

"He wasn't trying to kill you, Trippy. He was screaming for your love, for your help. He is desperately in love with a girl he can't have. He fathered a child. He is in pain. He has no one in the world to turn to. He doesn't need more rejection right now. He needs someone on his side. He needs you. I know this for a fact. He admires your leadership and respects you more than you know. He just has a hard way of showing it."

"He beats the shit out of a guy he respects? Now, that's a new one." I wasn't even close to cooling down, still enraged at the embarrassment of Creighton intermediating. I was more concerned about my own standing, my embarrassment, than I was at having a bulging eye, a quart of blood on my face, still dripping.

We sat down on a log and talked, really talked in a way I was no good at. A conversation where I lacked any experience. A conversation, rare even for this thoughtful man. Both of us listened. On that day, on that log, I learned how to listen. We didn't have to reach a compromise or bring in an arbitrator. It was obvious what the answer was.

At the risk of further undermining my authority and respect; at the risk of bringing sand into the tool shed; at the risk of burning down all the fences; in that moment, mad as the crew may have been, their respect for me began to grow, because I took the time to look at the man instead of his malevolence; to look at his future instead of his fury; I matured ten years. Retribution and revenge were poor management tools. This incident, others like it, could never be stopped with retaliation. Fighting violence with violence never brings peace. Hate plus hate never equals love or redemption. I had come a long, long way, learning to practice love, understanding, tolerance, forgiveness. These emotions were frequently lost in the brutal conditions and the isolation of wilderness living. Creighton warned me from the beginning that it could be a place that either saved you or buried you. I was nearly buried in my own gray ash. My anger that day frightened me. I didn't know then that my simmering rage was fueled by my own loss of a woman I deeply loved. I wasn't angry, I was still mourning. I should have been the first to recognize the depth of Spackman's desperation, but I was blinded by my own.

It took a long time for everyone in camp to comprehend what happened between Creighton and me. Spackle stayed. Even though he wanted desperately to leave, we talked him out of it. No one in the camp could figure it out; firing him one day then begging him to stay the next. Spackman had broken every rule we had in place—pay attention, protect the animal, rewards come to those who work hard, and don't speak harshly of one another. In other words, don't break the unsigned oath: the team comes first.

But there was one other rule that we followed. If you were given a lamb for a gift or for a debt, you have two choices. First, lamb chops. Eat the young, tender meat. Nothing like a very young chop or a rack of lamb roasted on a spit over hot coals. You get a few really good meals from the young animal that you can't get later from mutton. Or, second, you can raise the lamb, feed it, breed it, shear it, and sell the wool for a good price; start a small herd of your own. Repeat for many years.

Two choices—the pasture or the spit. Eat it now, or grow it for the future. Spackman, a very fine shearer, and an even finer human got a second chance that day. Violence led to calm, white water crashing violently over rocks, calmly settling into flatlands where deep pools created the ideal habitat for lazy rainbow trout.

We sent Spackle to pasture. We both needed some pasture time. Day ten of that encampment was winding down, the last bunch of sheep roasting in the heat, desperately needing to get a weighty pelt off their backs. We were looking forward to Sunday, a quiet time to rest and recuperate. We finally finished up at around 7 p.m., the spectacular mountain air coming down the canyon, cooling our depleted bodies. And cooling emotions. Reweaving torn threads.

Pelts had been counted and tallied. The final few were going up to be bagged. Machinery off, floors swept. The shearers cleaned lanolin and wool from their feet and blades, wiped sweat and pieces of wool from their nostrils, ears, and face. The quiet of the mountains returned.

At the end of each day, Creighton would record the tally in his ledger. This is how he calculated weekly totals and payroll, adding five dollars for each bell ringing.

Spackman's astute, scientific observations helped drive up production. Creighton called out, "Fagan 206 (a new high for him). Kirkpatrick 219, very nice. Apidale 223, impressive. And today's gun . . ." he paused for effect. Everyone thought they knew who would be at the top. Three guys always set a blistering pace, Kiwi frequently at the top.

"Today's gun, a personal best, with 224 pelts, Garrett Spackman. Spackle get up here and ring this bell."

A thunderous roar echoed around the valley. Birds suddenly took flight. Moose lifted their heads, wet moss hanging from their chins. Big Springs may have stopped flowing. The cheer roiled around the base of Sawtell Peak then rose up the slope like heat rising on a summer night. Even Mary left the kitchen trailer and joined with the crew lifting Spackle upon their shoulders. He was going to ring his first bell. "Put me down, put me down," he begged. The gang went silent. "Set me down. I'm not ringing that bell. It's not mine to ring. It was you, every one of you that patched up my mess. And it was a big damn mess. I'm on the mend, I think. I've worked hard these last few weeks trying to deal with emotions I've never felt before. Thanks for your patience. I got my strength from all of you. This isn't my bell. There's one guy who has never rung the bell, this is his day.

"Trippy," he waved to me. "Get up here." I made no attempt to hold back tears and neither did most of these filthy, stinking men, covered in a slimy goo of lanolin and wool. Together we walked to the bell, and I grabbed the leather strap. My first and only bell was a symphonic wonder. Spackle took the strap and pulled on it so long and hard the entire strap and bell came crashing down. His first bell was a disaster. He bent down, scooped it out of the dirt, and threw it deep into the trees.

We put the plant to rest and settled in for a very quiet night, ready to move on to a new place tomorrow. "What's next?"

—⁓⁓⁓⁓—

Normally, I wasn't a good sleeper. I had too much going on in my head most nights. That night I was nearly comatose, crashed at eight o'clock, and didn't move until sunrise. Instead of regret and anger about the Spackman matter, I found an inner peace. I wasn't reprimanded, I wasn't countermanded, I wasn't embarrassed, or undercut by a boss. I was taught. I was taught by a teacher of men with genuine love for his fellow man. He taught me that none of us can see too far down the road to see what's coming next because our expectations may never match what's up there. He taught me to live what he always called "breakfast to dinner." Get up and think about what you need to do, things you ought to do, don't worry about the things you didn't do, the lame promise "been gonna do."

We walked downriver to a beaver pond one afternoon. We marveled at their ingenuity. He said to me, "Trippy, you think a beaver wakes up one morning wondering if he placed a stick at the wrong angle? Or that he hadn't put enough mud on one spot and feared the dam would leak. That beaver wakes up every morning and starts cutting wood, mixing mud, getting the den ready for the day. He deals with what's right in front of him. That's all he knows."

Creighton would tell me if you spent too much time looking backward, you'll find your regrets hanging around, lurking. Spend just enough time looking back to remember it's your shortcomings and your failures that helped shape you and build you, much more than the things that came easy. It's okay to look back occasionally to remind us of what impossibly hard lava we had to crawl through to put down our roots so we could begin the push up to the sun. Never forget the cracks in the lava, then push on.

This mountain sanctuary once again soothed me and rocked me to sleep in its arms that night. I grew to love it even more. It may not be the most beautiful place in the world, but it is one of the most compelling, one of the most curious. How did so much beauty spring up from such a violent event? A magma flow, eons ago, burned every trace of life with a ruthless and unstoppable heat, leaving behind angry detritus in the form of unusable, worthless, impenetrable rock.

Given enough time, the most resilient forms of life restored the natural order and created something better than it had ever been. The rock is still here, right below my feet, a firm reminder that I'm just a short-term vagabond stopping on the earth for a time. The lava will be there forevermore. But you can't see the rock for all the beauty on the surface. The trees live on, the wildflowers live on, wildlife lives on, the huckleberries continue their secretive existence. The water at Big Springs, which refused to be dammed up by the lava, keeps flowing, keeps inspiring those like me who come to the water to be cleansed and purified, renewed and invigorated, redeemed, and reclaimed.

Just as Island Park isn't the most beautiful place, Creighton was never the smartest guy that ever lived. I knew that. He knew it as well and never pretended to be. His self-awareness was the source of his humility. He was, in my mind, exactly like this land, this place—rugged and intimidating, yet at the same time calm and reassuring. He had a beautiful spirit about him, something I'd never comprehended. I'd never seen these qualities in a man before because I didn't know they existed. I didn't know how to look for them. He was strong and resilient and never stopped looking for ways to take care of his family, his workers, and anyone who crossed his path, armed with the belief that anyone can find the strength to start again, not knowing how good they may end up.

He taught me how to shape men, carving with a sharp knife, rounding rough edges, watching the good emerge.

So many guys came through our camps, rough and untethered. We watched many of them move on to other endeavors, leaving with a Master's degree in endurance and perseverance. They developed strong legs to carry them long distances and stand tall wherever they put their feet. Because of the cruel, desperately long days, they developed strong arms to defend themselves, to lift a friend in need, and to protect others, even the smallest of creatures. The shearers, their unusually soft hands from lanolin in the wool, demonstrated the irony—tough, rugged men with a tender touch and a soft spot for others. They left with strong backs, able and willing to carry the burdens of others who needed help. And they learned an important lesson while being paid by the pelts they cut, and it is this—nobody gives you anything of value for free. Rewards come through discipline and effort.

Creighton taught me the lessons of the lamb—pasture or spit. Instant gratification or long-term rewards; harsh judgment or a second chance; retribution or redemption.

I took a moment to rub my eyes, resettle my man parts, and stand up from the recliner for a stretch. It takes me three or four attempts to get up these days and just about as long to sit back down. Hanging on the wall down the hallway is a picture. Junior followed me. "Look at this photo. This is the day I married your Grandma. This is my best man, Garrett Spackman. Now let's go finish up this torture you're putting an old fart through."

CHAPTER FORTY-ONE

Portable fencing was important to our success. Banging, bumping, stampeding sheep, and the wear and tear of constantly moving and shipping it over the next couple of years began to wear out the wood fencing. Hans's clever system had been brilliant but needed some tinkering. We needed more cut lumber. There was, obviously, plenty of timber, but very little of it cut for fencing. We didn't have the saws even if we had the time and manpower.

Hans and I were looking for a solution, talking it over as we filled a truck up with gas. Pond's Lodge was being rebuilt, logs stacked and ready to be put in place. They put in gas tanks before starting on the lodge. Mrs. Pond passed by and said hello, her eyes looking down. She and I had a peaceable enough friendship, but we found it hard to spend more than a few minutes talking. I saw in her Christina's kindness. She saw in me a broken heart that she didn't know how to mend.

She did hear us talking about lumber and told us where she thought we may find some. Before heading back to camp, we turned onto the Two Top Mountain Road where loggers had been working the last three years cutting trees for railroad ties.

An obscure fork in the road appeared to the east, just where Mrs. Pond had described. Half a mile in, timber was neatly stacked, pine-scented sawdust covered much of the ground. A man, a very small man was hewing a log with an adze. *Was it a young boy?* His face was too mature. We both squinted to see if our eyes were lying. Our mothers would have slapped us for staring. We were used to seeing only very large men, laborers, lumberjacks, equipment operators. We were surrounded all day by forty-foot trees that forced us to look up.

This half-size human was out of balance with the forest. We were forced to look down. All 6' 5 of Hans Herrman, heron legs, unfolded from the car. The peculiar 4' 11 dwarf, midget, shrunken man, carnival sideshow, greeted Hans who was completely flummoxed by the size disparity. He shook the small hand, delicate but calloused, and the little man welcomed him, his small voice squeaky and bearing a pronounced German accent. Hans about tripped over his own size 16 boots, falling forward, ready to flatten the runt.

I shouldn't have called him a runt. He turned out to be a friend who helped rebuild our fencing.

He and Hans immediately struck up an all-German conversation which was later shared with me in detail. This guy's name was Johan Sachs, but the American version was Johnny Sack. He was well-known and well-liked by everyone in the area. Here he was cutting timber, virtually alone, and had built himself a cabin, all by hand, all with logs. Its most prominent feature—its size, about half the size of normal cabin dimensions. It seemed a perfect fit for this very small bachelor. I walked around inside a bit, but Hans couldn't get in the front door. The architecture was remarkable. The logs all fit together in perfect order, cut and built by this little man. Tiny, handmade log furniture dotted each room.

Jonny Sack and Hans became buddies. Bonded by their common language and love for their fatherland, they set about building and fixing fences, stabilizing them, and improving the connectors for even faster setup and take-down. They shared a European respect for nature; taking old growth, leaving the new, cutting selectively to allow for regrowth. Lumberjacks coming down timber road frequently slowed their trucks to glimpse one human, nearly half the size of the other, connected by their common ancestry, both oblivious to the odd pairing and disruption to all sense of balance in nature.

They moved Johnny Sacks' little cabin over to the edge of Big Springs years later. Perhaps the Forest Service thought its small size made the springs appear bigger, more deserving of its generic name. The smallness of the cabin against the sweeping panorama of the forest changed the balance a bit. The area around Big Springs came back to life for me, and I gained a new perspective about a lot of things.

That cabin sits there to this very day and looks just about right sitting next to Big Springs, balance and order restored.

CHAPTER FORTY-TWO

We didn't see a lot of guys in suits and ties come around the camp. There were plenty of bankers, buyers, and others involved with our company, but they would mostly meet in the cabin at Phillips Lodge where I first met our partners. Businessmen rarely came out to the muddy campsites where we were shearing. It was impossible to miss a new Dodge sedan, burgundy paint, oversized running boards, and fenders as it slithered into camp. The car resembled a train engine, much smaller, with a sleek front end housing a powerful engine—the massive 60-horsepower.

The driver's shoes were immediately covered in the ever-present mix of sheep shit and volcanic ash as he stepped from the car. Black shoes were a dominant fashion choice, perhaps because it was the only choice. Someone should've been making gray shoes, less likely to show dirt, less likely to give away "big-city-ness."

His light-colored tweed suit, far too hot for summer, demonstrated at least a slight awareness he was walking into a wool-related industry. He was a moron. No one wore wool on a day like this. His jacket quickly gave way to a shirt, vest, a holster for his FBI-issued service revolver.

Peering into the holding pens, casual and curious, his left, muddy, gray shoe, rested on a fence rail, his demeanor calm. The twitching foot told another story. While feigning bravery, he wondered how often 500 sheep may have broken down temporary fencing, escaping in a rush. He didn't break character with his practiced G-man image, scrupulously hiding a fear of animals.

Creighton glanced up from the repair table where he was working morning and night to keep clippers running. He joined the G-man at the fence who asked, "How many sheep do you shear in a day?"

Creighton answered, "On a good day, two thousand."

He replied, "Impressive. I've heard you guys are doing a great job out here. I've never seen this part of the world. You picked a nice place to run a business, far up in these hills," clearly inferring that it was seemingly out of reach of the Feds.

Creighton, picking up immediately on the tone, asked, "Where you from?"

"I was born and raised in Carolina. North Carolina. I'm currently stationed in San Francisco with the FBI."

"Either of those places is, indeed, pretty far away from these Idaho mountains."

"I had a little trouble finding you." He paused for effect.

Creighton stared at the sheep.

The G-man said, "I'm looking for a guy named Tripp."

Creighton squinted his eyes as if searching his files.

"His name is Lester Tripp, but he might be using some other name." "Don't know a Lester Tripp," Creighton replied. "Sorry. You came all the way out here just for that? Good luck," Creighton said, dismissively.

"Listen," the agent explained, "there was a major robbery in San Francisco a few years ago. A bunch of guys ambushed a truck carrying rubber tires. They're a high-demand item, and they took them across state lines to sell them. That's why I'm involved. It looked like the perps knew when the delivery was going down like they worked with tires and cars. Probably an inside job." He paused, waiting for a reaction that never came. "The driver was beaten up and died a few days later from head injuries. This is a dangerous guy we're looking for. You sure you don't know a Lester Tripp?"

Creighton must have felt betrayed in that moment. He had to have been shocked, wondering if there was any substance to an FBI inquiry that may implicate someone with my last name. He must have considered the possibility he had been lied to. The day in the car when he gave me the human polygraph test, my answers were truthful. He believed me then, and he, apparently, believed me when he looked the FBI agent in the face and said, "Good luck finding your guy," and went back to his repair table.

Picking up supplies Mary needed in the kitchen trailer was part of my weekly routine. My truck was loaded with provisions, and I pulled into camp, conveniently, at the exact time the FBI agent was pulling out. Both our heads swiveled as we passed.

The supplies unloaded, next stop, a conversation with Creighton, working at the repair table. We were running a couple of balky clippers that needed servicing. "Creighton, you got a couple of clippers patched up for me?" He handed them to me and said, "Good to go."

"That guy in the Dodge, the suit and tie guy pulling out just now, one of your bankers?" I asked. It seemed an innocent question.

"Nope," he answered, unconcerned. "It was an FBI agent from San Francisco looking for a guy named Lester, had some trouble over there a few years back. Some big robbery."

"Lester?"

"Yes," Creighton said crisply. "I told him I don't know a Lester Tripp. You don't know a Lester Tripp, do you? Any relation?"

"Creighton, listen, . . ."

"I don't need to listen, do I? You've always been a hundred percent truthful with me, so I don't have time to listen to your yammering. Are you going to take those clippers to the shed? You said it was urgent." I took the clippers from him and got to work. Creighton didn't blink when he told me of the visit from the Feds. Creighton's human lie detector appeared, to both of us, foolproof.

"Junior, that's enough about Creighton Hurst, for now. You've patiently listened to the details of our experiences in the world of wool and meat, but let's end it there. He wouldn't want to be glorified and it feels like I'm getting close to that. He would never want glory. Nor praises. He had no interest in seeing his picture in the paper. He was a humble family man. When prices and demand for wool dropped and competition got worse, he decided it was time to get back home and spend more time with his family.

"The loss of a son had devastated him. He never got over it. He farmed a bit and did carpentry work the rest of his years, unsung and unheralded. Unlike the story in the *New York Times* that championed his accomplishments and made him a bit heroic, he was less like the powerful industrialists building railroads and skyscrapers, more like the deliberate beaver building a safe shelter for his family, underwater, away and out of sight.

"Mary called in 1964 or '65, somewhere in there, and said Creighton died in a construction accident. I couldn't eat or breathe or move for days, not even to attend the funeral. When he died, I pretty much did too. The hardest chapter of my entire life was about finding strength to avoid not going back to the bottle when he died. Your grandmother stayed by my side, pulled me, for the third time, out of a river to keep me from drowning.

"We've talked about so many of the things he taught me. I'm glad you coerced me to tell the story."

Let me just say this. By the end of the third year of shearing, the ravages of the depression were in full "take no prisoners mode." We had kept a lot of people out of the breadlines, out of the soup kitchens, and gave them a bed at night, and a roof over their head. Our canvas roofs leaked a fair amount and *ra-ta-tatted* like a snare drum when the rains pelted them; much more like a tympani when it hailed. But there was always a roof. There was always a hot meal on the table.

On perfect nights, the stars were the roof. The big dipper was clear as if it were drawn in blue sand by a child on the beach. Orion, Ursa Major, Leo, Virgo, and the Centaur were also clear, as were three or four billion more stars than city living ever allowed. We didn't know the first thing about constellations or the vast size of the universe, where it began. The Big Dipper, with its North Star, was the only one we could make out because we didn't know where or how or when to look for anything else.

We would often enjoy sitting around the fire at night, making a racket, occasionally trying to entertain each other. We looked around the circle and saw an unintentionally planned variety of faces and features, broad noses, angular jaws, black hair, red hair, and fair. Brown and green eyes, blue and hazel and emerald. Jack Empey had one brown eye, one green. There were names unfamiliar to each of us when we signed on with the crew. So too the ethnicity from which the names came–Basques, Germans, Scots, Maoris, and a menagerie of other mutts and mixes.

Some had a song, some had a story to regale us. Others had a Scottish jig or a rain dance taught to them by the Shoshone or Bannock. Time, weariness, and familiarity helped us shed our inhibitions, and we had nightly performances around the fire. Everybody learned from everybody. Kiwi always sat with us by the fire but never had a word to say. And I should say he didn't actually sit by the fire. Kiwi never sat. Even after working ten-hour days, he was too restless to sit still.

Periodically the boys wanted to hear about Sam McGee freezing his tailbone off in the Yukon. I was happy to recite the whole thing. It was a manifesto of the wanderer. Patty had his guitar always at the ready, though seldom in tune. He played his three songs so many times they would eventually comfort us with their familiarity. He tried to yodel like a cowboy, but that sent the sheep into a fever. He was forced to give up his howling.

We were all very different, more so than I would have expected when setting out to round up these guys, my Ohio bias leaning toward homogeneity. They were the ones set in my path like they were meant to be around that fire each night. By the time we started the third and final year, many of them had moved on, and we had new faces, new names, new idiosyncrasies. We had a new singer, always about half a note off-key as he ran through his Hoagy Carmichael list of tunes. He was pretty good, but even our tough, inexperienced crowd sensed it was a little off-key. We were a very forgiving audience. The variety of personalities, temperaments, strengths, worries, inner longings, and dark secrets were all scattered under a patchwork quilt ("just like the one around my shoulders that Grandma made so many years ago").

As an Island Park summer limped into fall, wool demand was in steep decline, prices below costs to get it to market. We knew a downturn would eventually catch us, and one full year into the Great Depression, it happened.

The men were tired. The ranchers were going back to more and more cattle. Beef prices were increasing. The power station Creighton designed and built by sheer determination was older and weaker than all of us put together in terms of hours worked. Newer, more powerful engines were being built, and power clippers were now standard equipment in sheep camps everywhere. Mobile operations were the new norm.

We should have bought a license to exclusively sell the clippers in the US when we had the chance, but we knew less about all that than we did about the shearing business, and that wasn't much. This would be one of those "don't look back" moments. One American company did get that license and made a bundle of money.

As things were winding down, it became increasingly difficult to keep our energy up, counts high. Tens of thousands of sheep were back in the hills, grazing on nutrient-rich pasture. Shepherds pulled their campers and tents, still by horse, up the slopes, settling in for winter grazing. Still clinging to worries about giving advice, I hoped that the guys had put some money away for the winter, coming at us all like a small wooden canoe unaware of the approaching rapids. Some did, some didn't. The booze and the girls were always too much temptation.

334 | MARK HURST

Some chose the pasture, some the spit.

Everyone was either packing their bags or thinking about packing their bags. No one wanted to work. We still had contracts to fill. Like a good horse at the end of the trail, we headed for the barn, stumbling and staggering the last mile. Every one of the crew was deciding whether or not to head back home if they had one. A few stayed; this had been their home for the last three years.

The campfire at night was our solace even though it had an uncertain feeling about it. It was as if the flames burned a different color orange. Less heat. Less intensity.

Our equipment and our modernized techniques were amazing. The way a few simple guys changed the wool industry was a remarkable achievement. Helping get some families through part of the Depression was miraculous, seemingly more miraculous each passing year. None of those things were as memorable as one crisp August night when we were in our entertainment mode, around the fire, singing and carrying on. We were eating Huckleberry pie, the greatest miracle of all.

In a shocking twist, Kiwi wordlessly walked toward the fire and stopped just short of the hot coals. None of us would have been shocked to see him walk across the hot coals. He had carved himself a walking stick with designs on it to match his tattoos. He carried that stick everywhere he went and had it hanging on a post in the shed all day long. He slept with it all night. I've never known for sure if the big old Maori ever slept. He was up every morning before me and doused the fire at night. The stick was a lucky talisman.

In the flickering light of the embers, orange light danced across his broad, brown body. Tattoos on his torso appeared to come alive, moving animatedly as the firelight and its shadows moved across his body.

The permanent ink seemed to be telling us a story. He stood uncomfortably silent for a couple of minutes as if he had something to say. With a sudden jerk, he raised the wooden stick over his head, looked up to the North Star, filled his enormous lungs with night air and smoke, and let loose an unholy and eerie scream that echoed from the Canadian border down to the tip of Mexico. The trees heard it, the river heard it, elk heard it. It glanced off the volcanic tuff then shot heavenward where the North Star heard it. The sheep heard it and stirred, ready to stampede. Weary portable fencing rattled.

Then silence as quiet as the scream had been loud.

Kiwi gradually lowered the stick to his knees, horizontal, hovering, then snapped it in half as simple as a toothpick breaking on a tough piece of meat stuck in a molar. His massive hands, now tender as if holding a crystal vase, lowered the broken stick into the coals and waited for it to burn.

He turned from the fire to face his comrades, and began a haunting, soulful, ceremonial dance, at once both threatening and tragic. He stomped his bare feet on hard ground, enough torque to snap any of my fragile phalanges, pounding his chest and pulling horrifying faces uglier than what you might see result from an unholy coupling of a rhino and one of the hideous sturgeons. Only much worse. His tongue flipped in and out like a cornered rattlesnake as he chanted an ancient war cry, some language, something angry, mean, ready to scorch the entire planet with a ball of fire and then swallow it whole.

It was terrifying, and it was spectacular. It was intimidating; it was inspiring. As angry as it sounded to most of us, it was poetry, a song, to some who had their ears attuned. It was his farewell. Tears streamed down the cheeks of this angry foreigner, tall and strong as Sawtell Peak looming over the caldera. A man with the heart of a lion and the tenderness of a baby lamb. He was screaming, and he was crying. He was yelling and whispering. He was sobbing and celebrating, and he was saying goodbye, telling us we were his brothers and that we fought together and stood together and protected each other. He told us the gods would strengthen us as we left the mountain for the last time.

Three very long days stuck in a room with me, listening to my stories, left Junior drained. It sure as hell left me drained. Junior could tell. I was exhausted, yet completely filled with an overwhelming sense of gratitude for the amazing people who touched my life, saved my life, reclaimed me. I thought a lot about Christina these last few days, opened a few locked doors. So many memories of her had become a fog, a dissipating mist nearly seventy years on.

There was her beauty. There was her strong spirit, her toughness, and her kindness. The irony of her calloused hands in mine, softened by lanolin. Her instant love of the little lamb I gifted to her. It took a long time to lose my resentment, to move on and make sense of the loss. At age 90, I haven't come even remotely close to finding answers.

Christina didn't die because God wanted her to die. Preachers told me God took people he needed most. I needed her the most. Others would speak of an angry god, a jealous god, a vengeful god inflicting punishment on me. I can't comprehend a vengeful god, any more than a loving god. This makes it sound like there are two gods, contrary to the widely held view that there is just one. Everyone thought they had an answer. A balm. Strangers poured it on.

Friends poured it out. It was all just a bunch of spittle and steel shavings from a whetstone, a gray puddle of useless dreck.

Christina died because there was a fire. That's it. I met her because she was at the lodge the night of a fight, not because God made our meeting happen. I found her because she was there one night and so was I. No big deal, no stars aligning, it just happened. The night Creighton pulled me out of the river, he was there when I needed rescuing. It wasn't miraculous. Creighton never pretended it was any such thing.

Gazing at the stars in those clear mountain skies gave no brilliant insights other than the obvious reality that even though they're billions of miles apart, sometimes one of them crashes into something else, bursting, breaking. It's the breaking that keeps the universe growing. It seems impossible, given the vastness of space, but it happens.

It's enormous, the universe, the heavens, stars by the trillions we are told. Where does it begin? Where is its outer edge? It's inevitable that a meteorite or a broken star is going to crash into something else. When it does, massive explosions send rocks, dust, debris, and chemicals into the atmosphere. The matter doesn't disappear; it starts over. New life begins to form. The universe nurtures its growth. Collisions and explosions continue to happen even if they're too far away for us to ever see. Burning and freezing. Failing and falling. The universe evolves and adapts. It morphs, matures, and survives for another ten trillion years.

Studying the stars was a nightly occurrence after Christina died. I tried to imagine her as one of those lights, a new star, reborn. There she was, a spec hanging in the vast darkness. From that vastness, I heard her speak to me. It was as loud as a cosmic collision, silent as a falling star. I felt her finger poke me in the chest, and she said to me, "You've got to get up, get on with it. Get over it. You can't stay put. The water has to keep moving downstream."

Who could forget the mountains where we worked? As rugged as they were, they welcomed me. Enveloped and embraced me. Shaped me. When I needed it most, the mountains helped restore balance and perspective to my life.

Living in a caldera, just above slumbering magma, tempered me the way heat tempers steel. I grew harder, stronger, more resilient.

It was here, in this mountainous retreat, where the rivers redeemed me. The living water.

Everybody loves a river, the stillness, the sound they make, their effortless flow, the beauty of their randomness, and the irony of their sometimes violent efficiency.

Anyone can stand along the shore and watch the water go by. The insouciant water doesn't care if you're there or not. You can stand safely, cautiously on the shore, or wade in, feel the current tugging at your leg, daring you to come in further and toss a few dry flies to the impudent fish. Everybody loves a river.

You can take a ride through whitewater, riding the waves and avoiding large rocks that want to slit open your flimsy rubber raft or punch a hole in your aging wood.

You can stare in awe at the power of a waterfall, or stand under the waterfall if you dare, engulfed in its wash.

You can pull up a chair and try to paint a picture of the river and learn, as all artists learn, the impossibility of capturing a moving river in a still painting, because the water is liquid, moving, evasive. Everybody loves a river.

Some rivers they call lazy, some are beasts. Some rivers are in a big hurry to get where they are going, some take their time. Some are whisper-quiet, others growl, or roar, or make the sound of 10,000 stampeding sheep.

A river can gracefully meander through a valley or cut a deep gorge in rock. Rivers are relentless.

It may be the mighty Mississippi, or the Missouri, or the Columbia—rivers that took explorers to places where the white man had never set foot, carrying with them the seeds and the tools that built a nation, watering our cotton, our tobacco, our wheat, our corn, our potatoes.

Everybody loves a river—the history, the tales, the heroes they carried along when they needed a ride.

But everybody *fears* a river as well—its hidden currents, whirlpools, and eddies that'll pull you under in an instant if you dare turn your back. Or wade in too far.

I once shared with a moose the river that runs between Lewis Lake and Shoshone Lake in Yellowstone. I was curious enough to not bother her and her calf while they pulled moss off the bottom. They were kind enough to let me share the river and quietly set and reset my line, each of us envious of the other. I shared a river with an osprey who ignored me, insulted me, mocked me as he out-fished me with his ability to see fish from up in the air and catch one with a death-defying dive. Effortlessly. Instinctively.

Nature decided where the rivers would run, unconcerned about mountains and rocks along their assigned route. If anything got in their way, they slowly went around them, over the top of them, or in some cases, right through them. Nature knew exactly what to do. It was men that turned rivers into borders. The mighty Rio Grande became a barrier, a buttress between nations. They have been fighting over the water ever since.

Who doesn't love a river that continues running regardless of what man asks of it? They are big and long and rugged. They are short and calm. They are wide, narrow, straight, curved, and irregular. The same rivers that water our crops are the very same ones that, from time to time, flow over their banks to destroy those crops. Rivers cannot be trusted.

There are variations of what we call a river—a stream, a rivulet, a creek, a babbling brook, a fork, a tributary. Standing in this spot, the top of the Continental Divide, a small river chooses to run both ways, East and West, joining forces with its larger brothers and sisters, getting bigger and stronger with each mile. All rivers have their destiny appointed here.

Rivers travel across prairies, plains, gullies. They make their way down ravines, canyons, valleys, through unknown wilderness, jungles, swamps, and impossible places. They always know exactly where they are going.

Everyone loves a river that cleanses you, sustains you, renews and redeems you. A river welcomes you and threatens you. Abandons you. Always moving downstream.

Everyone can see the rivers because they are right in front of you, shouting at you. But few people ever see the headwaters of a river. They don't know where a river begins. They don't know because they don't know where to look. The river I knew, the one that begins at Big Springs, Henry's Fork of the Snake River, is small by any measure, but it is consistent. No one ever called it a mighty river as it silently creeps up from the middle of the earth somewhere deep and dark, 120 million gallons per day, rising up through impenetrable rock, appearing on the surface, miraculously, without complaint, this place where the river begins. I would call that mighty.

The river haunts me, hurts me, heals me, and reminds me to keep moving, that it does no good to stand still. It tells me I'm needed somewhere downstream from here, just around the bend.

"You want to know, Junior, why I never revealed the location of the secret huckleberry patch?" He nods, eyes big. "I didn't know where it was. I didn't know where to look. Creighton's secret was safe with me, just as he knew it would be.

"And here's the final thing I'm going to say, then you're going to turn off that damn recorder and leave me alone."

"Okay," Junior said, "one final word."

"Did you get what you came for? The evidence of the crimes we committed, the horrible atrocities against helpless sheep? Are you ready to write up your final report and have me arrested?"

"Yes, Gramps, I got exactly what I came for."

AFTERWORD

Virtually every night as I wrestled with sleep that wouldn't come, I got in the habit of reciting to myself the Robert Service poem, "The Cremation of Sam McGee." I'll tell it to anyone who asks, although that isn't too often these days.

The Cremation of Sam McGee

by Robert Service

Published in 1907

There are strange things done in the midnight sun
By the men who moil for gold;
The Arctic trails have their secret tales
That would make your blood run cold;
The Northern Lights have seen queer sights,
But the queerest they ever did see
Was that night on the marge of Lake Lebarge
I cremated Sam McGee.

Now Sam McGee was from Tennessee, where the cotton blooms and blows.

Why he left his home in the South to roam 'round the Pole, God only knows.

He was always cold, but the land of gold seemed to hold him like a spell;

Though he'd often say in his homely way that "he'd sooner live in hell."

On a Christmas Day we were mushing our way over the Dawson trail.

Talk of your cold! through the parka's fold it stabbed like a driven nail.

If our eyes we'd close, then the lashes froze till sometimes we couldn't see;

It wasn't much fun, but the only one to whimper was Sam McGee.

And that very night, as we lay packed tight in our robes beneath the snow,

And the dogs were fed, and the stars o'erhead were dancing heel and toe,

He turned to me, and "Cap," says he, "I'll cash in this trip, I guess;

And if I do, I'm asking that you won't refuse my last request."

Well, he seemed so low that I couldn't say no; then he says with a sort of
moan:

"It's the cursèd cold, and it's got right hold till I'm chilled clean through to
the bone.

Yet 'tain't being dead—it's my awful dread of the icy grave that pains;

So I want you to swear that, foul or fair, you'll cremate my last remains."

A pal's last need is a thing to heed, so I swore I would not fail;

And we started on at the streak of dawn; but God! he looked ghastly pale.

He crouched on the sleigh, and he raved all day of his home in Tennessee;

And before nightfall a corpse was all that was left of Sam McGee.

There wasn't a breath in that land of death, and I hurried, horror-driven,

With a corpse half hid that I couldn't get rid, because of a promise given;

It was lashed to the sleigh, and it seemed to say:

"You may tax your brawn and brains,

But you promised true, and it's up to you to cremate those last remains."

Now a promise made is a debt unpaid, and the trail has its own stern code.

In the days to come, though my lips were dumb, in my heart how I cursed
that load.

In the long, long night, by the lone firelight, while the huskies, round in a
ring,

Howled out their woes to the homeless snows—O God! how I loathed the
   thing.
And every day that quiet clay seemed to heavy and heavier grow;
And on I went, though the dogs were spent and the grub was getting low;
The trail was bad, and I felt half mad, but I swore I would not give in;
And I'd often sing to the hateful thing, and it hearkened with a grin.
Till I came to the marge of Lake Lebarge, and a derelict there lay;
It was jammed in the ice, but I saw in a trice it was called the "Alice May."
And I looked at it, and I thought a bit, and I looked at my frozen chum;
Then "Here," said I, with a sudden cry, "is my cre-ma-tor-eum."
Some planks I tore from the cabin floor, and I lit the boiler fire;
Some coal I found that was lying around, and I heaped the fuel higher;
The flames just soared, and the furnace roared—such a blaze you seldom
   see;
And I burrowed a hole in the glowing coal, and I stuffed in Sam McGee.
Then I made a hike, for I didn't like to hear him sizzle so;
And the heavens scowled, and the huskies howled, and the wind began to
   blow.
It was icy cold, but the hot sweat rolled down my cheeks, and I don't know
   why;
And the greasy smoke in an inky cloak went streaking down the sky.
I do not know how long in the snow I wrestled with grisly fear;
But the stars came out and they danced about ere again I ventured near;
I was sick with dread, but I bravely said: "I'll just take a peep inside.
I guess he's cooked, and it's time I looked"; . . . then the door I opened wide.
And there sat Sam, looking cool and calm, in the heart of the furnace roar;
And he wore a smile you could see a mile, and he said: "Please close that
   door.
It's fine in here, but I greatly fear you'll let in the cold and storm—
Since I left Plumtree, down in Tennessee, it's the first time I've been warm."

I'm frequently asked how to make Basque Talo, the flatbread that I love. My story seemed incomplete without the aroma of good cooking in pine-scented air. Here's the simplest way.

BASQUE TALO

1. *In a 2-quart pot, boil 2 cups of water.*
2. *When near boiling, add 1 Tbsp of salt.*
3. *In a large mixing bowl, place 3 cups of cornflour (not cornmeal).*
4. *Using a ladle, slowly add hot water from the pot to the flour bowl. Mix with a fork. Add more flour or water as needed to get a soft dough.*

Note: You need to use hot water to make the dough; cold water will make it less flexible, and it may break. The hot water also helps to precook the dough and activate proteins.

5. *Roll the dough into a large ball and let it sit for 90 minutes with a towel on top of it to keep it moist.*
6. *Make small, palm-sized balls from the dough.*
7. *Sprinkle flour on the counter or cutting board and on your hands. (Don't do this on a cold granite countertop.)*
8. *Take a ball of dough and flatten it with your hand. Pat the dough until it's the size you want.*

Note: Basque chefs often use both hands and prepare two pieces of talo at once.

MARY HURST'S CHILI

Mary Hurst always had an amazing chili recipe. She never wrote it down, but here's what she told me was her secret. Start with tomato sauce, or paste, or stewed tomatoes, some broth, whatever kind of liquid base you choose. Add the meat, some hunks of Basque sausage they called txistorra, like chorizo; add either buffalo meat, or elk meat, and any beef you may have around, sometimes a little of all three. The Native Americans used buffalo in their chili, and most historians credit the Mexicans for introducing chili in this country.

Mixing meats together makes a mighty fine stew. A couple of our Mexican hired hands would bring Mary poblano and green chilies and some of their kidney beans and black beans. Mary would use both types of beans. She would add cumin and chili powder, paprika, and a few other secrets. Add onions and enough garlic to keep wolves out of your tent.

Normally, she would throw in a half cup or so of coffee, and if we ever had any on hand, she would melt down some chocolate and pour it in there. Crumble up some of the sheep cheese and put it on top. The chili would be brown from the chocolate, red from the paprika and tomato sauce, and spicy from that Basque sausage that you can't find anymore.

–Mark Hurst

BIG SPRINGS

Where the River Begins

Get your paperback copies or eBook at

Amazon.com and IngramSpark.com.

Read the Back Stories at bigspringsbook.com.

Made in the USA
Las Vegas, NV
25 June 2021